CAIT LONDON

WHEN NIGHT FALLS

AVON BOOKS
An Imprint of HarperCollinsPublishers

AVON BOOKS
An Imprint of HarperCollins*Publishers*
10 East 53rd Street
New York, New York 10022-5299

First Avon Books paperback printing: August 2002

Avon Trademark Reg. U.S. Pat. Off. and in Other Countries, Marca Registrada, Hecho en U.S.A.
HarperCollins® is a registered trademark of HarperCollins Publishers Inc.

Printed in the U.S.A.

10 9 8 7 6 5 4 3 2 1

When Night Falls

"You were the only one who believed that my family hadn't set the fire to get insurance money."

"Lauren believed in you."

Mitchell nodded and studied Uma in that quiet, gauging way. "Would you like to see the rest of the house—the kitchen?"

The kitchen was ruined, cabinet doors hanging off their hinges as though torn by an enraged hand, burned spots on the Formica countertop, ugly marks on the carpet. The stainless steel stove that Lauren had loved and cleaned meticulously was filthy. The sight made Uma feel nauseated. "I'd better go."

"Uma?" Mitchell's voice was deep and gentle.

She fought the tears burning her lids and then angrily brushed them away. "I miss Lauren. She was a part of my life, a good part, and now she's gone—murdered right there in front of me on an ordinary night. I saw his face. Even without license plates, I could identify that car. And they haven't found him. How can that be? How can a murderer drive by and shoot her? What had she done?"

Other Avon Books by
Cait London

IT HAPPENED AT MIDNIGHT
LEAVING LONELY TOWN
SLEEPLESS IN MONTANA
THREE KISSES

PROLOGUE

"**D**o you ever wonder what happened to those Warren boys?" Uma Thornton asked her girlfriends. After their usual dinner-out, middle-of-the-week movie and visit to Peggy's Ice Cream Parlor, the four women stood on the small town's sidewalk. There they would lick their ice cream cones and chat before each went back to her home.

In Madrid, Oklahoma, Main Street stood just as it had around the 1930s, in the days of Bonnie Parker and Clyde Barrow, Pretty Boy Floyd, and the Ma Barker gang. Red brick two-story buildings lined the street, and the beautification club's flower boxes adorned the storefronts. High on the red bricks, between the apartment windows, faded advertisements recalled the vanished era of the "nickel-a-dip" ice cream cone. The only modern touches were the neon signs.

A distance from town was the rodeo ground, and the town's population included a hefty percentage of Native Americans, many of whom were descendants of those who had traveled the "Trail of Tears."

In the cafes—Ruby's Home Cooking and the other, simply called "The Italian"—life moved along Madrid as it always did.

The four friends knew each other so well—teasing, giggling, and gossiping. They'd passed through life together, first as babies on their mother's laps, then riding their bicycles down Madrid's Main Street, catching fireflies on summer nights, and then during the flurry of teenage romances. They'd grieved over Uma's divorce and before that, her three-month-old baby's crib death. They'd comforted Shelly Craig, an unwed teenage mother and the town's scandal, because Shelly wasn't naming the father of her baby. They'd wanted to shake Lauren Howard for letting her unfaithful husband use her, Lauren working at their real estate business while he played. And Pearl Whiteford was just Pearl—beautiful, spoiled, sometimes vacant minded, completely selfish, and driven to be Mrs. USA-Perfect.

They accepted each other as they were, because the years had woven them together in a tolerant, caring fabric.

Uma looked forward to the weekly girls' night out. After all, a thirty-six-year-old divorced woman living in her father's home had little excitement. Life in Madrid, Oklahoma, purred along safely, predictably, comfortably. She had her odd moments, of course, ones that lazily stirred the quiet, safe life she wanted. Tonight, she had even fantasized that she was the blonde held in King Kong's loving hand.

Why had the nineteen-year-old Mitchell Warren's anguished face just danced across her mind? That was eighteen years ago, a lifetime away.

Maybe she'd thought of him because of the June heat rising up from the pavement, the same as when Mitchell had told Uma he was leaving Madrid for good, and never coming back.

"Do *I* ever wonder what happened to those Warren boys?" Pearl, the self-appointed social class judge, instantly soared in to express her dislike of the Warrens. "Madrid is glad to be rid of them. I say good riddance and don't come back."

"Now, Pearl, I doubt they'd want to. Madrid didn't exactly make them welcome."

While the other women talked, Uma settled in to enjoy her friends and the flavor of her weekly strawberry cone. At ten o'clock, the night was heavy with honeysuckle, and moths fluttered against the neon lights of Madrid's closed stores. Inside Peggy's Ice Cream Parlor, the jukebox was playing Peggy's favorite housecleaning song, "La Bamba."

What was that ominous quiet within herself? Uma wondered. That stillness as if everything had stopped turning, waiting . . .

She studied the insects that twirled in the shaft of a streetlight as though caught inside an imaginary cage. The light pooled onto Main Street's pavement, gleaming on the few cars and farm pickups that passed beneath. Since the day Bonnie Parker had posed for a picture with Clyde Barrow on their "running car," nothing had ever happened or changed in slow-moving, safe Madrid. Crops and cattle and sweet iced tea on a hot summer night ruled, punctuated by small town gossip and tips on growing roses. Excitement ran to the town dances, high school graduations, weddings, and Norman Evans's old Holstein bull sashaying down Main Street. Every year, he ate the beautification club's "city-pretty" flowers, and the club threatened to barbecue him on the next Fourth of July picnic.

Uma licked the tiny trail of melting strawberry ice cream from the waffle cone, then inhaled the scent of honeysuckle and roses and newly mowed lawns. The ordinary night in a rural town seemed too perfect, as if time were held on a sliver of glass, balancing back and forth, waiting to be shattered. She'd felt that unnerving stillness the early morning she'd gone to her baby's room. *And then, her world had stopped . . .*

"I just can't make up my mind whether to keep this scarf or not," Pearl said suddenly, always vain about her appearance. She held out the brightly colored floral scarf. "Here, Shelly, you try it on. I want to study how it looks."

"Give me that." Lauren grinned and grabbed the scarf, swirling it around her cotton dress. She danced away from Pearl, who tried fiercely to grab it away.

Smiling at Lauren's teasing play, Uma barely noticed a car rumbling out of the night and passing under the streetlights. It was unfamiliar, but looked like any other car passing through Madrid on a quiet evening.

Within Uma, that fragile sliver of glass quivered and she turned slowly to study the car. It bore Oklahoma dust, this two-door Chevrolet Impala, just like Ed Jones's powerful '71 model, dark navy blue body, white hardtop. But unlike Ed's, this one's windows were tinted the color of death. Once more the glass shattered within Uma and her heart stopped.

Then, in the open window, a man's narrow face caught the light, and with a blaze of fire, the sound of gunshot split the quiet night. The tires squealed and the car shot out of sight.

Lauren immediately crumpled to the sidewalk, the rose sprigs of her bodice stained with a widening dark circle of blood.

Uma dropped to her knees. She prayed that her mini-course in emergency care would save her friend's life. She placed her hand over the wound, trying to stop the flow of blood. "Call the clinic. Get the doctor."

One glance at Pearl's stunned pale face and rounded eyes, and Shelly sprang to her feet. "Never mind. I'll do it. There's a phone in Peggy's."

"There's no pulse. She's gone," Uma stated grimly as she removed her hand from Lauren's throat and began to stroke her hair. A selfless heart, Lauren had never failed to understand, comfort, and support. *Oh, Lauren, why you? We need you.*

In that moment, with her friend's head upon her lap, and the police siren screaming in the hot, sultry night, Uma knew that all their lives had changed forever.

Then Uma heard a whisper, like the soft wind teasing the tendrils near her ear. *I'll always be with you . . .*

She lifted her hand and found Lauren's blood staining it—she was gone. Like a treasured pioneer patchwork quilt ruined by a willful child's scissors, their lives had been torn, and would never be quite the same.

ONE

---

*H*ome hadn't been sweet.

Mitchell Warren had grown up here, on this little forty-acre Oklahoma ranch, and he'd hated it.

Maybe back then, as a child and a teenager, he'd hated everything, including his parents. Or had he?

He'd come back home to put the puzzle pieces together, to make some sense of the emptiness inside him. He welcomed emotions, but his ran deep and remained locked inside him. In his sleepless nights, the past would haunt him. One look in his morning shaving mirror revealed hard, bitter lines. One look in the midnight black windows and his haunted reflection came back to him. The streamlined life he'd created seemed cold in comparison to those with families and warmth and love.

Once, he'd wanted only money, the security of it, and now—

Now he wasn't even doing his best professionally—he didn't know how to relax, and those sleepless nights were catching up with him.

It was the baby. Just a tiny, six-pound squalling baby he'd delivered in the back of a city taxicab. Holding that mewling scrap of life in his hands, wrapping it in his dress shirt, and watching his secretary, Emily, beam though she was in pain, had poleaxed him.

"I love you, Mitchell," Emily had whispered. "You don't know what a wonderful person you are. You should find that person, know him, and love him." Later, her husband's jubilation and the love shining between them, a contrast to his sterile life, had jarred Mitchell.

Emily's six-pound baby had torn away his life and made him aware of what he did not have, what he did not feel. *He did not feel and he didn't know how to stop the sleepless midnights, the restless quest, the nameless hunger that always moved within him . . .*

He realized that other people moved through their lives while he stood still, like a statue in the park, with life churning all around him . . .

Mitchell had never backed off from brutal assessments, and looking at his life was no exception.

Home? An almost clinical chrome-and-glass apartment.

Holidays? Spent alone—as often as not, going over business reports.

Friends? Yes—but all to do with business.

Women? An ex-wife who he liked and respected, and a few previous relationships that had had more to do with sexual need than companionship.

Sex? Lately the call hadn't been there. He hadn't even missed it.

He hadn't missed anything, and that was the problem. He wasn't lonely. He preferred the single life—no commitments, no bonds.

Mitchell slammed the door on his late-model Dodge pickup just as he had once slammed the door on the past and his dying father's terrified screams.

Yet right here, eighteen years later, standing once more on this unforgiving Oklahoma earth, he had felt the past yawn open. It impaled him in a darkness he had to resolve—or at least, try to ease. He didn't understand himself, the bitterness inside. When he looked in the mirror, his father's hard face stared back at him—there was that drop of Cherokee in the French-Irish-English mix.

As an adult, his brother, Roman, looked much the same as he—rawboned and big, with a slash of dark brown brows that matched his hair, unrelenting brown eyes, and skin stretched taut over sharp high cheekbones. But Mitchell's nose had seen its share of youthful brawls. The lines across his brow and on his face said he often frowned. That uncompromising mouth and jaw said he yielded nothing. *Had his father's bitterness become his own?*

Bracing himself against the vivid sunset he remembered only too well, Mitchell scanned the Oklahoma landscape— the lush rolling green hills in the distance and a well-tended patchwork of fields had once been a 640-acre homestead; it contrasted the Warrens' present forty-acre flat, barren ranch. In the second week of June, sunset and memories washed over him.

In the distance, oil rigs seemed to peck slowly at the ground like giant birds.

The old corral where he and his brother had broken horses had been savaged, the good wood taken. Angled from the burned, overgrown rubble of the barn, the corral's few remaining broken and rotten posts cast long, eerie shadows on the ground. Only the weathered small garage stood, in which the Warrens had once repaired their cars and machinery. No more than a weathered gray shack slanted with the weight of eighteen years, the building had a roof that was more rust than metal.

The windmill paddles—what was left of them—circled lazily above him, the soft whirring noise familiar. Crows roosted high against the sunset, claws gripping the weathered old boards. Someone had shot holes in the revolving rusted gray paddles. A rabbit bounded across a mound of overgrown brush that hid the charred remains of a barn . . .

That night. In a rush, the fear and flames of that night consumed Mitchell, sucking away his breath. At two o'clock in the morning, the barn had been in full flame, the old sorrel and the other horses whinnying wildly. The board across the barn door had been nailed shut, and Mitchell and Roman had worked furiously to pry it free. The barn's winter hay had ignited, the huge, airy space filled with smoke that curled and crackled into the lazy summer evening.

Mitchell kicked the tuft of grass near his shoe—an expensive, glossy city dress shoe that contrasted with the black T-shirt and jeans he now wore. As a boy, his shoes usually hadn't fit, the soles were thin and worn with widening holes.

He crouched to study the dirt, hard packed and worn out. He'd been only eight when his mother had gone, and he'd hated her for leaving them.

Maybe his father hated his sons, or rather, that bit of his mother that remained in them. But it was hard work and "no sass" for Fred Warren's two sons, and there was no mother to comfort them.

With palms up, Mitchell studied his hands, now broad and big, a workman's hands, despite years as a businessman. On his left hand, one finger had webbed to another slightly, the mark of burned flesh. The scars from that fire ran smooth and gleaming, unlike the jarring nightmares that still tore him from sleep . . .

Mitchell inhaled deeply, the imagined stench of smoke strangling him once more, though the evening was laced with only the scent of a rambling honeysuckle vine. Now his tools weren't a hoe and a rake, but computers and intercom buttons. As a top manager for a building supply chain, he wore suits tailored to match his powerful body instead of jeans. And now and then, just to remind himself where he came from and how much better he'd made his life, he worked in the stores, hefting lumber as if he weren't a top executive.

Choices, he thought, mulling them. Though he'd left Rogers Building and Supply, he could have his job back at a phone call. He could locate a builders' supply and garden complex in Madrid to show off who he was now, to push back at the community that had hurt him. But he wouldn't. He only wanted to steep himself in the town and see if the past was really as bitter as he remembered.

Mitchell wanted to know if his father's bitterness toward his mother had marred his life. With a divorce behind him, he knew it had been his fault; he was incapable of giving, of tenderness, of caring for anything but his career.

He rubbed his chest. For years he had felt empty and cold, and he knew that Serene deserved better; she deserved all the things of which he was incapable. *Or was he?*

He could rebuild the ranch, making it a showplace. But he wouldn't. *He'd worked too hard on this land, and he wasn't ever coming back to work it again.*

He shook his head. Buying the ranch back had been folly. He didn't intend to work it. He just wanted to possess it as he worked through his problems; and the memory of that bank foreclosure and eviction notice long ago still rubbed raw. A savvy businessman wouldn't have bought it, or the house in town. Even at bargain prices, there was no logical reason—

Why had he come back? He didn't know, but here he was, held suspended by the past that lay right here.

Reluctantly, Mitchell slowly turned to study a small mound of overgrowth. A patch of June's daisies appeared like lace against a dark shaft of charred wood.

The smells of that night choked him once more. The teenage brothers had been too busy with the burning barn to notice that the house had caught fire. Passed out for the night, too drunk to care, their father hadn't awakened until it was too late. His screams drew the brothers, and Mitchell ran to pry free the door that had been nailed shut, too.

Mitchell rubbed the burn scars on his thigh. He blinked,

his mind's eye catching an image of flames on his father's clothing as Mitchell had hauled him outside to the cold snow. Fred hadn't survived the twenty-mile ride to town. A man who had lived in the tough old cowboy ways, who had bitterly mourned the wife who'd left him, Fred had died in that pickup bed. He'd left his sons nothing but a mortgaged ranch and a world of bitterness.

Mitchell turned in the direction of Madrid and wondered idly if the town still hated the Warrens.

If they did, it didn't matter. He needed to settle the past, still brooding inside him, keeping him trapped. He needed peace.

He stood slowly, remembering the frustration of a nineteen-year old boy who'd lost everything and believed he was responsible for the fires—that his dismissal of a married older woman's attentions had lit her husband's murderous wrath. A powerful man, her husband had sent his henchman to the Warren farm.

Uma, a year younger, had come to tell him how sorry she was for his pain. She'd leaned forward, over his hospital bed, enfolding him with that fresh, untouched scent. It had taken only her tender kiss on his cheek to break his rigid control over the storms inside him.

Embarrassed that she'd seen the burns on his thigh, ashamed that he was helpless and weak and needy, he'd tugged her over him, her wrist too fragile in his callused hand. In pain and darkness, he'd taken that innocent mouth roughly, driven by the urge to salve the nightmare of his life.

Even then, he knew it was wrong to quell the wild rage inside him, to let his hand roam over those sweet uptilted breasts while pressing her hips against his hardness. The searing burns on his thigh meant little as he punished her for being good and sweet and knowing how badly he hurt.

He was striking out at the world, not Uma, and her slight whimper hauled him back to reality. He'd pushed her away, disgusted at showing his need to destroy, to take something that wasn't his, to ruin because his life was in shreds.

Mitchell inhaled grimly as the windmill's paddles whirred in the silence.

There was only one way to find out what drove him so ruthlessly, why he couldn't rest—he had to face the past before he could move on.

Uma wrapped her arms around herself and stood in her darkened office. In the night, the room was soft and quiet, whispers of her mother and grandmother stirring in the shadows. They had passed on years ago, leaving her a legacy to tend—the lives in Madrid. They had been called "keepers," and now it was her turn—to hold and treasure the lives of Madrid.

By habit, she took a fortune cookie from a glass jar, turned blue with age, and cracked open the confection. She raised the tiny slip of paper inside to the light coming from the street. "One cannot always be safe, but one can be glad for change."

Nothing ever changed in Madrid, where two-story flat-fronted buildings bordered Main Street, where Charley Blue Feather argued with Lars Swenson about the moles crossing between their well-groomed yards. These skirmishes had raged through the years, Lars claiming that Charley's moles were destroying Swenson turf. Charley's reply was standard: "What do you want me to do? Brand them?"

Then there was Edgar MacDougal, who believed it was his right to have his evening pee off his back porch and onto his wife's roses. Myrtle Hawthorne, his next-door neighbor and a spinster with ten cats, had objected fiercely, complaining to the police. In retaliation, Edgar had broadcast throughout Madrid that Myrtle had spied on him using binoculars every evening.

There was, of course, Sissy O'Reilly, a "fine, prime widow"

who knew exactly what men wanted and how not to let them have it—without a cost. Kitty and Bernard's pot-bellied pig, Rosy, was walked down Main Street every day, the big bow around her neck replaced by a sweater in the winter. Marcy Roper's husband was having an affair with Janet O'Neil, only one of many discreet liaisons in town.

On the second floor of her father's house, Uma's office contained a drawing table, a large graphic computer screen, a high-tech computer, a smaller one she preferred when not doing graphics, and printers. The bookshelves lining the wall were filled with books, her CD music collection, and a player. This had once been her mother's sewing room, and now Uma enjoyed that same mellow, peaceful quiet—that safe quiet. It was here, listening to her elderly grandmother, that she'd learned about the families of Madrid—she knew the darkness and the relations, the ugliness of greed and lust, and the sweetness of families mending and loving.

How many hours had she stood looking out this same window, watching people move through their lives?

With its sprawling porches and huge potted ferns, the house stood white and tall at the end of Lawrence Street, elegant yet comfortable and set amid her mother's treasured gardens. Inside was a massive remodeled kitchen, a parlor, her father's room, and a library. Her upstairs room was just down the hall, comfortably enlarged after her divorce from Everett.

From that room, she could see Lauren's house next door. From a higher vantage point, Uma could see the leaf cluttered gutters, the moss on the shingles, the broken branches. Below were the untrimmed rose garden, the herbs and arbors and trellises aslant and weighed by ivy and weeds.

Uma tore herself away from the dream that she might see Lauren working there—

Lauren was gone, and nothing could bring her back.

Images of seven-year-old Lauren riding her bicycle, laughing as they raced, stirred in Uma's mind. Then that deathly kaleidoscope of images—of the night, the car, Lauren falling to the sidewalk—passed through Uma's mind. One moment Lauren was standing, happy, teasing Pearl with the scarf. The next instant her eyes had widened in shock. The next she was sliding in slow motion to lie still, her new cotton summer dress red with blood.

Uma brushed away the tears that always came. She crushed the fortune cookie into crumbs, letting them sift onto her desk. First there were four women, and now there were three.

She rubbed the chill she felt on her arms, despite the June warmth fluttering across the rose petals by the open window. She should finish the article for her newspaper column, which offered tips on dating and life for singles. Earlier articles had been collected for a popular relationship book, *The Smooth Moves List*.

And no one knew she'd written it, or the columns. Using her pseudonym, "Charis Lopez," Uma wrote about how relationships should be, how to build them strong enough to endure—but then, she couldn't even save her own marriage . . .

In reality, Uma should have had a full, busy life, working as a freelance graphic artist, writing a few articles, and the column. The writing was her own private, joyful secret, and so was the pleasure that her insights were lauded as helpful. Her articles had flown across the computer lines and no one in Madrid was the wiser.

She ran a fingertip over the velvety soft petals of the lavender roses on her desk. The variety was more flat and open than a usual rose—smaller, too. Just the same, the color was unique—

She should have told Lauren, who had faithfully quoted "Charis Lopez;" Lauren had hoped Billy, her husband, would change, but he never had.

Uma turned to the knock at the open door; her father stood outlined in the hallway light.

"You have that look. You're thinking about Lauren. There was nothing you could have done to save her. You still have the nightmares, too. I hear you roaming the house."

Uma nodded and Clarence said, "You should call Everett. Ask him to come over and watch a movie, or take you for a ride. It will only take him a minute to get here. Or you can stretch your legs and walk over there. It's only a few blocks to his house."

"No, Dad. I don't want to bother him."

"Bother Everett? He wants to remarry you. He's over here more than at his house."

"Because you invite him. You've been playing matchmaker for twelve years, since our marriage ended, Dad. He's got to move on. *I* have."

"I've always felt that I destroyed your marriage, or rather, that having that heart attack did. You saw me through it and you never went back to Everett. He's a good man. You need to reach out and live—remarry Everett and mend. He'll find someone—"

"I hope he does. Give it up, Dad. I'm just fine," Uma said softly, used to the familiar prod.

Clarence was silent for a moment. He knew Uma's limits. "It's only right that I want to see you taken care of after I'm gone. He loves you."

"I know. That's why I want him to have a good life with someone who can love him, and not as a sister or a friend. That's all there is for me now. Don't push it, Dad . . . please, not tonight. I feel as if something is about to happen."

"It's just the summer heat coming."

"Maybe."

The silence stretched into the night as Uma refused to carry the discussion further. Then Clarence said roughly, bitterly, "That Warren boy bought Billy Howard's place next door. He's back to settle old scores. Billy shouldn't have sold it to him. He sold it and ran out of town two days ago, before we could hang him for the deed. Waited until the last minute, so no one would know. It was a hush-hush, long-distance deal."

"Which Warren?" *Roman?* That girl-crazy, fast-talking, reckless show-off?

Or Mitchell? Mitchell, trying to do his best in school when he was too tired from hard labor at Fred's ranch or working as a mechanic in their ramshackle town garage? Mitchell, hauling his father home from a drunk? Mitchell, lying rigid in pain in that hospital bed, trying not to show how badly he ached inside, grieving for his father, worried about his brother, and furious with life's bad hand?

He'd fought not to show anything, pain etched on his face, those light brown eyes shadowed. And he was so helpless and young, battling a town that wanted him gone.

And he'd misunderstood her need to comfort him, dragging her onto the bed with him.

"It's *that* Mitchell. The one who dragged old Fred out of the fire and spent a couple of days in the hospital. Billy sold him that old Warren farm and Fred's old garage down on Maloney Street," Clarence brooded. "You can believe a Warren didn't come by all that much money honestly. He's probably in with the mob. Or running his own gang."

"Billy is a real estate agent, Dad. It's his business to sell. Lauren and Billy lived in different houses. They bought them cheaper and remodeled them and they sold at a profit." Only it was Lauren who did the work, and managed the real estate office while Billy gambled and cheated.

"I didn't kill her, Uma, I swear," he'd said, paling as Uma had faced him that day. With people moving around them, pawing through the sale goods on Billy's lawn, buying furniture and household goods that Lauren had treasured, Uma could have hit him—she didn't want to think of the violence storming within her. A placid woman, always choosing a sculpted, neat, safe life, she had been stunned. But just then,

she felt as if she could ignite and hurl a fireball from hell at him.

"Did you cause her to be shot, Billy?" Uma had demanded, furious with the man who had used her friend, selling off anything of value from the front yard, people milling around, shopping for a dead woman's—Uma's friend's—bargains.

"No, I've been all over that with the law. Why does everybody think it was me?" he'd whined. *"You're all against me. The whole town."*

"Because you hurt her. Everyone knows how you treated her—the gambling and the affairs. And don't you dare sell off her personal things, or I'll be back and I won't be nice. If you run, I'll find you. Don't you dare sell anything that was hers alone, not one dress, not one piece of paper, not one memento of her life," Uma had said, meaning it. It was the first threat in her life, and she meant to keep it. Lauren's things wouldn't be thrown away in the trash.

Uma shifted the lace curtains aside to watch a late model pickup prowl out of the night, the streetlights dancing on the metal. The driver used only the parking lights, yellow in the night, like wolf's eyes, and Uma shivered slightly. Ever since Lauren's death, she'd noted every unfamiliar car in town, watched for the murderer's narrow, hard face.

Why hadn't they found the car or the man?

The pickup pulled into Lauren's driveway, just one house away. A door slammed in the night and a man slowly walked out into the pool of light from the street just past the house next door. He was tall and broadly built, and then Uma knew that Mitchell had arrived. There was no mistaking his height or build, the way he locked his wide spread feet, his hands on his waist.

And she wondered if Mitchell had come back as her father had said, "to settle the score."

She wouldn't like it if he did, not one bit. Madrid needed to remain just as it always was—safe.

* * *

The next evening, Uma stood on the sidewalk, looking at the house Lauren had loved. It was small and neat, a one-level white frame and red brick ranch. Just an everyday house that Lauren had made into a home circled by herbs and roses. The huge ferns on the front porch were dead from last winter, a rubble of tree leaves cluttered the meandering porch that Lauren had treasured. One of the upstairs windows had been crudely nailed shut, and a rusted rain gutter hung askew.

The wary old tomcat her father tried to seduce with canned salmon watched her from beneath an untended shrub. Only Lauren had managed to pet and hold the cat. "You miss her, too, don't you?" Uma asked.

While the cat seemed to wait, a small breeze swept through the hot, still night and Uma shivered, her fingers chilled despite the warmth of the casserole in her hands, seeping through the tea towel. *Lauren.*

She could almost hear Lauren's whisper curl around her. *I'll always be with you . . .*

Uma braced herself to meet Mitchell Warren again; he'd called her office to tell her that Billy had left Lauren's things with a note to call Uma. The beef stroganoff casserole she held was only neighborly, despite her father's bad mood— "You what? You're taking food to a Warren? No daughter of mine—" he'd begun as she had walked out of the house.

She had no time for bitterness or hatred, except for the man who'd killed her friend Lauren. Who was he? *Where* was he?

One press of Uma's finger to the bell and the door swung open; a tall, powerful man filled the space. There was that same shock of dark brown hair, neatly trimmed now, but his body had changed from a boy's lankiness to a man's more muscular throat and broad shoulders, all packaged in a dirty white T-shirt and worn jeans.

In his stocking feet, Mitchell was just as she remembered, and the eighteen years since she had seen him had stamped Fred Warren's features on his face—blunt nose, high cheekbones, and hard, almost cruel mouth. There was the same six-foot-three height and the unique amber, almost golden brown eyes, the same dark brown wavy hair, neatly trimmed.

His gaze traveled down her light green summer dress, the linen shift long and cool against the evening heat, her summer sandals practical in worn leather.

"Uma," he said quietly and quickly folded Madrid's small shopping paper, tossing it aside.

"Hi, Mitchell." She handed the casserole to him. "Be careful. It's a next-door neighbor welcome. It's hot. I thought you might like something filling and homecooked, rather than a summer salad."

"Thanks. You're right. I'm not much on salads." He held the dish awkwardly, big hands gripping the delicate tea towel she'd embroidered.

She pushed away the last time she'd seen him—hurting, striking out at the world, a boy too young to handle life's raw patch. "I'm glad you called my house today. Is this time good for you?"

Mitchell nodded and opened the door wider. "Yes, of course. Come in. Or would you rather look at Lauren's things when I'm not here?"

Lauren. Uma moved into the house, standing in the foyer. In the living room, she noted the red stain on the cream berber carpeting, and it reminded her of Lauren's blood seeping through her dress. *Had Billy hired someone to kill her?* "Now is good for me. Did you get your business done today?"

"Just the usual, filing deeds on the old place, the garage and this house—setting up telephone, electricity, whatever, just paperwork."

Small talk filled big uneasy spaces, she thought, aware of him standing and studying her with the light at his back. She accepted her ordinary appearance, well settled into the security of it. A plain, brown-haired, ordinary woman with gray eyes, of small bust and boyish hips, whom people would term "willowy." She preferred her long hair on top of her head, though a few tendrils escaped in the summer heat, curling at her face and nape. With only a light moisturizer and a little lip balm, long cool dresses and colors that were soft and soothing, she just wanted to cruise easily through life.

The deep line between Mitchell's brows marked a lurking sadness, shifted and changed now from hatred and frustration; it lay in the shadows of his eyes, the hard slashes beside his mouth. She ached for young Mitchell and what he must have faced.

In turn, he studied her face, just an ordinary face, she thought—a little too wide and Nordic to be called pretty.

"You're just the same. Soft and sweet and caring."

"No, I'm not the same. No one is. I'm a realist now, not a girl. I've been married and had a child, a sweet little baby. Crib death, they said." She tensed, closing her eyes as the familiar pain squeezed her heart. *Christina.* So soft and tiny and sweet, snuggling warm in her arms one night, and gone the next morning.

She smoothed a light spot on the wall where a picture of Shelly, Pearl, Lauren, and her as girls had hung. They had had such bright dreams . . .

She felt an embrace, just the brush of a kiss on her cheek, and caught a scent. *She could feel Lauren here—waiting. Waiting for what?*

The old tomcat eased through the hole in the screen door and tail high wound around her legs. Then he strolled to Mitchell and nudged and purred loudly. While Lauren had petted and coddled the old cat, Mitchell bent to scratch the gray tom's ears roughly and the animal leaned into the favor.

He crossed back to Uma and strolled across her shoes and then leaped through the screen door hole, back outside.

Only Lauren had touched that cat.

Aware that Mitchell studied her, Uma struggled to maintain the conversation. "I'm a freelance graphic artist now. I'm divorced, living with my father, and I've lost Lauren."

Uma held her breath. *She could feel Lauren, sense her needing something . . .*

Mitchell nodded slowly as the memories stirred between them. "I liked Lauren. I'm sorry."

"I am, too. It was absolutely senseless—without reason. I guess these things happen in the city, but Madrid has always been so safe. You look so tired, Mitchell. I hope you find the peace you need here." She glanced at the clutter, a broom and vacuum resting in one corner. In the hallway beside her rested a pile of cardboard boxes that had held dishes, silverware, a toaster; plastic that had covered a mattress and box springs set all stuffed into a refrigerator box large enough for a child's clubhouse.

"How do you know that I need peace, Uma?" he asked quietly.

"Because everyone does," she said and wondered if she would ever find peace and safety again.

He frowned and hesitated, then he took a folded note from his pocket and gave it to her. "It was a long day. I'll put this casserole—smells good—in the kitchen. Here—"

Mitchell stood by her as she opened it; he hesitated and moved into the kitchen. On the note, Billy's small, immature handwriting scrawled over a stain.

I'm getting out of this town and never coming back. I know you can understand that. They ran you out one time and that's what they're doing to me. Didn't have time to clean up. Sorry. Uma wants Lauren's things, all that junk in the back bedroom.

She crushed the note in her hand. *Lauren.*

The blood was still on her hands, the terrifying memory of that night. Uma moved through the house that Billy had stripped, trying not to remember how happy Lauren had been when they'd first bought it, how hard she'd worked, stripping cabinets, painting . . .

The master bedroom was large and freshly cleaned. A king-size bed, the only piece of furniture in the room, stood unmade. The scent of lemon cleaner came from the bathroom as she passed.

The second bedroom had a broken window, plastic stapled over the glass. It was dirty and empty, but the third bedroom, the tiniest room where Lauren had ached to place her baby's crib . . .

Billy said we should wait for children until we can better afford them . . .

When Uma saw the clutter carelessly stacked at one end of the room, she couldn't move, couldn't breathe. This was all that was left of Lauren—a haphazard dumping of the lovely person she had been. Unable to move, Uma felt her throat tighten and her eyes burn with tears; she leaned against the wall, her arms around herself. She squeezed her lids closed to seal away that terrible night, and yet it came back—shattering her once more. She couldn't open her eyes when she sensed Mitchell had come to stand beside her.

"I know how much she meant to you," he said quietly. "I'm sorry about your baby and about Lauren."

"They never found out who shot Lauren." She swallowed roughly, tears too close to breaking free. Automatically, she reached for Lauren's rumpled, discarded clothing and began folding, placing the neat stack on an old chair. A moment ago they were all girls, planning marriages and babies, and now— "Would you mind if I didn't collect all this now? I will, but not just yet. I can't bear—"

"It's fine where it is. I'll clean the room and straighten things a bit. Here's a key—you can come when you want." He took a key from his pocket.

She clasped the key in her fist and knew that he understood she would need time and strength to deal with all that remained of Lauren. "Thank you."

"Uma?"

She tried to shake herself free of the tears. "Yes?"

"I'm sorry about that—what happened that day in the hospital room. I'm sorry I grabbed you. I've always regretted that."

She shook her head, looking up at him. "I know. I know how difficult it was for you back then. You were just a boy, and in so much pain. You'd just lost your father and your home."

Mitchell moved away from her, his jaw hard and uncompromising. "I shouldn't have—"

"It's in the past, Mitchell. Please don't think about it . . . but if I had Billy Howard in my sights now, I'd never forget how he just tossed Lauren's life into one unloved pile. I'm so angry now. I'd better go. But first, let me help you make your bed. Two people can do the work quicker and you look so tired. Your wife will be, too. When is she coming?"

"I'm not married. I was. It didn't work out." Mitchell's light brown eyes were shadowed and steady upon her. "Billy told me about you and Everett."

"Yes. We're still friends. We had a child together. That doesn't go away." Uma smiled briefly; Everett had had other ideas, and she'd tried at first. It wasn't a matter of forgiveness for his affair after their baby had died and she sank into depression; it was that they just didn't fit anymore. And she felt as if something inside her had died with her baby. She didn't feel like a woman any longer; she felt empty, filling the days with her father and friends, her work.

She smiled at Mitchell. "Let's go make your bed. Billy sold

the washer and dryer and you don't look as if you'd mind sleeping on a board tonight, let alone brand new bedding that hasn't been washed."

· "I wouldn't," he said grimly, and Uma remembered how harshly he had grown up. Fred Warren hadn't liked spending money on household goods. He'd used every penny on the land, on the horses he had raised and broken and sold, trying to stretch the feed and grain bill with that of pasture seed, and veterinarian bills—and in the end, Fred spent what extra money he had on alcohol.

In the large master bedroom, Mitchell worked on the opposite side of the bed, placing the mattress pad on it and then the sheets. He was efficient and awkward, glancing at her as she neatly fitted the corners, and she knew that homemaking wasn't a usual task for him. She ran a hand across the smooth brown blanket and fluffed the pillows. "When are the rest of your things coming?"

"This is it. I thought I'd add whatever I needed as I went along."

She lifted her brows. "You have a whole house to fill. Try the secondhand store. You'll need some furniture, like a living room chair and maybe a television set. There isn't that much to do in Madrid. Do you have a job?"

"I thought I'd see what turned up."

"I'll help you, if you want. I could ask around."

"I thought I'd take my time and get the feel of things."

She could never jump into a life away from what she knew. She wondered how many times Mitchell had had to adjust to a new town, a new life. "I—please don't answer this, if you're uncomfortable with it, but did you ever find out who nailed the barn and the house door shut the night your father died?"

Though Mitchell's expression didn't change, she could feel him sinking inside himself, a darkness enveloping him. "Someone who thought I was involved with his wife—I wasn't. The man is dead now. He had a heart attack soon after that night . . . end of story. You were the only one who believed that my family hadn't set the fire to get insurance money."

"Lauren believed in you, and Shelly, and I think one of the deputies did, too. He was your father's friend. You remember Lonny? He's the police chief now."

Mitchell nodded and studied her in that quiet, gauging way. "Would you like to see the rest of the house—the kitchen?"

Uma hadn't been in the house since her last coffee with Lauren. She placed her hand over her heart. "Yes, I would. I've already seen the other rooms. Billy wasn't much on home maintenance or cleanliness. Poor Lauren spoiled him. She managed the real estate office and did most of the work there, too."

The kitchen was ruined, cabinet doors hanging off their hinges as though torn by an enraged hand, burned spots on the Formica counter top, ugly marks on the carpet. The stainless steel stove that Lauren had loved and cleaned meticulously was filthy. The sight made Uma feel nauseated. "I'd better go."

"Uma?" Mitchell's voice was deep and gentle.

She fought the tears burning her lids and then angrily brushed them away. "I miss Lauren. She was a part of my life, a good part, and now she's gone—murdered right there in front of me on an ordinary summer night. I saw his face. Even without license plates, I could identify that car. And they haven't found him. How can that be? How can a murderer drive by and shoot her? What had she done?"

Uma picked up the embroidered tea towel she had brought to cover the casserole and dabbed her eyes. "I'm sorry. I've got to go. Thank you for calling me about Lauren's things. I'll take care of them, but just not now."

When Mitchell said nothing, but only stared at the scarred linoleum floor, Uma knew that the past still held him. She reached to touch his arm and the muscle there hardened immediately. "Please don't worry about that time so long ago. You were just a boy in pain. I understood."

He smiled tightly, briefly. "It shouldn't have happened. Not to you."

She couldn't resist smoothing that rough, hard cheek gently, and sensed the power that he held in check, the darkness lurking around him. "Be good to yourself, Mitchell."

The answer came with a scowl and his hand gripping her wrist, pushing her hand away. "You think I deserve that, do you?"

"Yes, I do." But Uma's thoughts were with Lauren, and she had to get out of the house. She tried not to run as she hurried into the hot, honeysuckle-scented night. When she turned to glance back, Mitchell stood enveloped by the porch's shadows and the cat sat beside him, gently flicking his tail.

TWO

After Uma had gone, a moth circled the ceiling light, and Mitchell watched it as he thought of the woman she had become.

Still compassionate and considerate. Still the same thick waving hair, a rich mink brown that gleamed with reddish highlights as if it had trapped the warmth of the sun. He'd gripped it in his fist all those years ago and the silky feel had remained, haunting him. Or was it the sweetness, the honesty he'd held for just that moment, and in his pain, wanted to destroy?

He'd known Uma forever, the forbidden girl from the right side of uptown. Perfect. Complete. She'd always been strong in herself, sensitive to others, and poised. The first anger he'd seen in her was just now, when she thought of Lauren's death. Then her dislike of Billy was right there on the edge, smoldering in those smoky gray eyes.

A woman's passion was there, controlled and simmering.

How long ago was it that he'd felt as deeply?

He didn't want Uma touching him. He didn't want that longing inside him to lean into her gentle touch. He didn't want her pity.

He should have comforted her, said the right words about Lauren, but he couldn't. He didn't know how. His emotions were locked inside him.

She didn't blame him for his attack all those years ago. How could she not?

The telephone rang, and after he answered, a man's muffled voice asked, "Mitchell Warren?"

"Yes. Who is this?"

"We don't want you here." Another silence, and the caller hung up. Mitchell replaced the receiver slowly; he'd expected as much, his arrival certain to stir Madrid's gossip. The voice was metallic and smooth and sexless, as if it had been electronically manufactured.

He walked out into the garden, now overgrown and littered with broken limbs. A woman had once loved it, and now the white picket fence needed painting and repair. Roses bloomed amid the weeds—Mitchell stopped, surprised to see Uma in the garden.

Framed by the moonlight dappling through the oak tree, Uma stood, head bowed. Her hands were stretched out over the roses, not touching them. Her face was pale, eyes huge in the shadows as she turned to him. "I loved her so. These roses are from my grandmother's garden. They're Hansa . . . with that clove scent, they're typical of the Rugosas, and in the fall the hips are large and orange-red. In my garden, her grandmother's Russelliana is climbing on a trellis. We shared the roses, sometimes going to old homesteads and collecting starts—all of us, Lauren, myself, Pearl, and Shelly. Pearl wasn't that enthusiastic, but she came along to be with us. And Shelly really doesn't have time to tend a garden now, or the energy. Poor Lauren's are so overgrown."

Her voice was only a soft whisper in the night, her hand drifting across a tumble of tiny white roses in a half barrel. "Lauren would make sachets from the petals and from the lavender buds, and she'd make soap, too. She'd let Dozer come cut rose hips for his winter teas. I couldn't bear to come here . . . we've always been together. And now we're not."

She pushed the old swing tied to a sturdy oak branch. "She kept this here for the neighborhood children and loved to watch them play."

Mitchell understood the necessity of closure. She needed to reckon with Lauren's murder as badly as he needed to resolve his past, separating Fred's bitterness from him.

Her cheeks were silvery with tears, which she impatiently scrubbed away. She looked at her hands, studying them. "I'd better go. Goodnight."

"Uma?"

"Yes?"

"I'll prune the bushes." It was the least he could do, though the offer surprised him.

"Do you know how?"

Her tone was listless as she continued to study her hands, turning the palms upward. What was it that she saw in those slender, graceful fingers, those soft palms?

He'd trained himself to gauge people in business, to stay away from emotional entanglements. Yet he'd offered. Mitchell frowned slightly, uncomfortable with whatever she stirred within him. "I'll learn."

"Be careful of the thorns. The plants should be fed— manure tea, if you want, or something commercial, and a spray for insects who love to feast on them. Until tonight, I couldn't bear to come here to tend them. In another month or so, they'll be beautiful."

She scrubbed whatever she saw on her hands away, and slid into the darkness. She crossed the shadows on the sidewalk, just as she had crossed his thoughts through the years.

A cloud passed across the moon and Mitchell thought briefly about her marriage, the man's name she'd kept. Everett Thornton would have suited her, a man with the right kind of background. What went wrong?

In the still night and among the budding fragrant roses, Mitchell's parents' raging battles echoed; they stalked him while a slight breeze riffled the tops of the trees, whispering in the leaves. His mother had pleaded, his father cursed bitterly. And then Grace Warren had gone to her young sons, begging them to come with her. Their father's taunts had snagged their fierce pride and they'd chosen to stay.

Mitchell didn't want to think about the woman who was his mother. He didn't want to open the letters she'd sent through the years.

Blaming it on his dark mood, the homecoming that wasn't sweet, Mitchell tore away a rotting white trellis and tossed it into a fragrant, rambling bed of blooms.

Small town welcoming, he thought, as inside the house, he filled a paper plate with the casserole and dished out another smaller helping for the cat, who had followed him inside. Crumpled beside the dish was the tea towel that Uma had used to wipe her tears.

Mitchell ran his finger over the delicate embroidery, tracing the white thread of the flowers.

In her way, Uma Lawrence Thornton was dangerous to him. He didn't like the restless softness disturbing him now. Nothing was adding up, or could be logically dissected. Mitchell liked assessments and bottom lines from which to build, but Uma tangled his senses.

On impulse, he picked up the telephone and called Roman. A woman protested sleepily and Roman's voice was rough and deep in the Las Vegas night.

"It's Mitchell. Bad timing?"

"What's wrong?" Roman's tone changed to alert.

"I'm in Madrid. I bought back the old places—the ranch and the garage—and a house in town."

"My God. What did you do that for?"

"I had to. Don't know why. Here's my phone number and mailing address." Mitchell smiled. He could almost see Roman sitting up in bed, reaching for a pad and pen. In the background a woman groaned sleepily.

Glass shattered and Roman cursed, then muttered, "You're making a mistake, Mitchell."

"Could be." Facing the past was better than the terminal freeze inside him.

"You just walked out of a top job, back to that hick town?"

"Uh-huh. Seemed the right thing to do now, for me."

After he hung up, Mitchell smoothed the tea towel on the counter. *Was it the right thing to do? Could he find what he needed?*

"Mitchell Warren is back?" Shelly turned suddenly to Uma.

"I thought you should know," Uma replied.

Time seemed to stop as Shelly slowly placed a laundry basket on the kitchen counter of her small, well-kept home.

By nine o'clock that night, Shelly had already cleaned two houses and was picking up after her rebellious teenage daughter, Dani. Dressed in her standard T-shirt and jeans, Shelly was tall and leggy, and moved with the lean grace of a woman who was physically active. Sun had streaked her chestnut hair, tethered in a ponytail. The clean-cut planes of Shelly's face would age gracefully, her skin gleaming without cosmetics.

"Why? Why is Mitchell back? Why would he *want* to come back?"

Uma searched her thoughts and emotions about Mitchell. She could almost feel the hardness of his jaw now beneath her fingers, the way he tore her hand from him—and she'd ached over the bitter life he'd known, for the life he must have had. "He's very quiet and watchful. I think he's lost something, and he needs to find it. There's a deadly quietness in him that—"

"I wondered why you came tonight. You came to warn me. I haven't told Dani about her father."

Uma nodded; Shelly hadn't told anyone about her daughter's father, including her own family, who had cast her out. An unmarried teenage mother, she'd kept her baby, supporting them by doing housework. Despite pressure to place her baby out for adoption, Shelly had never wavered beneath the gossip.

"Dani could stand a few facts of life. You shouldn't be picking up after her."

"We had a terrible fight. I just found out that she didn't take her last high school exams. Her high school diploma was not in the folder they presented at graduation. I never knew she wasn't going to class. She's out with her friends—if you can call them that."

Shelly shrugged carelessly, though her daughter's behavior worried her. "She's determined to make me pay. She calls herself a 'bastard child,' and she's ruining her life. She's got the notion that I played wild and free as a teenager. I didn't. There was only Roman and that one night when he was hurting so."

"She's making you feel guilty to have her way. She's spoiled, Shelly."

"I know, but I guess I tried to make it up to her—not having a father, the whole town questioning her biological father, my parents not having anything to do with their own granddaughter. My mother is the only one alive now, and in the rest home. She still won't talk to me."

"She should. You're paying for her stay there."

"I do some special laundry and help out there, and pay when I can. She had Dad's small pension, but it wasn't enough. I hurt her deeply when I had Dani. My parents had big plans for me to go to college. Now I clean houses. And guess what? I like it better than my parents' accounting business and office work, too. I like the movement and the feeling of being satisfied, of looking back and seeing that I've accomplished something. Ironing is possibly the best therapy there is."

Shelly searched Uma's face. "If Mitchell is back, then Roman could come, too. The Warren brothers were always close. You're the only one who knows Roman is Dani's father. I couldn't trust anyone else."

"Maybe Roman should know that he has a daughter."

Shelly shook her head and slumped into a chair. She slowly studied her work-worn hands. "No. It was just that one night after the Warren ranch was burned and Mitchell was in the hospital. Roman needed someone, anyone. I found him in that old garage on Maloney Street—up there in the old office. He was furious with life, shaking. I didn't know what he would do, but he touched something inside me. It wasn't pity or sympathy, or anything like that. I gave myself to him because I wanted to. I wanted to hold and protect him and to love him. I wasn't expecting promises of forevermore. He isn't obligated to Dani, or to me. I'm glad he gave her to me. She's my child, no one else's."

Uma took Shelly's hand, studying the small pattern of burns. "What happened?"

"Grease splatters. Pearl was here, picking up her husband's shirts, and I'd forgotten to turn off the stove. We were deep into the usual conversation of how good she looks and she assigned my duties with her latest charity. Then there was the usual perfect family talk, how wonderful her daughters are, how special her husband is, how much she paid for her new furniture. If we hadn't grown up together, I don't think we'd be friends, but I know how much she suffered from her parents—they were so cold, so demanding. I remember when she came to school, the bruises on her arms, poor little thin arms. And she has been good to us. I seem to be so distracted lately. It's only a few little grease splatters."

"You're tired and you're worried about Dani. Do you want me to talk with her?"

Shelly shook her head. "My daughter is my problem."

"You've always been stubborn." Uma crossed her arms. "I

changed her diapers often enough, and I've watched you struggle to raise her. I don't know if I can keep quiet. You don't deserve what she's putting you through."

"Maybe I do." Shelly studied Uma. "You're angry about something else. What is it?"

Uma's fingers bit into her arms and she leaned against the kitchen counter. "Billy. You should see that house. He's ruined it. And he's put all of Lauren's things into one room— just heaped them there, like trash to be tossed. It was bad enough when he sold everything possible, but to just dump her albums and life like that— At least he didn't throw them away."

"He always was a disgusting, drooling, zipper-down swine. He exposed himself to me one time, and I couldn't stop laughing. He was so pathetic. That was the last time he bothered me. I think the only time I ever saw you really angry was when Billy started selling her things. He wasn't expecting you to light into him, and that was quite the sight to see—you backing him against the wall, your finger shaking in his face while you threatened him with—what was it? 'An eternal haunting?' and 'cursed with erection deficiency'?" Shelly moved to put her arms around Uma, rocking her.

"I got a little carried away. I was furious, or I'd thought of better curses." Uma leaned her forehead against her friend's. "He was a real dog. Lauren had no idea he was panting after every woman in town, and making passes at her friends. I don't care what the sheriff said, in my thoughts, Billy had something to do with her death."

"Honey," Shelly crooned, rocking Uma. "We're going to have to go on without her."

"I know, but I want her killer found."

Shelly wrapped her arms tighter around Uma. "That might never happen. We'll have to live with that."

"I don't know that I can let it go. I see that man's face over and over in my nightmares, the way the world seemed to stop, and that old car. And I feel Lauren's blood, sticky on my fingers, how she just crumpled like that, not a sound. I feel her needing me and I can't do anything about it."

"She'll always be with us. Let me know if I can help you with her things. I loved her, too."

"I'd better go soothe family feathers. Dad is not happy about Mitchell returning to Madrid. Or about me visiting him. He's going to be even more angry when he learns that I'm going back to sort Lauren's things. And yes, I'd like you to be there. In a way, I can still feel her there, waiting, as if she can't rest until her killer is found."

"It's been a year—"

Uma's hand rested on her throat, on the pulse. "I know, but I just feel myself stirring inside as if something is going to happen. I felt that way the night she was shot—that cold, still feeling, waiting—I felt that way when my mother passed and my baby . . . I'd better go."

Shelly's hand smoothed the tendrils of Uma's hair back from her face. "You're very sensitive to others, and caring. You watch everyone's lives pass beneath your office window, there in your father's house. You know more about this town than anyone, and if Mitchell is here to heal, he'll be asking questions of you. Just don't get hurt, okay?"

Later, as Uma walked past Mitchell's house, she noted him sitting on the front porch steps. He rose and walked toward her, towering over her in the shadows, the stubble on his face darker now, his appearance tough and dangerous.

Something quivered within her briefly, stirred and settled.

"I'll walk you home," he said slowly, the moonlight creating a silvery outline around his dark waves and broad shoulders.

She remembered a boy, lean and serious, and devastating when he smiled—but Mitchell-the-adult hadn't smiled. Did he ever? "I'm almost there. It's just next door."

He walked quietly, slowly beside her. "What happened with Everett? Or do you mind my asking?"

She shrugged lightly, long having dealt with the love that had always been more friend than lover. "We were comfortable together. We still are. But after our baby—Christina Louise was her name—died, so did I, just a little. I thought Everett should have more than what I'd become. I'm happy with my life now. It fills me, but it isn't right for him . . . we're here."

Mitchell scanned the white two-story house shrouded by towering oaks. Then he nodded and turned, leaving her alone in the night.

He disturbed her, her senses rustling, whispering. Why? Was it the past? Or the trouble he could bring with him?

"I read your article in the newspaper about Bonnie and Clyde's visit here in Madrid. I suppose writing things like that keeps you busy, since you're not married anymore. Shelly called me this morning. She knew I'd be upset, and I am. I couldn't believe that Mitchell-person would actually return to the scene of his crimes. I hope this isn't another one of her fantasies. She's been in another world since Lauren died. She can't remember anything now . . . is it true? Is Mitchell really back?"

In Uma's office Pearl stalked through the quiet shadows, her dyed hair gleaming, the cream linen suit reflecting her expensive taste. Pearl shoved her fingers through the heavy mass, preening before she sat in the single overstuffed easy chair. "I just came from the beauty shop and you haven't said anything about my hair. Some friend *you* are. Walter loves this Rita Hayworth style on me. Jessie has finally gotten the shade right."

Uma leaned back and saved the computer file on the travel brochure Everett had requested. The resort was new and upscale and sprawling, and Everett wanted her to go with him to sample it. She couldn't do anything to encourage him, though the thought of the luxurious spa treatments were tempting.

Pearl looked around Uma's small office, the white sheer curtains at the windows buffering the bright morning. "I remember sitting here when your mother was alive. She wouldn't have liked you going over there to welcome that Mitchell-person. Your father told me about that when I called this morning. How could you, Uma? You know he's here to make trouble. There's no way the Warrens could do anything else."

Uma watched Pearl smooth her skirt, a town matron out to protect Madrid's social class from infiltration of the "lower element." "Mitchell and Roman might have had a little teenage trouble, but they were never convicted—"

Pearl held up one perfectly manicured finger, and the soft light in Uma's office caught the huge diamond wedding ring, sending a brilliant pattern onto the seafoam colored wall. "Only because their father was friendly with the deputy at the time—Lonny. Fred Warren should have been put in jail and they should have been put in reform school. You never did say you liked my hair."

The penalty of an enduring friendship was to pay homage to Shelly's vanity. Uma often wondered whether, if they had met afresh, they'd have been friends. But childhood bonds had only strengthened through the years; their lives were tangled, and in her way, Pearl needed them. Always quiet and composed and capable to the public, Shelly could speak freely to Uma, Lauren, and Shelly.

"I just drove down Main Street and saw my yard man, Dozer, sitting right on the same bench with Mitchell. There they were, having coffee, seeing who could shave the longest wood curls, pretty as you please. Mitchell looks like he's been through hard times—probably prison. I want you to keep your distance from him, Uma. You've got a soft heart and just don't see the evil in anyone."

Uma ached for the trust that her parents had torn away from her as a child. "Pearl, don't get all worked up."

Pearl threw up her hands. "Worked up? *Worked up?* He's living in Lauren's house. He bought it and the old garage back on Maloney Street, and he bought back the old ranch, what there is left of it. Now, don't you just wonder where a Warren would get money like that? He's back here to stir up trouble. I told my girls to stay clear away from him. It's a good thing they're at Walter's sister in Connecticut and then leaving for their private school in September. I don't want them exposed to his kind."

Tired of Pearl's ranting, Uma changed the subject. "Your hair is the best I've seen it. I really do think it looks like Rita Hayworth's."

Pearl's blue eyes widened with pleasure. "You think so? You think Walter will like it?"

"Yes, I do." *Walter.* Nothing Pearl did was good enough for Walter. Uma studied the cardinals in the garden's bird bath and wondered if Pearl would ever recognize his sly, insidious abuse, the way he demeaned her. Maybe that was why it was so easy to serve her compliments, to try to build her self-esteem.

Immediately brightened, Pearl stood and smoothed her skirt. "I have to go. I'm hosting the bridge club this afternoon. Walter is thinking of running for mayor in the next election, and I'm going to do everything in my power to help him. Now, Uma, I want your promise that you won't speak to Mitchell. Leave it to me to find out what he's doing here. And Everett won't like it one bit that you went to Mitchell's house. Don't tell him."

"Everett and I are friends, Pearl. He'll understand . . . and I love that shade of nail polish. What is it?" Uma asked, to distract her.

Pearl blinked and stared at her hands. She smiled brilliantly as she did when complimented. "Delicate Bondage. Oh, not that Walter and I are into that sort of thing, that's just the name of the polish. I'd better go. I have so much to do today. I'm planning to take the girls on a shopping trip to New York soon, before boarding school starts. There's nothing around here that's suitable for their private school. And I have to have that chat with Dozer. You really should get a suitable office, one with modern furniture and not just some old bedroom."

"I'll think about it." But she wouldn't. Right here was where she learned the past from her grandmother, where she had become "the keeper." *Some people are uppity, but if they knew their family's history, they might be taken down a notch or two*, Grandma had said. *No sense in hurting people, but it's only right that someone know the truth they'd rather hide.*

"You do that. You know I only want the best for my best friend, and Shelly, of course. You're all I have of Lauren."

Tears shimmered in Pearl's eyes. "I miss her awfully. Walter says the murderer will never be found—probably just some city hoodlum out to make points with his gang."

Pearl's vanity and lack of sensitivity sometimes gave way unexpectedly to the childhood friend Uma cherished. In her way, Pearl was helpless and sweet, and their lives were finely, intricately woven together.

After Pearl had gone, Uma tried to concentrate on creating Everett's travel brochure.

Instead, she thought of Mitchell, of the darkness lurking around him, the coldness she sensed inside him.

And then she knew he'd come back to close the past, to watch and relearn through a man's eyes. He'd come to heal.

Uma smiled in the shadows of her office, the colors soft and smooth around her, the fresh flowers from her garden scenting the room.

She drew comfort from the gentle, whispering memories

of her mother and grandmother in the same room. Here, she was *safe*.

"I'll dress how I want, go where I want, and if you don't like it, I'm moving out. There are plenty of places I can stay—or go," Dani stated stubbornly in Shelly's small, neat living room. The sound system slammed loud hard rock music into the deadly space between Shelly and her daughter.

Dani's dyed black hair, styled in short, straight peaks, matched the black T-shirt, tight black jeans, and heavy eye makeup. With one leg slung over an easy chair, her boot thumping the wall, Dani sat in the chair Shelly had salvaged from the church sale and reupholstered. "You don't love me anyway. It's not like you wanted me, or anything. I'm just the aftereffect of when you were my age and running around—"

"I did not run around. I loved your father. You're a part of him," Shelly stated, her heart aching for her daughter. Dani was hurt early, when Shelly's grandparents refused to see her, to acknowledge her. Even now, her grandmother wouldn't look at her—"the bastard child of Satan."

"Yeah, right. You loved him so much, you won't even tell me who he is. And like he stuck around to be a parent."

"He didn't know. *I* didn't know when he left."

Dani shook her head. "Mom, don't hand me this bull. The apple doesn't fall far from the tree—you ran around and I might end up the same way—that's what your old lady said."

"*She's your grandmother. Don't call her that.*"

"So when's she ever been in my life? When's she ever recognized me as her granddaughter?" Dani demanded hotly. "Well, I'm not going to end up like you, slaving at other people's houses every day, cleaning toilet bowls, and washing and ironing shirts at night, scrimping for every dime—"

"It's good, honest work. You could try a little of it. Or at least finish school."

"It's a waste of time. I want to live and have fun. You did—"

"Dani, I was not hopping from bed to bed, and I'd better not find out that you—"

Dani leaped to her feet and slammed down the fashion magazine she'd been clutching. "Or? *Or?* What will you do? Kick me out? Maybe that would suit me."

Despite her tough talk, there were tears in Dani's eyes, and Shelly's heart wept for her. "I'm sorry you grew up without a father, honey. I'm sorry my parents were cruel. But I love you so much and only want the best for you."

"Sure. That's why you won't tell me or anyone else who he is. I have a right to know my own father's name." Dani was sobbing now, a teenager battling growing up and life and her love for her mother. "Face it, Mom. I'm just like you. Only I'm not ever getting caught with a baby I didn't want."

"I wanted you. I wanted you with every bit of my heart."

Dani dashed her tears away, leaving rough black smudges across her face. The color of her eyes was dark, rich amber now, the same as Roman's. "Sure. It wasn't easy being stuck with a kid in this town, was it? Boy, I just can't wait to get out of here."

After Dani stormed into her bedroom, slamming and locking the door, Shelly felt as if her strength was gone, too. She sank into the chair Dani had been sitting in and picked up the magazine from the floor, automatically replacing it on the stack of others.

How could she explain that night to her daughter, all the depth of tenderness that had given her the most precious gift of her life?

How could she share the intimate details of seventeen-year-old Roman begging her to go with him? Of her choice to remain in Madrid, the safety she'd always known?

She wiped away her tears and studied her broad working

hands. They were rough now, despite hand creams and plastic gloves, the veins pronounced. She would do anything to protect her daughter, and Roman's name would only launch Dani's search for him.

He hadn't been safe back then, and he'd already been sexually skilled and "fast with women." He probably wasn't safe now, either, and Shelly didn't want her daughter hurt.

Dani was like Roman—rebellious, passionate, and headstrong. If the two should ever meet, they'd either clash or bond. Either way, Shelly would be the loser.

If they ever met, she wondered how long it would be before either one of them added times and birth dates together and discovered the truth.

THREE

Dozer's gnarled fingers shook as he tried to open the lock on the chain tethering the old Warren garage on Maloney Street. "Locked it because no one was watching it, and the owner who bought it at auction lives away from here. He didn't care what happened to it. I keep my lawn mowers in here, the sprays and fertilizers and what-not. I'm going to sell my business pretty soon, so you don't have to worry about this junk bein' here no more."

Mitchell scanned the street, remembering the cars and trucks that once stood outside the old garage, waiting for Fred Warren's healing touch. He glanced up at the second-story window, a jagged, broken pane mirroring the golden sunlight. That was where, as a boy, he'd taken Grace's place in managing the garage's books and discovered he liked business better than ranching. But then, he didn't like ranching at all, not on a tiny forty-acre ranch where hard work got nothing from the dirt.

At eleven o'clock in the morning, Madrid was quiet; spears of sunlight cut through the shadows of Maloney Street. The city beautification club had not seen fit to treat the street, and the old oaks shading it had littered the ground with leaves and broken limbs. The drugstore had moved to Main Street, and the old two-story buildings were boarded, the sunlight catching broken windows. An elderly woman carrying her black purse and a small bag of groceries hobbled on thick ankles into a building that had once been the town's seamstress. His rocking chair braced against the front porch of what used to be the candy shop, a tiny, ancient Native American man smoked a hand-rolled cigarette and watched life move around him.

Just around the corner, where Maloney met Main Street, the buildings were still old, but updated with neon signs and flower boxes. Mitchell inhaled slowly—some of the past was worth keeping, and the rest had been shoved away. What was worth keeping in his life?

"That's Rosy with Kitty and Bernard Ferris," Dozer was saying, nodding toward the pot-bellied pig crossing the Main Street intersection. There in the middle of the street, while drivers of trucks and cars waited patiently, the elderly couple stopped to allow a little girl to feed the pig a treat. Rosy was obviously treasured by the tiny woman in a flowing dress and a huge straw hat whose gloved hand rested on the elderly man's bent arm. Once fed and admired, Rosy swayed to the other side of the street on the leash held by the elderly couple, and traffic began moving slowly.

Mitchell noted the friendly waves between the townspeople. There had been few of those when he was growing up. "Leave your lawn care things as long as you like. I don't have any plans for the building just now."

"What about that old place? Heard you bought it, too."

"No plans for that, either."

"Well, family things are hard to give up, especially land. Seems strange—you coming back here without a job in sight. People are already talking. Talk is that you might be in the mafia, setting up our town for a hideout. They're wondering how you got the money to buy this place, the Howard house, and the old ranch."

"I'd saved a bit. I'll manage." Maybe he *was* hiding out—from life. Mitchell gently took the key from Dozer, inserting it and unwrapping the chain securing the two big sliding doors. When they swung open, the musty scent and memories swirled out around him from the dark belly of the past.

His father's drunken yells once more tore through the shadows, Roman and him arguing violently.

Dozer's assortment of mowers occupied the space where cars had been parked. The mechanic's car lift had been taken. Boards, spotted with dust and littered with rubble, formed the workbench, and a pegboard rose above that. Once it held tools, now it was gray with spiderwebs.

"I sprayed for bugs and put some bait out for rats and mice," Dozer was saying, smoothing the handles of his new riding mower as if caressing a lover. "That's another reason to lock it tight, so no kids will come in here and get hurt. We had a murder in town about a year ago—a drive-by that killed poor Ms. Howard, sweet woman. She always used to make me Mama's recipes when I was sick. I missed my Mama's cooking and it chippered me right up every time."

Dozer looked around the gloomy building. "The first place I checked was here in case someone was using it for a hideout. Weren't no one here. I never saw Ms. Uma get so het up and angry at the law for not finding the killer, for not doing more. She went to Tulsa, went through the mug shots, and even hired a private detective. She's usually the nicest woman, but then there was pure fire in her. Ms. Lauren was shot down right in front of her and Ms. Pearl. Ms. Pearl came unglued and holed up, afraid to get out, I guess. But not Ms. Uma. She starting hunting that murderer right away."

It's your mother in you, Fred had yelled at Mitchell. *Grace didn't like good hard work and the land, and neither do you.*

One day you'll turn your back on me, on what my people left to me, and walk away, just like her.

Mitchell glanced at the stairs that led upward to the office, and the echoes of his dying father's sobs whispered around him. He remembered the desperation with which Fred had hugged him. *You're all I've got left of her. You and Roman. I loved that woman with all my heart.*

Mitchell rubbed the ache in his chest, the tightness clenching his heart. Then he turned and walked out into the sunlight, breathing heavily, fighting the storms in him.

Later, as Mitchell stood on the old ranch, the hot dry wind carried more dark memories—*Hell, no, you can't have a bicycle. Those are for city boys, and they cost too much. Warren men ride horses,* Fred had said harshly. *Just like your mother, always wanting things that cost too much.*

The old windmill turned silently, and the crows peered down at him, feathers blue black in the bright sunlight.

Mitchell noted the padlock on the old garage. It was rusted, but relatively new, gleaming in the hot sunlight. He remembered the relentless sun, the hours spent trying to eke a living from the worn-out earth.

He might as well see it all today, chew on it, and settle what he could. Mitchell lifted a broken crowbar from the rusted debris against the garage, placed it into the lock, and pushed. The lock held firm, but the metal plate holding it broke free from the weathered wood.

He pried open the old sliding door. From the shadows, a rat scurried past him and Mitchell used the crowbar to swipe away cobwebs. A heavy stench curled out into the fresh air.

The car filled the shadows, a big, powerful Chevrolet hardtop, dusty and laced with cobwebs.

The slice of sunlight bit through the space between weathered boards and skittered across the dusty windshield. Mitchell eased through the shadows and, disturbed, a bird fluttered out into the daylight.

In the driver's seat, head back against the seat, yawning with bared teeth and eyeless sockets, was a skeleton.

"The town has been quiet since you Warrens left—up until that shooting last year," the investigator said as the crime team worked within the perimeter of the yellow crime-scene tape around the garage.

Mitchell watched the men carry the black body bag to the ambulance. He recognized several of those who'd collected in a crowd nearby. Older, they were the people who'd expected the worst from him, the son of Fred Warren. They reminded him briefly of vultures waiting to pounce, waiting to destroy.

He smiled at them. Mitchell had learned a thing or two in the tough business world, and one of them was to smile in the worst times. Let them wonder what was behind that smile. He was here to stay until it suited him to leave. He'd been driven from town once, and it wasn't happening again.

He smiled briefly at Lonny James, the current police chief, who'd been a deputy at the time of the ranch fire. With skin the color of his Cherokee ancestors, heavy jowls, and a good-sized belly, the beefy mountain of a man was a longtime friend of Fred's; Lonny did more than his share in keeping the boys and Fred out of legal trouble—and right now, from his meaningful look at Mitchell, the police chief wasn't appreciating the "city boy" invasion.

"Don't leave town," the investigator was saying as he snapped his notebook closed.

Mitchell recognized the prick of suspicion lifting the hairs on his nape. "Am I a suspect?"

The man's smile was cold and professional. "Someone had to put that bullet hole in his head. Just don't make any plans to leave Madrid, okay?"

Mitchell didn't like the swelling anger within him. In the old days, the Warrens were accused of any misdeed, and that still chafed. "I just got here last night. The coroner suspects this murder is almost a year old."

"Just stay put, sir."

He moved away and Lonny spat a high-flying perfect arc into the hard-baked ground. "Dufus there had to run his little toy siren through town. It lit up all the dogs and when they howl, I get phone calls. Oswald Page just turned sixty-five and he was pretty upset last time the deputy used his siren and the dogs howled. Oswald's Viagra had just kicked in. Man, I do not want to listen to him harp on that again, or Mrs. Puckett worried about the invasion of space aliens. And I was up at midnight, listening to Myrtle Hawthorne scream about Edgar MacDougal's peeing off his back porch. After I got done calming her down, I felt I had to do Edgar justice and peed off my own back porch. Irma thinks Ralphie, our little Chihuahua, is turning her rose bushes brown anyway."

Lonny gathered up spit and sailed another high-gleaming arc into the air. "I been running some buffalo on your place, hope you don't mind. Their instincts tell them this is an old run. It was hard keeping them off."

"That's fine. Someone may as well get the use of it." Mitchell watched a late-model dark green Toyota come to stop a distance away. Uma burst from the passenger side, running toward the garage. Everett followed more slowly, his expression one of concern.

They were a good match, Mitchell thought, both with the same gentile background, and he wondered what had gone wrong—they seemed to care about each other.

Mitchell allowed the hard grip of Uma's fingers on his forearm, her eyes searching his. "Mitchell? Is it true? Do they think this is the car?"

"She identified the car in the drive-by shooting last year," Mitchell said to the investigator. He noted how Everett, no longer a boy, and dressed in a white business shirt and slacks, came to place his arm protectively around Uma. With black hair and blue eyes, he was well bred and successful in his travel agency, according to Dozer. They suited each other, and Mitchell looked away. He didn't know why, but the image of them together nettled him.

But Uma was ducking under the yellow crime-scene tape, hurrying toward the garage. She stopped suddenly as if frozen in place, her hand over her mouth. The hot wind tugged at her long dress, pressing it against her slender body, causing the hem to flutter at her ankles.

Everett and the investigator moved at the same time, and Mitchell settled back to study Uma and Everett. She leaned against him slightly, his arm around her again as the investigator spoke to her and she nodded quickly. Clearly, Everett knew how to comfort her, and Mitchell wondered when he had ever given a woman as much. Comfort wasn't a thing he'd learned in Warren 101 class.

While Everett helped Uma back to the car, the investigator returned to Mitchell. "I'd like to continue this discussion at the police station. Would you mind coming with me?"

"Am I under arrest?"

"We'd appreciate your cooperation for this investigation," the man said. "It seems you don't have exactly a good past with the people here in Madrid. There was a fire some years ago, right here, and your father died. You could have your reasons for coming back. I'd like to talk with you about that."

Mitchell inhaled slowly and thought that things really hadn't changed in eighteen years—

The interview in the police station was intense and pointed—with a suspicion that Mitchell had come back to settle old scores and that he'd been in Madrid when the shooter was killed. Mitchell slowly traced the rim of his coffee cup with his finger. "If I were you, I'd check out those bullet holes on the windmill to see if they match the body's."

"Windmill?" The investigator looked blank.

Lonny looked up at the ceiling and rocked on his heels.

His too-innocent expression said he'd noted the bullet holes, but the city boy had a few things to learn about treating a small town police chief nicely.

"Dufus" picked up his cell phone and quickly punched the keys. "Seth? Get someone up on that old windmill and check out the bullet holes. Get back with me right away and send one of the paddles to ballistics."

"Your boy better have a receipt handy," Lonny stated quietly. "That's personal property."

Dufus snorted, as if anyone would care about an old windmill.

Mitchell hadn't come to Madrid to be pushed. He jotted down names and addresses, then stood, tossing the pencil onto the pad. "I never met Pete Jones. I wasn't in Madrid until yesterday. I liked Lauren Howard when we were teenagers, and I remember her fondly. I had nothing to do with her murder or the man found in the car. These are my references, where I lived, my employer for the last ten years. This is my attorney in Seattle."

He gave Dufus time to recognize the law firm before continuing, "What I want to make clear to you is that I will not tolerate slander, or the public release of any personal information. I want to settle into this community with as little problem as possible. What I did before coming here is my business. Research all you want, but you do not have my permission to release anything about my life, that I was a top manager for Rogers Building and Supply. I am in Madrid on personal business—basically, I'm retired. That's all anyone here needs to know."

The investigator leaned forward, eyes narrowed, picking at details, ready to pounce. "And that personal business is?"

Mitchell wasn't letting anyone know that he wasn't exactly certain what he was doing in Madrid, but trying to make some sense of his life. He stood slowly and nodded to Lonny. "I'll call my attorney and tell him to give you what you need.

Meanwhile, I'm not going anywhere. But I will not tolerate slander, suspicions, or the release of any information on my private life."

He caught Lonny's quick, pleased smile before it was replaced by an impassive mask. Lonny had been the only person in the department back then who'd believed that the Warrens hadn't set the fire for insurance purposes.

Lonny followed him outside to his pickup and clapped a big paw on Mitchell's back just as he had done years ago. Mitchell had listened to more than one lecture about "keeping on the narrow path." "Seems you've learned a few things, like how to hold in that temper—it used to get you in trouble years ago. You know how to back up what you say and not with your fists, either—the times I had to pull you boys out of scuffles. . . . glad you're back."

"You might be the only one. Things haven't changed much when it comes to my family and Madrid's best."

"Your dad was a good man in a hard place. He wasn't a rancher, but he was trying his damndest. And there wasn't a better mechanic. He could make a dead motor sing. If you want it quiet about what you did before coming back, that's the way it will be. I've got a little pull around here, and higher up in the state. 'Hot-shot' back there needs to learn some manners. Welcome back to Madrid. See you around."

As Mitchell drove home, slowly cruising Main Street, lined with shady oaks and old two-story buildings, he noted the stealthy stares labeling him as a troublemaker. It was a look he'd known since childhood. "Uh-huh. Madrid is really happy that I'm back. And I'm not leaving."

"I'm sorry if I disturbed you. I had to come to be with her tonight," Uma said quietly at nine o'clock that evening when Mitchell opened his house door. She knew he'd been grilled for hours at the police station, and the shadows and lines of his face said he still carried those hours with him. She could feel the defensive shell around him, the vibration of his anger. It quivered in the fresh flower bouquet she held, the flowers Lauren had loved best. "It's late, I know. Please tell me if you'd rather not have me here."

He nodded and opened the door wider, and the smell of fresh paint matched the butter-cream spots on his bare shoulders, face, and hair. Unused to the certain raw masculinity that was Mitchell's, Uma looked away from the spots clinging to the hair on his chest. Mitchell inhaled impatiently, rubbing his broad hands on his jeans, also mottled with paint. "I'll get a shirt."

While she waited in the foyer for him to return, she angrily noted Lauren's beloved wooden tile, ruined by water stains. Billy had often left the door open, careless of the rain storms. It had been Lauren's duty to keep everything safe—

Mitchell returned, wearing a T-shirt. "Go ahead," he said quietly, watching her. "Can I get you a drink? The bottled water is top notch. If you like, I have something stronger."

Uma shook her head and searched his face. The lines were deeper now; the day's stubble covering his jaw also bore paint spatters. "Lauren loved fresh flowers. I hope you don't mind . . . you're tired. The discovery this afternoon, and all the time with the investigators, must have been draining. I'm sorry I broke down like that at the scene. Just seeing that car in the shadows with the crime people working around it was enough to bring back that night."

"Forensics people will be working on that bullet hole, trying to match it to a gun."

"Pete Jones, that's who they said he was, the car identification tracked to him, and so did the dental work his wife described. He isn't much—has a few stretches in prison behind him for car theft. He's the suspect in a car theft, a little black Miata convertible, but they couldn't pin it on him. The car is still missing. He's taken odd handyman jobs when he feels like getting off the couch—some alarm systems, some carpentry.

He's been missing since a short time after Lauren was killed. The mug shot of him matches the man I saw that night—I'd never forget him. Maybe it is over, and he's been made to pay."

"Maybe."

Uma looked at him sharply. "What do you mean?"

Mitchell looked away, the bald light above him hitting his harsh profile, his deep-set eyes in shadow. "Just that—maybe. He didn't shoot himself. That means whoever did might still be around. I put a chair in that back room. Let me know if you need anything else."

He hesitated, then said, "Maybe you should call Everett. I saw him with you today, his arm around you. He wants to protect you. Maybe you should talk to him, invite him here, if you need him."

Everett had wanted her to come home with him, pleaded with her to let him take care of her. His concern was honest, but she didn't want to slide back into that comfort, not when she'd struggled to find herself, what she was as a woman. It would be so easy, and then eventually she would hurt him. She couldn't bear sensuality now, the needs of an aroused man. And she couldn't be the woman Everett should have.

A woman crying softly was probably the worst sound in the world, worse than a drunken man's raging yells, Mitchell thought, as he rearranged his ladder to paint the kitchen ceiling.

He thought he heard a woman's whisper, then realized it was only the cat, watching him patiently. The cat's tail swayed against a window screen placed against the wall, creating the sound. Mitchell shook his head—maybe Uma was right, maybe the spirit of the dead woman was still here—if he believed that sort of nonsense.

The oscillating fan whirred, pushing the paint fumes toward the open window, and stirring the picture of Uma as she had arrived tonight. She was too pale, her eyes huge and shadowed, her hair long and flowing around her. When he'd opened the door, the streetlight had framed her, picking up the curling tendrils playing in the light breeze and draping her in silver. She belonged to the soft, gentle side of life, and looked like a fairy princess from another world, her mauve shift stirring around her.

His discovery of the car had freshened her pain, and she needed someone to help her. But he couldn't; he didn't know how. It was better to stay on the outside of her life. The cat suddenly leaped from the shadows and sat staring up at Mitchell—the animal's tail twitched as if he were waiting. And Uma's soft weeping seemed to roar.

Mitchell rubbed his hand across his face and stepped down from the ladder. Someone had to say something, do something to comfort her, and he was elected. He placed the paint roller aside, briskly rubbed his hands on the rag, and then stood at the kitchen sink, carefully washing them. What could he say to her? How could he help her?

In the end, he carried two bottles of water into the shadowy room to find Uma seated on the floor, an album across her lap, her back against the wall. On a small table near the open window, the red roses and daisies and blue batchelor buttons caught the slight breeze, the scents as soft and feminine as the woman on the floor.

He'd never been comfortable with softness, with the gentleness of women. That stark truth hit him as he eased down beside her, stretching out his legs. Her eyes were closed, her cheeks damp with tears.

If there was anything Mitchell did not want to do, it was to comfort a grieving woman.

He studied her profile, the sweep of her lashes, that perfect nose, the honed high cheekbones that said girlhood was years ago, the lips that were just as full and lush on the top as on the bottom.

Mitchell looked away into the night. He didn't want to

think about Uma's trembling soft lips, the glitter of tears on her cheeks—or the button of her dress that had come undone, just enough to show the curve of her breast above her bra. Each unsteady breath she took lifted that fascinating curve and he damned himself for the flick of sensual interest.

"What happened to you and your wife? You said you were divorced," Uma asked, the quiet question creeping out of the soft shadows to jar him.

He handed the water bottle to her. "Lots of things. It wasn't Serene's fault. It was mine."

Those lips curved slightly. "You're a cautious man. You always were guarded. Intimacy would be difficult for you. A woman needs that link."

He let that remark pass by into the night. But the next hit him dead center, too poignant to ignore.

"Your mother and father loved each other. It wasn't their fault that she left. You can't blame yourself for that, or for the fire that night."

"I don't want to talk about her." Mitchell sat in stony silence for a moment, then rose to his feet.

"You can't unwrap the past without her."

"How do you know I want to relive anything?" he shot back at her, surprised at the bald truth she'd served him, the penetrating boldness of it. She'd snagged his anger, pressed too close to what he didn't want to believe—or remember.

He was safer away from Uma than with her. He didn't like the feeling that he was emotionally running from her, but he was. And he was running from any discussion about his parents. Maybe he was afraid of whatever she knew—Uma had always known more about Madrid's lives than anyone. His father had said that her grandmother knew everyone's secrets, dark as they might be. An elegant woman, she had held a lynching mob at bay with those secrets, protecting a young man suspected of rustling.

Later the man was proven innocent, but the power of

Uma's grandmother was remembered as a soft hand in a lace glove, a sweet smile; she was a tigress when fighting for what she believed, with a backbone of steel. Priscilla Raleigh liked things quiet and peaceful in Madrid and had often guided the community into civilization with that velvet touch.

Uma's mother had once caught and held his ear painfully when he'd tried to steal candy; she'd held him there, stretched up on his toes until he promised never to steal again—and he never did. Now, just for a moment, Mitchell suspected that Uma had inherited that same unrelenting, ear-twisting quality.

And he wasn't about to get pushed around by her. His business was his, and he didn't like the mental image that his ear was grabbed, stretched painfully, until he was standing on his toes, ready to obey. He was thirty-seven and Uma was butting into his personal life.

Mitchell returned to the kitchen, to painting the edge of the ceiling. He tried to ignore the woman standing at the door, watching him, knowing that she'd come too close to his shadows. "Lauren would have liked that, a fresh coat of paint, the same shade as it was. We picked out that shade together," she said. "I'd like to help. I'll feel like I'm doing something for her, cleaning what she loved."

"I like working alone."

"Mmm. Do you?" Uma's eyebrows arched higher, her expression too bland.

He hadn't expected that touch of insolence, that mocking tone, that slight ridge of anger. He didn't want to look at that one untethered button, the gap it created in the soft curve of her breast.

He rammed a hand through his hair and a gob of paint plopped on his face. He knew what women's breasts looked like, all shapes and sizes in clothing and without. But dammit, he didn't want to think about Uma's breast, or how he'd foraged roughly for it when he was a boy in that hospital bed. "You'll ruin your dress."

"Give me something to wear—an old shirt, some boxer shorts." She wasn't backing off, watching him with those shadowed eyes, coolly drinking the bottled water. "It's going to be a long night for both of us, I think. You're furious now and it's showing. You're fairly bristling, that cool dispatched shield away for the moment—you missed that bit to the right . . . a little more . . . there, that's it. I would like something to do, here for Lauren. May I?"

He didn't like people ordering him around; he'd had enough of that growing up. When he looked down at her, Uma met his look. "You're bristling now. You don't like orders, and from a woman, right?"

Mitchell came down from the ladder, carefully placing the paint can and brush on the plastic sheeting covering the floor. He faced Uma and tried to keep his eyes on her face, not on the gap in her dress. He'd been a business manager; he knew how to control a situation—and Uma was a definite situation, a troubling one. "It's been a hard day for you. You should go home and rest."

She glanced at the whiskey bottle on the counter. "It's been a hard day for you, too. You resent the suspicions, don't you? I don't blame you. It must have brought back bad memories. You're emotional now and hiding it behind by growling. That won't do, Mitchell. Not everyone is your enemy."

She went right for the heart of his mood, leaving him nowhere to hide. Feeling raw and exposed to her, he decided to take a defensive shot—just a little warning to tell her it was backing-off time. Mitchell leaned back against the counter and crossed his arms over his chest. "What do you want from me? Bottom line? And by the way, your dress is unbuttoned."

He'd expected her embarrassment and enough distraction to send her on her way. Instead, Uma looked down; she slowly, methodically secured the button in its hole and then met his eyes. "The shirt and boxer shorts? Would you mind terribly if I helped paint tonight? Or are you set to growl some more?"

"Why don't you just run on home to Everett? Or back to your nice, safe house?" He didn't like revealing the bitterness in him, that lack of control, the edges that Uma could raise.

And she wasn't backing off, ignoring his warnings. "I could. But then I'd miss the fun of seeing you trying to bully me."

Bully. That's how he'd thought of Fred. The label shocked Mitchell. "Huh?"

"You're wounded and you're hurting and you're striking back. Madrid is a good town, Mitchell. Give us a chance."

How much of a chance had they given his family years ago? Instead of answering Uma, Mitchell turned away. "You lived one life. I lived another. Our viewpoints aren't going to match . . . my clean laundry is on the bed. Use what you want."

An hour later, Mitchell tried not to look up at Uma's bottom, cupped within his boxer shorts, or the muscles flexing in those long legs, her bare feet slender on the ladder.

He wasn't used to sharing his life or his personal space and Uma had stepped right into both. *Bully.* The word still burned. But then, he shouldn't be shocked, he was Fred Warren's son, wasn't he?

They'd worked quietly, effectively, noting briefly only the necessities. He turned away from the light fabric over her breasts, the uptilt of them as she raised her arm to paint around the ceiling. He didn't want to think of her as a desirable woman, one he'd want to carry into his bedroom, there to forget about the rest of the world.

But that was exactly what rode him, the poignant sensual restlessness of a man too long without a woman.

At three o'clock in the morning, they had finished the living room and Uma sat on the ladder, her head down. "I'd better go."

She rose tiredly, stretched, and shook free the hair she'd tethered in that loose knot, and the movement caught him, stunned him with unexpected sensuality. "I'm glad it's over now and Lauren can rest. Thank you for letting me say good-bye to her like this, restoring what she loved."

"Any time." Mitchell didn't want to remind her that someone else might have been involved; she needed whatever closure was possible. But more than likely, whoever had shot Pete Jones and the windmill was still around.

Dawn found Mitchell cleaning brushes and making coffee and wondering about the need to hold Uma tight against him, to wrap his fist in that long, waving soft hair and take her mouth.

But then his wife had said he was too controlled, too cool, even in lovemaking, hadn't she?

Lovemaking. Was that what it was called when two people served a mutual need, then separated as soon as possible, lying deep in their own thoughts, the air heavy with them? *Intimacy would be difficult for you. A woman needs that link.*

Mitchell sipped his coffee and moved out into the dawn and the blooming, unkept roses. He inhaled the fragrant, damp air and watched the rising sun catch on the dew. His homecoming and the discovery of the body, the interrogation, had raised his edges, riffling through the past, bringing the storms to life that had long been held in check.

Madrid's hot sultry nights and old memories could arouse any man, torment him into unfamiliar emotions. Uma's unexpected fire and passion when she faced his dark mood had fascinated him. The tag of "bully" still rankled. Yet she'd faced him with a steel he hadn't expected. It was disconcerting that someone so gentle could get to him—

He watched a bright red male cardinal light on a leaf-filled bird bath. He didn't like Uma prowling through his life.

" 'Intimacy,' " he muttered, disliking the taste of the word, the intrusion.

He'd streamlined his life for money and control and not emotions—definitely not for tenderness . . . or the raw edge of sexual need, driven by emotions, the primitive need to drag her into his arms and feast—

The cardinal flitted to a high limb, watching him with beady eyes. Uma was an instinctive woman, an intuitive one, gauging his mood, spearing right into his darkness without fear.

He really did not like that, or the bruising he now felt after the encounter. She'd called him "emotional and growling." Maybe he was.

But he didn't want anyone else noting that—especially the woman sailing by his house in the dawn, her legs long and gleaming in a free stride of a runner. It appeared that he wasn't the only one who couldn't sleep.

Uma seemed to float over the pavement, her pony tail floating behind her, her profile intent. Mitchell's gaze skimmed down her long throat to the soft cloth against her surging breasts.

He breathed raggedly; he didn't want to think about that soft bounce, the way she'd looked in his underwear.

He didn't want to think about those smooth muscles, or just exactly how Uma worked off her tension. He had enough of his own, humming quietly, unexpectedly in taut frustration.

He'd named himself "Clyde" after Clyde Barrow, a flamboyant 1930s holdup outlaw. With his gang and his girlfriend, Bonnie Parker, at his side, the real Barrow had led lawmen a chase across Oklahoma and other states. His legendary shootouts and robberies had sparked the interest of the press, and years later Clyde's bloody fatal battle still commanded attention.

Barrow, a man who took action to change his life, fascinated the person who now called himself "Clyde."

Life had been dull in the new Clyde's life, until he'd decided to take control. He wanted excitement, dangerous edges, and the power to take and give. His life had always been so commonplace, and now running on the edge was an addiction and a rebirth.

He wanted power, to feel fear churn in Madrid, to pay them back for their treatment of him. After all, it was only right that he make them pay . . . and he'd promised that by the end of summer, when the last rose petal fell in Madrid, he'd finish the job, killing all the women.

He hated roses; he hated the women who loved them. He hated the thorns and the beauty.

Clyde laughed silently. The four women had been childhood friends, their relationships too perfect, loving one another, sharing their lives now. They needed to be torn apart, to realize that life wasn't perfect. "Call it revenge," he whispered.

He shouldn't have trusted Pete Jones, that incapable clown, to manage a drive-by shooting. From now on, Clyde would do his own killing and Pete was just the first.

Studying his dapper reflection in the mirror in his hideaway, Clyde smoothed his three-piece checkered suit and straightened his tie. "It's true. Good clothes make the man."

He'd had quite the time convincing the tailor in Topeka to get just the right fabric and style. Clyde had explained that it was for a 1930s costume party. That was the same excuse he'd used for the other tailors—one in each city. Then, of course, they'd had to die and the records of the suits be removed from their files. Even the little dressmaker in Madrid had to die after she'd altered his clothing.

He couldn't afford to let Rosalie gossip about who he really was and his fascination for Clyde, his hero. It was really old Rosalie's time to die anyway, and the push down her stairs had made her death look accidental. No one suspected Clyde had helped—after all, Madrid was safe, wasn't it? Oh, he contributed to her funeral. It was only right. And he mourned her with the rest of Madrid.

Dresses for Bonnie, purses, and cloche hats were stored in boxes behind the closet's fake wall, a clever little door known only to him.

Dressed like Clyde Barrow, he could feel the excitement rushing through him, the power—

One lift of the board on the floor would take him to Clyde's favorite handgun, gleaming and deadly. The Colt Model 1911 .45-caliber automatic had handled well, peppering the Warrens' old windmill, a perfect moving practice target.

Clyde hated Madrid for what they had done to him, making him seem like nothing, when he was really better than they would ever be. They would pay for every put-down, every snicker, and he was getting really good at killing . . . and at waiting and planning. They still hadn't put the pieces together, the little accidents he'd planned, including poisoning Pearl's dog—Chester had barked too much, and Clyde didn't want the dog to arouse anyone to his night stalking.

Clyde adjusted the brim of his hat and polished his charming smile, a real lady-killer smile. Pearl might make a good Bonnie, but Clyde would have to be very certain of her first—she could be unstable and emotional, and he wasn't. He knew exactly what he wanted—to kill the women.

Mitchell had found the body in the garage and it was time to get Pearl working on gossip, using her to get Madrid worked up about the Warrens again. Clyde sucked in his stomach and straightened his shoulders. The Warren men attracted women, that tough, lean westerner look, and that irritated. *Uma and Shelly and Pearl had always been Clyde's, and Mitchell Warren wasn't interfering.*

Clyde scowled into his reflection. "Pete Jones really shouldn't have asked for more money."

Pleasure rippled through Clyde as he remembered Pete's surprised expression as he died. Clyde liked power and control, and that moment had been ultimate—Pete begging for his life.

They'd found the body and Clyde was ready for them. It wouldn't do to move too fast, because that would take away the pleasure, the anticipation, and he wanted their fears to grow, devouring them as his once had—before he'd discovered who he really was—Clyde.

Lauren was only the first to pay the bill Madrid owed him, and he was getting really good . . .

FOUR

Roman slid the Harley-Davidson near the sidewalk and kicked the stand down. The well-tuned FXRS's Low Rider motor died smoothly. He removed his helmet and scanned Maloney Street. The old garage had a padlock and chain, the boards were weathered and unpainted, the window broken.

He smiled briefly and wondered how many windows he'd broken in deserted buildings, a kid showing off his pitching arm with a rock. He removed his mirrored sunglasses and squinted against the morning sun. The street's pavement was cracked, blue-gray and still cool enough for a rabbit to hop across and into the brush of an empty lot. It was only the last week of June, and by mid-July, the pavement would be hot enough to burn the hand.

His cruise down Main Street proved it was the same as eighteen years ago—flower-basket clean and perfect. But behind that perfection lay the weaknesses, lusts, and darknesses of those who lived there. Just opening their stores, people still noted a newcomer, pausing on the sidewalks and slanting curious looks at him. A few "road apples"—horse manure—

were smashed flat. He'd recognized a few of the store owners' names, all people glad to get rid of the Warrens.

Awash with memories of the night his father had died horribly, Roman leaned against the Harley. He hadn't helped Mitchell pull Fred to safety. Maybe he wanted Fred to die. Maybe he wanted to be free of the hard work and the go-nowhere promises, of Fred's bitterness and taunts.

Roman had tried to become "someone." As a professional racecar driver, he'd wrapped himself in fast cars, fast times, and faster women.

On the run through life, he didn't have to think about bitter times—or how he stood back, not helping Mitchell with Fred.

Mocking himself, Roman decided that the hot-shot, know-it-all teenager hadn't really gone so far. He had everything he owned in the bag strapped to the Harley, a bum knee from a racing wreck, the twinges of a hangover from the night with the last woman—whoever she was—and no money in the bank. He'd lived fast and ended back where he'd started.

He bent to knead the aching knee that would never be perfect again, not quick enough for racing. There on Maloney Street, visions of racing wins, of champagne and beautiful, exciting women, cruised around him. Darkness followed the brilliance, the agony of the wreck, rolling over and over, the pain.

Roman lived with the bitter realization that he would never again be top dog, that he could settle for the racing pit, a mechanic's job or nothing . . . and just as suddenly as it had come, his fame was gone, along with friends and money.

He might never have come back—except Mitchell was here and staying, apparently. With a body discovered a week ago in the ranch's garage, Mitchell was likely to have the old suspicions rise around him.

After leaving Madrid, they'd argued bitterly about Roman finishing high school and "straightening up." But he wasn't letting Mitchell take the place of Fred's parenting. Roman had finished high school because he'd wanted to, and through the years, as men, they had come to an easy relationship.

Roman smiled briefly, coldly. There was just enough stubbornness in the Warrens to stay put amid the town that had never liked them.

Whatever troubled Mitchell enough to bring him back to this godforsaken town, Roman wasn't letting his brother face Madrid alone—especially not with the murdered man raising old bitterness.

He shrugged lightly. He had nowhere else to go. He'd come full circle. A few miles back on the highway, a big sturdy road sign looked like a way to end it all.

But Mitchell might need him, and Roman would be there.

He listened briefly to the sound of poorly tuned motorcycles pulling closer to him, stopping, and he slid on his sunglasses. The tough kid with sideburns and tattoos had insolence written all over him. Roman knew the look—he'd worn it as a teenager. He also recognized the slit-eyed appraisal of his bike, gauging how much the machine would bring when sold.

The other kid was the follower, trying to emulate the tough guy, a cigarette pack rolled high into his short sleeve.

The girl was all spiky dyed black hair and hard black makeup, unmatched dangling earrings, blue fingernail polish, tight red top and tighter jeans; she wore silver toe rings and black sandals.

Roman kicked a piece of crumbling sidewalk with his scuffed biker boot. Did he feel guilty about not helping, not answering Fred's cries for help in the burning house?

Maybe. He definitely felt guilty about Mitchell's bad burns and his pain.

Sliding from the past, Fred's terrified cries careened into

the bright afternoon sunlight and died in the hot, dry air as Roman forced them away.

"The name is Jace. What's up, man?" the tough kid asked, with a threatening edge to his tone that said he didn't like being ignored. The hard-looking girl with knowing eyes looked Mitchell up and down, appraising his faded "Sturgis Is for Real Bikers" T-shirt, black jeans, and biker boots even as she draped an arm around the kid. Roman knew that look; women liked him and he liked them. Women and motors, he thought, they both hummed to his touch, and it still wasn't enough to fill the hole inside him.

"Not much."

"Nice bike."

"Thanks." It was all he had left—that, and a Lamborghini stashed in a friend's garage because he couldn't afford to pay insurance and upkeep on it.

"You want to race? Maybe bet a little? How about it?" the kid asked slyly.

Roman automatically noted the kid's bike leaking oil on the pavement; it probably needed new gaskets and the boy's pants were wearing a fair amount of the sprayed oil. He shook his head and swung onto his bike, revving the motor and swinging out onto the street to circle back to Mitchell's house.

"I thought you'd come," Mitchell said quietly as he opened the door to his brother. Roman seemed to appear whenever he thought Mitchell might need him. The ties were there, if not expressed. They'd struggled through a childhood and teenage years together. "How's the knee?"

Roman's shaggy hair and scruffy look matched his road miles. But he bore that hard Warren look, the brown wavy hair and amber eyes, and the attitude that said he wasn't taking any more knocks from anyone. Mitchell noted the lack of Roman's watch and ring, both given to him for winning races.

"It's cooler here than Las Vegas. LV isn't my kind of town anyway, but I thought the dry heat might heal up my knee. Nothing is going to," Roman replied with a shrug, but his narrowed eyes watched Mitchell closely, gauging him for trouble.

"Just to soothe your mind, I don't have a terminal disease," Mitchell said easily. Daytona and Indianapolis were really Roman's kind of towns, where racing flowed through the veins of the pit-men, the champions, and the bars. But Mitchell knew that his brother was too shamed and aching every time he heard the racing motors rev, the flag go down; Roman couldn't settle for being a top pit-man.

Roman shoved the leather bag into Mitchell's chest, a little less than gently, but that was the brothers' way. "I wasn't worried about you. I just came to live off you for a while. You always were an easy touch."

"Uh-huh. Sure. Come in."

As Mitchell led the way through the house, Roman took in the ladder and paint supplies, the big cardboard boxes of washer and dryer, the rolls of linoleum, an array of new power and hand tools spread across the kitchen counter.

Mitchell dropped the bag onto the floor of a bedroom they had just passed. "You'll need a bed. I'm short on furniture until the floors are covered. And I'm not picking up after you, or doing your laundry. I did enough of that when we were young."

"Man, we weren't ever young," Roman stated flatly and opened the screen door out into the overgrown rose garden. Then there was the silence as he turned to Mitchell, that quiet assessing stare.

But he didn't ask what Mitchell sought, what he needed, why he was back in Madrid, a town that had never wanted their family. Roman turned on the faucet and placed his head under it, then caught the towel Mitchell threw at him. He glanced at the new light fixture on the floor, waiting to be installed, then took the beer Mitchell handed him. "What's the deal here? Who trashed this house?"

"Good old Billy Howard. He married Lauren. She's dead, a drive-by, and he took off."

"I read a rehash about her death in the newspaper article last week—thought I'd check up on the old town after you moved here. Too bad. Nice girl." Roman browsed through the new refrigerator, selected bread, lunch meat, and cheese, and began building a sandwich. Leaning against the counter, he watched Mitchell heft the light fixture and begin up the ladder. "You need me, don't you? Admit it. You're looking for cheap labor and you found that body just to bring me back to this hick town."

Mitchell dismissed Roman's tease, and came down the ladder. "You may have enough problems without mine."

Roman neatly sliced a tomato, a quick one-slash that said he'd spent time cooking for himself, and plopped it on the sandwich. "What's that?"

Mitchell sipped on the beer he'd opened and handed the news to him straight, because the brothers didn't dance around the truth. "Shelly Craig has a daughter. A seventeen-year-old named Dani, and Shelly has never married. According to gossip, no one knows who the father is. Shelly's folks kicked her out and she raised the girl by herself. She's had a hard time of it, cleaning houses and ironing. Shelly is paying the bills for her mother in the rest home, and Mrs. Craig won't claim the girl. The old man died years ago, but he was even worse."

He watched Roman frown slightly and methodically place aside the sandwich on a paper towel. On a drunken binge long ago, Roman had mourned taking the virginity of a nice girl in Madrid. The time line coincided with Shelly's daughter's birth. *That could just make Mitchell an uncle, and uncles were supposed to be responsible. If the girl needed help, he would give it.*

Roman studied the linoleum that Mitchell had started peeling away. He was quiet, his hand running across his chest as if soothing an ache there. "You're going to need help here, with this house. I might stay a while."

"Then you'd better get used to a few things. One is that I don't care for anyone to know my business, other than that I'm retired. It might come out, but I'm not spreading it around. Two, someone put that bullet through Pete Jones's skull, so there is an ongoing investigation. Three, they still don't like us."

"So what else is new?"

"Those are Lauren's things in the back room. I told Uma Thornton that they could stay. She's still pretty broken up—so are Shelly and Pearl."

"They were always close, the four of them." But Roman's tone said his mind wasn't on Lauren's death, or the murder of Jones. He was thinking about Shelly and her daughter, his mind flying back through the years to that night—and the possibility that he might be a father.

"Take it easy, Roman," Mitchell advised slowly, understanding that Roman was torn by the past and his emotions now. He could be impulsive, passionate, emotional—and he was bitter about the shattered knee and lost fame. In truth, Mitchell didn't know what Roman might do—they were men now, with too much time apart. "She's built a good life."

"Always trying to protect the vulnerable, right, Mitchell?" Roman asked softly, and Mitchell took comfort from the half-smile. "So do you want help with that light fixture or not?"

He looked like a warrior fighting the brambles of Lauren's old garden, the cat high on an oak limb watching him. Mitchell Warren was clearly at war, the weeds and trimmed brush piled high in the back of his pickup.

Coming back from her morning run, Uma stopped,

stunned by how he moved through the rose bushes, careless of his bare chest and the thorns in his bare hands. He battled through shadows and rising dawn, a powerful surge of muscle and strength. Curious as to what he fought—himself, or the garden—she moved through the overgrown shrubs between their houses, on the stones placed just so. She wondered what could bring such savagery, what he sought and what he battled. Clearly the garden was a battlefield, the bushes cut to nubs, a pile of rubble waist high. Roses in full bloom splashed across the stark, leafless stalks. Broadleaf lilies-of-the-valley, past their blooming, had been trampled. Lemon balm and mint, torn from their rambling beds, scented the air, and a coffee cup was perched upside-down on a garden fairy statue's head. "Good morning, Mitchell."

Then she knew—he fought himself. That fierce "don't come near me" look, the bloody scratch across his unshaven cheek and more on his shoulders, all said he was wrapped in something far worse than trimming an overgrown backyard garden. Sweat gleamed on his shoulders and plastered his hair to his head and his eyes were as dark as the mood he wore.

He bristled nicely, Uma decided as she stood in the shade, smiling at him, waiting to see what he would do next, now that his kingdom had been invaded. Odd, that she should be so curious about him, fascinated by the raw power and the emotion driving it. Mitchell hurled the pruning shears he'd been using point first into the rich ground.

He came back from whatever fury he fought and the air stood still as he slowly took in her sweaty tank top and shorts and legs and running shoes. Through the bed of lavender, over the tarragon and lemon balm, the impact of Mitchell's raw sexual energy hit her. It quivered in the rose of Sharon bush, and danced along the spiderwebs heavy with dew. Deep and slow and husky, his voice snared her.

"I remember you standing just like that on the playground, watching everyone like you were fitting all the pieces together—so solemn, as if you cared about everyone and knew something they didn't. . . . I'm hauling the brush out to the ranch. Want to come with me?"

When she hesitated, thinking of all the reasons she shouldn't, Mitchell braced a hand against the wall beside her head and leaned down to whisper, "Afraid?"

He was too close and too big and too—Uma sucked in air and pressed back against the wall. She could almost feel the damp texture of his skin, the heat pouring from him, the raw sexual need. Was she afraid? Not of him, only of whatever lurked within her that she didn't want to release—had never released.

Mitchell was watching her reactions closely and she looked away to his hand, wide and open near her head. "You probably got that temper from your mother's Irish blood. She fought, too, though in a gentler way. Those thorns in your hands really should be removed."

He blinked and frowned and considered his hand, turning it palm upright to reveal the rose thorns embedded there. "I hadn't noticed."

"Let me take them out."

"I can manage, and my mother has nothing to do with me. She gave up that right."

"Is everything going to be a fight with you? Can't one neighbor help another?" she asked, half-teasing, half-serious.

"What do you know, and what do you want?" he returned softly, easing a tendril back from her face. His finger lifted her chin, those dark eyes prowling on her face, too close and seeing too much.

What did she want? Peace and safety and harmony, and none of them were in his eyes.

In the kitchen, while Mitchell was retrieving the antiseptic and cotton, she felt Lauren calling to her, that warm brush of air, almost like a hug. Uma leaned against the counter and noted the expensive black leather briefcase, the letters opened beside it. At a glance, one letterhead stood out—"Mr. Mitchell Warren, Vice President of Sales, Corporate Office, Rogers Building and Supply."

She recognized the company name—Rogers Building and Supply was a major national warehouse chain, where customers could find everything from building needs to gardening supplies.

A printout beside it said "Position terminated amiably by employee" and showed that Mitchell had transferred stock and funds from his company retirement fund into personal investments. The total took Uma's breath away, and yet he appeared to have little, other than his pickup and the family property he had purchased.

When Mitchell returned, wearing a shirt, he glanced at the briefcase and shoved the letters aside. His silence said he suspected she'd seen the correspondence.

She felt Mitchell watching her as she bent her head to tend those big broad torn hands, easing out the thorns with a needle, dabbing antiseptic on the scratches. His breath was warm upon her cheek and she sensed his study of her. "You really should wear leather gloves and be more careful. But then, you know that, don't you? You were in a mood this morning and taking it out on poor Lauren's garden, just ripping and tearing because you felt like it."

He snorted at that, dismissing her.

Finished, she studied the hard craggy face, the bloody scratch on his cheekbone and dabbed the cotton ball with antiseptic on it. He rared back, glaring a "don't touch me" at her, and without thinking, Uma reached for that rich shaggy hair and held it tight in her fingers.

His eyes narrowed, flashing at her, yet he let her hold him as she continued to cleanse the scratches. "You like that, don't you? Having your way? Running things?" he asked darkly.

She screwed the lid back onto the tube, forming her words

carefully. "Maybe I do, when someone like you doesn't know what's good for him. These could get infected."

"That's my business."

"You always were difficult and bull-headed."

Without pausing, Mitchell shot an edgy taunt at her. "And you like things nice and easy, don't you?"

She didn't understand the shifting emotions, and frowned up at him. Mitchell pushed away from the counter and turned on the faucets full force. He bent his head beneath the running water and scrubbed his face.

"What's with you?" she asked, trying to understand how she'd upset him.

When he straightened and deliberately wiped his face while looking at her, she knew he was washing her touch from him. "You," he said as he ran the towel roughly over his hair, leaving it in shaggy peaks.

Mitchell wasn't in a mood for gentleness or understanding as he hurled the kitchen towel into the sink and issued his challenge: "Coming?"

Uma's reply surprised her. She wondered if his bristling mood was contagious as she lifted her chin, staring at him boldly. If he wanted an argument, she could give him one. "Only if you ask nice."

Mitchell considered her face, the way her body tensed as his look raked down and up. "Terms?"

"You could call them that. I don't like feeling like a tagalong. Either you invite me, or you don't."

She didn't trust the way his mouth curved slowly, or the low husky intimate tone, "Well, Ms. Thornton, would you mind accompanying me this morning?"

"That's better. Yes, I would love to, Mr. Warren," she said very properly and wondered why she had agreed. Why Mitchell fascinated her. Why she wanted to reach out and shake him.

At the ranch, or what was left of it, Mitchell tossed the brush onto a pile and glanced at Uma; she didn't deserve the backlash of his dark mood. With a bad, restless night behind him, he'd battled the garden for physical relief.

And found that he liked it.

All those years when he'd worked his way up the corporate ladder, he actually liked the physical movement, the tending of trees and plants. Just one more thing he didn't know about himself, that he enjoyed the simplicity of working with his hands.

The truth of the matter was that he didn't know how to react to those soft, caring looks, that light sweet touch of her fingers upon his skin.

He should apologize, but he—Mitchell hurled a limb onto the pile. *He never apologized. Never.* The morning was cool, with just enough warmth to foretell the day's baking heat, and he remembered that his father had never apologized. *People take apologizes as a sign of weakness . . .*

Mitchell frowned and studied his hands locked to the pickup's side panels. The pickup jolted and he looked up to see Uma standing on the bed, taking the old broom in the back and sweeping out the leaf and twig clutter. "I can do that," he said, nettled that she would be helping him, working with him.

And he wondered why.

There, moving tall and leggy, silhouetted in front of the bright morning sun, capable and lithe and all slender curves, Uma looked like any other woman, not the cool artist-type who preferred her shadowy office and her quiet. Or was she?

Mitchell could almost feel his fingers locking into those hips, smoothing those long, slender legs. In his mind, an erotic flash of skin against skin, of those long legs circling his hips as he drove into her, just sex and heat and woman making him forget everything—

When she put down the broom and made to leap from the back of the pickup bed, Mitchell stood in front of her. He wondered what she would do—

"Move," she ordered and he took pleasure in that tight tone.

"Or?" He wondered how far he could push her before—

She placed her hands on her waist and looked down at him. "Mitchell Warren, you are as perverse as you were as a boy. Just every bit as ornery. Now, step back."

With his hand sweeping low in front of him in a bow, Mitchell stepped aside and Uma leaped to the ground. "You just love doing that, don't you? Challenging me? Why?"

"Because you're here and I like getting to you. You sizzle, just a nice smothered sort of anger, all very ladylike—and I wonder what it would take to get you really riled. Call it entertainment."

Uma's gray eyes narrowed, then she lifted her head and walked away from him to the overgrown rubble of the house. He rarely entered other people's lives, but Uma seemed so complete and strong and yet feminine.

He wondered how any man could let her go and why she didn't want remarriage to a man as gentle and upstanding as Everett; why she didn't want a home of her own and a family when she suited the role.

He wondered why that lurch of possession shot through him, to hold her, to have her. He came to stand behind her and heard himself ask, "Do you like being single?"

"I do. I like my life." She pushed an old board with her foot as the old windmill slowly whirred nearby. "Tell me about that night."

"No."

Those gray eyes turned to look up at him, searching his shadows. "Afraid?"

"Of telling you? No." She was pushing, trying to understand something he couldn't. To give himself thinking room, removing himself from the passion inside, he said, "The Warren homestead was originally 640 acres. Now it's only forty."

She knew everything, but still those gray eyes studied him and the night of the fire pushed out of him, something he'd never shared with anyone else. There, in that cool summer morning, amid the old burned house, that bitter night slashed out of him as fresh as when it had happened—the living terror of seeing the barn blaze.

"Roman and I saw the fire first. Dad was drinking and we couldn't rouse him. The horses went wild, the smoke so thick you couldn't see, and you could only hear those awful sounds. The barn doors had been nailed shut. By the time we found a crowbar to pry the plank free and get the horses out, the house was on fire and Dad was screaming. The doors to the house had been nailed shut while Roman and I fought the fire. It was arson . . . payback for something I'd done, or didn't do."

The smoke of that night choked him, the fear wrapping around him as he turned away. "There's not much after that. Dad died on the way to town."

Tell Grace that I've always loved her, his father had whispered amid his pain. *Everything was my fault. Take Roman and go to her . . .*

But he hadn't; he needed Roman perhaps more than his younger brother needed him. He couldn't bear the thought of Roman going to a mother who had left her sons and husband. Mitchell looked down to where Uma's slender pale fingers held his own, and then up to the softness of her eyes. He tore his hand away, rubbing it against the other and studying the two fingers webbed by fire.

"You still feel guilty, don't you?" Uma asked quietly at his side. "You think that you could have done something to save him, that you failed in some way."

"I should have seen it coming. At nineteen, I had some idea about what a woman could do. Tessa was a woman who always got what she wanted. I didn't want her."

"Tessa Greenfield?" Uma's sharply indrawn breath said she understood immediately.

"Her husband was dead of a heart attack by the time I put the pieces together and got Roman under control. When I walked out, Tessa was still screaming, cursing at me."

A slight breeze riffled through the tops of the old elms, broken by fierce Oklahoma storms, and Mitchell heard his father whisper, *Tell Grace that I've always loved her. Everything was my fault. Take Roman and go to her*—

"Tessa just lives across the county line, not eighty miles from here. She sold the ranch and moved when Max died, so she could have more of a social life than on the ranch. You came that close to Madrid and never came back in all that time?"

When he shook his head, Uma looked off into the distance. "And that's when you decided money meant everything, that and power. I saw the letters on your kitchen cabinet. Money and prestige weren't enough, were they? You can't get over this. You're still wearing that guilt—that you were the reason he died and your family lost what was left of the old homestead."

"I think about it sometimes," Mitchell said, unwilling to give her everything. "I imagine your father had a lot to say about—"

"His feud is his own. But in a way, you both are alike, carrying dirty old laundry with you, when there's nothing to be done about it. How does Roman feel?"

"I don't know."

"You mean, you don't talk about it, right? You just locked it up and—"

"Lay off."

The slow rise of color in her cheeks told him that she didn't like his attitude. "Don't forget you're in my town now, Mitchell Warren, Vice President of Sales. I know the people here. I love them, and I won't have you storming around, brooding, tossing off all sorts of porcupine needles—"

" 'Porcupine needles?' " Mitchell stared at the woman pacing back and forth in the sunlight. He could have picked her up and carried her into the truck and used her passion in a way that would satisfy them both—or could he? He wasn't exactly certain what would satisfy Uma.

"Well, invisible barbs when someone comes too close."

In his adult lifetime, few people had lectured Mitchell. He didn't like it; in his youth he had taken enough orders from Fred. "Anything else while you're at it? Just what's bothering you about me?"

"Just don't forget that you're in *my* town. If you've got any big ideas about tearing everything apart—forget it."

He leaned back against the pickup and crossed his arms. "My, my, my. How you do talk. And by the way, it'd suit me if you'd keep my private life private."

She waved her hands again and shook her head. "As if I'm a pipeline to the world. I know what is private and what isn't. Don't fight me on this, Mitchell. You'll lose."

After her morning with Mitchell, an afternoon with Everett was soothing. Uma hadn't expected Mitchell to be able to rile her, but he had. He'd stood there, tall and powerful against that black beast of a pickup and his expression said he was amused.

Amused. She amused him.

Uma trembled slightly. Unless she was mistaken, Mitchell's look at her was purely sexual—raw, vibrating through the bright sunshine and locking within her. The ride home had been silent, and he'd driven right to her home—something that was certain to irritate her father. Mitchell had reached across her and opened the door, his arm brushing her breast.

In that frozen moment when neither moved, Uma's heart

stopped, her senses too aware of the currents between them. "Better go inside," Mitchell had said softly, tauntingly. "Where it's safe."

She shivered again as she realized Everett was speaking to her—"Uma, we could still have a good life together. I love you. You know that."

Uma wiped the counter in the kitchen that had once been hers to tend. Designing Everett's travel and advertising brochures often led her back here, to the home she still loved, because it was a part of her—the old dreams that she didn't want now. It was a good time and a good house, she thought fondly.

His office in the home they had once shared had been designed by her. She'd also shared his office on Main Street, her graphics computer set up across from his desk. They'd been high school sweethearts, their courtship gentle and secure, encouraged by their families. They'd gone to college together and had returned to be married. How exciting that time was—just married, working together and planning a home, building it. Life had been so perfect—once.

Then Christina, their baby, had died.

Uma tugged herself away from the pain, that ache. She folded the dishrag and placed it beneath the sink. "Everett, I love you, too. You're a wonderful man. We've been friends forever, but you deserve more than that."

"There's never been anyone but you, and you know that. I—I made a mistake, my affair with Lorraine. I can't explain it—"

She turned to him; Everett's black, waving hair and soft blue eyes had been his gift to Christina. He was a gentle, good man, and very attractive now in his navy and white striped dress shirt, open at the throat and rolled up at the sleeves, his suspenders in good taste and his navy suit pants flowing down to polished dress shoes. The suitcase at the front door said he'd be leaving on business soon and as always, she'd come to water the plants—ones she'd chosen long ago to decorate the house—and check on his home, no longer hers.

But the attachment was there, the long hours spent in planning and painting—

How hard they'd both worked to set up their businesses—Everett taking over his family's travel business and Uma starting out as a freelance graphic artist. That was the arrangement they'd always had, the Big Plan. According to the steps in the Big Plan, when they had children, her graphics office would be moved into their home—if she decided to continue working. They'd seen each other through the grief of dying parents, been together through so many wonderful and horrible times.

"I can explain Lorraine easily," Uma said softly. "After Christina, I was depressed and withdrawn. You needed comfort, too. I understood, I told you that. I think you have someone now."

Everett frowned and rubbed his chest. "I won't lie. It's convenient for both of us. We're friends and she has a little girl. I . . . like that little girl, and Anna understands that we don't have a commitment. She knows I love you."

"You're a man who should have a family."

Everett rubbed his chest, and she thought how he had looked as a young father, cradling his baby daughter and so proud. The past tethered him, and it was unfair. He should have other children, a woman who loved him as a wife should. Uma loved him as a longtime friend.

His statement came from his heart; she'd never doubted him. "I will never forgive myself for being gone when Christina was born, or when she—"

Uma placed her hand on his, covering the ache she knew was genuine. "You were away at a conference, both times. It was essential to Thornton Travel. The company was growing, it still is. You've set up branch offices, Everett. You could move anywhere you want, but you're staying here."

"Home is where the heart is, haven't you heard? I want you with me." His other hand covered hers, his expression sincere. She'd seen the high-powered salesman in him, she'd seen the tender lover, the honesty—and the desire.

She couldn't stand the desire, was chilled by it.

Uma eased her hand away, and Everett shook his head. "Uma, you've locked yourself away from life. You watch and you care, and you love, but you don't live, not for yourself. Come with me on this trip. It will be good for you. You haven't gone anywhere to relax since Lauren—"

She allowed herself to be drawn close to him in that old protective way, the friendly way that reassured her, comforted her. Everett rocked her against him. "I know, honey. Life's not turning out like we planned, is it?"

She shook her head, mourning the old dreams in the house around her. The time had passed, and that's what she felt as a woman—that her time had gone on without her.

"Shh. Just let me hold you. Friends, okay?"

"Sure—friends," she returned, resting against him. After a moment, she drew away, and with the familiarity of the years between them, smoothed his hair and adjusted his collar. She did care for him, this genuine man who couldn't move on either, and who deserved so much more. "You have a plane to catch, don't you?"

"Uh-huh. Just send that design on to the printers, will you? Sign my name?"

"Okay. A hundred thousand copies, was it? Due at the end of the month and to be sent to your branch office in Chicago?"

"You got it, kid. Thanks."

The working familiarity was there, the easy arrangements, the same old Everett. She raised her face to kiss him on the cheek, her friend, their lives merged. Instead he turned slightly, their lips meeting. The warmth was pleasant, lingering—and then Everett breathed heavily and moved away, and she knew he wanted more.

That afternoon, in Uma's second-story office, Shelly sat hunched in the overstuffed chair. In her familiar shirt and shorts and her hair in a ponytail, Shelly brought with her the scent of lemon cleaners and fear. Her hand shook as she replaced the tea cup in its saucer, then gave it to Uma. "It's always so safe here, so quiet, as if nothing ever changes. I remember being here, playing with the doll blanket your mother sewed for me, the way your grandmother cuddled me in this chair. Your mother fitted me for maternity clothes here. She held Dani—what am I going to do, Uma? Roman is back and I heard Dani talking to her friends—I really don't like them—about this hunky guy on a Harley. It's Roman. The talk is all over town. He and Mitchell went down to the lumberyard and got supplies and then to the thrift shop for a bed. You said Mitchell had a bed, so that means Roman is probably staying. What should I do?"

"Maybe he won't stay."

"Dani is determined she's going to have him. I heard her talk about how she was going to have a real man take her virginity and he just arrived in town. I think that is all a ruse to force Jace to commit to a solid relationship. I've got to stop this now, somehow. Roman is her father!" On her feet now, a lithe, active woman, Shelly wrapped her arms around herself, her ponytail whipping around her face as she turned. "Tell me what to do. You're the only one who I can talk to."

Uma placed aside the tray with the tea service on it. Long ago in this same room, she had learned how women sharing tea led to peace and clear thinking. "You have to tell Roman."

Shelly rocked herself. "I just can't."

Uma let the silence settle her point and Shelly sank once more into the chair, her head on her knees, arms around her legs as she rocked. "I don't have a choice, do I?"

"Not really. Mitchell has been here for a week. He's been in town quite a bit, buying fix-up stuff for Lauren's house—"

"Lauren's house—I forgot to tell you. Pearl went over there and told Mitchell that you'd sent her for Lauren's things. She intends to sell them at her church thrift shop. Did you really tell her she could have them? I thought we were all going to sit down and—"

"I did not." Uma reached for her telephone, punching in Pearl's number. Pearl was obsessed with her post as manager of the thrift shop. When she answered, Uma tried not to let anger enter her voice; Pearl could be disoriented and pitiful, whining when faced with anger. Raised in a verbally abusive home, she had married a man who enjoyed tormenting her. "Pearl? I hear you collected Lauren's things from Mitchell's house."

Pearl's voice was at first confident, explaining that she didn't want Lauren's things to be where "that man could paw through them." "Pearl," Uma said carefully. "You are to put Lauren's things in a box and not leave one of them out. I'm coming over there to collect them."

"Did I do something wrong?" Pearl was immediately distressed. "I just didn't want my friend's personal mementos in that man's possession. And I think she would like the idea of making money for the church thrift shop, some little girl wearing her old bead bracelets, that cheap stuff she wore."

"I think Lauren's things should stay in her house for the time being. I sense she would have wanted it that way."

Alarm rang in Pearl's hurried questions. "You don't think that she's a ghost now, do you? Haunting that house?"

"Pearl, just put everything in the box; I'll know if anything is missing. I went through everything very completely the other night." Uma replaced the telephone and met Shelly's look. "Sometimes she can just make me—"

But Shelly was still thinking about Roman. "I can't tell him."

"You don't have any choice, Shelly," Uma stated softly. "I'd better go over to Pearl's right now. She's probably coming apart right now. I hate to be firm with her."

"She needs us, that's for sure. She always has. She's a part of us and we're a part of her since first grade. I've got to get home and start supper." Shelly's blue eyes were worried. Dani could be headstrong, just like her father. One more clash, and Dani could leave home . . .

Shelly heard her own sob. She'd do anything to keep Dani safe.

FIVE

Mitchell settled back in the stool at Clyde's Tavern, named after Clyde Barrow. Memorabilia of the 1930s Oklahoma outlaw drenched the small, dark room, from the framed pictures of Bonnie Parker and Clyde, and the Jesse James and Ma Barker gangs, to hangers of reputed outlaws' various coats and clothing, and guns all covered with a layer of dust. There were lipstick kisses on Pretty Boy Floyd's glass-covered picture.

After treating Roman to a homecoming dinner at The Italian, it only seemed right to walk down the street to Clyde's Bar. Roman had already centered in on a curvy blonde in a tight red sweater and tighter jeans, and the local boys standing at the bar weren't happy.

Mitchell looked closer through the shadows. A Remington "Whipit" gun, similar to Bonnie Parker's, was dusty. But the Browning automatic rifle, of the type favored by Clyde, lacked cobwebs, and gleamed in the shadows. If Mitchell had been the curious type, he'd wonder if the guns had been disabled. But then, he wasn't looking for answers or for trouble.

Brewing trouble was something the Warrens knew how to do, Mitchell thought idly; they were bred to it. He sipped his

beer from the bottle, rather than the uncertain cleanliness of
the mug. The smells were the same, of alcohol and smoke, of
old-timers' stories of the Land Rush and the Dust Bowl.

The darker memories circled him: how many times had he
hauled his father out of here?

He glanced around the dark, smoky shadows of the tavern, gauging Roman's chances if he let his hands get any
lower on the blonde's jeans as they swayed to the jukebox
music.

Mitchell didn't like thinking about Uma's bottom, the way
it curved as she stood on the ladder, as she painted the ceiling
trim; the way it tightened and swayed as she had paced on the
ranch, the way her T-shirt pressed close to her breasts when
she put her hands on her hips.

She'd worn his clothes and the sight of that had set him off
in a way he didn't understand.

Mitchell sipped his beer and watched Lyle Nelson eye Roman and the girl. The men at the bar wore plaid western
shirts and worn jeans and boots that had seen more than
their share of manure and stomping fights. They were whip-
cord lean from ranch work, and he recognized most of them
as going to Madrid's schools.

"Hey, crip," Lyle called to Roman. "That's my girl. How'd
you like that other leg tromped?"

Mike, the bartender, threw down his bar towel and
reached for a baseball bat. He patted it into the palm of his
other hand in a silent warning, but Lyle wasn't watching.
When Roman leaned close, nuzzling the girl's ear, Lyle started
to walk toward him.

"Outside," Mike's voice boomed over the music.

Mitchell shook his head as Roman leaned in to kiss the girl
and then slowly walk past Lyle out to the back alley. Lyle's
three buddies sulked after him.

Lonny came in, spotted Mitchell and walked to his table;
he slid into a chair Mitchell's foot shoved at him. He

slammed his book down on the table, *The Smooth Moves List.*
"Nice quiet night."

"Uh-huh."

A big crash sounded against the back alley door. "Cats in
the garbage cans again," Mike said easily before he went back
to the bar.

"Real big cats. 'Cats' means Mike thinks whoever is having
a go at it should be left to settle it," Lonny noted as another
crash sounded. He took a deep breath and looked at the Indian peace pipe on the wall. Someone had hung a white plastic rose and purple Mardi Gras beads on it. "Irma says I
should try that Viagra stuff and read that. She wants us to
have a relationship like in the book. I need to develop my
feminine side, she says, and be more sensitive. She wants 'intimacy' . . . we've got three grown kids, now she wants sex
and intimacy. What the hell is that? Women. They stick together. I guess Uma recommended it to her."

Uma. Mitchell thought about how she bit her lip when she
was concentrating, how sweet and soft she could look, and
wondered when was the last time he'd had sex—just good
old-fashioned plundering until you couldn't move, couldn't
think, temporarily blinding sex.

"Once a month is good enough for anyone, especially old
married couples," Lonny was brooding. "What do you think?"

"I think I appreciate you not telling everyone what I did
for a living."

"You left a hell of a high paycheck. Going back?"

If I had any sense I would. "Don't know. I'm here now.
That's all I know."

"Well, you'll figure it out. You kids had a tough time, but I
always liked your dad. He was honest, anyway. I don't think
he really wanted that land, the obligations it brought, but he
thought he owed it to his family, to his sons, to keep it in the
family. It was the right thing to do for you, buying those forty
acres back, and the garage."

"I'm not going to work that land," Mitchell stated firmly, just in case Lonny had that idea.

"You'll do what's right." As thunder rolled outside, Lonny got up to play the pinball machines and brood about Irma's sexual expectations.

The crash in the alley sounded again and the blonde started swaying her hips to the jukebox music. She turned to Mitchell, and he shook his head at the sultry invitation.

He wondered what it would feel like to hold Uma close and tight. He wondered what it would feel like to press those gentle breasts against his chest, to smooth that long, swaying back, to be inside her, with her flowing beneath him, over him—

The hard throb low in his body was unexpected and unwanted.

With a rough sigh, Mitchell got up to see if Roman was holding his own and to maybe ease a little old-fashioned sexual tension.

Uma ran through the early morning mist brought by last night's thunderstorm. The layers hovered over the neatly cut grass of the houses on Lawrence Street, and curled damply upon her skin. Bordering each side of the street, houses were draped in it, puddles shimmered and rippled as rain dropped into them from the leaves.

The first week of July, Mrs. Riley's sun tea sat on her front porch; Mr. Thompson had just let out his poodle for lawn duty. Looking as if he'd just gotten out of bed, his gray hair standing out in peaks, Lars Swenson was madly shoving a spike into the ground, cursing moles. Steel devices with spikes were placed in a row, poised to shaft into the ground, killing the "varmints." In an hour, Etta Harmon's boy would be sailing his bike down the street and tossing rolled papers into bushes.

Uma had met Roman at the hardware store last week. He'd

been wearing a split lip and had winced when he'd shot her a charming grin. Mitchell had been wearing a scraped cheek and a scowl.

The brothers were bound to stir up Madrid, and everything had been quiet, except for the Warrens' hammers and saws. She glanced at the well-trimmed hedge, at the spiderwebs catching the fog. Everything was the same, yet it wasn't. Her shoes sounded rhythmically on the sidewalk; her heart was racing to keep up with her stride, her lungs sucking for air. She could feel Lauren against her, breathing with her, the loving hug, the sadness. What did Lauren want?

Lauren's things were safely back in her old house— Mitchell's house, now. It wasn't time for them to leave, to be sorted and packed away in another place. Lauren wasn't ready—then Uma felt the coldness, as if someone feared— feared what?

Returning from her morning run, Uma's free stride matched the pounding of her heart. She caught a scent and it reminded her of Lauren, and then, just as the old gray tomcat ripped across her path, she saw Mitchell crouching beside his pickup. He stood in the layers of mist, coated by the half-light, his chest bare and powerful. The dark boxer shorts led into powerful legs planted far apart like those of a gladiator ready to fight. His dark, fierce expression seemed dangerous, predatory as the mist swirled around him, the rain still dripping from the trees when all else was quiet.

Perhaps Madrid was his arena, Uma thought, where he would face his battles and either win them or be defeated. He'd been here three weeks and even coming to his house, helping to select carpeting and paint colors, she knew little about him except that he fought the past.

She could have told him what he didn't want to hear—the secrets of Madrid were in her keeping. But he wasn't asking.

She had already fought her battles—and lost. She'd started with dreams and ended wanting only peace. She slowed and stopped, noting the four flat tires as she placed her hands on her knees and tried to catch her breath. "What happened?"

For an answer, Mitchell glared at her, burning her in the heavy fragrant mist. The look was long and intense and caused a heated tingle to shimmy up her body, despite the cool layers of fog swirling between them. His stare took in her body from worn shoes, up her legs to her loose blue shorts and damp, clinging navy tank top, up her sweaty throat and face to the red terrycloth headband.

She could almost feel the bunching of his muscles, the electric sizzle in the layers of damp air between them.

She straightened, placing her hands on her waist, breathing deeply—from her run and from whatever raw and primitive feelings quivered in the air between them. She didn't understand the exact challenge of that narrowed, grim, penetrating look, but gave it back to him. *Whatever rode Mitchell wasn't going to upset her.*

He opened his fist to reveal four nails. "Same old town," he said quietly. He reached down to pick up a power nail gun, used by carpenters. "So much for the nail gun we missed the other day. I thought it was just misplaced, but someone had a better use for it."

But Uma couldn't look away from his arm, the muscles surging beneath the tanned skin, the leap of power that ran up to lift that flat dark nipple and the lightly furred power of his chest.

She swallowed as she followed that line of hair from his chest to his navel, the indentation marking the line that continued lower—

If she could just place her hand on that flat, muscled stomach—Uma rubbed her palm on her damp chest and forced her eyes to his face. There was no reason she should want to touch and smooth and curve her fingers around—

Mitchell nodded toward Roman's Harley, lying as if it had been pushed down. "Sweet and homey. I get the message."

The brooding clouds overhead matched his expression and Uma knew that he'd gone back to another bitter time. A woman who cared unselfishly about the pain of others, she leaned closer to touch his cheek and expected the flash of his eyes, his temper riding him. "I'm sorry."

She jerked her hand back from the heat of his face, the hard bones pressing against his skin.

Whatever lay inside Mitchell now was too primitive to examine, and yet a part of her wanted to touch and to heal.

"Sure." Mitchell tossed the nails into the truck bed and walked toward the house. The screen door slammed behind him.

Uma's own edges rose and trembled and heated, like a hot wind causing waves across cool grass, stirring it. She walked up the front walk, around the new wood stacked there. She knocked on the screen door. "Mitchell?"

"What?" Roman's sleepy voice preceded his pushing out of the house, almost knocking Uma aside. In his boxer shorts, Roman barely glanced at her as he came out to stand on the porch. Belatedly, he glanced at her. "Uh, sorry, Uma. Mitchell said that—"

He swung around to study Mitchell's pickup, parked on the curb, the flat tires. The string of low curses followed him as he tramped across the yard in his bare feet to the Harley, lying on its side. He hefted it as if picking up a bruised baby, adjusted the kick stand, caressed the metal and the leather, and leaned back to study the flat tires. "Someone is going to pay," he said grimly as he walked back to the porch. "Are you coming in or not?"

Past Roman, Mitchell stood in the shadowed hallway, his fists at his side. His body seemed coiled, the muscles defined in the dim light. "I'm not in the mood to hear anything about the good people of Madrid, Uma. You'd better go home, back to your safe little tower where everything is sweet and good—"

"I don't know that I like that remark. You're not taking that bad temper out on me." She loved Madrid, and Mitchell wasn't painting evil over the entire town, just because—"I didn't do it, Mitchell."

But people weren't happy about the Warren brothers back in town. The old bitterness had stirred in the gossip, wondering what revenge they were planning, what crimes, and more than a few people believed that Mitchell and Roman knew something about the dead man in the old ranch garage.

He disappeared into the kitchen. Roman shook his head. "It's that punk kid. I'll have to have a little chat about him repaying the damage. Mitchell is making coffee. You might as well come in."

She shouldn't enter their lives. She pushed away the challenge that Mitchell had thrown her out on the street, an unfamiliar taunt. But then, she couldn't ignore that challenge either.

Or the call to soothe the surly males in their lair. She didn't want a minor war, more back-alley fights, that could tear Madrid apart.

She stepped around the standing power saw on the front porch and came into the house, moving across the foyer and down the hallway. Roman followed her into the kitchen.

The sight wasn't pretty—carpentry tools spread across a counter, wallpaper half stripped and the rest lying in a tangled mess on the floor. Kitchen toaster, microwave, and assorted pots and pan boxes lay tossed in one corner. Mitchell held the coffee pot, pouring it into two mugs. At the sight of Uma, he added another mug and stared at her darkly. "Don't start on me."

"Have I ever? What makes you think you're worth the effort?"

He poured the third cup and replaced the coffee pot on its automatic holder with a click that sounded like a door ending all conversation. Mitchell picked up his mug, cradling it in his hands as he leaned back against the counter. Roman did the same, and Uma, faced with two brooding, unshaven men in their shorts, took the third cup.

"I hate it when you're like this," Mitchell said after a long, heavy silence.

"Hmm?" In peacemaking, she'd found it was better to let the other person speak first.

"She's a woman," Roman stated darkly, as if her sex determined that she was illogical.

What was she doing standing between these men, trying to understand and soothe? "Yes, and I'm right here. Don't talk over me."

"We have to. You're shorter than we are," Mitchell said slowly as if explaining a basic fact to someone who should know the obvious.

"I may be shorter, and I may be a woman, but I am definitely smarter—" she began.

"You're sweaty, and you *are* definitely a woman. No maybes about it," Mitchell stated flatly, as if nettled.

Uma stared at him and fought to keep her control. "You are in a bad mood, Mitchell Warren. And you want to start a fight with someone. And for some reason, you'd like that someone to be me. Why?"

After a silence saturated by Mitchell's brooding, Roman answered, "Because every time you run by here, he's locked onto every move. Why do you think he's up at this hour? To wait on me? I'm taking a shower and going down to the old garage. If I catch that punk kid or one of those guys, I'm going to get either some money or some new tires out of them."

"Oh, fine. Start looking for fights first thing in the morning. That's the way to make friends," Uma said and reached for something to lighten the moment, the brothers' childhood names. "Same old Hawk and Eagle. You really shocked very few people when you rode into town, bareback, and wearing only war paint and breechcloths."

Both men stared at her darkly.

"I hate that peacemaking crap women do," Mitchell murmured after a silence, ignoring her again. "I've been here just three weeks, and that's long enough to find out just what Uma does—she's part matchmaker, part town historian, protector of abused women; she writes newspaper articles, and does pro bono graphic work for civic clubs. In short, she runs this town her own way. She likes everything to be nice and sweet, and as for her life, she's got enough to do managing other people's. She comes in here, tells me I should make peace with Grace and a few other things. And I am not a bully."

"I don't want to have anything to do with Grace," Roman said. "She walked out on us. No mother should do that."

"Oh, did she really? I'm sure you know all the facts, don't you? I'll bet you don't talk about this either, or try to understand anything past a ten-year-old viewpoint." Uma didn't care if her tone challenged them; she understood exactly in facing these two brooding, stony-faced men why Grace might have given up and left Fred. According to Uma's mother, communication wasn't Fred's strong point—evidently he'd passed that lack of ability onto his sons.

"Eight," Mitchell stated. "I was eight. He was seven. Don't try to make it right. That won't work."

She looked from Mitchell to Roman and back again. She could only handle one at a time. "So you've been brooding about that all this time? It was a logical suggestion. I do not manage other people's lives. And what's wrong with wanting no trouble?" Uma demanded, staring up at him. "Madrid is a good place to live."

"Because it's a lie, and I was talking to my brother. Not you."

"I'll bet you two have absolutely no meaningful conversations anyway. I can understand you being upset about your tires. But I can't understand you being surly with me."

"Yeah, well, it's all a little package, isn't it? And by the way, men don't have *intimacy*. It isn't a requirement."

"Maybe *you* don't. I don't know what you mean about the package, and the way you say 'intimacy' makes it sound like a bad word."

"I heard about you meddling in Lonny's love life."

She'd tried gently to help Lonny and Irma's troubled marriage. "I . . . did . . . not."

"Books aren't life, honey." Mitchell's tone was sarcastic.

"I'll leave you two to your squabbling." Roman shook his head and took his mug with him, heading for the bathroom. He ignored the wad of wallpaper that Mitchell tossed at his back.

After a moment, the shower started and Uma, circling just exactly why Mitchell was up and watching her run in the morning, stood very still. She sipped her coffee there, leaning back against the kitchen counter with Mitchell, dressed only in his shorts and bad mood.

She looked down at her legs, smooth, gleaming slender-strong. Next to hers, Mitchell's were bulkier, lightly furred, and definitely more powerful. An electric jolt skittered over her skin and slammed low into her body, and she decided to concentrate on the style of the brown pottery mug. She'd known sensual excitement in those first days with Everett, and she didn't want that tug with Mitchell.

She held the mug with one hand, and smoothed the other hand up and down the surface, sensitive to the textures under her hands. She lifted the mug and blew lightly into the brew to cool it.

Next to her, Mitchell shifted abruptly, as if he were uncomfortable. In the ominous silence, his next statement roared, though he spoke quietly: "You've got sweat between your breasts and they bounce when you run. When you bent over to catch your breath I could see enough of your breasts to want to know how they'd fit in my hands, taste in my mouth. When you put your hands on your waist, trying to catch your breath, the whole package is there, sweetheart, nice and curved and soft. Your butt has just enough quiver to make a man hard, and those shorts should be illegal, showing off—"

She stared at him and blinked, trying to equate his dispatched brooding with the raw sensuality churning from Mitchell now.

Mitchell slowly placed his mug and hers aside, then turned back to study her. The tip of his finger lifted to push beneath her chin gently, closing her parted lips. "What's the matter? Didn't you think I'd notice? That any man would notice? I may be trying to sort things out, but I'm not dead. You smell like a woman. You sweat like a woman. You move like a woman. You *are* a woman. Or is reality just too much for you?"

She couldn't breathe, couldn't think. She saw Mitchell's hard expression ease, his eyes lower to her lips, and then his head was slanting, coming nearer.

She saw his eyes close, those thick lashes gleam as his lips brushed hers, and when he straightened, studying her, she forced herself to breathe shakily. Those gold eyes were soft and warm, amused, just like the slight curve of his lips.

She continued to stare at him, trapped by what had just happened as Mitchell leaned back, crossed his arms, and smiled.

She hadn't expected that boyish grin, that delight as he watched her. Or the flush rising up her cheeks.

"Surprised?" he asked. "Are you going to come out and play or not?"

"What do you mean?"

His grin widened and he said softly, "I bet you're rosy all over. I didn't know women still blushed. It's fascinating, the way that pale skin changes to pink, how it sort of blooms like a rose."

He was obviously flirting with her, enjoying unraveling a self-possessed woman, a woman everyone saw as functional and quiet and in control, the wallflower she preferred to be. "I'm not. I've just run and—"

In slow motion, his finger reached to hook her tank top, just between her breasts, and he tugged lightly. His finger trailed across the neckline, brushing her skin, before moving away.

Those light brown eyes traced her face, the heat upon it. "Sure. Tell me another one. It's been a long time since I've seen a woman react like you did out there on the street, all engines humming and heating."

"Mitchell! Don't talk like that."

There was that slow, devastating smile, that sexy look of a male—

She wished she hadn't looked downward—but then, how could she stop?

Mitchell was definitely aroused and ready, and those humming motors were definitely gearing up.

Uma held very straight, lifting her chin. She wouldn't let him unnerve her, she understood herself, he wasn't getting to her— "Thank you very much for the coffee. I have work to do. I'd better not keep you from your business."

"Okay," he said easily, those gold eyes still amused.

Uma cleared her throat. "Yes. Well. Goodbye."

She sensed him watching her as she forced herself to walk slowly out of the kitchen and down the hallway, her heart pounding to a rhythm she didn't want.

She wanted safety, and Mitchell definitely wasn't that.

Later, in her shower, Uma leaned back against the stall, lifting her face to the streaming water. She could just feel his kiss, feel the need behind it, the testing, the sensual current dancing between them.

In another life, one of dreams and forevermores, Everett had kissed her like that, just a brush of his lips. He sometimes kissed her now like that. Years ago, she'd enjoyed lovemaking, the safety of a man committed to his marriage and to her, the gentleness of it, the friendly comfort, the assurances in the afterplay. Everett was the kind of man who would be there in the morning, and the next day, and the next.

She knew his body, the pleasure of it. And yet her desire for him had slowly died.

Mitchell wasn't meant to be a gentle man or to comfort. His words this morning said he wanted, and that desire ruled him, nothing more.

She opened her lips and let the water inside, still tasting that kiss.

She couldn't take him seriously. *Are you going to come out and play or not?*

"Not," she whispered as the shower streamed against her skin, sensitizing it. *When you bent over to catch your breath, I could see enough of your breasts to want to know how they'd fit in my hands, taste in my mouth.*

Mitchell stood in the shower, letting the cold water stream over him. He tried not to think of Uma's smoky stare, the way it had taken in his body this morning. He could feel her awakening, the stark stirring of her sensuality there in the mist—and knew it was wrong. With a failed marriage behind him, and enough relationships to tell him that life with him was hard on a woman, he could only hurt her.

He closed his eyes, and the image of her breasts, quivering as she ran, and the rounded shape as she bent to catch her breath, tantalized him.

He shook his head and wondered what had possessed him to reveal his desire, a controlled man who shielded his emotions from everyone.

He sighed roughly. Uma was inside him, stirring him, and with her, it wouldn't be sex-on-the-go, it would be problem after problem. He had enough to do sorting out his life, and he was flirting with her this morning, just like he was on the make and she was in the direct line of fire.

The worst part was how much he enjoyed her reaction, all that rosy, warm soft skin heating up, her confusion, the elegant ladylike way she pulled herself together.

No, the worst part was how much he'd wanted her, there on his bed, in the cool, fragrant morning. Worse yet was the way he'd exposed how he'd wanted to touch her, taste her.

Mitchell briskly soaped himself. He felt raw and bristling and surly, as Uma had said, and he didn't like the knowledge that at his age, sex still created enough pressure to waylay him from clear thinking.

Roman shoved open the door of the old garage on Maloney Street and inhaled the musty past. The morning sunlight was warm on his back, spreading between his legs and over his head and shoulders to lay his silhouette on the old concrete floor.

There were Dozer's lawnmowers, the riding and the push ones, and his assortment of pruning tools and chain saws, the bottles and sacks of weed killer, insecticide, and fertilizer. The bagged fertilizer's sharp tang mixed with echoes of Roman's father's voice, the shadows stirring memories around him. Fred was a really good mechanic, not a rancher. He was best with tools in his hand, bent into a humming motor.

Maybe it was that frustration that he chose to take out on Mitchell and Roman.

Roman didn't want to think about the bitter memories associated with Fred. He pushed away the night of the fire but couldn't drown out the sounds of his own voice echoing from the past, "The old man deserves what he gets."

Maybe he did. Maybe they *all* did. Life had never been easy, growing up in Madrid.

Maybe he'd always been racing back here. Roman shook his head. He'd come full circle, through the fame and the money, back to Poor Town. He had enough to think about—Shelly might have given him a child, a daughter, and he hadn't known. Whatever he was, he would have stood by her.

He scanned the shadows, the mechanic's pit without the lift, the workbenches, and frowned when he saw pale, fresh sawdust on the floor beneath the steps. He glanced up at the old office and eased up to the top steps. He crouched to run his finger across the rough planks and then angled around to look at their underside. Someone had sawed the boards just enough that weight would cause the board to break. And the cuts were fresh.

Roman shook his head. Eighteen years ago, someone had nailed boards across the house, setting it afire. And his homecoming present was Lyle's kidney punch and nails in his Harley's tires. People were watching from behind their curtains, suspicious of where he went and what he did. Things hadn't changed much.

He turned to go down the stairs and then momentarily slowed as he saw the tough-looking girl standing in the shadows, watching him. Without the hard look, the punk and the paint, she might be around Dani's age.

She watched him walk toward her, the buttoned leather vest and cutoffs making her seem very slender and young. "Saw you walking past the house and followed you here. Heard you had tire trouble."

"You can tell your friend that I'll be expecting his money for the tires."

Within the hard black makeup, her eyes widened. They were light brown, he decided, catching the dim light and changing into a dull gold—just the shade of his. "Oh, no. Jace wouldn't do that. He wants that bike and said the tires alone cost a fortune and that he could get a good price for them."

"Someone nailed them. I'll be finding out who. They'll pay for my brother's truck tires, too." He wanted to find out about Dani. "You go to school, kid?"

"Hell, no. I'm out." When she shook her head, the spiked hair caught the light and he wondered about the true color—rich and auburn and soft, like Shelly's?

"Summer vacation?"

"I'm just out." She held out a slender, small hand, the wrist layered with beaded bracelets. "My name is Dani. I hear yours is Roman. Nice. Like gladiator stuff, right? I heard you can handle yourself, too. I like a man like that."

Dani. This young girl, slender, had Shelly's clean-cut Nordic features, and eyes the same light brown as his. He forced himself to breathe, his heart pounding. He wondered, *no, he knew, she was his.*

"You okay, guy?" she asked, frowning up at him. "You look like you forgot something."

How could he forget that night? Why hadn't he checked on Shelly after that? She'd been a virgin—a sweet, giving virgin. "I'm fine, kid. I'll feel better after I have breakfast. What's the best place to eat around here? Show me and I'll buy."

"Ruby's is good. Home-cooking and good pies and sweet tea made in the sun. I work there sometimes." She grinned at him, and Roman's heart stopped. There was Shelly, young and shy and tender—all pain and edges and uncertainty—beneath layers of paint and hair dye and leather. *This was his daughter.*

The rumble of a motorcycle preceded the young tough he'd met earlier. The boy paused in the yawning opening of the garage, and Roman knew exactly what he was, because that's just how he'd been—girl crazy, taking what he could get, showing off just how tough he was.

He held back the impulse to rip the kid from the seat and threaten him. That wouldn't help him with Dani.

The kid purred the bike inside and Roman didn't like his dark look at Dani. "Hop on," the kid said in a tone that warned.

Jace could have been Roman as a teenager, just there, framed in that square of sunlight, revving his motorcycle. And Roman knew exactly what kids that age wanted—and his daughter wasn't going to be ordered around, or used. He had always been very careful to stay within the bounds of girls—okay, older women—who knew the score. He had preferred older; Shelly was different that night and he'd needed her in a way that was soft and warm. "She's with me."

"Oh, yeah?" The tough revved the bike and Roman knew what would happen next—he'd be fighting a boy for his own daughter!

Roman glanced at Dani and found her eyes bright and hopeful—and worshipful of a man she wanted for her own.

Well, hell. What would a real father do in his place?

First things first. "Dani said you wouldn't have nailed my tires or pushed my bike over. Did you?"

The kid's eyes widened, showing his youth, not that hard, tough look. "Not me. I wouldn't do that to a Harley." He spoke the name with reverence.

"If you pick up who did, I'd appreciate the lead. But Dani and I were just going down to Ruby's. How about coming with us?"

The kid revved his bike. "I've got business," he said and back-walked the motorcycle out.

When he roared away, Roman asked, "Are you going to have trouble over this?"

"I can handle myself," she said and the inviting look she gave Roman shocked him.

"Old guys aren't fun," he said sternly and surprised himself at the paternal protective nudge. Dani needed someone to—oh, well, hell, what did he know about what a father could teach a girl, or how to protect her from users? "You shouldn't try a come-on with me. Just how old are you, anyway?"

Dani shrugged and her tone was casual, as if she knew

everything there was to know about life and accepted it. "Jail bait. I'd lie, but you'd find out if you stay around town. But I know the rules. I'm the same as my mom, and she never told anyone who my father was."

But Roman knew, and he wanted to know more.

SIX

Uma leaned back in her desk chair. After hours of trying to understand what had happened to her computer, why all the files had been erased or corrupted, she still had no idea. At five o'clock in the morning, she had a deadline for her Charis Lopez column in two days, and a layout for a real estate company, and now she had to start all over. The backup CDs she was meticulous about making were not readable, either. She had to reinstall all the programs, write the column, and—

And it was the third week of July, hot and dry. *It had been two weeks since Mitchell had—since he had been so, so intense, and had kissed her.*

Mitchell was a concentrated male package—taut, edgy, brooding, concealing his thoughts. And emotional. She had merely caught his dark side, that bristling male shield that wanted to put her off guard, to defend his inner emotions.

She tapped the pencil she was holding. Naturally Mitchell would be emotional, coming back to Madrid, remembering—

But then, she should be worrying about her deadlines, the way her computer had crashed.

She looked past the window's sheer lacy curtain onto the street. Earlier, distracted by her computer problems, she hadn't noticed the two holes in the window. She picked up the BBs on her desk. Her father wouldn't be happy, and she'd have to make a point of telling the Ellison boy to not shoot at birds. His father had been irresponsible, showing little Nicky how to shoot at birds, and she'd complained at the cruelties. She would again—just as soon as she could talk to his father.

Her own father was still snoring, the sound cruising down the hallway like a revved chainsaw. Tracking the Warrens' movements through a network of townspeople, what they bought, where they went, was exhausting work.

Other than the crashed computer, and the BB holes in the window, everything else appeared normal. Ellie Long was on her morning walk, pushing her baby's stroller in front of her. Life in Madrid was as usual, Mrs. Simpson trying to fit her big Lincoln into Maggie Fenton's driveway.

Uma still tasted Matthew and the sensual electricity surrounding them. She'd been off balance since then, nettled and sleepless and angry with him—and with herself for letting him get to her. She'd avoided looking at his house, though she badly wanted to help him restore it.

On the roof, shingling at dawn a week ago, Roman had called out to her. She'd waved, but hadn't met Mitchell's quiet look. She passed by two women who had suddenly started jogging up and down Lawrence Street, both single, very young, and man-hunting. Dressed only in jeans, the brothers were quite the sight, strong bodies gleaming, muscles surging, Mitchell's back all broad and tanned and—

Sex. Mitchell wanted sex. He was obvious enough about that, stunning her. Saying those things men just did not say to her, and she was far past any excitement a bad-boy image could stir.

Did he have to say those things? Holding and tasting her—

Uma shivered and broke the pencil she'd been holding, as she made notes of all the computer's damage. The hardware seemed fine, but the files were lost—

And Mitchell could do with a good dose of Charis Lopez's takes on relationships, on intimacy, on tact, and—

Uma quickly tied on her running shoes. If she couldn't concentrate on her article or her work, then she would run out the tension that thinking about Mitchell had created.

On her front porch, she stretched and whipped her hair back into a ponytail, placing the terry sweat band around her head. Everett was back, and she had enough to do straightening out her computer and meeting her deadlines.

The Warren brothers were stirring up everyone in town. While people wondered where Mitchell got his money, they didn't hesitate to take it at the plumbing and electrical stores, or at the small lumberyard. Served them right, the gossip said, that Lyle and the boys "fixed" their tires; they'd learn to leave Madrid's good women alone.

Gossip told her that the two men were working nights: "Busy as bees, the two of them. Working as if all hell were after them. They'll have that place fixed up in no time. Probably want to sell it, or bring their buddies in. Wonder what they plan to do with the garage—run a chop shop, and paint stolen cars? Or that old ranch?"

The speculations about the ranch had reached fever pitch. After all, what would the Warrens do with the dead bodies now? They were just lying low after the first one was discovered, but the town speculated that there were more.

Uma stretched her arms high. She couldn't worry about Mitchell; Shelly needed her—she'd seen Roman standing out on the street, watching the house. Dani spoke of nothing but him, and Shelly was terrified that Roman would find out about her daughter and that she would lose Dani.

Uma started to jog slowly, warming up her stride as the dawn promised a hot, dry day. She passed her neighbor's house and ran faster, determined not to notice Mitchell. She glanced at a runner coming out of the dawn and smiled,

"Hi, Everett, I didn't know you were still running."

Today he had already shaved and wore the sky blue T-shirt and matching shorts she had chosen for him—to match his eyes. She liked to shop for him. Was it because that was all she could give him, and not what he wanted?

He was solid and good and dependable. "We used to run like this. It was good. I'm out of shape. Thought I'd try to keep up. Thanks for the casserole you left for me the night I came back."

"You're welcome. Let's see what you've got," she teased, running faster.

Then Mitchell was running at her other side, his chest bare and his shorts and shoes with a very expensive trademark. "Thought I'd try getting in shape, too—unless you mind?"

You've got sweat between your breasts and they bounce when you run. . . .

Uma tightened her muscles and decided to buy a sports bra. No one had ever commented on her running gear before. Or her sweat. *What kind of a man would mention a woman's sweat?* "No, of course not. We don't mind, do we, Everett?"

Everett ran grimly, silently. Mitchell's scruffy jaw and shaggy haircut emphasized the difference in the two men, though they were the same height. In comparison, Mitchell looked rawly masculine and unsafe, especially when he glanced down at Uma's chest.

Uma tried to ignore him, but couldn't resist glancing up at his face, which had a grim look she didn't like. They cruised two blocks to Main Street, where the smell of the bakery mixed with Ruby's morning coffee, and Lorraine Jarvis's big black Labrador fell in behind them.

Uma tried to ignore the people who had come out onto the street to watch the two men and her, the window shades being drawn aside in the two-story apartments.

Unable to stand being the town's spectacle, running beside the two men, Uma took the first opportunity to escape. "I forgot something," she said and turned around suddenly, heading for her house and safety.

Everett and Mitchell grunted at the same time. When she ran a block back, she looked over her shoulder to see the two men running full speed in the other direction, the Labrador replacing her position.

As she ran past Lauren's house, Roman was just setting out the sun-tea jug. It was comforting to see Lauren's customary summer tea on the repainted porch. Uma badly needed comfort; she didn't care if people were peering at her from behind their blinds.

She ripped off her sweatband and stopped to talk with Roman; if Madrid wanted to gossip about her after all this time, that was just fine.

"So how's it going?" Roman asked, grinning at her.

"You know how it is. There I was, running between two men. My ex-husband, who is nice, and your brother, who isn't."

"A lot of women like that competition kind of thing. It suits their egos."

"Not me."

"My brother isn't here now. He said you wouldn't come in if he were here, and I know how you felt about Lauren—nice girl. Would you like to see the house? We've done quite a bit of restoring. It was a shame her husband trashed it. The house has got a certain—soft feel to it, I guess."

She was grateful for Roman's consideration. "Yes, I would. Thank you."

That "soft feel" would be Lauren—waiting. The house had been repainted, carpeted, and cleaned. Barren of furniture, it was achingly lovely in butter-cream walls against the dark wood trim. The stained glass window Lauren loved created softly colored patterns on the cream carpeting. The damaged entryway flooring had been replaced. The kitchen was stark and clean, two bar stools the only furniture. Beyond that was the utility room where laundry was humming and then the door to Lauren's garden. In the room where Lauren's things rested, a vase of fresh roses scented the air, a contrast to the masculine scents of soap and shaving lotion.

"I don't know what to do with them," Uma said as Roman came to stand beside her. "It's all so wrong. I should get her things out of your way."

"Take your time. Mitchell put the flowers in there. I did go through the albums and the class yearbooks. Seems like a long time ago, forever, in fact, when we were all young. Hope that was okay."

Uma knew that he was battling the past, the same as Mitchell, and probably remembering Shelly. Dani's fascination for him was no secret. "Be careful, Roman," Uma advised softly.

He inhaled and slowly released his breath, watching her. "What do you know about Shelly's daughter Dani?"

Uma knew about Dani, and about Grace Warren's struggle to save her marriage. The Warren men weren't an easy breed. "I think you need to be very careful with Dani. She's got your eyes."

Roman studied her. "You know, then."

"Everything. But tell me anyway."

He sighed roughly and ran his hand through his hair. "I haven't done much with my life, but I'm trying. I sold a car I wasn't using. Not much money to start working the old garage again, but Mitchell is helping. I'm good with cars and motors, same as the old man when he was on top of it. And with this bum knee, I'm not good for much else."

"I think you'll be marvelous," she said quietly, aching for him, for all he had gone through. "Did you ever find out who put nails in your tires?"

"Someone who didn't like us," Roman stated. "And I don't think it was Lyle and his friends. But that knife rip through the back screen door wasn't sweet. The town would like to see us leave. We aren't. Come on in the kitchen. I'm great with toast."

"I should be going." The hallway table was a paper-cluttered improvised desk with a copy of *The Smooth Moves List*.

"Okay, but I want your opinion on something. Do you think that book is any good? Or is it just something women like to dream about—" Roman reached for the book on top of colorful garden books, and a stack of papers slid to the floor.

Uma bent to pick them up and noted the Rogers Building and Supply letterhead with Mitchell's big, bold signature.

At a slight noise behind her, she turned to see Mitchell leaning against the doorframe, lifting a water bottle to drink heavily. He was sweaty and thunderous. "Snooping again?" he asked overpolitely.

She handed the paper to him. "What made you choose now, after all these years, to come back to Madrid?"

He glanced at the paper, then crushed it into a ball, hurling it at Roman, who grinned and ducked. The wadded paper hit the wall and rolled back onto the floor between Mitchell and Uma. He stared at it as if it were condemning evidence. "I delivered a baby in the back of a cab for my secretary and it changed my life. That's the whole damn truth of it, as near as I can figure. So you'll come in the house when I'm not here, huh? And why would that be, I wonder? Could I have possibly said something to upset you, Mrs. Thornton?"

Before she could think of an answer, Mitchell turned and walked toward the shower, slamming the door behind him.

Roman was looking up at the ceiling, which was good, because Uma didn't want him to see the anger bubbling inside her. "So what about this relationship book?" he asked. "Is it worth reading?"

"It's very, very good. Your brother could take a few pointers from it. I've got to get home. My computer crashed and I've got a deadline—ah, a brochure that needs to be finished. I've underbid the project as is, but I intend to deliver on time."

In the shower, Mitchell braced his hands against the smooth tile. The ties between Uma and Everett ran deep. Everett was a husband-guy; they deserved each other. And here Mitchell was, trying to fit into a neat little threesome. He had ended up flopped in the small city park, too out of breath to move while Everett ran on.

Lonny had come to sit on the park bench beside him. He handed Mitchell bottled water. Mitchell poured it onto his face, then opened his mouth and let it stream into him.

The policeman's laughter roared. When he caught his breath, he wiped away the tears. "Out of shape? That was quite the sight back there, Uma running between her ex-husband who still wants her and you."

Mitchell strained to lift an eyelid. "He's in shape. I'm not. I'll work on it."

"He's been working on it for years. She's not buying. She may be one of those women who doesn't seem to need men. Seems just happy living a quiet life with her father. So what are your intentions? With Uma, I mean."

"I'm not talking about Uma," Mitchell had said tightly and heaved himself to his feet.

"Well, okay then. You boys are busy as bees over at that house. Makes a person wonder what you're trying to get out of your system. People are keeping tabs on the delivery trucks parked in your driveway. Now, if there were a Rogers Building and Supply in Madrid, you wouldn't have to go ordering in supplies. You could do a lot for the town, if you wanted."

"I don't. I'm just trying to live, that's all."

"Sometimes that's all we can do." Lonny looked up at Mitchell, his mood changed to serious. "Still haven't found any news on that shooter. Dufus Boy just figured out that someone pushed the car back into the garage after the shooting. I knew it when I saw the marks on the front bumper and the window open. The bullet went clear through and we can't find it. That shot was fired outside the garage, or it would have been stuck in the wall—probably by the same person who shot up the windmill with the .45. If anything turns up out there, you'll let me know, won't you?"

"Sure. I suppose I'm still under suspicion."

"Only Dufus's. He did that background check and knows who you are, but he'll shut up. We had a little chat. If someone else wants to check you out, I can't stop them."

Mitchell nodded, his stare locking with Lonny's. "You want to play this real quiet, don't you? You're keeping the town from panicking, right?"

Lonny spat that arc into a bed of fuchsia impatiens. "Just let me know if you pick up anything. I'm just praying Dufus Boy doesn't muck up this investigation. His prints are probably all over the car by now. Hadn't you better be running along? If you can?"

"Lay off." Mitchell knew what panic could do—guns, people shooting too quickly at suspected prowlers, and innocent people hurt.

To save the shreds of his pride, he forced himself to jog back to the house, where he had found the irritating, fragrant, soft, womanly problem of his sleepless nights. It had been easier to take a shower than to face her.

But Uma was still waiting for him when he came out of the bathroom. Roman was leaning against the wall, his arms crossed in front of his chest, wrapped in the look that said he wasn't going to let anything happen to Uma.

Mitchell knew that Roman had a protective streak when it came to women—but when it came to Uma, Mitchell wasn't exactly certain what he did feel, other than wanting to dive into her. He didn't like feeling like a boy, chasing a girl he wasn't likely to have, and Roman understood too well, moving in to buffer Mitchell's mood. "She didn't get her daily fortune cookie. Her computer has crashed and checking the online I-Ching and her horoscrope is the way she starts her work day."

"And you've embarrassed me in front of the whole town," Uma said, clearly launching her attack. She crossed her arms in front of her, as Roman had. "What were you thinking?"

Since he was wearing only his boxer shorts, Mitchell had the advantage. Uma was trying to focus on his face, determined not to be embarrassed. Now, that was sweet, and he almost felt sorry for her—but not quite. "I'm thinking that it's a real good morning," he returned pleasantly.

Always the lady in control, Uma said quite properly, "You've done a nice job with the house. I haven't looked at the garden yet. Nice furniture in the living room."

Mitchell glanced at the big screen television and the two huge leather recliners that had been a necessity for Roman and himself. Between them, a rickety metal TV stand served to hold their dinners, beer, and popcorn. "Thanks. Are we done here? This little conference?"

The banging on the front door and Uma's father's bellows said the morning was just revving up. "You Warrens. Come out. I know you're in there."

"This wonderful, peaceful morning isn't over yet," Mitchell said quietly as Uma walked quickly to the door. Beyond her was Clarence Lawrence in his undershorts, his hair standing out in peaks and his expression furious.

"Dad! What's wrong?"

"Someone just shot out every one of our windows. BBs all over the floor. These hooligans—" He motioned to the brothers as they came out onto the porch. He thrust out his hand, BBs rolling in the palm. "Here's the evidence. They need to be arrested, and—"

"It was probably little Nicky, Dad. I'll talk with his father."

"It's *them*. Those Warrens. They used to go around shooting up old buildings with the BB guns, and Fred didn't make them stop. Now they're men and they haven't changed their habits. They have to pay for the windows. Don't you dare defend those rapscallions. You know what they did when they were boys, and now it's worse."

Mitchell pressed a warning shoulder into Roman, who had just moved forward at the accusation. "We didn't break your windows, and we're a little old for BBs."

"See there? They even admit what they used," Clarence snapped to Uma. "I forbid you to come here."

Uma straightened and smiled pleasantly, but those gray eyes were as dark as smoke and packed a sizzle; the temper was there, the independence. "We'll talk about this later, Dad. Let's go home."

When Mitchell returned to the kitchen, Roman tossed him a bottle of water. Mitchell mulled clashing with Uma when all he wanted was to lay her down and—

The stack of decorating magazines mocked him. He had no idea how to make the house look like a home. He had no idea about handling Uma, which he wanted to do in a very up-close and personal way. One more disenchanting fact about his life popped in front of him—he wasn't good at developing relationships of the friendly and persuasive kind, and that's what it would take to treat Uma right. It was very important that Uma be treated well, that he give her everything she would want.

The word "intimacy" taunted him and he scowled at the bottle of water.

"Old Man Lawrence needs to get laid," Roman remarked coolly. "Maybe you, too. Take it easy on Uma. She's just like everyone else, trying to make a life for herself. Her kind has things all planned out for them, the Life Plan, and hers didn't work out. Now she's trying to make the best of it. She's the kind of woman who should have a houseful of kids by now, seeing them off to school in the fall—and you don't like that picture, do you? All those little rules and a woman calling the shots? I know I don't."

"Lay off."

Roman swigged his bottled water and said quietly, "Dad used to do that, you know—close up, get sour, go hide. I remembered when you tromped off to the bathroom. He and Mom would argue and he'd go hide out somewhere while she cried. I hated the sound of that."

"Let's skip the good old days, okay?" Mitchell said. He didn't like comparing himself to Fred, but that's exactly how he had acted. He'd handled tough board meetings, but handling Uma set him on edge. He enjoyed nudging her control too much, picking at it to see the woman she concealed—a fascinating woman.

"Sure."

When the phone rang, he answered, and Uma's cultured voice cruised over the lines. "My father extends his apologies. Please come to dinner tonight. Roman, too."

She'd been at work again, making peace in her perfect world. Her father grumbled darkly in the background, and just to irritate him, Mitchell said, "We'll be there."

Maybe this wasn't such a good idea, Uma decided, as Everett, her father, and Mitchell sat at her dinner table. Roman's excuse not to attend had been thin, but passable; he probably was enjoying a much-publicized boxing match on television. Each man dressed in a summer short-sleeved shirt and belted slacks. The men were grim; the conversation ran between silent gaps as she foraged for a common topic.

The bouquet of roses that Mitchell had brought had stunned her. Each bloom had not opened fully, yet was not a bud, and the thorns had been removed. The fortune cookies in a china blue bowl had also been a wonderful surprise from him.

After a hard, frustrating day of restoring her computer and retrieving the extra set of backup disks she had in the bank security box, Uma had hurried to cook dinner, an easy pot roast, vegetables, and salad. Everett had brought a freezer churn of ice cream, his pineapple recipe and her favorite.

While Everett managed an awkward conversation about weather and travel, her father was ominously silent, his disapproval thundering around the dining room, jarring the antique Blue Willow dishes her great-grandmother had bought long ago. The battle with her father still raged, echoing about, "Not in my house. Not a Warren."

"I want this resolved," she'd said. "There is no sense in this war continuing years after his father is dead. You embarrassed me this morning and we're going to make some gesture that we're not still living back in feuding land rush days."

"Oil and water don't mix," he'd protested. "Neither do Warrens and Lawrences."

"They will tonight," she'd stated firmly. "May I remind you of Mother's impeccable hospitality? I'm only doing what she would have done. If that isn't what you want, tell me now. Our living arrangements can be changed, because I don't know any other way of life than to be neighborly."

"I heard about him running with you this morning. That gossip is all over town."

"Everett was there, too. I don't own the streets, Dad. He can run where he wants. Now I issued a dinner invitation. Are you going to be difficult?" she asked, and tried to toss away the image of Mitchell running on one side of her and her ex-husband on the other.

In the end, her father had sulked, but agreed. Uma had worked furiously on her computer—she could function now, but it would take a full week to get everything up and running. She reassured herself that the dinner would flow nicely, and all the tension would settle down. Everett, her father, and she often had dinner together and the conversation flowed easily.

But tonight only Mitchell, the outsider, seemed at ease. Clearly he had been in difficult situations before, managing the ebb and flow of everyday conversation. He commented on the sweet tea brewed in the sun, the pies at Ruby's Cafe, and the old gray cat that would wander into the house and sprawl to watch him work.

When her father stiffened, Uma ran her finger around the iced tea glass's cool rim. For years, her father had been cultivating that old half-wild tomcat, trying to make friends with him with a can of good salmon.

Mitchell took second helpings while the other men deferred. He actually seemed to be enjoying himself. "I see you collect Native American artifacts and pioneer goods, like that old wooden bread bowl," he said directly to Clarence.

When Clarence ignored the tentative conversation, Uma filled the silence. "My father has always been interested in western Americana. Much of what is in this house is from our family."

"Is that right? I'd be interested to hear more."

Then Mitchell smiled at her, a too-pleasant, innocent smile, and a wary tingle went up her nape. Or was he enjoying her discomfort every time those amber eyes locked with hers and the sensual impact sailed to plummet and heat her body?

Was this what she'd been seeking when she'd dressed so carefully in the print summer dress, piling her hair just so on top of her head, smoothing cream on her legs? Why she had smoothed the material over her hips and stood with her back to the mirror, steadying the fit? To get Mitchell's attention? Why?

What was that raw, tense emotion simmering inside her?

It felt like sex, and more sex, and a woman on the hunt. But that couldn't be her, not Uma Lawrence Thornton. Those jungle drums that beat when Mitchell looked at her were some—she could only give it one word—"temptation."

She braced herself and looked down to see Everett's hand possessively covering her own, his expression impassive as he looked at Mitchell. Everett's thumb slid over her third finger, left hand, a stark reminder that she had once worn his ring. From the slight mocking curve of his lips, Mitchell hadn't missed the possessive move.

Uma withdrew her hand and placed it on her lap; whatever cat-and-mouse game the men were playing, she wasn't going to be the prize. She belonged to herself now, and she was keeping it that way. Some women were meant to live in Single City—quiet, peaceful, controlled lives—and she was one of them.

"I'll help you replace those windows, Clarence," Everett was saying without looking from Mitchell.

"You know, we're about finished with the house, and I'd be glad to help you, too," Mitchell offered lightly.

"No," Clarence snapped, his control breaking. "Not you. I'm leaving on a trip to Arizona tomorrow, to stay with a friend for a month. You are not to come in my house."

She knew better than to press the situation; her father loved her, but there were limits to his control. "My, it's a nice night, isn't it? Too bad Roman had another engagement," she said instantly to soothe the obvious snub, and smoothed her hair from her neck.

She dropped her hand quickly when she saw that Mitchell's eyes had narrowed on her and whatever was happening between them pulsed hot and stormy across the table.

She looked away from Everett's close study to the Blue Willow platter standing upright on the decorative shelf. She was certain that the tension in the room was enough to make it vibrate and jiggle.

Uma wondered whatever possessed her to think she could bring a fraction of neighborly peace between her father and Mitchell. She wondered why suddenly she was caught between two men who seemed to want her for different reasons—Everett, for the long term . . . and Mitchell, who wanted sex, pure and outright, with no strings attached.

* * *

•

Clyde smoothed his suit's wide lapels and straightened from his crouching position near the Warren brothers' house. They weren't home; Roman was at the old garage and Mitchell was dining with Uma, Everett, and Clarence.

Mitchell. The background check on him was easy enough with Clyde's connections. Mitchell had left a high-paying job with a building-and-supply chain, and now he was working as a yard man. Sweating didn't make sense when someone else could do the work; his only purpose in coming back to Madrid had to be revenge.

From the shadows of a stand of pampas grass, the gray cat hissed, his back arched and his fangs showing white. Half-wild, the cat would be hard to catch and kill, and he'd damaged Clyde's suit. When Clyde had bent to use his mini-battery-powered saw, the cat had reached out to scratch him, and in flight, ripped across Clyde's arm, snagging the fabric and digging holes into his arm.

Clyde was angry and could have used killing that old cat to release his frustration. Uma thought the BBs were a child's prank, and not the threat Clyde had intended. He'd have to make his message—that Uma stay away from the Warrens—much clearer. The mini-battery-powered saw was handy, sliding through the rungs on the ladder easily. He didn't like physical work, not like those sweating Warrens. Clyde was more of a thinker and a planner, and now he was thinking that the mens' weight would break the tampered rungs. If one of them fell just right, eliminating him, so much the better.

Uma really shouldn't be cozying up to the Warrens. She needed a lesson, and so did the cat.

The evening breeze was sudden and cold, whipping a climbing rose branch against Clyde's face. The thorn's scratch was slight, but an eery sensation enveloped Clyde, as if Lauren were protecting her home and those in it. The hairs at his nape lifted, his body chilled suddenly as fear clawed at him.

He pushed away the idea, sneering at his weaker side, and hating that vulnerability. He'd always been too vulnerable, and not tough enough. Now he was handling his life, paying back those who had belittled him.

He'd caused Lauren to be killed, and he'd killed Pete Jones. Exactly how could a dead woman hurt him? he scoffed as he tore a full rose bloom from its vine. It was July now and he had only a couple of months to complete his mission—to kill all of the women—before the last petal fell from the last rose in Madrid.

The dinner had ended uncomfortably—Everett stubbornly taking his place with Clarence for a game of checkers, and Mitchell returning to his home. Later, craving a peaceful relief from the bristling males—Everett and her father—Uma drifted into her moonlit garden. The gray cat slid from the shadow of a trellis, eyes glinting silver in the night, while lightning bugs blinked across the small lawn.

On another night, in another time, Uma might have talked quietly with Lauren, sharing their lives.

The roses' heavy perfume wrapped around Uma, and a drift of silky petals washed against her cheek. She could almost feel Lauren—waiting, wanting . . . fearing.

Uma rubbed her hands, the image of Lauren's blood staining them.

The cat watched her, then turned to a noise, and suddenly Mitchell towered over Uma. Moonlight caught on his brow and cheekbones, his eyes deeply shadowed. Unbuttoned against the night's heat, his shirt hung loosely down his chest.

Uma fought the leap of her heart, the pounding of her blood, as Mitchell took a step closer. His hand looped around her wrist, bringing her hand to his chest, smoothing her palm against the rough hair there.

"I'm sorry dinner wasn't more pleasant, Mitchell. I

wanted it to work out. My father can be very stubborn," she whispered as his other hand released her hair from its knot, his fingers prowling through it.

He studied the effect of moonlight on the strands, lifting them away from her face and lazily twining them around his fist. He gently drew her closer and bent to nuzzle her ear. "Dinner was what I expected. Nice. Cool. Tense. You controlling the situation, keeping a lid on it. I wonder what you can't control—what makes you look afraid and sweet and sexy, all at the same time. I wonder what would happen if you lost it—that control, the cool exterior jerked aside and the woman inside released."

He looked down to her fingers, smoothing the hair on his chest, and when he slowly looked back into her eyes, she read the desire heating him, leaping from him, pounding at her.

Then his gaze lowered to her mouth, heating her skin as it traveled lower to her breasts beneath her summer dress. "Do you know that I wake up hard every morning, wanting you?"

"Mitchell, you shouldn't say—" She couldn't speak, sensations from his open mouth on her throat riveting her. At first, she thought the tropical warmth came from the night, and then she knew it came from within; she was quivering and aching and needing to possess him, to pit herself physically against Mitchell, battling him, taking his challenges.

Excitement skittered over her body, a primitive hunger to take and to torment—

She had to have his mouth, to taste him. Uma caught his face, bringing it to hers, taking his mouth.

The jolt of his parted mouth, the heat coming from him, poured into her as he tugged her close and tight against him. His kiss wasn't sweet, but erotic and intense and pulsing through her, demanding that she give everything.

Uma held his hair in her fists, accepting the gentle foray of his tongue into her mouth, raising up on tiptoe to be closer to him, to feel that burgeoning heat of his body against hers.

She realized slowly that Mitchell was easing away, and when she looked up at him, she found his mockery.

"So now we know, don't we? You can pretend with someone else if you want, but not with me," he said before turning and leaving her alone and shaking and hot in the night.

Upstairs in her bedroom, Uma gripped her arms and tried not to think about revenge. On the other hand, revenge was the only payback that was acceptable for Mitchell. He'd deliberately set out to prove his point—that she was susceptible to him—and he'd succeeded.

She looked down at the well-trimmed area between their houses to Mitchell's back porch. If he would just come out, she had just the present for him—

Meanwhile, she worked furiously on her column, "Takers and Givers." Takers had to be shown the boundaries of a relationship, the equality of it, the intimacy. *And they definitely did not walk away from romantic—sensual—interludes, as if they had never happened. They did not use sexual attraction as a tool.*

Two hours later, Mitchell lay on his bed. His body ached and he should have known better than to try to prove his point with Uma. The tense dinner had left him raw, the image of Everett's hand holding hers.

So now we know . . . Mitchell had been jealous and out for revenge, and Uma didn't deserve his arrogance.

He'd wanted to claim her, to make her remember him that night, and not Everett—not exactly a class-act thing to do, leaving her simmering and himself aching.

Unable to sleep, Mitchell launched his taut body from the bed and went outside into the garden beneath Uma's darkened bedroom window. It slid open, the lace curtains moving, and Uma leaned out slightly. "Having fun? Gloating?

And do all the men in this neighborhood prefer to run around in their undershorts?"

"I'm in my own backyard, sweetheart. Proper attire is casual. And I was just making certain that you didn't get confused about which man you're kissing," he returned, still nettled by Everett's possessiveness.

"I see. For the record, I'm not going to be controlled by you and I don't like hit-and-run attacks."

"I wouldn't exactly call it an attack. Why don't you come down and we'll discuss it?" he invited, enjoying the tit-for-tat with her. She gave him pleasure in more than the physical sense. "Or maybe you'd like a second round."

"Or maybe *you* should learn some *manners.*"

The cold water hit Mitchell in the face, drenching his body and undershorts. Before he could think, he was in motion, propping a ladder up against her house, and climbing up to her second-story window. On his way, he plucked a perfect rose.

Stunned, she stared out at him from the open window, and a surge of boyish pleasure hit Mitchell. He couldn't help grinning as he handed the rose to her. "Are you going to invite me in?"

"Good heavens, no."

Backed against the wall, with her hair in braids, wearing a loose T-shirt, and clutching a rose to her chest, she looked adorable. *Adorable.* Now, when had he ever thought a woman looked "adorable"? "Want to come out and play?"

"Good heavens, no. Mitchell, you've got to get down before you get hurt."

"I'll need a kiss to take home with me." Teasing Uma could be addictive, he decided. She looked all flustered and cute.

"You had a kiss, and a pretty good one at that. Then you left me."

"I apologize. My manners need improvement. The next

time I kiss you, I'll finish the job, good and proper. Good-night."

Mitchell almost chuckled as he descended the ladder and replaced it against his house. When he saw Uma staring down at him, her arms crossed, he bowed deeply, then blew her a kiss. The window closed quickly.

Inside, Roman was waiting and laughing. He handed Mitchell a towel. "You're lucky her old man didn't spatter your backside with buckshot. I thought you were too old and stiff for playing games."

"I'm learning a few things." Mitchell toweled his wet hair and shoulders, crossed his arms, and leaned back against a counter. He wasn't exactly pleased that his brother had seen him acting like a lovesick, horny boy. And the knowledge that he actually would have crawled through that window to have her poleaxed him.

Even now, he could feel her warm, soft mouth beneath his, slanted, and fused and giving. He could feel her tremble, her body tight against his, every curve—

Mitchell sighed roughly. It was going to be a long, hard night.

"By the way," Roman said slowly. "Our friend has been busy again. He works fast and he's good. He knows we use that ladder. When I came home, it was in a different place than we left it. After the nail and tire incident, I checked and he'd been busy, sawdust on the grass. I fixed it, pronto."

Mitchell tossed the towel aside with the violence he felt. "It is someone who knows a lot about everyone and he's giving notice that he's not happy."

Clyde leaned back into the shadows. He listened to Edgar MacDougal peeing off his back porch, just a few inches from Clyde's well-polished shoes.

Mitchell had used the ladder, handling its weight easily as

he'd propped it up against Uma's house. In fast motion, he'd used his arms to power up the ladder, and not his full weight, as a working man might do.

Clyde frowned; he'd have to remember that Mitchell moved quickly for a big man. That size meant a bigger target, but Clyde didn't want to just shoot Mitchell. He wanted to enjoy his pain.

SEVEN

Shelly stopped her Wednesday night ironing, poured a long cool glass of sun-brewed sweet tea, and held the icy glass up to her hot cheek. The third week of July baked the streets during the day, and heat hugged the night.

Tabor Street was quiet; the houses along it settled into the night beneath the towering oaks. During the day, the trees gave some relief from the hot summer sun, and in the winter, they sheltered the homes from the fierce winter winds that would sweep across Oklahoma. The basic "starter" houses with small yards were owned by a mix of newly marrieds just starting out, and retired people on strict pensions.

And everyone knew what happened along Tabor Street, who visited who, for how long. It was a friendly gossip, neighbors checking on each other, and as a single mother, Shelly usually appreciated the safety and comfort. But with Roman prowling in Madrid, she wasn't certain she wanted her life inspected.

She pressed a hand to her aching back—today was her every-other-week floor cleaning day, scrubbing and vacuuming at the Millers' big two-story house. She was tired and hot and her ancient air conditioner had broken down and Dani could be anywhere. Shelly turned her face to the oscillating fan, letting it blow the damp tendrils around her face as the washer and dryer hummed near her. Her cotton tank top and the cutoff shorts didn't ease the heat and she debated asking for an advance on next week's cleaning to repair the living room window's air conditioner. The small window unit in Dani's room did little to cool the small house.

Shelly rubbed a healing cut on her arm and looked down at her bare feet. She didn't have control of her life or her daughter, and there was only one thing she could do about Roman—tell him the truth and hope . . . for what? What if he wanted to step into their lives now?

Shelly looked outside her kitchen window to see Roman standing beneath the streetlight. She pivoted, tossed the dishtowel aside, and leaned back against the counter. She crossed her arms, locking her fingers into the flesh, and still they continued shaking. Dani spoke only of him. *Shelly had to talk with him. He had to know that Dani, the girl infatuated with him, was his daughter!*

She took a deep, steadying breath and turned off the iron that she had been heating to press her customer's shirts. She hesitated at the back door, then firmly jerked it open and stepped out into the hot, quiet night. The heavy scent of her neighbor's honeysuckle met her as the police car cruised by and she waited beside her ancient Toyota pickup until it passed. Taking another deep breath, she walked out on the sidewalk where Roman could see her.

She wanted to run, but she couldn't. She had to protect Dani.

Roman turned to her immediately and started walking across the street. He came to tower over her and said nothing. The oak trees on her lawn hid them from the street, the shadows engulfing them. His face was so hard now, his body lean, but heavier than it had been in his youth. The black shirt he wore stretched across shoulders that blocked out the night, his jeans flowing into long legs and biker's boots.

But the hair was the same, unruly and shaggy and damp, his scent that of soap and the tang of aftershave—and of anger. She could feel it tremble over the softer sweet scents of the honeysuckle in the hot night.

In the streetlight, one side of his face caught the light, the other was in shadow. Those long lashes shadowed his deep-set eyes and created shadowy fringes on his tanned skin. His jaw gleamed, that high ridge of cheekbone jerked just once as he looked at her. She wasn't a girl any longer and that close study tore at her senses; she gripped the white fence post for support.

He looked slowly down to her hand, the knuckles sharp in relief, and then back up to her face. The pinpoints of his eyes lasered at her, and she sensed that his slow breathing, that slight flaring of his nostrils, was forced, a man keeping an edge on his emotions. *Back then, he'd been so desperate to hold her, to love her, as if he needed an anchor to tether him to life . . .*

Roman's stance, hip-shot, that arrogant tilt to his head, said he hadn't come in peace.

It had been so many years. Her heart raced as she tried to force just the words she had practiced from her lips. "I . . . there's something you should know."

His expression tightened and the bitter low tone slammed into her. "That Dani is my daughter. That you—"

"No, she isn't," Shelly lied fiercely.

"Oh, she's mine, all right."

Her carefully constructed words flew out into the street, still heated from the sun. "You don't know that."

"I can do basic math. Her birthday counts back exactly nine months from that night. We've been talking. I know quite a few things."

He wasn't sparing her, slapping her with facts. "You must know that you've got to leave her alone," Shelly said.

"No, I won't. You know I won't, but I haven't been bothering her—not that way. What do you think I am, anyway? She's my child, and dammit, you never tried to contact me. There were people here who knew where Mitchell and I had gone. They should have, they ran us out of town as soon as Mitchell left the hospital."

"You were a boy. There was nothing you could have done."

"I would have taken care of you somehow. Away from here. I asked you to come with me at the time, but you couldn't force yourself to leave Mama and step into the big, wide world. And what would you have had? You would have probably ended up hating me."

Shelly felt herself fading, sliding—then Roman's hand was on her arm, holding her upright. "Let's go in. You need to sit down."

"You can't come in. If Dani came home—"

"She'd see me. We'll handle it."

Shelly let herself be propelled into the kitchen, eased into a chair, and took the glass of water that Roman handed her. "Drink."

He was taking in the tiny neat kitchen, the rolled dampened laundry in the basket, the already pressed dress shirts hanging on the rack, the waiting ironing board. She couldn't move while Roman quietly prowled through her two-bedroom home, clicking lights on and off as he went.

Shelly scrubbed her rough hands across her face and knew how he would see the used, reupholstered furniture, the curtains she had sewn, the old sewing machine that she used to patch things, the basket beside it. The bathroom was tiny, cluttered with Dani's makeup; her bedroom was plastered with posters, clothing on the floor. It was quiet now, without its usual earsplitting rocker music.

Then Roman was back, sitting in a chair, looking down at

her worn linoleum floor, his hands dangling at his knees. Her "Roman—" set him off and he lurched to his feet, slamming an open hand down on the yellow marble Formica table. He went to the kitchen counter and braced his hands against it as he looked out into the night.

Then he looked at her and the flashing anger in his light brown eyes, his too-quiet tone, held her. "Want to tell me about it?"

"No." She didn't want anyone to know what her parents had said, how the town had speculated about the father, the pressure she'd been under from the minister, and the censure of everyone, the lurid stares from the men. But worst of all was the livid coldness of her parents, the way they wanted her to put Dani up for adoption. "I had friends," she said, not wanting his pity.

"Uma, Lauren, and Pearl, right? What about your parents?" he demanded as he tested the buttons and knobs on the dead air conditioner. Then he turned back to fire the next volley. "Dani told me how wonderful they were. They didn't recognize her as their granddaughter. That really hurts the kid."

"I know. Only my mother is alive now and—"

"And you're paying the tab at the nursing home and she still won't talk to her own granddaughter?" His tone was low, quivering, and shaking the room with emotion.

She loved her mother, and through her pain, she'd understood. Her parents had such plans for her—college, a good marriage, security . . . "There are worse things. I was able to work. I did. I work at the nursing home to help expenses. Mother has a small retirement. We managed. Like I said, my friends helped—Uma and Pearl. Pearl and Walter were wonderful. Pearl gave us so many things she didn't need. Uma babysat and was my rock."

" 'Managed.' " The flat tone and Roman's dark scowl challenged her.

She didn't like him criticizing the best she could do. "You have no right to judge. Just stay out of Dani's life."

"She's my kid, too. And she's headed for trouble, just like I was. I know better than you about this and how she could end up. I don't want that to happen."

"You don't have any say in our lives."

Roman's smile wasn't nice. "Honey, from now on, I'm making you and Dani my business."

Shelly leaped to her feet. "Don't you dare hurt her."

Roman frowned and lifted a finger to trace the year-old scar along her temple. "What's that? How did you get it?"

She brushed his hand away. The burn had hurt fiercely, just searing her scalp which bled horribly. She didn't think it was necessary to see a doctor, and she could ill afford the luxury, using butterfly bandages and good antiseptic. "I hit my head on something the night Lauren died. A branch or something tore my skin when I was coming into the house. I'd been outside, trying to get Dani's cat in out of the storm, and—"

His eyes narrowed, his expression cold. "Uh-huh. That was quite some branch. . . . it's always Dani, isn't it? That's why she's spoiled and doesn't care if you work yourself to death, while she's partying."

"*I love her.*" Her statement vibrated in the air and Roman watched her carefully, the protective mother fighting for her child. She didn't try to hide her emotions; she'd already fought many, many times for Dani. She'd fight with her last breath.

He shook his head and studied the wide satin strips hung carefully over the door. His hand cruised down the hot pink satin and he lifted the brightly flowered one beneath it. "What are these?"

She didn't like him seeing into her life, inspecting the bald, poor edges of her pride. "Ribbons for Rosy, the Ferris's pig. I launder and iron them for free because I love them and her.

The Ferris's low retirement pensions aren't paying their bills now, but I can do this for them. And I will."

He scanned her arm, the bandage running across it. "What happened?"

"An accident."

Roman's deep voice was quiet and fierce, demanding an answer. "I asked you what happened."

"A knife. A butcher knife that I forgot I'd placed on the cans on the closet's top shelf. I reached up and it came down. No harm done."

His dark brows jerked into a fierce frown. "Is that where you'd usually place a knife?"

"No . . ." She didn't want him to know the series of accidents that had happened in the last year; they had increased since her preoccupation with his arrival in Madrid.

Roman's expression said he was caught on the edge of a decision and she again tossed him an escape. "I don't want you to have anything to do with Dani. She's my responsibility."

His low tone shook the kitchen. "She's my child, too. I wasn't there then—but I am now. She's not going to end up like me, or ironing someone else's clothes. The kid is running with the wrong crowd. She has to graduate from high school and get an education."

"*Stay out of our lives. I know what she needs and it isn't you.*" She leaped to her feet, her fists at her side. She hadn't meant to sail that order at him and in the silence, it boomeranged back to her.

Roman rubbed his chest and looked at her, a heavy pulse beating in his throat as she locked her gaze with his. She'd really only fought for one thing in her life, and Dani was it.

"I'm going to be around," he said as the washer started bouncing and chugging and moving off the blocks she'd placed beneath it for balance on the sagging floor. Roman tested the soft flooring with his foot. "Termites, more than likely."

She hadn't had money for the exterminators and now pride forced her to stay quiet. Roman caught her frown and shot it back to her.

"I'll be around," he said quietly as he bent to lift the washer slightly and readjust the cement block beneath one corner. He stood, looked at Shelly, and served her worst fear to her. "Explain it to Dani however you like, but I'm going to be a part of her life. I'll be around. See you."

At the door he turned to stare at her. "Dani tells me that just after Lauren was killed, your car caught on fire when you turned the key. Is that true?"

"Yes. I'd been having trouble with it and the engine just seemed to explode. The mechanic said a gas leak—"

"Did you have a gas leak with it before? Any smell of gas?"

"Well, no, but it was old and everything needed repair on it. I smelled gas that morning. One of the old hoses, proba-bly—"

"Uh-huh," Roman said grimly and closed the door behind him.

"You can't just come in here and take over, Roman War-ren," Shelly stated shakily to the yawning, quivering silence. *I'm going to be a part of her life. I'll be around. See you.*

"Shelly, Shelly, Shelly," Clyde murmured as he watched Ro-man step out into the night. "You're not making this any eas-ier on yourself. I made a mistake with Lauren, hiring someone else, but I won't with you. I was angry that night with Pete and let my temper get the best of me, shooting at you—missing you. It's just as well that you wear my mark, that scar. I like that. So much better for the game, then actu-ally shooting you between the eyes. I like the game with you. You can look so distracted, so confused. I'm amused, I really am. But that won't help you. You've trespassed, and you've got to be removed. Because if you live too long, you might tell, and I couldn't have that."

He tipped his fedora slightly and sank into the shadows as Roman walked by on the street below. Clyde didn't like the Warrens in his town again, stirring up Uma and Shelly and Pearl, because they belonged to him.

Roman stood inside his father's garage, the moonlight slicing through the boards on the windows.

If there was any place he didn't want to be, it was Madrid.

If there was anything he hadn't planned, it was being a father.

If there was any woman he didn't want to tangle with, it was the good kind—and Shelly was still innocent and sweet and fiercely a mother fighting for the child they shared. Dani had said that Shelly didn't—hadn't ever—dated, and that meant that . . .

Dammit, the slam of desire still rode him. One look at those long legs gleaming in the moonlight, the crevice of her breasts as she sat looking as though everything she'd loved would be torn away from her, that hair—the sleek, silky movement when she turned her head, and those eyes—green as meadow grass and so soft when she spoke of Dani, the love shining there, the fierce protection of a mother fighting for her child.

He should have been here. He should have—what? Maybe she was right, he was just a boy . . . Shelly had faced everything by herself . . . she knew how to love, how to give. What did he know how to do? Race? Find a party and a willing woman?

How the hell did he think he could give her something, anything, now?

The shadowy, musty air closed in on Roman, squeezing his chest. He rubbed the ache there, thinking of all the time that had passed, and the life he'd lived, the women he'd known. Shelly was a virgin when he took her that night, and she was still—he heard a noise and turned to see Dani in the shadows. *His daughter, his child.* "Hey, kid. A little late for you to be out, isn't it?"

"Nah. I'm going to be eighteen soon, and I'm a woman already. I do what I want, whenever I want. What are you doing here?"

He knew the tough talk; it had been his. "I'm thinking I'm going to start a garage. What do you think?"

She shrugged, but he caught the excitement in her pale face beneath the paint. Then Roman asked, "You said your mom does cleaning and laundry. I'm going to have to trade fix-up and car stuff for what I need, until I get on my feet. Do you think she'd buy that?"

"I can help you. I'll do anything, wash your clothes, rags, whatever—even help clean this place. I love motors."

"Do you wash your own clothes?" he asked, pushing her, resenting all the work that Shelly had had to do to pay their way. Just the way Dani turned her face was enough to remind him of Shelly, that wholesome, clean look.

"Sure."

He knew she was lying. "Look, kid. Help me out. I don't know many people here and it takes a bit to build up business. Your mom knows everyone and she's got a good rep and I don't. She's a way in, if you know what I mean."

Dani considered the thought. "Sure. I'll fix it."

"You do that, and when I'm on my feet and something comes in that is hot and fast, I'll show you what I know about racing. You don't need to be any biker's girl. Not with your looks. And if you weren't wearing that paint, you'd look that much better—like your mother. Besides, there isn't anything like racing. You'd look real cute beneath a helmet, behind a steering wheel."

I'm your father, a little bit late, but I'm trying. "And kid, get this straight—what you want, between us, isn't going to happen. I'm not looking for jail bait trouble. And I'm not going to be used to keep Jace in line, getting you what you want."

Dani huffed and stomped out of the garage, slamming the front door behind her. He thought of going after her, of following her, and then he heard the rev of a motorcycle.

Roman rubbed his jaw and couldn't help smiling. So the kid had a temper, just like her old man. Maybe that wasn't good, but at least he understood. He probably understood better than her sweet mother.

The one thing he did not want to do was to hurt either Dani or Shelly. They'd both paid enough for him.

Then a motorcycle cruised outside and stopped, purring roughly. In another second, Dani slammed into the garage. She stood, legs braced, her hands on her slender hips, glaring at him.

"Wear a helmet when you ride, kid," he said, just to get her going, to see why she'd come back.

"You've got a thing for my mother, don't you? A lot of men do. They think because she had me with no old man taking the blame that she's free and easy. Well, she isn't, and neither am I. I can get what I want without the payoff."

"Maybe I am interested in her. I don't know yet," he answered slowly, truthfully, and didn't bother to tell Dani that she might not have a choice about the "payoff." Some men just took. Was that what he did?

"I won't be happy, you know. And I'm not her. No one is going to walk all over me and leave me flat like my old man left her. If I want a man, I usually get him, and I don't put out."

"That's hard talk from a little girl." The kid was honest, and he could deal with that. He heard the motorcycle rev outside and knew that Jace was just as hot-blooded as Roman was years ago. The boy would have to do some running to get his daughter, or he'd be in for a little lesson.

When Dani slammed out again, he wondered how long it would be before she put two and two together and realized that he might be her "old man."

* * *

Clyde stroked his chin and watched Dani stalk out of the garage a second time. The girl was as willful as her mother, defying the good folks of Madrid. He would do the town a favor by getting rid of the pair of them—mother and daughter. Shelly, because she knew too much, and Dani—well, because Dani was evidence that threatened Clyde.

After a week of working to rebuild her computer programs, getting the brochure electronically uplifted to send to the printer, meeting her Charis Lopez syndication deadline, Uma stepped out into the dawn. In a few hours, the sun would be high and hot, baking the streets. She began her warming up exercises for her regular morning run. Her body was stiff from too many hours in a desk chair, and her senses were still humming from Mitchell's light kiss—and the tense dinner she'd planned to make peace among the three males. The dinner's only reward was another Charis article, "When Men Bristle."

But Mitchell hadn't. He'd been enjoying the tension, and the gold watch on his wrist proved that he had battled his way up to a fat paycheck. He knew how to handle himself in conflict.

She lifted her hands to the gray dawn, spread her fingers, and let the light filter through them. With her father in Arizona, enraptured with the new Zuni pots his friend had acquired, the house was quiet. She'd never lived alone, and once the window's glass had been changed and the repairman was gone, she enjoyed the freedom.

A week without Mitchell had been peaceful—relatively—until she'd remember that devastating, tormenting kiss. Everett was traveling again, attending a tourism conference in Vermont. Uma gathered the morning around her, planning her day. While the last week of July baked the days in

Madrid, mornings were perfect for gardening, and since the computer crash, she'd let her mother's garden go far too long.

And the mornings were apparently good for mole hunting, she added, as she noted Lars Swenson prowling across his yard with what looked like a harpoon. Periodically, he waggled the handles of the pitchforks that were stuck in the ground. The theory was that moles could be driven by the vibrations, and Lars had lined up the pitchforks to face Charley Blue Feather's house. One by one, Lars moved the pitchforks closer to Charley's yard, driving the herd back to their home base.

Mitchell walked out to set his sun tea on the front porch, and Uma caught her breath. The dawn gleamed on his chest, and in his bare feet, he had that scruffy, just awakened look, his jaw dark with stubble. He glanced at her, scowled, and then walked across to Lars's house. The old tomcat, tail held high, strolled across to join him, winding around his legs. It was all very neighborly and it didn't concern her.

She now wore a good support sports bra.

Mitchell was not going to bother her with those hot, dark looks, she decided as that quivering, sizzling sensation began to warm her.

Pearl's stinging call of yesterday morning still rang in the quiet air. "Dozer has been my yard man since Walter and I got married. Can you imagine him quitting, just now, when my garden is in full bloom, and me with a garden party coming up next week? Dozer sold his business to that—that criminal, Mitchell Warren. He can't possibly know anything about gardening. Yet here he comes, pulls up to my yard, and starts unloading the riding mower from his pickup. Well, I tell you, I went out there and fired him on the spot."

Later that afternoon, Pearl had called again. "I've called everyone in town I can think of. That Warren man has got all of Dozer's business. No one else is doing yards. I'll do it myself before I let him prune one bush or tree."

Uma started jogging easily, refusing to look at Mitchell's house as she thought of Shelly, terribly frightened of what Roman might do—or if Dani would discover her father's identity.

Uma tensed as Mitchell nodded to her, the two men standing and pointing and apparently discussing the "mole herd." She noted that his pickup was loaded with the riding and push mower and the open garage door gave her a full view of Dozer's old business, from push mowers to insecticides and tree trimming gear.

She sailed into a full, fast run, crossing the pink dawn striping the pavement. The Warren brothers had certainly stirred up Madrid; gossip said that Roman was going to open the old garage and that he was now living in it. And "gossip" knew that he'd gotten the money from big syndicate crime partners who were just looking for a small town to use as a hideout.

The sleepy town was stirring, fierce arguments in the barber shop and the cafe and at the gas station. Bred from Native Americans and homesteaders, cowboys and frontiersman, half of Madrid knew they would endure whatever came their way. Those wanting to stimulate Madrid's cash flow recalled Bonnie and Clyde days, how the lawmen, reporters, and tourists had piled into the city. For a town built in one day during the Land Rush at the turn of the last century, anything seemed possible. But the "civilized" element, the society class in which Pearl moved, were outraged.

Gossip also said that Everett and Mitchell had shared a booth at Shirley's Ice Cream Parlor the morning after her make-peace dinner. Whatever could they have been discussing?

She ran down Main Street, cool and quiet in the morning, before the stores opened. Then, at Tabor Street, Shelly swung into a run beside her. Since Shelly's energies were necessary to her house cleaning and laundry work, Uma was surprised.

The two women ran in stride down Main Street, and then Shelly said between breaths, "Roman is at my house, fixing something, every day. Dani is furious, but she's not telling him why. She thinks he's interested in me, and she wants him. *Him* . . . interested in *me*. I could kill him. Dani thinks it is a trade-off, an exchange—my laundry and patching for his house repair. He's already fixed the air conditioner and he's starting on the flooring. I do not like having him around. He's making me feel as if I can't take care of anything!"

Uma frowned slightly; Shelly wasn't a person to complain, but the Warren brothers could excite even the most placid temper—and clearly Shelly was frustrated, using running to work off her early morning mood.

"You wouldn't understand," she continued. "But I haven't lived with a man around the house—you have. They leave the toilet seats up. That is unnerving, and so is the way Roman looks at me—let alone if I tell him I can't afford the work that he is doing—ironing and laundry just won't cover it. The whole town is lit up and gossiping. It's only a matter of time before someone—you've always got good advice. What can I do?"

Just then Mitchell's black pickup cruised slowly by Uma. " 'Morning, ladies," he said, and Uma unconsciously picked up speed, nudging Shelly down a side street.

Shelly looked at Uma and shook her head. "Roman's garage is down Maloney Street. I'm not going down there. What's wrong?"

Uma shook her head, preferring silence. "May I help you, Mitchell?" she asked finally, politely, pointedly as she looked at him.

"Dinner at my place tonight, Uma. Just a neighborly pay-back for dinner the other night at your house," he said, with a narrowed smile she didn't trust. Mitchell didn't wait for an answer, pulling forward on the street.

When his pickup slid onto a side street, enveloped by the cool shadows, Shelly studied Uma and noted, "You look as if you're going to give him a very nasty hand sign."

Mitchell's invitation wasn't sweet, and ran more to the dictation of a powerful man expecting his orders to be obeyed. "I wouldn't. I've never done anything of the kind. But that man can really get to me."

"Excuse me," Roman said as Shelly stood at the sink, wiping the counter. He leaned close, his arm went past her, his bare chest warming her back as he turned the faucet and let the water run cold enough to drink.

She didn't move, feeling Roman's body close to hers, his breath against her cheek. He turned off the water and both his arms came down on the counter to frame her. "Problems?" he asked too softly.

Problems? Roman was too close, and whatever leaped within her all those years ago was threatening to do the same now.

After a week of him hammering and running a power saw, putting in new windows, and putting in new pipes in the kitchen and bathroom, she had a definite problem that stretched into her sleepless nights, her tense days—Roman. She was apt to find him anywhere, lying with his tools on the kitchen floor, head and shoulders beneath the sink, grinning at her from on top of the roof, at a window he was repairing from the outside, caulking the tub—

The lowered intense look of those gold eyes could stop her like a doe caught in headlights. She'd argued with him logically, fought with him, and yet just there, riding on the edge, was a sensual pull she didn't want.

She looked down at her hands near his, white knuckled as they gripped the counter. His thumb slowly cruised over the back of hers. "I've told you that I don't have the money for the repairs, for the materials. You're making me feel as if I can't cope, and it's only a matter of time before Dani discovers that—"

He blew on her nape, shifting the tendrils that had come free from her ponytail. "What are you doing running early in the morning, Shelly, when you've got a full day of work ahead of you?"

Trying to figure out how to deal with you. "I like the fresh air," she said, and regretted the trembling of her body.

He blew those tendrils again. "Tell Dani that I'm your boyfriend. Let her get used to the idea before this all breaks and someone says the wrong thing to her about me. Putting dates together is easy enough with all the gossip in this town."

"No."

He shoved back from her and Shelly pivoted around to face him, her hands behind her, locked to the counter. Roman served her one of those hot leveling looks at her faded shirt, cut-off shorts, and tennis shoes, and walked to the refrigerator. He jerked it open and took out a can of soda, popped the top, and lifted it to drink.

Raw and masculine, the appealing package was all there— the shaggy sweat-damp hair, the gleam of tanned sweaty skin over his arms, his lean and powerful chest, and that flat plane of his stomach and lower where his jeans sagged just a bit. From there on down to his bare feet, he was all long and strong.

Shelly breathed uneasily; life in close quarters with Roman set her on edge, her senses clanging with big warning bells.

He tossed the can into the trash, braced a hand on the refrigerator, and leveled one of those dark, burning looks at her. "I've got a bum knee and no money to speak of. I got into that fight the first night I was here because of a woman. But that's not happening again, not unless the woman is you. I can't make it up to you, but I can help you with Dani now. You don't have a clue about the darker side of life and that's where she's headed—I've been there."

What might happen to Dani terrified her. She'd read of girls who'd run away, but Roman in their lives now wasn't possible. More than once those honey-colored eyes had ripped down and up her body, leaving a tingling path. "I've managed this far—"

"Deceive yourself, if you want. You need help on this one, honey. Call me a dreamer, but I'd like her to know that I'm her father."

"You didn't come back because you knew that. You might not have come back at all."

His hand slapped at the refrigerator hard enough to shake it, rattling the apple-shaped cookie jar on top. "Well, I'm here now and the kid is making moves on me. I'm not leaving. I had a mother who ran out, and I wasn't here for you or for her. I know what a kid feels like, all torn up inside because a parent didn't care enough to stay around and see her grow up. I'm staying, honey. Get used to it, and I'm going to talk with *your* mother, too. She's Dani's grandmother, for God's sake."

Shelly's secret had been her own—with the exception of Uma—for all those years. She couldn't bear to reopen the past, the heartbreaking arguments, the venomous accusation that her "whoring" was responsible for her father's death. "You can't just come in here and—"

"Try me."

The words hung in the air. Roman made his way to the back door, never taking his eyes from Shelly. Horrified at what he might do, she couldn't move—then she heard him say, "Hi, Dani. I'm just leaving—going out for a ride."

Panic drove Shelly to the door; Dani wanted more than anything to ride behind Roman on the Harley. "I'll be with you in just a minute, Roman. I've never had a motorcycle ride."

Their stunned faces did look alike, the same light brown eyes, the same turn of their parted lips—father and daughter. Roman stopped drawing on his T-shirt, almost comical as it paused above his stomach. Then Dani frowned. "Maybe you're too old to hold on, Mom," she stated nastily.

"Nah," Roman said easily, jerking his T-shirt fully down. "If you want a ride later, kid, that's okay, but I'd already asked your mother. See if you can't fold those towels on top of the dryer while we're gone. If there's one thing that makes a woman look bad, it's not carrying her share of the work. Work hard, play hard."

Dani blinked, and Shelly caught the subtle taunt—Dani already thought she was a woman. "I carry my share," she tossed back and slammed into the house.

"Hurry up, honey," Roman said, watching Shelly. "Or would you rather not finish what you started?"

EIGHT

"I really shouldn't. I need to make canapes for Pearl's dinner party tomorrow night. Some caterers are coming in, but Pearl—I don't know what to do. I've never ridden a motorcycle before," she said honestly as Roman carefully fitted the extra helmet to her. She didn't know what to do about anything—Dani glaring at her through the kitchen window, the music blasting loudly enough to disturb the elderly couple next door, the man who wanted to be a part of Dani's life.

"Then it's time you learned. You look about seventeen yourself just now, all steamy mad and frustrated. Only you were sweet back then and now you're ready to fight for what you want. You learned plenty and you managed. You'll learn this," he said, tipping up her chin with his finger and smiling down at her.

It was an intimate, heart-stopping smile, and though she knew he'd given it to many other women, it was still very dangerous. "Maybe I won't."

He swung onto the seat. He turned to look at her, challenging her with that steady half-lidded look. "Hop on."

"You wear your helmet, too." She wondered how she could sit on that seat without touching him.

He shrugged and reached for his helmet. "Anything else?"

She looked down Tabor Street and saw the elderly couples walking at sunset. They'd seen Roman's motorcycle in her driveway for the past week. They'd seen him use Mitchell's truck to haul boards and plumbing supplies to the house. "Heaven only knows what they're thinking," she muttered, as she eased into the narrow black leather seat behind him.

He back-walked the bike with both of them on it, and ordered, "Put your arms around me."

She placed her hands on his waist, then gripped his shirt in her fists as he revved the motor. "Doesn't this hurt your knee?"

"Everything hurts my knee. But I'm not on painkillers any more. I'm not going through that mess again, if that's worrying you."

The instant small lurch of the mechanical beast threw her backward, then Roman stopped it, only to jerk once more. "Told you to hang on. Put your feet on the pedals."

Shelly glanced at the newlyweds just down the street, the bride snuggling against her husband, as they watched. "You know what this looks like."

When he didn't answer, but jerked the motorcycle again, Shelly eased her arms around him. He was hard, inflexible, powerful, the muscles rippling as he drove the motorcycle from Tabor Street on to Main Street, where the whole town watched them pass.

She wanted to fly, to let the wind flow through her hair and over her body, to laugh with the pleasure and the freedom of the ride. Images of houses and trees and of Lonny sitting in his police car sped by her, then a green spread of pastures dotted with Hereford or Angus cattle.

Glorious, mindless freedom. Shelly inhaled escape as though it were heaven, if only for a moment.

She realized she was smiling, just a silly, pleased, mindless smile, when Roman drove onto the old Warren spread. She was still smiling when Roman parked the bike and she was still gripping him tight.

"Off," he said in the quiet of the sunset.

Shelly realized that her escape to momentary freedom with Roman had landed her alone with him. She scampered from the machine and Roman eased off more slowly, favoring his knee and freeing his helmet.

He reached to take Shelly's and hang it beside his. When he turned to her, she couldn't move, pinned by the dark intent in his eyes.

"Let's start all over again, shall we?" he asked huskily as the old windmill whirred and the stormclouds brewed and the wind rose to tug at her hair, licking at the ends.

She couldn't move as he bent to brush his lips against hers, gently asking, wooing . . .

She found herself leaning into the kiss just as Roman stepped back, studying her. "You're just as sweet, Shell."

Blushing, she turned away into the sunset and the rising storm and the wind. The contrast of beautiful day and incoming storm was as mixed as her emotions. "We can't go back, Roman. And I'm not—"

"What I'm used to? A fancy woman, if the other words are too hard for you to say?"

"I was going to say, you're very experienced. I have a daughter to raise, I can't just—"

"*Our* daughter, Shell. It's time she knew."

The secret that only he and Uma shared shook violently within Shelly, trapped by years of silence.

Roman looked off into the storm coming toward them, its furious dark churning clouds. The wind lifted his hair, pulling it back from his face, the bones stark and thrusting against his skin, the resemblance to Dani caught in the last gold of sunset. "I haven't got anything to offer her, or you, to make it up. But I'd like to try. I'm asking you to give me a chance. To let me be in your lives. I'd like to get to know my own daughter, Shell. And I'm really sorry about what you went through. Just—please . . ."

The word quivered in the air, as if Roman had asked for little, but this was important enough for him now to bend his pride. "Dammit, Shell. I am really sorry. I'll do the best I can from here on out to be a father to my daughter."

He hadn't looked at her, that muscle in his cheek contracting. "I'm not like my mother. I don't run off when things get rough—I wouldn't have run then either . . . if I had known."

"I don't know what is right now," she stated honestly, feeling the storm wrap around them just as fiercely as their emotions.

"Neither do I. But I want to try."

Her life was so safe now, but Roman wasn't. She believed him and yet she feared Dani's reaction; the tempest of father and daughter could rock all their lives. Her link with Dani was tenuous at best, the teenager ready for flight.

Roman was right about one thing—he understood Dani's wild side better than Shelly did. "I'll think about it."

Clyde lifted his face to the wind, inhaling the dampness of it. Excitement throbbed in the storm, because tonight he felt the strength of gods swelling in him; he tasted revenge. Once he had been powerless and ridiculed, and now he was strong. Those who had taken what was his would pay.

While the thunderstorm raged outside, rain slashing at the windows, Uma sat in candlelight, folding laundry and brooding about Mitchell's so-called dinner invitation. As often happened in Madrid, telephone service was out, and with the violent weather outside, Mitchell couldn't possibly expect her to arrive at his house.

She hadn't had dinner with a single man, other than Everett and her father, in her lifetime. The situation would have been far too uncomfortable because Mitchell wasn't an easy man to understand; she was better off staying at home and catching up on laundry and dusting.

Dusting was therapeutic, the scent of lemon polish filling the room, the old heavy antique furniture from the 1880s gleaming in the candlelight. After her father's ancestors had staked their land rush claims, the furniture had followed in wagons. It was old and dear and she loved easy nights when she could wear old clothes, have a glass of wine, and polish the old wood.

She smiled to herself, wrapping the safety of the house around her. Her father was thrilled with his Arizona friend's collection, swapping stories and pots, and his visit might take at least two months as they scouted possible historical sites. No doubt her father would hear of Mitchell's pickup cruising beside her this morning, and that she had gone to the ranch with him—and then, and then there was certain to be another revival of the "damned Warrens" and the Lawrence feud with them.

Uma pushed away the future discussion with her father. When he'd had his heart attack, her move back into the house had served their purposes—she'd needed some thinking room in her marriage—but the silent understanding was that once she was uncomfortable, she might move. Clarence's expectations and most of Madrid's were that she would remarry Everett.

Everett deserved better. She'd just have to work more on finding him someone to date, a wifey sort of woman—just as she had been. She reached for the pad on the sofa beside her and wrote, "Charis Column, due next week—Expectations: Wifey or Partner or Single Lane?"

Mitchell was definitely an alpha-single male. He clearly wasn't going to move into the intimacy lane. Next to her note, Uma added, "He who wants sex alone may not be partner material." Many of her notes sounded like fortune cookie readings, but it was true enough.

Sexual need fairly hummed from Mitchell. The problem was, she was picking up those vibrations, and they had moved restlessly within her.

Did *she* want a life partner, or even a temporary one? She added to the note, "One must understand one's self prior to a relationship, the goals and expectations. What are they?"

She shook her head and folded a fluffy seafoam-green bath towel, running her hand across the soft texture before slapping it on the stack near her. Mitchell wasn't pushing her around, making her feel unneighborly.

Making her feel. Her hand shook as she reached for the laundry basket at her feet.

She wondered what it would be like—

A shadow moved on the front porch, and in the flash of lightning a man's large form was silhouetted in the glass of the front door. Uma's hand went to her chest, the rapid fearful beat of her heart. Lauren had been killed, and the murderer of that man had never been found . . .

"Uma, open this door," Mitchell's deep voice demanded after the next roll of thunder.

Fearing that he might be hurt, or struck by lightning, Uma hurried to the door.

Holding a big cardboard box covered with painters' plastic under one arm, Mitchell stood towering over her, his hair plastered to his head, his black silk shirt damp against his chest, revealing the powerful width of his shoulders and chest. A blast of wind and rain tore at him and his hair caught the wild tempest; the man and the primitive elements seemed to be one. "Mitchell! What on earth are you doing out on a night like this?"

He smiled tightly at her and then stepped into the house, gently shouldering Uma aside. His foot kicked the door closed behind him. "Did you really think a little bad weather would keep me from you?"

*   *   *

Still wrapped in his dark mood, his plans for easing into a very personal relationship with Uma waylaid, Mitchell took one look at her wide gray eyes, her slightly parted mouth and lower, to where the men's large T-shirt pressed against the twin shape of her uptilted nipples and draped loosely to her upper thighs. They were smooth and slender and probably very soft and with the candlelight behind her, he could see every curve of her body, the gentle flare of hips, and the place where her thighs met, and the wind swirled around him to press the thin material against her breasts.

Her hair was free and fragrant and waving to her shoulders, just the way he'd imagined it would be when he loosened that prim little knot on top of her head, or eased his fingers through those braids, the sensual softness dragging against his skin.

He forgot the danger, a chilling new discovery that murder still lurked in Madrid; he knew only what he wanted and had to taste.

"There's only one way to see if I'm reading your look right." Mitchell placed the box on an elegant little carved walnut table, steadied it with one hand, and then reached for Uma with the other. He caught the back of her neck, tugged her to him, and brought his other arm around her, drawing that soft, curved body closer against his.

For a moment he couldn't breathe. She felt so right, a part of him, flowing and soft and warm. He'd wanted that body heat and more, but he hadn't expected the tenderness that came with it, pulsing along between them.

She angled her face up to his—stubborn, strong, and defiant. "I'm so sorry I couldn't make your dinner invitation, such as it was. And the phones were out," she said very properly.

Uma's cheeks began to color, her eyes flashing beneath the shadowy lashes. "Well? What do you have to say for yourself?" she demanded huskily, as her eyes traced his hair and her hands reached to smooth it back. "You're all wet. You'll probably catch cold and summer colds are really bad. I'm not taking care of you."

She fascinated him and Mitchell couldn't resist kissing her just a little, beside that soft mouth and then on the other side to see how she would react. She quivered and heated beautifully, her breath catching. The sensual package was all there, warm and trembling and aching—his instincts told him that he could make love with her.

But would she regret it? He couldn't take the chance.

Taking a long, deep breath, Mitchell pushed down his instincts to take her and worry about the consequences later. He couldn't resist kissing the soft palm that cradled his cheek.

"I've been cooking all day," he said quietly, watching her, feeling her heart beat against his chest, and raised a hand to open on her back, pressing her lightly against him there. He should be warning her of the danger in Madrid, the fear that the sound of thunder could cover a spray of bullets from a Browning automatic rifle, a favorite of Clyde Barrow's. Lonny's report of the ballistics check had proved the Warren windmill had been laced with the same, a few dug from the weathered wood.

And the bullets Roman had dug from beneath the ivy on Shelly's back door matched Clyde's favorite Colt Model 1911 .45-caliber automatic. A thunderstorm had erupted the night Shelly had gotten her scar; it could have been the graze of a bullet fired at the same time, too. The murdered Pete Jones's skull damage matched that type of handgun.

And Mike, an expert at that period of guns, wasn't talking.

Mitchell should tell Uma that someone had recently sabotaged the steps at the old garage and sawed the rungs of his ladder.

Instead, all he could think of was the woman in his arms—holding her, loving her. "Spaghetti. It's all I know how to make. I made plenty of it when Roman and I were on our own. The salad is a premix, the dressing is bottled."

She studied him, her brows lifting slightly, and he could feel the heat pulse from her, her bottom soft within the cup of his hands. "Your hands are wandering, Mitchell."

His smile mocked himself and his uncertainty. He wasn't usually distracted from his logic, which told him that Shelly was definitely in danger, and by way of her friendship, Uma was included. She should be told and he'd planned to gently ease into—

Ease into the woman, feel her close around him, heat him as he'd never been before . . . "I'm having a little problem, Uma. You're it, and you know it."

"Your memo this morning wasn't exactly a friendly invitation. And your technique is certainly to the point," she whispered huskily.

He thought of the floor and of the couch and of the upstairs beds and Uma beneath him. "Not exactly. There are detours I hadn't expected."

He wanted her to want him just as badly. Why? Or did it really matter?

"I'm damn fragile, Uma," he admitted huskily. She could wind softly inside him, making him uncertain. He hadn't been uncertain since he'd been the older brother, in a parental role, trying to manage a rebellious younger one.

And he'd never had trouble with women, that is, wondering what they were thinking—because they hadn't mattered. "I suppose this intimacy thing is going to be a big deal and this just might be my first time in that neighborhood."

Her eyes widened at that, and pricks of electricity skittered between them. She cleared her throat and shook her head, and he felt that quiver run the length of her body. All his sensual antennae leaped in response.

The moment hovered tantalizingly between them, then

Uma said softly, "How nice of you to bring dinner. Please excuse me while I change into something more appropriate."

That wasn't what Mitchell had hoped for, that cool, ladylike withdrawal, but Uma was setting her own terms and he wasn't forcing her. He nodded and lifted his hands away. "Yes, of course."

She hadn't moved away from him, and he understood that she was considering—what? Intimacy? Sex? If there were negotiations to be made, conditions set, he would rather take on a boardroom of difficult stockholders.

"If you don't mind, we'll have dinner here, on the coffee table," Uma said. "This is an old house, and there is a slight draft in the kitchen and dining room. Candles do best here when the electricity is out. I've never liked kerosene lamps. I'll be right back."

"Yes. Your shirt . . . is all wet . . . from me." He allowed himself a long, slow look down her body, to the breasts he ached to taste, and lower to the dark V between her legs.

Her breath caught again and that little quiver almost tipped him over the edge, his body aching to hold hers, to slide within the warmth—

She looked down and then up to meet his eyes. "I think your blush just hit your forehead and is rising to your hairline," he couldn't help saying.

"And you're enjoying yourself. You're smirking. Please excuse me." The dismissal was there, with just a touch of anger, wrapped in the invitation of a perfect hostess.

When Uma turned, Mitchell enjoyed the view of her hips moving beneath the light cloth, the shadows making his mouth dry and his body harden. The night wasn't turning out at all and Mitchell frowned as he walked to the couch and grabbed a towel from the laundry basket. He swiped it around his face and hair and tossed it back—the edge tipped a small pad and it toppled to the carpeting. He picked it up and

"Charis Notes," written in Uma's handwriting, caught him.

Click. Well, well. Uma was just chock-full of surprises, wasn't she? Mitchell replaced the pad where it was and began unpacking the dinner he had prepared. All he had to do was to study the book she had written, treating her as she suggested. Okay, so he had one basic priority—sex. But good sex. The kind that both of them would enjoy slowly, thoroughly and—Mitchell didn't turn when he sensed her returning to the room. He continued laying out the dinnerware. Now that he knew her game, he could play it back to her.

"Mitchell?"

"Umm?" He'd study intimacy; he'd—

"One who wishes more conversation should come upstairs to bed."

He froze and slowly placed the fork he had been holding onto the plate. Or he tried to put it there. The fork fell from his fingers onto the floor. When he straightened, he noted the candlelight moving up the stairs—with Uma. *One who wishes more conversation should come upstairs to bed.*

Uma. Every molecule of his body locked onto that feminine scent, hardening, tensing. Mitchell sucked in the air he'd forgotten to breathe and rubbed his trembling hands against his damp jeans. He wasn't prepared; he hadn't read *The Smooth Moves List.* Trust Uma to waylay him, ruin his plans—

With the certainty that she could interfere with anything he planned, Mitchell slowly began up the stairs.

"Your father isn't going to like this. For starters, he didn't want me in the house, much less in your bed," Mitchell said as Uma lay naked beneath the sheets. She wanted him as much as he wanted her. She wanted that heat and passion and the primitive instincts that drove Mitchell to her, and her to him. It was no impulse of the moment, rather, she had selected the man she wanted to share her bed and body—for the night.

She trusted him. She'd known him all her life and Mitchell had always tried to do the right thing.

He was her torment, and he would be her lover. She'd known that when he'd come through the storm to her. *Did you really think a little bad weather would keep me from you?*

"I'll tell Dad and protect you."

A man who had made his own way in a tough life, Mitchell snorted at the suggestion he couldn't defend himself. He moved into the room, studying it in the flashes of light from the storm outside. He noted the sturdy Amish furniture, the clean lines of wood, and placed a hand on the chaise lounge she'd bought, just the thing to read by the window. "I expected something more feminine—ruffles, that sort of thing."

"I've had that all my life. I wasn't certain what I wanted when I moved back here to take care of Dad. But I wanted something uncluttered, so that I could make up my mind exactly who I was as a woman, and what I wanted. It just seemed to stay that way. My office has more of the rest of the house. I wanted the comfort of having my mother and grandmother near. They taught me so much."

"Some people called your mother 'the Keeper' because she knew almost everything about their lives. Now you're the Keeper, right? You know and you don't talk."

She ached for him. He wasn't ready to accept the truth, but she would offer that gift—"If a person comes to me and asks about their private family matters, I would tell what I knew. I would tell you about your family, if you wanted. How it was between Fred and Grace—"

He cut her off with a curt "No."

She knew what he was thinking, a male uncertain of his position in her life. Lovemaking with Mitchell would change their lives forever, yet Everett would always be there. "No one has been in this bed but me, and Dani, when she stayed overnight. She was frightened of storms just like this and Shelly was sick and needing rest. I enjoyed playing auntie."

"You would." Mitchell's dark eyes found her body, locking onto her body, heating it. "Do you know how badly I want you?" he asked in a low, rough tone.

That was the glorious part—she *did*. Whatever ran between them was primitive and raw and real, her senses pulsing with it. Did he really want her, to consume her as his expression said he did?

"You're on your own, buddy," she whispered into the shadows between them.

"Am I? We'll see, won't we, unless you change your mind—and you can. I'll understand," he said, challenging her with a slow, seductive smile as he began to undress.

There was the sensual impact, the desire, the heat and the hunger—and the endearing uncertainty. Mitchell wasn't certain he was in control of the situation or himself and that would bother him.

She realized that he would always challenge her, and that she would always rise to it. Whatever ran in him, the wildness and the strength, the sweetness and the tenderness, she wanted to ride on that river with him, trusting him as her body told her to. "I'm not changing my mind," she stated huskily.

Uma held her breath as Mitchell tossed away his shirt and unbuttoned his slacks, letting them slide to the floor with his shorts and stepping out of them. The flash of lightning hit him—all angles and strength, the desire hardening his face.

Truth. It rode in the moment like the rising beat of the sensuality, pounding at her. Whatever happened after Mitchell's lovemaking, she would remember that she wanted him as well.

Mitchell sat on the bed, his back to her. Drawn by the flowing muscles of his body, she smoothed his skin and felt the quiver of flesh and heat and desire beneath her fingertips, the tension held there. He wasn't certain of her yet, only the desire between them.

Then suddenly, he turned, pinning her down full length with his heavy body, framing her face with his hands. "Is this what you really want? Just this?"

She'd traveled through life step by step on the path that had been set for her. She didn't resent her life, but tonight Mitchell was her choice, just for her, without expectations or commitments. Perhaps she was a rebel, after all. Perhaps she hadn't known what lurked inside her until Mitchell came back to Madrid. Perhaps tonight would prove the circle fully joined. She reveled in the freedom and the storm and the passion racing through her—passion he could cause by one sultry look, the pulses racing, heating in her body. "Just this."

He tensed and closed his eyes, then opened them again as he slowly eased aside to draw away the sheet over her body. Lightning flashed again and the hard ridges and planes of his face caught the light and the intensity that darkened and grew as his open hand moved slowly over her body, following the softness, gently trapping her breasts in his hand before moving lower.

"You quiver," he whispered raggedly. "When I touch you, you tremble and heat."

She tried to breathe and couldn't, excitement dancing inside her. She felt like an adventuress about to make her life's biggest discovery; she was both drawn to it, and afraid, and yet she couldn't resist. "I know. I can't help it. I would, if I could."

"No, you wouldn't like revealing that much about the woman, would you? You like control as much as I do, only this is something else, isn't it?" He cupped her intimately, stroking the dampness there slowly.

She arched upward, responding shockingly to that light touch, wanting more. The quickening drew her hands to his arms, her fingers locked to that so-warm flesh, the muscles flowing beneath it. "Mitchell, are you going to play games?"

"No," he stated honestly, bending to place his lips against

hers, to take that first hot, deep kiss that left her breathless and aching.

He meant to claim her, she knew, taking and possessing, but she had plans of her own, circling his shoulders with her arms, turning to him, arching as his mouth moved lower, open and skimming her throat until he found her breast, sweetly tormenting her.

When she cried out, Mitchell moved over her, his face locked in passion, in the truth she wanted between them.

She hadn't expected him to ease so slowly into her, to be so careful, the trembling of his body telling her of his effort. Then deep inside, rich and fully lodged, he pressed deeper until she held her breath, the exquisite tightening of her body telling her it had been too long . . . too long.

"Say my name," he whispered roughly against her throat, nipping gently at her, as his body began to flow with hers.

"Mitchell . . ." But she was already climbing, burning, crying out, locking him to her.

"Say it again," he demanded with an arrogance she'd expected.

"No," she whispered, pushing, testing.

He smiled against her throat and eased slightly away. "I can make you."

Despite the driving need within her, Uma knew the cost of his control, his body shaking with it, and when he lifted to torment her with those mind-drugging kisses, she gently bit his lip. "Do it, then."

Minutes later, Mitchell lay heavily upon her, and she stroked his hair, his skin damp and warm and fragrant against hers. He eased slowly aside, those dark eyes slitted, watching her, seeing too deeply. "Well, that was interesting."

Interesting? Interesting? Her body was still trembling, still remembering his, the pounding fever between them, take and take and give and the pleasure—she'd been tossed into a burning hungry furnace of sexual pleasure, all systems flowing, pulsing, beating. . . . Interesting?

"So now I know, don't I?"

"You know how to ruin a moment," she said tightly.

He toyed with her hair and grinned when she looked away. "Well, then," he said as his hands began to wander and caress and find just the right places to send her quivering and heating and aching. "Let's see if I can't do better this time."

Who would want to hurt Shelly? That bullet graze at her temple said someone did. Roman had seen enough wounds like that to recognize the scar.

And Mitchell had called, identifying the bullets lodged beneath Shelly's ivy, and the bullets that had battered the old windmill. So Pete's likely killer had had Shelly in mind. Why?

From the window in the garage's upstairs office, Roman looked out into the night, the lightning bolts spearing almost straight into the ground, the thunder rattling the windows he had just replaced. He rubbed his bare chest and the ache in it, then shoved his hands into his jeans pockets.

I had a daughter—have a daughter, he corrected, and he hadn't been around; he didn't know anything about what he'd missed or how to be a father. A wash of leaves swished across the glass and he thought of the color of Shelly's hair, like fiery autumn, golds and reds overlaying rich browns. It moved silkily, freely, just as her body did.

Shelly had the long, clean lines of the Lamborghini he'd just sold, and she was just as classy.

The laundry she'd done for him, hung pressed and neat on a standing rack, his underclothing folded neatly on a chair. She'd survived by cleaning and hard work and ironing until she couldn't move.

Every time he saw her drag herself to the ironing board, he wanted to pick her up in his arms and rock her. But he couldn't. He couldn't touch her; he'd ruined her. She deserved better than a life of hardship, a daughter who had her father's rebellious blood and a mother who had disowned her.

And just what did he have to offer? Fixing up her place a little here and there, and no cash to hand over to her, nothing to give her or Dani?

He couldn't go back and undo the harm he'd done by reaching out for something he'd hadn't had—tenderness, understanding, and maybe even on that night, love. Roman took in the darkened, spacious single room he had finished cleaning. Unfinished wood scrubbed clean and disinfected, the walls no more than planks, the room held the smell of bleach and of old oil. A hot plate and some bargain pots and pans served for the kitchen, the used refrigerator chugging nearby. The thrift shop bed and mattress he'd used at Mitchell's was comfortable enough, so was the chair near the desk—or rather, the long, low shelf serving as a desk. He'd taken the luxurious recliner that was Mitchell's offering, along with enough borrowed money for a starting bank account. The tiny bathroom's fixtures' gray stain had finally come off.

Downstairs was a mix of used mechanics tools and machines that probably needed repair. An ex-boxer who Roman had helped through rough times had done well with the Lamborghini money, loading the requested parts into a truck and hauling them to Madrid.

Along with the junk was a wrecked Harley-Davidson Sportster 1200 Evolution that had been used for scavenger parts by an unskilled hand. It was just about the only thing Roman could give Dani, if he could coax it back into life. Not exactly a college scholarship or a good start in life, but it was what he knew.

So here he was, just as broken down and pitiful as the

garage. Maybe they were a good fit, the wrecked bike and himself, two has-beens.

He studied the row of old posters, Alberto Vargas calendar girls, carefully tacked to the walls. As a boy, he'd drooled over the pictures and they'd caused more than a little discomfort. "Well, dolls, here we are. Not much, huh?"

He studied the slender curved bodies and long legs of the 1940s paintings, and thought how much they resembled Shelly's. He shook his head and mocked himself for dreaming of her posed and seductive . . . and that wasn't going to happen.

Roman frowned when lightning flashed and he saw the small figure dressed in a yellow slicker bent against the slashing rain and wind. A bolt seemed to shoot straight into the ground near the person and she froze—her face pale and terrified.

Shelly!

NINE

Roman cursed as he hurried down the stairs, his bad knee aching. There was probably only one reason Shelly would be out on a night like this—Dani.

He hurried outside into the slashing rain and crossed the street. Her eyes were huge in her pale face, her long hair whipping wildly around her. Roman wrapped one arm around her shoulders and hauled her back across the street, pushing into the garage. He slammed the door behind them. "What's going on?"

Was that rain, or was it tears falling from her lashes? He couldn't bear to think of her crying—and she'd probably already had her share of it because of him. Her lips moved and no sound came. Then the whisper: "I can't find Dani. I was getting ready for bed and I didn't think she'd be out on a night like this. I went into her room, just to check on her . . . I think she might have gotten so angry with me this afternoon for riding with you that she might have run away. I . . . I knew it would happen, sooner or later. She doesn't like rules and I—"

"You tried, Shelly." Roman knew his daughter's rebellious

attitude all too well. "Do you have any idea where she might be?"

She looked as if she might collapse. Roman shook her gently. "Shelly, listen to me. I want you to go upstairs and make some coffee and drink it. I want you to wait here for me. Will you?"

"I can't. Dani—"

"I'll bring her back," Roman promised softly and hoped that he could. Madrid hadn't changed much in eighteen years and the old hangouts still looked the same. For example, that barn just outside of town. He'd seen Jace's motorcycle and others, the kid parked there, along with cars painted with stripes and cut low to the ground, and high big-tire pickups.

"I'll go with you. I'm her mother—"

"And I'm her father. Let me do this, Shelly. Just go upstairs and make that coffee and drink it. You won't be any good to her if you're in shock or catch pneumonia." Roman pushed open the sliding door and walked back to rev up his bike. He knew the machine he'd rebuilt, and tonight would push them both to the top of their limits. "Close that after me."

"You don't have a shirt or a raincoat. It's terrible outside—" Shelly stripped off her yellow slicker and handed it to him. "Here."

Roman jerked on the slicker and then stopped, his mouth drying at the sight of Shelly's body. Her light cotton nightgown was damp, clinging to her, molding every curve. She was his Lamborghini and his Vargas calendar girl all rolled into one sweet package.

And she was real . . . he reached for her, dragged her into his arms, and took her mouth, and in the next heartbeat, that wild, sweet heat poured out of her as her arms wrapped around his neck. Then she stepped back, breathing hard, her breasts taut and peaked against the material.

He revved the motor and put on his helmet and knew he'd

never forget the sight of her standing there, holding her arms in front of her, pleading with him to find her—*their*—daughter. Then Roman soared out into the storm, leaning into it, and prayed Dani would be all right. The storm, a raging wind and cold rain, slashed at him, the headlight barely burning through the sheets of rain.

Roman glanced at the old deserted motel near the highway, carports linking the four units. In disrepair, it hadn't been used for years. Walter Whiteford had purchased it for his wife, because she loved the old European roses growing there. Madrid's rumors said that Bonnie and Clyde, on the run after a holdup and a shootout, had once stayed in the old motel.

The buildings served as a marker to Roman, just a few more miles to where Dani might be—was it too late? Had she left Madrid?

He'd find her. He had to. Roman couldn't let Dani travel down the same road as he had—

He battled the wind, rounded a corner, skidded and righted, and settled into the storm, fearing for Dani. A lightning bolt shot straight down into the field beside the road. If she were riding behind Jace on a night like this—

The old barn had lights, and he didn't expect the door to open. But when it did, pushed aside by two youths, Roman drove inside. Jace's motorcycle was there, and so were the other teenage toughs and the girls, all smoking and drinking beer and settling in for the night.

Roman tried to bank the anger inside him, a father's rage that his daughter would be hanging her arms around a surly punk kid. But then he'd been a punk too, right here, with the same kind of friends. He let the bike idle beneath him, ignoring the ache in his knee caused by his cold, damp jeans and the stress of the ride. "So, Dani. How's it going?"

She nodded, watching him with those painted eyes, the

defiance locked into her chin. "Just peachy. A little old to be out tonight, aren't you?" she asked, tossing his remarks back at him. "I thought you might be getting cozy with Mom."

He saw no reason to coddle her. She looked like she'd taken enough torment and had become hard because of it. If he guessed right, she understood straight talking better than anything wrapped in candy. "A little hard to do that when she's worried about you."

"Big Daddy," Dani scoffed. "Being nice to get to my mother. I went all through that for years. She didn't have what it took to hold my old man and you'll be on your way soon enough."

He had something she would want very much and he played it. "Hop on, kid, and we'll talk about your old man when we get back to your mother."

Dani was just a young girl again, stepping from behind her hard mask for a moment. "You knew him?"

"That's for your mother to say."

"She's not going," Jace stated, stepping forward with a few of his buddies.

"What's she worth to you?" Roman asked as he stripped off the slicker and buttoned Dani into it.

"Gimpy Guy. Think you can take all of us?"

Roman hoped that Jace's pride was more in his motorcycle than in keeping any girl. "I think I can probably make those junk piles you have purr. They're needing a real mechanic. It's a trade-off. Come around the shop and we'll talk. But not tonight."

"We were cutting out tonight . . . headed for the coast," Dani said softly as she swung behind him, strapping on the helmet he handed her. "Then the storm came up."

Roman watched Jace hesitate between getting his bike tooled and taking the girl he'd probably ruin and leave. Was he any better?

He nodded to Jace, who nodded back and said, "See you, dude. Later, Dani."

He wanted his family together and safe, Roman thought as he fought the wind and Dani, wearing the raincoat, folded herself close to his back. He feared each bolt striking the ground, the rushing streams of water crossing the road that could toss them off the bike. He knew the fear that Shelly must have felt, raising Dani alone, the responsibility of having a young life depend on her. Dani was a part of him that would go on, the best part, and she had to be protected. By the time they reached the garage, it was hailing, the icy pellets hitting his bare chest and arms.

"Inside," he yelled as the storm crashed around them, and pushed her into the entrance door.

Shelly was at the top of the stairs, wearing his cotton shirt over her nightgown. She looked almost as young as their daughter. "Dani!"

"Stay put," he ordered as Dani hunched beside him, black makeup streaming down her face. "Dani and I are going to have a little talk."

He read the fear in Shelly's eyes and shook his head. He spoke quietly to Dani. "See that bike in the corner, kid, or what's left of it? I know how to make motors purr, and that one is yours if you'll cool it with your mother tonight. You don't need to ride behind any guy. You can ride your own bike. Pink, I thought. A real sassy pink, with a helmet to match. Stick around and I'll show you how to rebuild it."

Dani scanned the machine. "It's a pile of junk," she scoffed, but Roman caught the excitement, recognized it— she saw the beauty of a finely tuned machine in those boxes just as he had.

"Uh-huh. So was the one I ride—it was a beauty before some rich dude was showing off and slammed it into a brick wall. I had some down time with my knee, and rebuilding her helped. It takes a real mechanic to love a good piece of machinery back to life, someone with talent. But then, she's your baby and you understand her every rumble. You can feel her purr beneath you, know her limits and her strengths. This Sportster is a good machine."

Dani considered the parts carefully lined up on the garage floor. "You might know what you're talking about. You ride okay, I guess."

"Thanks. So can you."

Sure, bribe her into the much needed time. He watched Dani weigh her options, and saw the fear. He prayed she'd have enough sense to bend her pride—he hadn't.

"What's the deal? How do you know my father?" she demanded, and he recognized that one-track stubborn streak as his own, too.

"Let's go upstairs, shall we?"

Shelly fought tears as Dani and Roman slowly ascended the stairs—Dani because she was reluctant to face her mother, and Roman because he was soaked through, aching and favoring his injured leg. They were so much alike—mulish, rebellious, passionate, and strong. It had cost him tonight to ride into the storm, but he had—for their daughter. He shot Shelly a look that said it was up to her and reached for a towel, roughly mopping it over Dani's head and face. He flipped open the raincoat and jerked it from her, tossing it aside. "We're here for a little while. You can use the bathroom and soap to wipe that mess off your face."

When Dani sulked into the bathroom, Roman spoke quietly to Shelly as he dried himself with the same towel and jerked on a black long-sleeved T-shirt. "I told her I knew her father. The rest and how much you want to tell Dani is up to you."

Shelly gripped his arm. "But—"

"Up to you," Roman repeated as Dani returned. He went

to the hot plate and poured the coffee, sipping it as he watched Shelly and Dani.

"He said he knows my father," Dani stated abruptly. "Who was he?"

Who was he? The question hung in the air, the only sound in the room was the hail pounding the window.

Shelly turned to Roman, seeking his help, but his expression was impassive, giving her nothing. She felt her world crumbling, falling onto the bare boards at her feet as she fought for control. How could she tell Dani that Roman was her father?

Dani leaned back and blinked as though she had been slapped. *"What did you say? He's my father?"*

And then Shelly knew she had spoken aloud, the secret locked inside her for years circling the silence. "I . . . yes, he is. I was young and he was—he was injured, so terribly wounded. I'd always loved him, I think, and I wanted him to know that love was real and good and strong. It was only for a night, and he didn't know I—he gave me you. I've never regretted being with him, not for a moment."

Dani was staring at Roman in shock. "Take it easy, kid," he warned slowly as her temper brewed. "Leave your mother out of this one, okay? Let me have it. I deserve it, not her."

"If you knew what my mother went through . . . how hard she had to work . . . the way my grandmother, if you can call her that, treats her . . ."

Shelly blinked, Dani had turned on Roman, defending her mother.

"I'm going to take care of her from now on, kid, and you, too. So are you up to trying this, or not?"

"Exactly what?" Dani screamed, her thin body taut. "You just come in here and think you'll take up with my mother again and hurt her and leave her like you did before? No way, buddy."

Roman smiled that devastating smile at Shelly, who

couldn't follow what was happening between him and Dani. "I like this kid. You did an okay job, Mom."

"I'm going to have to think about this," Dani said slowly, carefully, as she plopped down into his chair. "I have to think what's in it for her and for me, because she's been through plenty."

Roman scratched the stubble on his jaw. "How about some eggs and toast while you're thinking?"

Dani just glared at him and then at Shelly. "Boy, you sure know how to pick 'em."

To Roman she said, "I heard your mom ran out on you. I figure you've got the same blood and could do the same."

Roman leveled a look at her and the room was dead quiet as he said, "Kid, I'm staying for the duration. It may not be sweet, but I'm what you drew, like it or not."

Dani glared at him, and Roman's expression said he wasn't backing up or "making nice." Shelly tried to say something that would soothe the moment, but what was there to say? Instead, she went to the window and watched the storm.

She had no idea how to cope with the two of them. And she sensed a bond between them already—a stubborn, rebellious one that said they were set to slash and hack things out between them.

Then, as Roman fixed toast and eggs and placed them on the shelf that was his desk, Dani said in a low warning tone, "You get my mother pregnant again, and you'll pay big time."

Shelly closed her eyes, leaned her forehead against the cool glass, and wished this were all a nightmare.

"So how far has Jace—"

"Roman!" Shelly exclaimed, disbelieving the whole conversation that had moved around her, sweeping into its own storm.

"I can handle him, Mom," Dani stated baldly. "I'm still sweet, Pops. Now, *you* tell *me* how you felt about my mom all those years ago."

For a moment, Roman scowled at her, his lips clamped shut.

"It's a trade-off, Pops. Truth time," Dani nudged ruthlessly.

"I thought she was the sweetest thing that ever happened to me. She's about as close to love as I ever came, and I knew then that I didn't deserve her. I don't now," Roman said slowly, looking at Shelly. "I dreamed about her. I'd hoped she'd settled down with a guy she deserved and had all she wanted. I never thought that—"

Shelly looked away, her hands trembling as she locked them, fingers digging into her flesh.

"Yeah, right. I've got some serious thinking to do," Dani said. "And we're not going to be friends."

"Oh, boy, I sure wouldn't want that."

"And I don't want the whole town knowing the deal, either . . . not until I'm ready to handle it right."

"It's up to you. Your call."

Dani pushed on. "If Mitchell is my uncle, he might have a different take on you, so I'm going to talk with him. Better let him know. And if I've got another grandmother, she has to be better than the one in the rest home, that icy old bag. I want to know everything about your mother, and I want to meet her, too. It's my right, get it?"

"Hell, no. I'm not having anything to do with that woman."

Dani met his scowl with her own. "That 'woman' is my grandmother, and I want to meet her. Then I'll figure it out for myself."

"Get your butt back in school and we'll talk," Roman seemed to growl.

"Don't I have anything to say about all this?" Shelly asked, frustrated with the easy back-and-forth bargaining Roman could manage with Dani, when she couldn't. Dani kept her word.

"No," they both said in unison and looked at her with that same frown that changed to surprise. Father and daughter stared at each other.

"Maybe," Roman said finally.

"Sure. Maybe she has something to say, but that doesn't mean I'm going to agree. She's got this—"

"Upright soft streak?"

"Yeah. Always believes the best of people. Probably no one but her would have anything to do with an old has-been like you." But Dani's look at her mother was that of love and tenderness and of understanding, the first in a long time.

Roman waggled Dani's head. "A has-been, am I? Gee, not too long ago I was a 'stud.' We'll see about 'has-been' when we get the bikes up and running. I'm expecting you to do your share—if you want it—and to help your mother, too."

"Oh my, no. Dani can't—" Shelly stopped when Roman and Dani both frowned at her again. She tried for as much dignity as she could manage while standing there in her nightgown and Roman's shirt. She wanted home and safety and no Roman while she worked through what had just happened. "I think we'd better just have a good night's rest before this goes any further. The storm is letting up now and Dani and I can walk home."

She resented Dani's questioning look at Roman, who nodded. "Later."

Mitchell leaned back into the shadows of Uma's bedroom, studying the woman curled on the bed. Through the soft rain at the window, predawn crept softly into the room, fingering over the curves of her body in tempered, blended hues of pink and yellow. Her arm was still curved in the position in which he had left it after easing from her. He could still feel her softness against him, hear those little hungry sighs, feel the shudder of pleasure deep within her. Her hair spread across the pillow in waving strands, rich, mink-brown hair that he had plunged his fingers into, holding her desperately when he couldn't get enough.

Couldn't get enough . . . of what? Of sex? Or of the woman, Uma, that excitement, the challenge, the magic?

His body told him he'd definitely had the sex, but his mind was as troubled as last night's storm.

She wasn't a woman to leave.

He wasn't a man to stay.

Mitchell rammed his hand through his hair and caught her scent upon his skin. His body reacted instantly—hardening, wanting. If he went back to bed, he wasn't certain he could leave. If he stayed, he wasn't certain what he could say.

She was a woman who deserved commitment from the man who wanted her body. Okay, just maybe he wanted more.

That wasn't on his life-menu, and neither was running out on Uma just after they'd made love. He wanted to reassure her that—what? What safety could he give her?

Uma was unraveling him in ways he didn't understand. Sex—sure. Sex with Uma—not sure, because it was more than that. It was magic and fascination and tenderness. He wasn't certain that he wanted tenderness.

Mitchell decided the safest thing was to make coffee and then clean up the dinner they had forgotten. He picked up his jeans and eased quietly down the hallway. The slight draft from her office suggested that she might not have closed the window against the storm.

He frowned; a thorough woman, Uma would be careful of her equipment. A ripple in the shadows drew his attention to the lacy curtain at the window. Drawing the curtain aside revealed a perfect round bullethole.

On the opposite side of the cozy room, a vase had tumbled from a shelf onto the overstuffed armchair, the roses that had been in it spread onto the floor, water dampening the chair fabric. Realizing how much Uma cared for her family's treasures, Mitchell automatically picked up the vase and lifted it—

The bullethole in the bookshelf was fresh, and the angle from the window sighted down to the sidewalk across the street. Mitchell replaced the vase; he took a large cardboard poster featuring the Cayman Islands and placed it over the window.

Downstairs, dressed in his jeans, he sipped coffee and studied the homey kitchen. Maybe he should make toast and cut some flowers and take her a breakfast tray—to see if she was okay after the lovemaking that just might be branded in his mind forever. *Uma. Flowing, soft, hot, hungry.*

The thought of a bullet tearing through her sickened him.

He turned to see her wrapped in a short pink cotton robe sprigged with delicate rosebuds that came just to her knees.

They were beautiful knees, and he wondered about kissing the backs of them and working his way upward over those slender-strong muscles and higher—

Mitchell couldn't move as her hand slid through her long hair, easing it back, her gray eyes locked with his. "These rainy mornings aren't for running, but more for relaxing, don't you think?"

He couldn't think, his senses humming. He'd caused those shadows beneath her eyes, that sultry darkness in her eyes, the swollen fullness of her lips. He'd tasted those peaked breasts, felt the riveting response that ran the length of her body.

He didn't like the burn of jealousy over knowing that another man had seen her like this, soft and warm and sleepy . . . and sated.

Still walking toward him, Uma came to ease her body against his, laying her head on his shoulder, her lips against his throat. Mitchell placed aside the coffee cup and eased his arms around her carefully. He closed his eyes as her scent caught him, wrapped magically, tantalizingly around him, and her breasts nudged him gently. Her hand stroked his hair, and something dark and tremulous settled within him.

"You're a cuddler," she whispered against his throat. "You like to snuggle. I hadn't expected that."

Mitchell straightened and frowned down at her. "Huh?"

She grinned up at him. "You like to cuddle. I thought you might be someone who likes his space on the bed. Oh, you're blushing. I didn't mean to embarrass you!"

Mitchell eased away from her. He'd never blushed in his life. Embarrassment was something he hadn't ever been able to afford. He felt as if his whole life had just flipped over.

Uma drew back, studying him. "I'm not going to hide this, Mitchell, unless you want me to. You don't know what to do, do you?"

"I'm not into chit-chat." He didn't know how he felt and Uma was far too close, those solemn gray eyes filled with his reflection. He wasn't certain how he liked that "cuddler" remark; it sounded a little feminine.

Uma was opening the refrigerator, taking out a carton of eggs. She began cooking breakfast as if they had shared it every morning. Mitchell held very still, dealing with the "cuddler" remark and the enormous normality of her beginning the day calmly—dealing with his newly discovered possessive streak made him uneasy. He tried to sound casual, though every sense centered on Uma's answer to his question: "Do you still cook breakfast for Everett?"

She turned slightly, one delicate eyebrow questioning him. She plopped a thick slice of ham into the skillet, then began to crack eggs on the rim of a bowl, emptying them into it. Each movement was deliberate, as if she were carefully placing her thoughts in order. She began to whip the eggs, then placed the bowl aside and looked directly at him. "We didn't eat last night and I'm sorry your lovely dinner was ruined. . . . yes. We're friends, and he's often over here in the morning, chatting with Dad."

"And?" He hated pushing, needing to know.

Uma removed the ham and slid the eggs into the drippings. "And I love him. He's my best friend. What was that conversation about at the ice cream shop? The one between you and Everett?"

While the eggs sizzled and the toast popped, Mitchell wasn't certain he wanted to answer. "It was a man-to-man thing. You wouldn't understand," he began evasively.

"Try me. And if this is a bet between you, I'll kill you both."

"He doesn't want you hurt," Mitchell answered slowly. "He knows I want you."

"That would be nice to hear. You didn't talk last night."

"I was busy."

"Mmm."

That slight sound dug into his nerves. "What do you mean, 'mmm'?"

"Just that. Set the table, please."

Her control and that "mmm" irritated him while he was awash with uncertainties. As soon as he could get his hands on the book she'd written, he might understand. He'd never tried to understand women before. He decided that "mmm" was a silky-soft weapon that could disarm and confuse him.

And he had to warn her, to protect her. "I came here last night with a purpose."

He stopped, enjoying Uma's brief knowing, sweet smirk before she pushed it away and asked coolly, "Which was?"

He hated to disarm that intriguing little smirk, but—"I think you're in danger, and Shelly definitely is."

Uma frowned and the telephone rang. She took it from the wall. "Hi, Dad . . . oh, hi, Pearl."

As Mitchell cleared away the dishes, he heard Pearl's shrill voice, noting the way Uma held the telephone away from her ear. "I know, the garden party is essential, everything has to be just right, your annual late July dinner and dance party is the prime event of the better people in Madrid . . . the storm felled a tree on your English garden maze? That's awful."

Uma looked at Mitchell. "Yes, I know that Walter isn't meant to do manual labor. Uh-huh. An investment banker can't spend his energies dealing with storm damage. Yes, I'm planning to help you serve tonight. Shelly said she would help, too. Dozer is in Florida, Pearl. He sold his business to Mitchell, remember?"

She held the phone farther from her ear. "You can't find anyone else? Mitchell is the only one I know. I hear he's good with shrubs and flower beds . . . yes, he has all Dozer's equipment, including a chain saw. You might try him."

Mitchell couldn't help grinning. Whenever Pearl passed him on the street or in her car, she turned away immediately, a definite snub.

"No, I'm not going to do this for you, Pearl, and don't ask Shelly to, either. You'll just have to ask him yourself."

After replacing the telephone, Uma turned to Mitchell. "You will be nice to her, Mitchell. Pearl is a bit high strung, but if you knew how badly she was treated when she was younger, you'd understand."

"Maybe. I'm not promising anything. Come here." When Uma walked to him, Mitchell tugged her onto his lap. He eased her against him and rubbed his chest against her breasts, gazing down at them with that dark look that could cause her to heat—as if he had been starved and she was everything he wanted. Just that look was enough to make her want him equally. "I'm a cuddler, huh?"

"First class." She sucked in her breath and closed her eyes when Mitchell nuzzled the crevice of her breasts.

Then he leaned back, watching her face flush. "You're not so cool and untouchable, you know."

There was that boyish victory grin that sent her senses tumbling. She struggled to focus as his hand closed over her breast, framing and testing it gently. "You're so perfect," he whispered unsteadily. "How do you feel this morning? I'm a lot bigger and stronger and I . . . I didn't mean to touch you like that. I wanted . . . I wanted to be very gentle—I wasn't."

"I think I managed to hold my own," she whispered against his lips. "What was that you were saying about danger to Shelly?"

Mitchell frowned and leaned back. "And to *you*. I think the broken windows here were threats, somehow. You've stepped on someone's toes. And the bullets in Shelly's house and that scar she's wearing say someone doesn't like her."

"Bullets in Shelly's house?' Her scar? The one she got the night Lauren died?"

Mitchell spoke carefully. "Roman says it looks like a bullet grazed her. He dug slugs out of her house, beneath the ivy at the back. Lonny had a ballistics check on the windmill, then compared the damage to Pete's skull, and the ones found in Shelly's house. They're all a match. Whoever killed Lauren might have wanted all of you—"

"But no one said anything—that there was any trouble. It's been over a year since Lauren's death."

"Shelly has been having a lot of accidents since then. There's a black spot on her driveway where her car ignited and burned. She was lucky to get out of that one. She told Roman that her ladder broke while she was cleaning windows. He dug it out of that shed in her backyard. It had been sawed just enough to break with her weight."

"I can't believe anyone would want to hurt Shelly. She's always the first to help those in need."

"What about Pearl? She was there the night Lauren was killed."

Uma circled through the past year, itemizing Pearl's catastrophes. "Her car's brakeline leaked and she nearly ran into a building. She almost had two car wrecks while traveling and couldn't recognize the other car. Her dog ate something and died . . . they thought it might be the poison put out to kill moles. Walter and the girls were devastated and Pearl had an elaborate pet funeral. Oh, my, Mitchell . . . this is awful—if someone is trying to—"

He ran a finger over the roses she had placed on the table. Mitchell suddenly looked too dangerous. "All in this year, since Lauren's death?"

She shook her head, aligning the incidents that all spelled calculated harm to her friends. She began to chill and shake and Mitchell drew her close, nestling her head against his shoulder. "Anything else?"

"I don't want to think about this—that we could have someone here who is so evil—"

He rocked her gently. "Tell me."

"Several cows were shot—wounded. Opal Udell's favorite little Guernsey cow, more of a pet, really. Lilly Belle was shot with an arrow. The vet who took care of the cows thought maybe it was hunters again, but it was a practice arrow—you know, with a metal-pointed tip and not the arrowhead type. Gerald Van Dyke's tractor ran over him, crushing him while he was in front of it. His sight and hearing aren't good at eighty, but—oh, Mitchell, no one would want to hurt Gerald. But you can't just take ordinary farm accidents and careless hunters and kids with air guns and put them all into a package with a label that says 'murder.' "

"The nails in Roman's and my tires weren't exactly friendly."

"Lyle Nelson didn't like his girlfriend dancing with Roman. It wasn't nice, but that happens, too."

"Lonny talked to Lyle and his friends, and so did Roman and I. None of them knows how to operate a power nail driver. If they did, they'd be shooting nails into their boots."

"Oh, my," Uma heard herself say once more.

"That is partly why I came last night. I don't want you staying alone. Lonny doesn't want to panic the town, and it seems that the Warrens have stirred up whoever isn't happy."

"That's so terrible." Uma began pacing back and forth. She didn't want to think about anyone in Madrid—she knew all their lives, and there was no reason for anyone to want to kill . . .

Mitchell rose slowly. "Come up to your office. There's something I want to show you."

Upstairs, he leaned against the doorway as Uma pulled away the curtain, then he lifted the vase aside to expose the dark hole in the wall. "I'd say it's a .45 slug. They didn't want to hurt you. If they did, the light at the window would have made a perfect shot. They shot somewhere you weren't, just for a warning. You can call Lonny after I'm gone. He doesn't need to know that I've been here."

She moved into his arms, needing the safety of his body. She held him tight and Mitchell immediately scooped her closer, tucking her head beneath his chin. "This is terrible."

Mitchell stroked her hair. "Just one question. Where are we sleeping tonight? Here, or at my place?"

TEN

That night, Mitchell settled into the shadows of a rose arbor and watched Uma as she served guests at Pearl's garden party. While Oklahoma was settling in for August's dry season, Pearl's rose garden, styled after an English maze, was watered, lush and green. Japanese lanterns softly lighted the sprawling redwood deck. Citronella candles had been strategically placed to repel mosquitos.

In the soft glow of lantern light Uma danced with the man who had brought her—her ex-husband, Everett. With heads close together, their conversation appeared very intimate. Everett's hand pressed Uma's onto his chest—

Mitchell realized he had just snapped a lathe board on the trellis, and released it from his fist, smoothing the foliage over it. Everett would, of course, know how to be "intimate" with Uma either in conversation or in bed.

Pearl's glance at him barely veiled her dislike. He smiled briefly at her, just a lazy show of teeth to antagonize her. She turned away, a definite snub, and that was exactly what he wanted while he brooded about Uma.

He rolled his shoulder beneath the light cotton shirt. His

muscles ached slightly, unused to the chain saw he'd needed to remove the fallen tree.

It was good, hard work, and he'd enjoyed pitting himself against the old oak—it wasn't exactly the physical release he'd wanted for today, but it had helped. After trying to get everyone else in town to work for her, Pearl had been reduced to calling him. Apparently, she had used up her share of goodwill with neighbors and friends. She had hovered and fussed over the repair and clipping of her garden. And later, while he'd picked up fallen limbs and packed them into his pickup, Pearl had spied on him from her lace-veiled windows.

It was really Dozer's garden. His notebook carefully noted the roses' care, their historical beginnings, if they had been found near homesteads or cemeteries. The layout of the shrubbery was also carefully marked. Pearl knew little about the roses. She only knew how she looked in a summery dress, a large straw hat, and gloves, and holding a basket for gathering bouquets.

Earlier, while stacking storm-damaged rubble into his truck, Mitchell had purposely insinuated that he could be induced to move faster—if he were invited to the party. There would be dancing, as Pearl had noted when she'd told him to clear away the redwood deck first, so that she could arrange the benches and side tables. After a night of making love with Uma, Mitchell did not want to think of her dancing in Everett's arms. Mitchell wanted Uma in *his* arms, and he wanted to take her home later.

He'd wanted to feel emotions when he came back to Madrid, to know what stirred him, and he'd gotten a dark wallop of jealousy, something he hadn't expected.

Pearl's expression had been furious and haughty when he'd asked if he was invited. "Oh. Yes. Of course, you're invited. Please shower first and . . . and try to wear something nice, will you? Nothing with—uh—spots or holes," she'd said in a tone that would freeze the still damp roses.

Pearl had been careful to place him far from her at the catered dinner, and Uma had been seated by Everett.

Who does she want? Mitchell wondered as he studied her dancing in Everett's arms, a charming ex-husband who was deliberately keeping her very busy.

Mitchell shrugged mentally; if he were Everett, he'd work to keep male poachers from Uma, too.

The crowd was small and elite, from the best long-established families in Madrid and surrounding countryside. Shelly moved by Mitchell, dressed in a prim black and white maid's uniform, and holding a serving tray she had no doubt polished. She looked distracted, her smile distant but pleasant. Mitchell had seen her carry in plastic-covered trays to the Whiteford home—to the back door, of course.

She was probably working through two problems— Roman's entrance into her daughter's life, and the danger in Madrid. She had spent the day working at Pearl's, and when Mitchell had seen her, she'd looked dazed—but then, Roman telling her that he was staying the night, sleeping on her couch, might do that to a woman who'd managed her own life and her daughter's.

Uma had also been drafted to work the party, and probably not for pay. Neither woman seemed to mind the hushed orders from Pearl as she bustled about in her designer roses-on-silk hostess gown. Uma's apparent function was to circulate and to act as a sub-hostess, making certain that everyone was comfortable and well fed. Mitchell, desire humming through him now, didn't like seeing the woman he wanted being treated like a servant.

Nor did he want to see her in Everett's arms, with that friendly, intimate laughter between them.

Across the garden, Uma's dress was cool and long, light yellow with a delicate cream pattern. Tiny tormenting buttons ran from her bodice to her ankles, concealing what Mitchell had held and kissed and caressed the previous night.

"Having a good time?" she asked pleasantly while her smile said she knew he wasn't.

Okay, maybe he wanted a commitment from her, something he'd never considered from any other woman. "No. I'd rather be in bed with you. I'm feeling about as wanted as a mongrel at a pedigree show."

Her eyes widened and her color began to rise; there was that delicious quiver that told him she responded to him beautifully. She was wearing that prim little knot on top of her head, the tendrils catching the garden night's dampness and curling along her skin—skin he wanted to taste.

The perfect richly gleaming pearl studs in her ears reminded him of another precious intimate pearl within her that he had not yet—

"That certainly was to the point." Her words were prim, but her voice was low and husky and drenched with the heat of last night.

Mitchell noted with satisfaction that the pulse in her throat had quickened, a visible reaction that he'd affected her. He needed the reassurance that last night had really happened. He wasn't certain how he felt about missing her, or why he felt alone as he walked back to his house this morning with the neighbors watching him.

"Some electricity problem last night. Just had to reset the breakers," he'd called to Charley Blue Feather, who was watching Lars Swenson's antics with a pitchfork, driving it into the mole runs. "Was yours okay?"

Mrs. Riley's hair was in huge pink curlers as she placed her jar of sun tea on her front porch. "Mine was just fine, Mitchell. But I'll remember that you're handy the next time there's an outage."

Edgar MacDougal finished zipping up his pants; he strolled into his house after a smirk at Myrtle Hawthorne, who was already dialing Lonny. The brown look of MacDougal's wife's rose bushes said he wasn't changing his habit.

Keeping the lid on an intimate relationship in Madrid was impossible; Mitchell didn't want Uma touched by gossip—he knew the damage gossip could do, and he'd never cared before.

He sniffed at the damask-scented bloom brushing his shoulder, and blamed his uncertainty on the perfume as Uma said, "You're scowling, Mitchell. You look so fierce."

He knew his smile down at her wasn't nice. He shrugged the bloom from his shoulder and ignored the clinging petal. "Maybe I had plans for tonight that didn't include a crowd or an ex-husband. . . . someone here could be Pete's killer. And the person behind all the so-called accidents."

Uma scanned the crowd and shook her head. "I doubt it. Lauren barely knew these people, though she helped Pearl with these parties. These are the contributors to Pearl's charities."

"Lauren didn't like them, did she?"

Uma turned to him, frowning. "Not especially. Why?"

He shrugged, unable to explain the sudden insights that had come to him since he'd been living in Lauren's house.

Uma took his hand, clenching it urgently. "You feel it, too, don't you? That Lauren is still here, waiting? That she wants to tell us something? Oh, I can't tell you how many times I've felt that. As if she's not ready to rest yet. I feel her moving strongly in that room where her things are. More than anything, I want to help her rest, Mitchell. Tell me what you feel."

He couldn't; it wasn't logical. Since he'd lived in the house, some of his feelings seemed illogical . . . and feminine, like making certain the decor would not be too cold and sterile, but more welcoming and soft. Now he thought of lighting the rooms, how the shaded glow would affect the wall's colors. Brown, sturdy, and bold had always been reliable, and yet now whispers of "comfortable" and "welcoming" curled around him.

He served Uma a diversion, a fortune cookie saying, "One can only see what is real or one can be put in the nut house."

"Ohhhh! You are so—"

"Yes?" He allowed himself a pleased smirk. She'd been well satisfied, and he knew it. Sexually, he knew. He hadn't had time to study the intimacy she'd written about in her book—probably one element of which was holding her hand on his chest as they danced. But then, he hadn't danced with her, had he? When he had the relationship-intimacy elements in his armory, his bargaining position to get Uma into his bed would definitely be better. "So how is it going with old, dependable Everett?"

"You're in a nasty mood. I'd already told Everett that he could pick me up tonight. I needed him to help carry the petit fours I'd made."

"I imagine I can carry a tray of petit fours just as well as any man."

"But I had already asked Everett," Uma returned firmly. "You realize that this is a situation that has to be handled gently."

"Why?" he asked bluntly. To him, the situation was simple. He was now Uma's lover; Everett was no longer in the picture.

"Because that is how I am going to handle this, Mitchell," she said in a firmer tone.

The scene on her porch had been awkward, Everett carrying food from her house when Mitchell had arrived. Since he was obviously dressed to go out, and there was only one soirée in the whole town of Madrid, Mitchell had no choice—he had followed the woman he'd made love to last night . . . and her ex-husband . . . to the Whitefords. The feeling that he was a tagalong wasn't one he wanted repeated.

The dinner and dance and socializing party was a mix of

upscale clannish bankers and wealthy investors. They now knew that Pearl's "yard man" had been a vice president of a national building and supply chain, and they weren't certain how to approach him—how to bridge the gap from years ago, when they'd looked down on his family to getting what they wanted from a man who could be influential in Madrid.

He could have eased into the chatting groups and made that bridge easier for them, if he'd wanted to. He much preferred watching Uma; so did Everett. Mitchell had never needed reassurance and now he did, working his way through that fragile zone. He tried to appear casually disinterested in Uma's relationship with Everett, but every nerve in his body tensed. He casually lifted a rose and sniffed its fragrance. "Have you told him about last night?"

She misunderstood his underlining of the changed situation. "No, Lonny wants to keep everything quiet. He thinks everyone would be panicked and the—whoever—would slip away. Everett would definitely be upset. He'd probably want to sleep over—oh, don't scowl like that. He has before, in the guest room when a tornado went through and damaged the roof on our house."

Our house. Everett had shared her life, and he was perfect for her. Mitchell didn't fit into the domestic picture, and as a Warren, he didn't fit into tonight's crowd . . . and he wanted to pick up Uma and carry her out into the night.

"I meant something a little more personal than that bullethole. Have you told Everett about us—together? Last night?"

Her color rose and she looked away, the soft light glowing on her skin, the sweep of her lashes. "I'm trying for the right moment. This is a difficult situation."

"I will, if you want."

She turned to stare up at him, her eyes flashing silver. "You wouldn't dare."

"Just try me."

"Someday, you're going to learn that I don't like being pushed," Uma said firmly.

"It's better out in the open, clean and neat. The guy isn't going to be happy and right now, neither am I." Mitchell wasn't too certain about Uma now, as those gray eyes met his.

Uma tapped her foot and seemed to be counting under her breath. "That's how you would do it, would you?"

"Seems appropriate and less complicated. Unless you've changed your mind."

"Women are more tactful. This isn't a black-and-white is-sue. You're thinking like a man."

"The last time I checked, I was a man. Maybe you noticed last night."

That delightful color returned to her cheeks and Mitchell couldn't resist stroking that warmth. She impatiently brushed away his touch, and just as he expected, when she was flustered, Uma responded with a typical fortune-cookie statement. "When teased, it is wisest to wait for one's best time to return the favor."

Everett was working his way to them, stopping to chat with Walter Whiteford, a tall, slender man with a potbelly that said he liked beer. Mitchell recognized the look of a man intent upon corralling a woman as Everett started toward them again.

His arm circled Uma and she sent a warning frown at Mitchell. Everett's smile was cold. Could he have known that Mitchell was with Uma last night? Could he have fired that shot?

"Nice night," Everett said coolly, as the men's eyes met and locked.

"It's okay." Mitchell picked an old European rose, "Au-tumn Damask." The blossom carried the light pink shade of Uma's blush; its double and ruffled bloom was as lush as the manner in which she gave herself to him, and the fragrance reminded him of her body. He carefully, meticulously eased it into Uma's hair. Maybe it was a possessive reaction, but that was how he felt.

Everett frowned slightly, then picked another rose, "Maggie," which was a fuller, richly red bloom, a perfect match to the heat deep within her. He handed it to her. "My dear."

Mitchell pushed down the sharp shudder of jealousy; Everett showed his teeth in a wolfish smile.

Uma frowned at one and then the other. "Mmm. Thank you, Mitchell. Thank you, Everett."

Mitchell looked at Everett. "I really hate it when she does that 'mmm' thing. It could mean anything."

"I know what you mean. The fortune cookie sayings aren't that easy to translate, either. One counters the other."

"I'm right here, boys," Uma said, softly enough to make the roses in her hair barely tremble. "Mitchell has a habit of overlooking that, but I didn't expect it from you, Everett—"

"Why, so you are here," Mitchell drawled, after wanting to hold her all night.

"Dance?" Everett smoothly offered Uma, with an intimate smile that Mitchell could have crammed down his throat.

But he wouldn't; he was being "civilized."

She looked confused, glancing from Mitchell to Everett and back again, and she wasn't choosing Mitchell's company that quickly. "I . . ."

Just then, Mitchell spotted Lonny's patrol car across the street and Shelly arrived with a tray of petit fours. Mitchell decided that the party didn't need him and he didn't need it. Uma fit in perfectly; she always had. The old fences were still there; he still didn't fit in her crowd.

"Excuse me. You two kids enjoy yourself. It's time I left the ball," he said as he took the tray from Shelly and with it high, eased over the Whiteford's hip-high wrought-iron fence. If he couldn't have Uma tonight, he'd at least enjoy her petit fours. He walked down the yard's slope and across the street to where Lonny waited. Lonny's jowly face was illuminated by the flashlight he held as he read a book.

"Dinner time," Mitchell said, as he eased into the passenger side and placed the tray on his lap.

Lonny snapped off the flashlight, put the sandwich he'd been eating back into the sack, and chose a small frosted cake with all the daintiness of a child selecting a special candy. He paused and held up a finger. "Wait a minute. These little cake things need a drink to set them off. I've got an extra cup here somewhere. You've been made . . . the whole town is gossiping that you're here to scope out the site for your company."

"I know. I've been getting hints all over town. Lots of friendly people here, all of a sudden . . . all except the old ruling class. They can't bring themselves to ask me anything except to do their lawns. Lucky for them, I like lawns and yard work."

"It's good therapy. Not like fishing, though. Irma wants to be my friend, my buddy. She wants to go fishing with me. There are just some things men need to do alone or with other men, and fishing is one of them. I don't want Irma for my buddy. Life's rough when your wife is in the moody hormone business and having a midlife crisis about how she looks and wanting to be your buddy." Lonny fished in his cluttered back seat and found a stack of foam cups, pouring coffee into two of them and setting one on the dashboard. He gave the other to Mitchell, who was already chewing on the cake, but not tasting it.

While Mitchell circled his gloom and his empty bed, Lonny ate two of the cakes and sipped his coffee. "Got a report of a prowler last night. Seems some big guy walked right up to Uma's door in the storm and she let him in. I hung around for a while outside, but Irma likes me home during storms and the Lawrence house was real quiet. So that shot was either before I arrived—and whoever Uma let into the house—or after. The Lawrences sure do have a problem with windows—and with visitors . . . heard you fixed some electrical problem there last night."

Mitchell ate another cake and tried not to focus on the laughter floating down the hill to the police car. Or that Uma was probably dancing with Everett again . . . her ex-husband was probably cuddling her. "Did you talk with Mike?"

Lonny delicately patted his mouth with his handkerchief. "Had a nice quiet talk with Mike. He doesn't know anything. Whoever our friend is, he likes long-distance work. There's only one thing to do, and that is to sit on this one and hope that whoever he is, he makes a mistake. I figured you Warrens would stir up trouble, and I figure you can handle it. Roman is taking a liking to Dani, and he's over at Shelly's. I just thought I'd see that she got home safe . . . this tray is almost empty. I'd like to take a look-see at who is at that fancy party. I'll take it back up to the Whitefords, if you want to mosey on somewhere. Or you can sit here with me. I'd appreciate a man's opinion on this book and just how much sex he can tolerate before he goes blind."

Mitchell had gone blind about three times last night, and his body told him that he wasn't finished with Uma. "No, thanks."

"Uma, wait!" Pearl called as Uma stood alone in the Whitefords' rose garden, admiring Mitchell's work. Retrieving a garden from a vicious storm had meant trimming broken branches and stems, and now the garden looked untouched.

She certainly wasn't untouched, Uma thought with a quiver that ran through her every time she thought of Mitchell's body against hers, within her, the passion and the fever, the hunger that prowled through her.

Uma watched Pearl make her way through the English

maze, frowning as her hostess gown caught on a rose bush. She jerked away her skirt and hurried toward Uma. "I want to talk with you."

"Your party was wonderful, Pearl." Pearl needed reassurances; her parents and her husband had left her fragile and wounded. Her mother was a cold, determined woman, and as demanding as her father that Pearl be the perfect child. When she failed, she was punished.

"Thank you, Uma. I think my esteemed ancestor from Boston, Matilda Radford, would have been proud of me tonight. I'm told she threw wonderful soirées that the social set back then wouldn't miss. Shelly seemed so distracted that I had to get on to her several times tonight. I pay her well, you know."

Pearl's parents' financial bias left little room for sentimentality. "She loves helping you. You've been so good to her and Dani."

"Yes, I have. But I want to warn you about Mitchell. Body language tells, and tonight, you were definitely very intimate with him—as if you'd been in bed with him. I know you very well, Uma, and you're usually so cautious. Mitchell isn't for you. I don't care if he is supposed to be an executive looking for a site for a new building and supply complex or that Madrid needs the financial stimulation. I cannot allow you to—to give yourself to a man who is beneath you. You know that his father was a drunk, and the whole Warren family, dating back generations, couldn't keep a family homestead, selling it off piece by piece. The neighbors saw him coming out of your house this morning, still wearing his overnight beard. Don't you dare dishonor your mother, your family, by having an affair with that low-class—"

"That's enough, Pearl." Pearl was on one of her favorite tirades, just getting warmed up to list all of the Warrens' misfortunes and Fred's drinking.

Pearl was determined to have her say. "Thank goodness my girls are visiting Walter's sister in Connecticut. I wouldn't want them to know that the woman who they think of as an aunt is . . . is interested in a Warren, one of the lowest families in this town. Don't tell me that you can actually stand there and think that he is an equal to you, with your background. He doesn't fit into Madrid, not the class that you're in. He's a lowlife, Uma. His great-great-grandfather was hanged for horse thieving. His great-great-great-grandmother was part Indian, and there's some shanty Irish blood in there somewhere. I just cannot let you get involved with someone whose family bloodline reads like a criminal report. Now, you just listen to me—"

"Pearl, you need to stop," Uma warned, and wished her temper wasn't rising. Pearl's ideas of class lines had been drawn by her parents, and there were secrets that Uma had guarded, handed down by her grandmother and mother.

Anger rippled through Pearl's body like a snake, hissing and hot, and her blue eyes glittered. "You already have Everett wanting you. He's the best man, with a perfect family line behind him. What could you possibly want with a no-account Warren?"

"Pearl—"

"Living right next to you, just like any honest person. His brother is going to fail at that garage business, because Warrens are lazy—"

"Mitchell did you a favor with this garden."

Pearl clenched a rose blossom and crushed it in her fist before dropping the petals to the stone pathway. In the moonlight, her face was pale with rage. "I paid him, Uma. That doesn't mean he's my social equal. He forced me into an invitation, and I only invited him to show him how he doesn't fit. His blood is tainted—"

The leash Uma had been holding on her temper snapped. Pearl's gossip had hurt more than one family, and Mitchell didn't deserve more of what Pearl's family had done to the Warrens.

Whatever Uma felt for Mitchell ran deep and true, and she would protect him. "Pearl, if you want to talk about family lineage, let's talk about yours."

Pearl straightened and said frostily, "Mine is impeccable. You should know. Your mother and grandmother knew everything. Don't even speak my family's name or Walter's in the same breath as a Warren."

Uma shook her head, aching for Pearl even as she served her the truth. "Pearl, maybe it's time you knew a little more truthful story of your great-great-great-grandmother."

"Matilda? She was from Boston, from the very best social class."

"And she ran a bordello. The very best one, back in drover days, but a bordello nonetheless. Before she earned enough to buy that house, she was employed in that occupation herself."

For a moment, Pearl looked blankly at Uma, and then her hand rose and slapped Uma's cheek. "You're just saying that to protect Mitchell."

"If I have to, I can prove it." With Pearl's slap burning her, Uma still ached for her longtime friend. "Don't push me any more, Pearl. You're welcome to come talk to me when you've cooled down."

Uma left Pearl standing alone in the garden—rigid, pale, stricken, and shaken. Uma ignored Walter's leer and let Everett help her into his car, packing the serving trays into his back seat. "Something wrong?" he asked, taking her trembling hand.

"Pearl. She's on her high horse again. I'm afraid I lost it this time."

"You must have had a good reason."

"I did, and I regret explaining a few facts of life to her. She's had such an awful time growing up, and now with Walter. She's so fragile, and I should have handled it better."

Uma knew why she had been brusque with Pearl, when she usually handled her very carefully. Apparently Mitchell's dark moods were contagious.

Shelly noticed that Lonny was following her home, but decided that he was just on his way from Clyde's, where he'd often get Irma her favorite nighttime movie-watching snack of hot sausages and pickled eggs. Lately, Lonny had been patrolling more at nights and he'd looked exhausted and almost hunted. On the other hand, Irma seemed younger and chipper, almost girlish.

Shelly pulled into her driveway and sat for a moment, trying to push away the rock-hard headache she'd gotten tonight from Pearl's demands. Pearl paid well and had always been supportive of Dani, but she wanted perfection, and was always on edge at her parties. Walter's obvious belittling comments added to Pearl's demands until she was almost frantic and brittle. Shelly felt sorry for Pearl; in a way, she'd had a harder life in her upscale family.

Drawing on the last of her energy, Shelly eased the leftovers from the party out of the car. More than once, Pearl's leftovers had buoyed her tight budget. Pearl was generous and Shelly had always been grateful. She carried the boxes and plastic bags into the house and found Dani's note on the kitchen table.

At the garage.

The papers near Dani's note and under a can of Pepsi were applications for a course to get her diploma. Shelly shook her head. How many times had she argued with Dani to complete her high school requirements?

One stormy night, and Dani was making bargains with Roman—and keeping them.

Shelly noticed that Lonny's car was parked on the opposite side of the street. It pulled off when Roman's motorcycle rumbled in the driveway.

She smoothed the scar at her temple. Was it really possible that someone wanted to hurt her? And Uma and Pearl?

And Dani? Fear streaked through Shelly, freezing her as Roman and Dani came into the kitchen.

Roman's eyes narrowed, ripping down her maid's uniform, the neat black dress, ruffled apron, and tiny ruffled hat.

Shelly hurried to hug Dani; she didn't stop to notice that they were both sulking. Dani pushed her away and tromped back to her bedroom; soon the blaring sound of hard rock vibrated from her room. Roman's grim expression became a scowl as he stalked back to her bedroom and knocked briefly.

When the music didn't stop, he opened the door and walked in, clicking it firmly behind him. Fearing the tempers of them both, Shelly ran to open the door just as Roman punched the off button on Dani's sound system. She glared at him from the bed.

"Anyone for leftover sandwiches from Pearl's party?" Shelly asked, trying for a distraction. "Umm, Roman? It's late. Shouldn't you be leaving?"

"You can't always protect the kid from herself and her temper, Shell. And no, not until we've talked and I'm ready." He scowled at Shelly's maid hat and eased it off her head, tossing it aside.

Dani glared at him. "Great. Move in and make everyone miserable. Then I'm heading out."

"That's your choice, little girl," he snapped. "Keep that music down, or wear headphones. Your mother is dead on her feet and she needs some peace and quiet."

"You're sure not it, Pops."

"I'm fine, really—" Shelly began, and they both scowled at her.

"Don't women usually soak in a bubble bath or something to relax?" Roman demanded. "You look like hell."

Dani glanced at Shelly, and the hard, angry look in her kohl-lined eyes turned to amusement. "Sweet, isn't he—my pops?"

"You two are going to drive me nuts." Roman shouldered by Shelly and went to the bathroom. The sound of running water followed his order to "Get in that bath and stay there. I poured some purple stuff in. It makes bubbles."

Shelly stood her ground. "You are to stop ordering my daughter around."

Dani was on her feet, her body taut with anger. "I'm one thing, because I haven't got it figured out yet how I'm going to make your life hell. But don't you dare order my mother to do anything."

Roman slowly looked at Dani, and when he turned back to Shelly, his lids were lowered. But there was no missing the satisfaction and pride in those gold eyes, that slight pleased curve to his lips. "Uh-huh. Then I suppose you'll have to stick around to see that I don't. She's pretty easy to push, maybe blackmail a little, huh? Make her worry about you, just to get what you want?"

Dani's flush said she had known exactly what she was doing, those digs at Shelly to get her way.

Shelly couldn't bear for Dani to be hurt. "Roman, leave us alone."

Anger flashed and rose on the pinpoint of flame in those gold eyes, then he pivoted. His back was taut as he walked out of the house, slamming the door behind him.

"Go after him, if you want," Dani stated tightly. "He's sure not much and he knows exactly how to get to you. Anyone can see he thinks you're hot—my mom, the babe."

Shelly closed her eyes and tried to push away Dani's bitterness. Her daughter looked miserable, just as she did when she was terribly hurt. "Tell me the worst in all this, and we'll work through the rest."

Dani's mouth softened and then trembled as she dashed tears from her eyes. "Jace turned me over like I was a piece of property—he traded me, Mom, just for a few hours in a garage tuning his bike. I thought we were going to get married and—"

Shelly thought of other ways that Jace might turn Dani over—after he'd had his fill—and she was grateful to Roman for exposing the boy. "That's the worst?" she asked, fearing that there was more.

"Yeah. I can handle the old man. I know how he thinks; you don't."

Dani ran her hands down her clothing, smoothing it. "I may be a virgin, but I feel gritty and used. I thought I could change Jace and make a life, you know? I thought we'd start out easy, work into something special. He's not going to change. But there for a while, I thought I could use Roman to nudge him into—mind if I take that bath first? I'll clean up the bathroom and run another for you, if you want—you look like you could use it."

"Sure. Go ahead." Dani had never offered to clean after herself, or had been very thoughtful, unless it served her purpose.

Shelly noted a shadow outside the house. *Roman had said that someone had just shot at Uma's window during the storm, and a whole series of incidents proved that the danger in Madrid was not over.*

Heartbeats later, with a cast-iron skillet in her hand, Shelly eased outside the house, quietly closing the screen door behind her. She flattened to the wall and heard brush rustle in the backyard. The broken limb was big, and someone was moving—

Whoever the man was, he was big and powerful, trying to pull the branch away from the house where it rested. She moved closer, her skillet raised, and just then Roman turned.

His foot caught in a branch, and with a stunned expression, he tumbled backward into the deep foliage of oak leaves. A solid thud and grunt sounded, and then nothing.

"*Roman?*" Shelly tossed aside the skillet and ran to help him.

She bent into the darkness of the heavy leaves and prayed—Roman's hand shot upward, caught her wrist, and tugged. With a cry, Shelly toppled onto him.

When she braced away, Roman held her and grinned as the branches and leaves enveloped them.

"Not funny," she said sharply. "I thought you'd left."

He toyed with her hair, winding her ponytail around his hand and studying it. He brought the strands to his face, closing his eyes as he inhaled the fragrance. "I moved my bike into the shadows, under the tarp where the lumber for the new flooring is. I don't want anyone to know I'm staying here."

"You're not. You can't possibly stay here."

"It's dangerous, babe. Give me a break. I'd feel pretty guilty if anything happened to you and I wasn't here. I just want to stay here and know that you're safe." Roman sighed and stretched luxuriously beneath Shelly. "You feel good."

"Stay here? In my house?" she asked incredulously.

"Right here."

"Oh, no. People would talk."

"People have always talked. The important thing is that Dani and you are safe. That's all I want, Shell, to know that you're safe."

She thought back to that night when his father had died, how shattered Roman had been. "We can manage."

"With what? A skillet? Whoever is out there is playing for real, Shell. I've got some experience in dealing with that; you don't. Do you really want to know that you could have prevented something from happening to Dani and you didn't?"

Shelly's heart froze. "Nothing can happen to Dani. She's everything to me."

"I watched part of my family die once, and it's not going to happen again, not you or Dani. It's settled, then. I'll bunk on the couch for a few hours at night. That scar says someone is real serious about you and they move at night."

His voice had lowered into a seductive whisper as his body hardened beneath her. Shelly tried to push away and Roman held her, still grinning. "You look sexy in this uniform."

He was bigger and harder than she remembered, but his smile was even more fascinating. Shelly tried to ignore the ripple of anticipation in her, that feminine urge to linger with him. But Roman was about as volatile as a flash fire and just as unpredictable. "Let me go, Roman."

"I did once. That was a mistake. I'm not going anywhere this time." His smile slid away into an intensity that burned. Then the caressing fingers at her nape slowly drew her down to his lips. "This won't hurt a bit. How I've missed you—"

The gentle brush of his lips was a beckoning, an enticement of magic and beautiful secrets that she couldn't resist . . .

ELEVEN

At home, Mitchell's big screen television and reruns of NASCAR races weren't any substitute for needing Uma. The house moved softly around him, soothingly—if he hadn't been thinking about Uma and Everett, and the irritating way Everett held her hand to his chest. In the bare window, where Mitchell had drawn away the sheet he'd hung there, Everett's car slowed on its way to Uma's and Mitchell snapped off the television. Comfortable in only jeans, he sat in the dark, ignoring the beer and the decorating magazines on the metal tray at his side. He had no right to think he had any hold on Uma, that she had any commitment to him—one night of the best sex he'd ever had was no reason he could expect another.

He'd been a powerful vice president of a national company, and he wanted to carry a damn tray of petit fours to a party more than he'd ever wanted to negotiate top money projects . . .

Mitchell sighed heavily. At least Uma would be safe with Everett—maybe. Mitchell would wait until later, and then go out into the night, circling the Lawrence house to see if anyone was stalking her.

Then Everett's car prowled by in the opposite direction.

Uma was either in it with him, or she was alone—and in danger.

Mitchell sat in the dark, tensing as he heard a key rattle in the front door and the deadbolt turned, unlocking. He eased to his feet and flattened himself against the wall, next to the door. Whoever it was would think he was out for the night or asleep, and he intended to—

The intruder stepped into the doorway and Mitchell grabbed a fistful of shirt, hauling him into the room.

Delicate fabric tore and Uma's body flattened against the wall with a solid thump.

She glared at him while he tried to absorb that the "dangerous intruder" was just a woman whose dress was torn. He held part of it in his fist; and the rest was sliding down to her waist with her bra. She crossed her arms in front of her chest.

Then she let the dress and her bra slide to the floor, and still glaring at him, stepped out of it. She turned and walked down the hallway to his bedroom, an erotic picture with her tapered back, mauve cotton panties on her swaying hips, those long legs, and her practical flats.

Mitchell let the torn scrap flutter to the floor. He wavered between going after her with excuses and picking up her dress, stuffing it in a bag, and waiting to see if she'd ever speak to him again. He sank into his recliner, which seemed to be the safest place in the house. Following Uma into the bedroom was definitely dangerous.

He couldn't face Uma when she came to stand beside him, but a side glance at those long, smooth legs said she was wearing his shirt. She picked up the remote and clicked through the stations—golf, world news, how to build a bird house, NASCAR races. "Anything good on?"

"Not much," he said as the lead car slowed with a bad tire and maneuvered into the crew pit; the crowd went wild as another car hit the side wall and ricocheted into the path of another, driving it off the track. But Mitchell's heart was pounding for another reason—*Uma had come to him. She needed him.* "I'm sorry about grabbing you. I'll get you a new dress."

"You *bet* you will." Uma needed Mitchell's truth after the blistering argument with Pearl, after hurting her. She felt guilty, yet Pearl had to be stopped.

Mitchell had that closed-in look, as if he were expecting the worst. She couldn't resist smoothing his hair . . . clearly he'd been running his hands through it, as it stood out in peaks. Uma noted the stack of fortune cookie paper strips piled beside his chair. "Find any answers?"

"With you, there aren't any," he brooded.

"That's because I don't know them myself. I feel like I'm being taken over. I like my independence, and I like being single, making my own decisions."

He felt bruised and vulnerable and shielded those emotions with a brusque "So? So do I."

"I know tonight was difficult for you and you're upset, but don't take it out on me."

"I don't know where any of this conversation is going," he stated bluntly, needing to know if Uma had told Everett. He recognized jealousy and tried to push it away. It stayed to lurk and taunt. *Everett was perfect for her.*

Uma straightened the sheet that Mitchell had drawn away for a clear view of the street. "Why didn't you ask me for a dance?"

Because he would have picked her up and carried her away. "You were busy. I was busy."

"I'm sorry Pearl can be so awful. But I'm glad you came. I needed you there. I've just had an incident with Pearl that I may regret. She's so fragile that anything could push her over the edge. But sometimes, she just needs—I'm glad you're here now. I needed to see you."

She needed him. Hope inched a centimeter higher in

Mitchell Warren. He noted with an inner pleased smirk that she was wearing *his* rose, and not Everett's. "Everett was there, fitting right in," he nudged, needing to hear more.

She lifted an eyebrow. "Don't tell me that you couldn't fit in if you wanted, Mr. Vice President. I'm certain you've done your time at dinner chit-chat, and I'm certain that when you set your mind to it, you're very good at anything you want to do. One chooses his own path and who he wants to walk with on it. Tonight, you chose to walk alone. Lonny returned the tray, by the way, and stayed to help himself to quite a bit of food while he chatted with the guests. Pearl was not happy. One who is not happy in her own home cannot be happy within."

In the shadows, Mitchell tried not to smile at the typical Charis Lopez notation. "Why are you here?"

"To ask you not to be so distracting when Everett is nearby. You two were glaring at each other like dogs fighting over a bone."

Mitchell couldn't resist running his hand over her smooth thigh. "The description doesn't quite fit. He wants you back."

"Mmm."

Mitchell withdrew his hand and concentrated on that "mmm"; it could mean anything.

"You could do with some furniture." Uma eased onto the arm of his chair and took his left hand, studying the webbed fingers, smoothing them. "You said earlier that you could sense Lauren's feelings."

Mitchell didn't want to explain the softness that rose in him sometimes, especially when he was working in Lauren's garden or her kitchen. The feeling was stronger in the room that held her things, like a long, sweet aching sigh that couldn't be heard—as if she hungered for life that would not come.

He'd never been sensitive, but the uneasiness could curl

around him, as if the shadows wanted something from him. What was that prowling inside him?

Uma slid her fingers through his, holding their hands on his lap. Her finger traced the scarred, webbed fingers of his left hand, and when Mitchell would have drawn away, she held tight. "Lauren wants peace. I want her to have that. I think she's talking to you and you're resisting. Tell me what she wants."

The thought that a woman might be moving inside his mind took Mitchell to his feet. He rammed his hand through his hair and walked into the kitchen—a cozy kitchen where a woman's love had created—he stalked past the laundry room where she had neatly folded towels and ironed tablecloths and—

He jerked open the back door and surged into the cool, sweet night, with its fragrance of roses. The storm from the previous night had swept a flurry of color onto the lush grass and lavender bed. She'd wept here, sadly acknowledging that her husband was unfaithful and that she would never have the children she wanted. The incredible sadness enclosed Mitchell tighter than rope. Lauren would have loved to have held the baby he'd delivered in the taxicab that day.

Mitchell rubbed his aching forehead; he sensed that Lauren *did* know about the baby, how just holding it had made him wonder about the "more" of life.

Lauren should have had the babies she'd wanted; she should have been able to love them and see them grow—

Women needed babies to cuddle, and Uma's had died. The sorrow within him surprised him and clenched at his heart, an aching that Lauren would have felt for Uma. "Listen. About Lauren's things in that room—I don't have plans for it. Why don't you do something with it—say, a nursery, or something she would have liked."

Uma was quiet, and then she said, "I don't want to decorate another nursery ever again. But I will try to make it into a room Lauren would love."

Then her arms came around him from behind, her hand covering his racing heart. "She was the sweetest person, Mitchell. I wish you could have known her."

Maybe I do. He tossed that thought away, fearing it. "I knew her as a kid—remember, we grew up together. She was always with you and Shelly and Pearl. How the heck did you and Shelly and Lauren stay friends with Pearl all these years?"

Uma nuzzled his bare back, kissing his shoulder. "Pearl needed us. She's been wonderful to Shelly. We've dug old pioneer roses from the homesteads together and with our mothers. Our mothers were in the same activities—your mother, too."

"Leave Grace out of this." *I've always loved her . . . go to her,* Fred had whispered as he died. Mitchell had forgotten that echo through the years, and now it was back.

When he began to move away from her, Uma linked her hands, holding him tight. "Dani wants to know her grandmother. She has that right. You should know her, too. Fred loved her."

"You can't make this work, Uma. Don't try."

"One question: Roman was driving the night your father died, and you were in the back of the pickup with Fred. Did he say anything?"

You're all I've got left of her. You and Roman. I loved that woman with all my heart. Tell Grace I've always loved her, his father had whispered amid his pain. *Everything was my fault. Take Roman and go to her—*

"Did you ever tell Roman whatever Fred said?" Uma pressed gently.

"No. It's better he doesn't know."

"You should tell him, no matter what it was."

She nuzzled his back and Mitchell's anger slowly slanted precariously into soft wooziness and hunger.

"I missed you today," he admitted roughly, and sucked in his breath as she eased away slightly, her hands sliding from him. His shirt fluttered to the ground, covering the rose petals and the lavender, followed by her panties. Then she was back, her breasts bare and warm against his back. "Tell me what you feel, Mitchell. Just what you feel. . . ."

"That this is right," he whispered rawly as he turned to catch her in his arms, seeking those soft lips. Uma's lips opened to his, the seal perfect and hot and tormenting, pulsing with hunger, her arms tight around him, her body waiting—

He couldn't wait, bearing her gently down to the shirt spread upon the lavender bed. In his mind, he wanted to take her gently, yet that plan slid away into the rose blossoms crushed by their bodies. Uma unfurled to his needs, hungry, stormy, her hands gripping his hair, holding him as he stripped away his jeans.

She was ripe and sweet and tender and intense, flowing beneath him, closing her eyes as he entered her.

"Does it bother you?" he asked roughly, needing to know. "The scars on my leg?"

Her hand smoothed the uneven skin, and Mitchell waited, his heart pounding. Early in his life, more than one woman had hated the sight of the scars. "No, they're a part of you. A badge of your bravery. You'll always face what comes, even this, between us," she whispered unevenly.

He lifted her face to the moonlight and Uma kissed his hand. "I don't know that I can wait, honey."

"It is wise to take what is right for one when the moment arrives."

"Good advice." Then Mitchell couldn't think any more, his body needing the depth and the heat and the tightness of hers, the flowing together that made them one—a oneness he'd never had, diving into the tempest, feeding on it . . . *the Oneness* . . .

Uma understood the primitive taking, welcomed it. Mitchell's honesty was undiluted, stripped of civilization. His breath became hers, his body lodged deep within hers, surging powerfully as she met him thrust for thrust. His lips, his whispers driving her on, that tight clenching taking what she needed to soothe the ache within her.

For just one heartbeat, she opened her eyes to the man above her, the power and truth in him, his features taut with desire. His hands ran down her body claiming her, finding her, and the first jolt of pleasure tossed her against him, his mouth sealing hers as it went on and on.

Uma tried to breathe, fought for control, needing to make the pleasure she'd waited for all day last and last. When it came, peaked, and drove her higher, Mitchell held her tightly—she gave him everything, trusted him to care for her.

Then he was lifting her gently into his arms, easing her into the house and placing her upon his bed.

Mitchell came to her again, needing her, filling her, hungry for her just as she was for him, meeting him passion for passion, taking and giving—

Later, a very well-loved Uma sighed and drifted off to sleep in his arms. The soft drape of her arms and legs was luxuriously feminine and sweet. He liked holding her, listening to her sigh sleepily, wondering at the slight frowns and secret smiles as she slept. The scent of crushed rose petals filled the room, and shadows stirring softly as if Lauren hovered nearby, pleased at the tenderness he felt for Uma, the need to protect her. Mitchell looked at the moonlit shadows on the ceiling and smoothed Uma's hair, easing the soft strands across his chest.

Who would want to hurt her? Or Shelly? Or Pearl? Why?

Someone did, that was a certainty. Another certainty was that he wanted nothing to do with his mother.

Mitchell gathered Uma closer, smiling a bit at her notation that he cuddled. He really had to read her book, he decided sleepily as Uma began to stir beside him. Her eyes opened slowly, silver in the night. "You're not getting your way," he whispered.

"Oh, aren't I?" she asked as she rose to straddle him, her eyes silvery in the night, then closing as she accepted him gently into her warmth. The rosy flush of her cheeks told him that she was unfamiliar with taking what she wanted, and yet she wanted him enough to step outside her boundaries.

"Well, maybe."

Mitchell frowned at the doorbell. He was just studying the grass stains on his shirt, the rose fragrance delicate and precious as he remembered Uma arching up to him, her body pale and curved in the moonlight—

One petal clung to the material, pressed and flattened and bruised into the fabric and he smiled fondly at it, remembering. He brought the shirt to his face, nuzzling it and inhaling the scent.

He frowned again when the doorbell rang again and the tom who had clawed at the back screen, ruining the wire mesh to get inside, raced to the front door.

Mitchell didn't want company; he had other plans—like joining Uma in bed with the breakfast he'd just cooked and a bouquet of freshly picked roses; making love on a bed of rose petals was an experience he intended to repeat. He glanced at the filled plates he'd placed on a scrap of board and the huge bouquet of roses. He'd chosen "Paul Neyron," a cabbage rose with blooms of six to seven inches wide—more petals to lie on with Uma. Lauren had left excellent notations in her handwritten garden book, "Big and juicy and luscious, but a little overpowering. Quite persuasive when used in the proper setting."

The shower sounded in his bedroom and he smiled to

himself, picturing Uma wrapped in steam and nothing else. He just had time to scatter the rose petals on the bed—

Mitchell shook his head; he was not thinking like Lauren. He was not influenced by her gentler, feminine romantic notions. Her presence was not in the house . . . just the showering woman he intended to join. He wanted to persuade Uma—of what? To live with him? That he was a stable, well-rounded, courteous guy capable of intimate feelings and sharing himself?

He jammed on the jeans he'd worn last night and hurried to the front door before the intruder could ring again. On his way, he jerked on the shirt Uma had worn, wanting to keep her close to him.

Maybe he was beginning to understand intimacy, yin and yang. One thing was for certain: he was on a winning roll that he wanted to strengthen this morning—without the intruder.

As a man with deep upward mobility tendencies, Mitchell was dizzingly happy. "I might even make it to the petit four tray-carrying stage, at this rate."

One jerk of the door opened it to a familiar woman. Through the screen, she was older, harder-looking, and definitely uncertain. There was no mistaking the thick ring of diamonds that glittered on her shaking hand as she raised it to smooth her bleach-damaged hair. "Tessa?"

He sensed rather than saw Uma behind him in the hallway. "I invited her, Mitchell. Please come in, Tessa. We're just about to have breakfast, weren't we, Mitchell?"

Caught between the two women, Tessa Greenfield, who years ago had accused him of being her lover and had fueled her husband's rage, and Uma, the woman who had just taken his hand, the woman whose hair still carried the scent of roses, freshly showered and dressed in one of his shirts, his jeans rolled up at her ankles, Mitchell said bluntly, "Not with her, we're not."

Tessa paled more beneath her heavy makeup and Uma's

dark smoky eyes locked with his. "I invited her, Mitchell, after . . . yesterday morning. She has something to say, and it
will not be said with a screen door between you and on a
front porch that everyone in the neighborhood can see."

"Busy little bee, aren't you?" he asked, and didn't spare the
sarcasm as he withdrew his hand from hers. "One should not
act in the business that does not concern one."

Uma's head went back with the verbal blow, and her lips
tightened. "Mmm," she murmured. "Come in, Tessa."

"Yes, come in," Mitchell invited tightly. Uma had stepped
into the intimate corners of his life, the edges he didn't want
touched and had ripped them wide open. Maybe she needed
to see just how ugly they were.

Tessa glanced around the barren, newly repainted home.
"I can't stay . . . It's so soft in here. Like love," she whispered
in awe as the old tomcat rubbed against her legs.

"Remember Lauren? This used to be her house," Uma said
softly.

"I remember her. She was sweet, like sunshine." Tessa
hadn't been a loving person, always out for herself, but she
bent to pick up the insistent tom and cuddled him close. He
purred and seemed to smirk at Mitchell.

"What do you want?" he thrust at Tessa and arched as
Uma pinched his butt, just enough to warn him.

"I'm sorry about Fred—your dad. I didn't know that my
husband—you know Max died of a heart attack right away—
I didn't know that he would even do anything like that. I
should have known—I'd seen him with animals, and with
men. We had a terrible fight that night—after I'd found out
what he'd done. When you came to the house, I was more furious with him and myself and I—I reacted badly to you.
Back then, maybe I was terrified of Max, too, of what he
would do to me. It was so awful, what happened to Fred."

Mitchell heard his father's dying screams echo through

time. "You were just an innocent bystander in all this—right, Tessa?"

Her face seemed to crumble beneath the makeup, aging her instantly. "No, I caused everything, and I'll have to live with it for the rest of my life."

"Such sympathy." He frowned at Uma, who had just pinched him again; he wasn't used to being prodded or told to mind his manners; Uma would have to get the rules straight. Then he bluntly asked Tessa, "Anything else you have to say?"

"Only that it was Fred that I wanted. I couldn't believe he still loved your mother. When he turned me down, I decided to—to take something he loved just as much as her. That was you. And you weren't buying. I was spoiled and young and—and I'm so sorry, Mitchell . . . so sorry," she sobbed. "It wasn't you, it was him. And it was my fault. He never once wanted another woman, only Grace."

Mitchell couldn't move, couldn't think, locked in the nightmare of that night. *You're all I've got left of her. You and Roman. I loved that woman with all my heart.* "Get out."

Then, because Mitchell was in pain and couldn't bear to let anyone see so deep inside him, he scowled at Uma, "You, too. Get out."

He turned and walked down the hallway, into the kitchen where breakfast and the rose blooms waited. He waited for the tom, his only male alliance in the house to follow—the doorway remained empty.

Uma heard the crash and placed her arm around Tessa, who was shivering and holding the old tomcat tightly. "He'll be all right. Thank you for coming."

Before he'd closed his expression into that tight dark mask, Mitchell's pain had seared her. When he had turned and stalked away, his clothing bore stains of roses and grass, his body taut as if last night's lovemaking hadn't happened. Yet that one lush red petal had clung to his shoulder, refusing to be tossed aside.

Uma knew how badly he ached; she wanted to go to him, needed to comfort him—and herself. But all his edges were up and bristling, cutting her out of his life. *Get out.*

She shivered despite the morning's warmth. Mitchell had just severed what they had without a second look back at her.

"He's so fierce, just like Fred," Tessa whispered shakily as they moved out into the morning sunshine. "And honest. You can see the truth in him, and the strength. That unbending strength. That's what I saw in Fred, why I wanted him so badly. I knew that if he wanted to love me, he could make everything right. I had only my body to bargain with, and still I was no match for Grace. Mitchell is like that. If he ever loves, it will be just one woman to the end, but he's a hard man to understand."

There, in the fresh August morning, Uma knew exactly what Fred had said as he was dying. When a man loved a woman that deeply, he'd speak of that to his sons.

And Mitchell had clenched that inside him all these years, withholding it from Roman. Both men were firmly against Grace, and yet they didn't know how much she had tried, how the failure of her marriage had wounded her.

Through her mother, Uma knew. And she knew that Dani was right in wanting to meet Grace.

Get out, Mitchell had said, slamming the door shut on her and the past. He was more like his father than he knew, proud and stubborn, and just as skilled at hurting. . . .

Uma brushed away the tears burning her eyes. *Get out.*

Later that morning, Uma put the finishing touches on a new logo for Mrs. Westerfield, a client in Oklahoma City who wanted to market designer bags inspired by vintage styles.

The duct tape over the bullethole in the window reminded Uma that danger circled Madrid.

The ache inside her told her of Mitchell's pain, the way he could easily close her away from him, even after two nights of lovemaking. She'd opened herself to feeling, to wanting desperately, to sensuality and hope and—

And Mitchell had crushed it in his fist.

Tessa had been shaky, but steady enough to drive; and Uma had almost run for her house and for safety. She felt as if pieces of her were scattered along the sidewalk from Mitchell's house to hers.

Uma let the tears gather inside her and roll down her cheeks, the sobs growing, choking her, until they burst into the quiet room.

Out of habit, she reached for her fortune cookie jar. Her fingers trembled as she broke one open to extract the small paper that read, "Your actions to help another are justified."

She crushed the paper in one hand and the cookie in the other. She watched the crumbs fall into her wastepaper basket. Of course she was justified. She was half in love with a man who brooded about a death that wasn't his fault. She wanted to protect Mitchell, to soothe him, and what did he do?

Get out. The words rang cold as steel, as if he'd never kissed her like that, and she'd opened her body and her life to him.

Did she regret the giving?

No, it was honest and true, just as Tessa had said of Mitchell.

Uma cried until the anger came, fierce and unrelenting, and needing release. They'd made love perfectly and Mitchell had torn the magic into shreds. Later, she would be reasonable and regret any hasty actions.

Later would be too late; she needed to find Mitchell and nail him. "If truth be held in your emotions today, release them," she muttered. "Holding darkness within withers the beauty . . . strike while the iron is hot . . . waste not, want not."

Mitchell had reached inside her, taken away her safety, and given her beauty, and now he had to pay for his *Get out.*

Uma ran to her room, where she had shed his clothes, bent to gather them into her arms, and hurried to his house.

Mitchell wasn't there; his pickup gone. Uma hurried back to her car, tossed his clothes into the passenger seat, and shot back out of her driveway. Her tires squalled as she left Lawrence Street, passed Tabor Street, and bulleted down Main Street onto Maloney, cornering sharply enough to make her tires squeal.

His pickup was parked in front of Roman's garage. Her brakes screeched as the car slid sideways a bit, nicked Mitchell's perfect back bumper, and stopped. Fiercely angry, now that Mitchell could dismiss her so easily, she ignored Lonny's patrol car easing to park in front of the garage.

Uma grabbed Mitchell's shirt, jeans and belt that she had worn and hurried into the garage.

"Where is he?" she demanded of Roman, who had just hefted a small motor from out of a dishwasher and stood holding it. A long rubber hose was draped around his neck.

Roman, clearly wary of her mood, nodded to the truck, and to the two feet extending from beneath it. Uma didn't think; she reacted. She walked to the work boots she recognized as Mitchell's, dropped the clothing, and bent to grab both of them.

When she tugged, he grunted and the bump beneath the truck sounded like he had hit his head. She tugged again and the roller bench he lay upon slid from beneath the truck. Mitchell lay there scowling up at her and rubbing the grease mark on his forehead—it spread across his forehead like war paint.

War, that was what she wanted—war on the man who had made love to her and then had told her to "get out."

"Here," she said, bending to pluck up the clothes and dump them on his face. "I forgot these this morning. Thank you for the use of them. Goodbye. And by the way, Tessa was doing her best this morning, and you were just plain evil. About three years ago, she went off into a ditch—she was tipsy and sobbing and guilty over what she had done. She'd been visiting your father's grave. We had a chat over tea and she explained everything. I thought you should know. I thanked her for you. And I refuse to be dumped like garbage."

Mitchell slammed the clothes aside. "You what?"

"I said, I refuse to be dumped like garbage on the morning after. You needed to know the truth. I just didn't have time last night to prepare you. I was very busy. I contacted Tessa because I cared—I cared, or last night wouldn't have happened. You think that I am the sort of woman who has flings because—because?"

Uma paused to suck in air and anger, just getting warmed up. "You've been feeling guilty all these years because you thought you caused that fire by turning Tessa down. It wasn't you she really wanted, it was Fred. So you'll have to stop hiding behind all that self-installed guilt, *because it doesn't fit anymore.* She served you the absolute truth. If you can't handle that, then you're not the man I think you are." She kicked his boot for emphasis. "And by the way . . . I'll pay for whatever damage there is to your pickup. It was in my way. I hit it."

"You *what?*" he demanded again, this time louder.

"I hit your pickup. It was there and it reminded me of how awful you were this morning, when I was just trying to help—"

"You've been crying," he noted softly, as if seeing her for the first time. "Your eyes are all puffy and red. The braids look nice, though. Your mother used to put ribbons in them . . . pink. What's that stuff in your hair? Bread?"

Uma brushed the fortune cookie crumbs from her hair and then her face where they had stuck to her tears. "Mmm. I didn't notice my eyes were puffy and red. However, thank you for being so observant and noting that I'm not exactly looking tip-top this morning, for some reason," she said and tried to walk out of the garage with as much dignity as she could manage.

Then she turned and walked back to Roman. "Your brother hasn't told you everything about the night Fred died, and it's important that he does."

"What?" Roman tensed, and his expression closed.

Uma knew instantly that Roman carried his own secrets and wasn't releasing them to his brother.

"Ask him." She pushed her torn dignity into a heap and marched out to the sidewalk.

" 'Morning, Ms. Uma," Lonny said uneasily.

"Lovely morning," she returned on a sound that she hoped wasn't a sob. She knew he'd never seen her so irrational or angry . . . and she'd been taught always to act like a lady. Uma had just thrown every bit of her mother's "quality" teaching into the trash can and Mitchell had caused it. "How's Irma?"

He looked at her warily. "Okay, I guess."

"I'm glad. Please tell her that I said hello, will you? Why are you looking at me like that? Is there a problem?"

He blinked owlishly and glanced over her head to where Mitchell stood. "Uh. No. No problem."

"Good. Then have a lovely day. See you."

She didn't turn when Mitchell said "Women" in that dark tone that somehow explained his thoughts about the whole sex.

Sex. Her hand trembled on the steering wheel as she reversed; metal squeaked as her car pulled back from his pickup. *Oh, yes. They'd had plenty of sex, hadn't they? That was something they both understood. But was there anything else in a man's heart who could tell her to get out of his life so easily?*

After driving a few feet, Uma pressed her foot to the brake, and the car screeched to a stop. *How could she want Mitchell so, and how could he could slam all the doors of his life to her?*

She shook her head and began driving again, only to stop the car abruptly. *How could she possibly understand him?*

Uma gripped the steering wheel and slowly pulled a few more feet, before stopping with a screech of tires. She decided that—"While he's mad, I may as well make him good and mad, because Dani deserves to know her grandmother. And because Grace didn't deserve what she got. And because I know everything that happened."

When Uma looked in her rearview mirror, she saw Mitchell, Roman, and Lonny standing in the street. They looked confused and uncertain. Lonny was scratching his head. Roman was standing hip-shot, bending to rub his damaged knee, and Mitchell was rubbing his forehead as if he had a headache. There was no reason for his obvious confusion. She was being perfectly logical after the man she'd made love to for two nights and who could be so endearing and sweet and tender had just told her to "get out."

Oh, she would all right, but Dani and Grace deserved to know each other. "Men," she said, using the same tone Mitchell had, and soared off to her home. Too angry to work, she sat down to write a searing Charis article on the benefits of releasing anger upon the one who has acted poorly. She inserted "justified" in front of "anger." Yes, her anger with Mitchell was justified.

Later, Clyde crushed the roses in Pearl's English garden. He needed the empty-headed twit, chattering all the time, pretending people actually listened to her. Right now, Pearl served his purpose—using her could bring Shelly and Uma right into his hands.

Too bad that Mitchell and Roman Warren had come to town. Too bad for them.

And Uma wasn't taking hints, like the bullethole in her window, a perfect warning served at the same time thunder struck.

Soon, he'd have to stop warning and the games would end. Lauren was just the start, then that dimwit Pete Jones, who had asked for more money after the shooting. He shouldn't have done that. No one messed with Clyde.

He tugged up his black gloves and smoothed his new tailored suit and adjusted his fedora, fueling the hatred inside him. Uma had to die, of course; she knew too much. And she'd only angered him by aligning herself with a Warren, and everyone knew they were bad news. Gossip about them ran through Madrid like wildfire. *Clyde really didn't want Uma whoring. It wasn't ladylike.*

Clyde skimmed his dapper appearance and thought about Walter, whom he had seen earlier, parked on the street outside his home. If Walter thought that the dying sunlight hid the gleam of his elegant hip flask as he tipped it high, he was wrong. Clyde had known Walter since childhood and knew his weaknesses.

Walter was apparently very angry, flinging the hip flask into Pearl's garden. Obviously in pain, he eased out of the car and slammed the door. He rubbed his genitals as if they ached and cursed, "Bitch. That Uma is going to get what she deserves."

Clyde watched Walter hobble up the elegant walkway. Apparently Uma was one woman with whom Walter could not score. Clyde had kept very close count of Walter's affairs, because they'd make excellent blackmail fodder—when he chose to act.

The fever rose to hurt something, anything, now. Uma, Shelly, and Pearl would have to wait, because Clyde didn't want to kill them without enjoying their fear . . . he rummaged for what would squeal and pleasure him and thought of Rosy, the Ferris's pot-belly pig. Clyde had stepped in Rosy's mess once, spoiling a perfect shoe shine.

Yes, Rosy was a perfect candidate for tonight.

* * *

"But I don't need a dishwasher," Shelly said as Roman and Mitchell muscled a dishwasher into her house. "I can't afford one."

"You can this one," Dani said with a grin. "The old man tuned up a throwaway down at the church thrift shop and put a new hose in her. He sure can make a motor hum."

Shelly had discovered that Roman knew how to make women hum, too; his kisses in the fallen tree branch were sweet and tender and hungry. She'd just managed to tear herself loose, fighting her way out of the leaves and twigs to her feet. Roman was frowning, obviously in pain as he had bent to rub his knee. She'd fought running and her conscience. "Can I help you?"

He'd scowled at her and struggled to his feet. Though obviously favoring his knee, he had refused to bend and rub it. "No. Get away from me."

Uma had been crying and angry, because apparently the brothers shared the same defense, slam-door-shut style. Shelly had seen Uma angry only the one time she'd confronted Billy with his treatment of Lauren.

Now, Shelly wondered if anger was contagious as Roman continued to interfere with her life.

The men ignored Shelly as they discussed how to hook the dishwasher to the sink. A new empty space beneath the counters had greeted Shelly when she'd come home from Uma's house. To make matters worse, Roman was quietly explaining installation procedure to Dani, now lying on the floor beside him, her head under the kitchen sink. When he asked for a tool, she dug into the battered box and hauled out the right one.

Mitchell stood, his arms folded, watching Roman and Dani. Then he looked at Shelly. "Saw your car at Uma's. Is she okay?"

"No, she's not. I could kill you."

His eyebrows shot up. "I didn't do anything wrong."

"You think she just—?" Shelly glanced at Dani, who was suddenly sitting on the floor, watching the exchange with Mitchell.

"What did he do, Mom?" Dani asked, rising to her feet and scowling at Mitchell. "Did he hurt Uma?"

"Not exactly. Uma tried to help him, and—"

Mitchell's hand slashed the end of her sentence. "She shouldn't have."

"Sometimes I wonder if the Warren family has any couth at all," Dani murmured, shaking her head.

"Not much," Mitchell said. "Goodnight, ladies."

"She's . . . making . . . Christmas fruitcake," Shelly leveled at him. Her ominous tone spelled trouble.

Dani whistled through her teeth. "Man. He really must have pulled one. The last time she made fruitcake was—when she went after Billy Howard, right there on Lauren's front yard, amid everyone buying her things. I've never seen Uma so mad, as if she could have picked up six-guns."

"She bought all the maraschino cherries, raisins, pecans, and walnuts in the grocery stores, got a bottle of rum from Clyde's Tavern, bought Mrs. Clover's frozen on-sale candied fruit, and enough flour and eggs to cause a real shortage."

"It's only August, ladies," Mitchell said warily, as if he were trying to connect the guilty dots—and they all led to him.

"Well, she might cool down a bit by Christmas—just maybe. Or like the fruitcake recipe she has that requires aging to get the best flavor, maybe she's just warming up. If I were you, I would either apologize or leave town. And I swear, I will help her with any plans she has to show you some manners."

Mitchell's head went back at the threat, his eyes flashing. He started to say something, then nodded grimly and walked out the door, slamming it behind him.

"Let's try this baby out," Roman said as he rose awkwardly to his feet. He glared at Shelly as if reminded of his disability.

She was still wrapped in Uma's heartbreak. "Do you ever talk about what happened the night your father died?"

"Why the hell would we want to do that?" Roman's fierce scowl said he didn't want to open that door to the past.

"How you felt. Do you ever talk about that? Or your mother?" she pressed him.

Dani stood still, clearly fascinated by her mother's reaction to Roman. "Get him, Mom. Let it all hang out."

"Stay out of this, Dani. You're in my face, Roman, pushing me. It's only right that I push back. My turf, my house, and you're in it. My neighbors are gossiping all up and down the street, whispering about you being here so much, about Dani being at the garage. I will not have her slandered."

"Your mom is a real tiger, kid," Roman said too softly. "Too bad she's revved up over the wrong thing."

Shelly's hands went to her hips. "What does that mean, exactly?"

"Figure it out," he said darkly before slamming out of the house.

Dani ran to the kitchen window and peered outside. "They're out there, leaning against Mitchell's truck. They're not talking. How can guys do that, just stand there and not talk?"

She jerked open the window and yelled, "I want to meet my grandmother, and no one is stopping me."

"I am, kid," Roman shot back.

Both men glared at her, then Mitchell jerked open his pickup door, got in, revved the motor, and backed out onto Tabor Street.

Roman entered the kitchen to scowl at Dani and Shelly. "You know that there is some maniac here in town, up to no good. The pieces aren't fitting together yet, but they will. Meanwhile, the two of you better get used to having me around."

Dani gripped a kitchen chair, swivelled it, and straddled it.

She braced her arms over the back and rested her chin on it. "Here's the deal. You can stay here—on the couch—and I'll hit the books and play Little Miss Nice. But you'd better be nice to your mother—*my grandmother*—if and when she turns up."

"No deal. She ran out on us."

Shelly recognized Dani's expression, just as stubborn as Roman's, but aching, too. "I've heard that Grace was a good person."

"Sure, a mother who deserts," Roman scoffed. "I don't want to talk about her anymore."

"He's holed up like a wounded old bear. I guess it's up to us, Mom."

Roman eyed them. "Don't get any ideas, either of you."

Shelly returned Dani's look, smiled slowly, and asked, "Who, us?"

Later, Roman was sitting on the couch, watching television and brooding. After her shower, Shelly decided she could ease the tension in her by ironing. In the kitchen, she inhaled the scent of freshly pressed clothes and ignored Roman, who came to stand, leaning against the counter and studying her.

Instead of wearing her usual nightgown, Shelly had decided to wear a T-shirt and shorts, her freshly shampooed hair dampening the cloth. "I really don't like you staying here," she said, flipping a man's long sleeve to the opposite side and ironing it briskly. "I want you to leave."

"Those bulletholes in the ivy aren't exactly friendly. How would you feel if they'd hit Dani instead?"

Shelly shivered, terrified by the image of Dani crumpling as Lauren had. "We'll be careful."

Roman rubbed his jaw and the sound of stubble grated in the silence. "I want to do something. It's late, but I want to protect my daughter and you."

Shelly locked her eyes with his. "I don't want you here. I need to be comfortable in my own home."

"So be comfortable."

"You're a whole invasion, Roman. We're not used to having a man around. There's the toilet seat up and things changing, and I—"

"I'd like to hold you, Shelly. Just hold you. I know that you're scared for Dani and Uma and Pearl and you can't forget how Lauren died—"

"Do you know how many times Uma looks at her hands every day? Still seeing Lauren's blood?" Shelly wrapped her arms around herself and shook her head. "Do you think whoever it is will try to hurt her?"

"Mitchell will take care of her—if she'll let him." Roman hesitated and then came to look down at Shelly. "Here," he said simply and folded her into his arms, bringing her close to him.

Shelly closed her eyes and absorbed the comfort she needed so badly. "Dani—"

Roman's lips moved against her temple. "I know. You're worried about her. I am, too. Our guy likes to make his moves at night. Let me stay, Shelly. Please."

She knew how much that soft "Please" had cost him, a proud, arrogant man. He'd used it only once before, asking to be a part of Dani's and her life.

"For Dani's sake," she agreed slowly and moved away from him. "I couldn't bear it if anything happened to Dani."

"Nothing is going to. Tell me why you've never married or dated," he asked rawly, tension humming around him, ricocheting from the silence into her heart and lying there, pounding at her.

Roman stood still, his hands at his sides, looking so lonely she ached. She turned away, because she wanted to hold and comfort him, too. That wouldn't do, not with what hummed inside her, the need of a woman for a man. He'd been her only lover, and her body hadn't forgotten his in those eighteen years.

The truth was that she'd never wanted anyone else. Inside her, she knew that she'd bonded with Roman Warren, that he was in her blood and staying there . . . and now the fever was hot and mature and explosive—just like him.

"I thought about it."

"Dani said they were after you—some with marriage on their mind, and others who wanted to play."

Shelly thought of Walter Whiteford exposing himself to her, as if she'd be hungry for the likes of him.

"I don't owe you any explanations, Roman. I've got plenty to do without you interrupting me with talk all the time." With that, she whipped another shirt out of the plastic bag and began fiercely ironing it.

"You sure don't owe me anything," Roman said softly as he stood watching her, his arms crossed. "But I'd like to help."

She brushed away the tears burning her lids, her emotions frantically tumbling through her. She burned her hand and cried out, bringing the small wound to her mouth.

Then Roman took her hand, inspected it, and brought it to his chest. "I'm not much, Shelly, but I'm trying. I don't know if the station is a go or not, but I'm not leaving this time—unless you tell me to."

His eyes locked with hers and he brought her hand to his lips. The gesture was humble and honest. "That's all it would take, Shell."

When he turned and stood by the window, his hands braced against the countertop, his back stiff, she knew then that Roman probably needed redemption more than she needed her pride.

And she knew that she'd never stopped loving him. "Thank you for the dishwasher," she said quietly.

"Sure."

Roman stared into the night and wished he could take back all the years, the bars and the women. He had absolutely nothing to give a woman who had paid so dearly.

But he'd work his heart out trying . . .

TWELVE

"Hello, Everett. Nice night." Taking care to let Rosy work her way up Uma's front steps, Mitchell nodded to Everett. Uma's ex-husband sat on the front porch; his oak rocker creaking on the painted wood. The glass of iced tea at his side said Uma had been hospitable; Mitchell wasn't expecting any real welcome, yet he had to see Uma.

Images of her passionate anger at the garage stormed at him, generating an uneasiness that she would never speak to him again.

Whoever had tried to hurt Rosy had also served Uma a warning with that bullet; and he was definitely going to tuck Uma under his protection, too—if she accepted his apology or not. He wasn't letting whoever prowled Madrid and knew the habits and lives of the city hurt Uma. *Who could it be?*

Everett, as an unseated potential lover-husband, was a definite suspect to serve Uma a warning, but not to hurt her.

"Took you long enough. I thought you'd show up, and I wanted to be here when you did." Everett flung into the hot, honeysuckle-sweet August night. His usually neat hair was standing out in peaks and he hadn't shaved, his tie askew on his short-sleeved dress shirt. Mitchell recognized the ominous signs of Everett's bad temper; on the other hand in the last three hours of mulling at his house, Mitchell had shaved and dressed carefully. While pasting toilet paper on the tiny shaving cuts caused by his concern for Uma, he'd practiced his apologies to the mirror, and tried to put a logical spin on his actions as he tried to explain to Rosy.

His logical spin was very important, because Uma had to understand that he took care of himself. He didn't need a nurturer and a fixer; he needed Uma, his lover.

On the other hand, he'd hurt her. That was unforgivable, and he felt like a lowdown cur.

But then, a man had his pride. He couldn't have a woman meddling in his life. Once the rules of who stepped where were established, Mitchell intended to share Uma's bed every night. The segment in *The Smooth Moves List* on "Make-Up Sex" taunted him. He really needed to reach that bonding, to know that lovemaking with Uma had really happened.

The taste of her skin, her body swirled around him, those soft, hungry sounds had pursued him all day, contrasting with the pain in her expression when he'd ordered her to "get out."

Then her anger at the garage had shocked him.

Mitchell frowned at his highly polished shoes. Women's volatility and moods weren't something that had mattered and he sensed that what preceded the make-up sex, referenced in her book, was very, very important. He wasn't that easy to stun, and Uma the lover, Uma the hurt, and Uma the angry had battled across his mind all day. He'd snarled at Roman's sensitivity lecture, Lonny's silent accusations, and every time he looked at the dent in his pickup, smeared with Uma's car's red paint, he knew she had declared war.

By evening, Shelly's jab and the ominous fruitcake-baking warning had made him see how badly Uma ached. When a woman resorted to making fruitcake, the circumstances might be critical.

He just wanted to hold Uma—and keep her safe. If she wouldn't let him near her, he couldn't protect her.

If she didn't let him near her, he couldn't make love with her.

Careful of the peacemaking bag of Chinese fortune cookies he'd brought and letting Rosy plop onto the front doormat as he held her leash, Mitchell eased into the rocking chair next to Everett. Mitchell felt like a schoolboy about to be lectured. He wasn't certain how he liked that served by an ex-husband.

"I ought to beat you to a pulp," Everett snarled. "She's all worked up in there. You hurt her somehow. She's a good woman and she says she has feelings for you. She told me so last night at Pearl's."

Get out. Mitchell's words echoed in the night as the cat came to sit on the railing, yellow eyes studying the two men, tail twitching slowly as if watching a game to be played. Rosy snorted as if in agreement.

And within his home, Mitchell sensed that Lauren wasn't happy, either. The house had a closed feel to it, as if she had shut him away for hurting Uma. Mitchell shook his head; dealing with Uma, all revved and angry, and the sensations that Lauren might possibly still be in the house and not happy with him were enough to make him take a bracing drink while getting ready. He'd managed tough boardrooms; he decided he could manage two women, one alive and one not, who somehow managed to make him feel like a guilty brute-clod.

The cat had pushed the glass off the counter, breaking it.

On Uma's front porch, Mitchell stretched his taut neck within his collar. He had the uneasy sense that Lauren used the cat to transmit her feelings. Women and eerie sensations were enough to throw a man off-balance. That unsettling softness within him didn't feel right, not like a man's clear-cut emotions would feel.

When he walked into a board meeting, he was usually prepared with alternatives which would still get him what he wanted. However, this wasn't a business meeting. He'd wounded her and he'd have to apologize.

He had to apologize *delicately,* and yet firmly hold his line that she didn't step into some areas of his life. With Uma, that balance might be impossible. Her weapons weren't graphs and reports and surveys. Her actions all came from her heart.

"What's this about Uma baking fruitcakes?" he asked Everett.

"It's not good," the other man replied flatly.

A screen door creaked at the MacDougals' and Everett said, "Old Edgar is watering his wife's roses. At least he has a wife. I've been waiting years for Uma to see that we belong together. Then *you* come into town, and you don't have one damn intention of marrying her. I've waited twelve years since our divorce for her to realize that we are meant to be together. *Twelve years, and I don't regret a minute of being her friend, but I am going to be her husband again.* I heard about today—how she ran you down. Lonny said she was hot-tempered. Uma never gets angry or frazzled; she's a very safe driver, and Sissy said that Uma rounded the corner from Main to Maloney on two squealing tires. Someone has to protect her from you, and I'm that someone."

Mitchell stared at the cat. Uma hadn't exactly been in control last night—neither had he.

Apparently Everett was just getting worked up, his face tight with anger reflected by the rest of his body. Mitchell ran through the consequences of brawling with Everett—Uma's lifelong friend. They were a couple; he was an outsider trying to get an edge . . . rather, possession of Uma.

Everett's expression said he knew that Mitchell was determined to be a solid contender for Uma in round two. "You're pure trouble, and everyone in town knows it."

The door creaked open and from behind the screen Uma said, "Shoo. Get off my porch, both of you. The whole neighborhood is watching."

Mitchell turned, with his best smile, and found Uma scowling at him, a streak of flour across her cheek. She was definitely still simmering.

"No," Everett answered as the scent of baking cakes swirled out into the night. "I'm staying right here until I know you're okay. *He* can leave."

Mitchell wasn't going anywhere until he saw Uma and spoke to her—privately. He'd handled this morning wrong and knew it, and he didn't want Everett seeing him grovel. Uma was worth groveling over, though—but Everett was not included in the sorting-out mélée. "I could, but I won't, not until I've talked to Uma."

Uma stepped out from the screen door, holding it as if for protection. The circles beneath her eyes said she hadn't rested, her skin pale as her eyes flashed gray steel at him. Had he done that to her? Made her afraid of being hurt?

She looked down at Rosy, who had refused to leave the comfortable doormat, and blocked the full opening of the door. "I'll call Lonny."

Mitchell took in the flour on her hair, that precious little topknot, the tendrils swirling around her flushed face. He watched that delectable pulse throb in her throat and traced the flour dust over her checkered shirt and jeans and sandals, over the curves he wanted to hold close to him. He knew instinctively that deep inside her was the warmth and oneness that he craved.

Oneness. He wanted that all the time with her, not just sexual.

Not just sexual, he repeated mentally. She'd ruined him for other women—of course it was sexual, but it was different, too. And he didn't like being vulnerable. "You just do that. I'm sure the neighbors would like excitement."

The cat twitched his tail, waiting and watching the two men.

The door slammed and silence circled the front porch;

Mitchell hoped she would offer him a glass of tea. He'd never wanted an indication of welcome so badly in his entire lifetime.

"I've loved her all my life," Everett said slowly, fiercely. He reached to grab the sack of fortune cookies, dropped them to the porch, and stomped on them.

"Take it easy, Everett," Mitchell warned softly as Rosy grunted and stood, happily rooting through the plastic sack to the crushed sweets.

Everett's blue eyes blazed. "Just what's going to be left of her pride when you decide to move on, Warren? You going to desert, are you? You don't come from people who stick around."

"Lay off," Mitchell warned again. He'd heard enough about his mother. Also, Tessa's eye-opening jolt this morning, combined with Uma's hissy fit, were riffling his emotions. In a boardroom, he could close any discussion he wanted, if he wanted. Uma, on the other hand, acted because she cared with a nurturer's instincts, and he would be that brute-clod if he didn't find a way to negotiate an interaction with her—a oneness sort of discussion and an amenable finalization to the negotiations, which he hoped would end in make-up sex, concluding any more riffs in their alliance.

Everett lurched to his feet, the rocking chair he had vacated continued rocking and creaking. "Go away. The whole town is gossiping about how you were involved with Lauren's death, yet you have the nerve to—"

Mitchell heard a warning trigger cock inside him. He stood slowly, facing Everett. "I had nothing to do with that."

Everett's fists clenched at his sides. "I was wrong to leave Uma when the baby was due, and wrong to be gone so much after Christina died. I understood how empty she felt later, how when her father had a heart attack she wanted to stay here—and I made a bad mistake. But I always knew that Uma and I were meant for each other. She knows it, too.

With her father away, I'll take care of her. You're not wanted here."

"Let her tell me that."

"Don't you get it? She feels sorry for you," Everett shot back, as Roman's motorcycle purred to the sidewalk and Dani hopped off. Holding a small sack, she raced up the sidewalk and the steps.

"She's out of brown sugar and eggs. Mom sent some over," Dani panted as she glanced at the two men, facing each other. "Hi, Rosy," she said, bending to scratch the pig's head. She hurried into the house, and after nodding at the men, Roman looked up, suddenly interested in the stars.

Everett's temper showed in the vein in his temple, and Mitchell knew his wasn't far behind. Both men smiled tightly at Dani as she eased back out between them and hopped on Roman's bike.

With a look that said Mitchell would have to handle his own hot-tempered woman problems and his mistakes, Roman eased the bike into the darkness.

"You're leaving," Everett said tightly, his fists balled at his sides. "Now."

"Am I?" Mitchell smiled just enough to show that he wasn't going anywhere until he was ready, until he'd had his say with Uma—to tell her that he'd try not to act so hard-nosed about his private life, but that it was his own.

He watched Everett draw back his fist, prepared to block it—and then saw Uma peering through the lace at window.

Mitchell took the punch and knew he deserved it as he held Rosy's leash. He also hoped it would buy him some time with Uma. In bargaining negotiations, a loss could mean a good gain.

The connection stunned at first, and Mitchell allowed himself to waver just enough, before crumpling to the porch. He moved aside slightly because Rosy was rooting for more crumbs close to his face.

Uma was outside and Everett was hurriedly explaining—"Uma, I didn't hit him hard enough to—"

"You can help me get him into the house and then you must leave, Everett," she ordered primly.

Certain that his sacrifice had won him the prize—a few moments with Uma—Mitchell forced his pleased smile into an aching groan.

"I thought you might be pruning roses—when you're like this," Mitchell said warily as he sat in Uma's kitchen with a washcloth filled with ice cubes on his jaw.

"Like this?" she challenged instantly. She was still angry with him, and because she wasn't a vengeful kind of woman and because Mitchell had changed her, Uma frowned at him. Whatever Mitchell stirred in her, she wasn't on the outside of life looking in—she was in the center of the storm and enjoying the battle.

"Looks like you're working out a problem."

"I am. A big one—you." She had a computer full of work, a newspaper column due, stacks of paperwork, and because of Mitchell, she was baking fruitcake.

Several men in Madrid had chosen today to make themselves perfectly horrible. There was Mitchell's "Get out," and Everett's firm argument that she needed his protection, and then there was Walter.

Pearl's husband had decided that Uma needed his studly service—since it was apparently obvious to the entire town of Madrid that her years of abstaining from sex had ended.

Uma tore open a carton of mixed candied fruit and plopped it into a bowl, jabbing it with a wooden spoon. She'd managed for years to be retiring, helpful, and non-combative. Now she felt like taking up a sword and shield and issuing a Valkyrie call to announce that Mitchell had ended a sexual fast she didn't even know she'd had. She had two choices: to explore the new Uma . . . or not. *Who was she?*

After seeing her this morning, running back to her house and crying and wearing Mitchell's too-large clothing, the neighbors had quickly spread the gossip. They had added, of course, that Mitchell's former "painted woman" had come to claim him and that was what had hurt Uma after spending the night with him.

Edgar MacDougal, in his nightly rose-watering chore, had seen her enter Mitchell's house last night. As she had gathered her fruitcake makings throughout town, Uma had heard the whispers, and Pearl hadn't been quiet in the grocery store—launching into "You ought to be ashamed of yourself, Uma Lawrence Thornton. You should have remarried Everett a long time ago."

Uma still felt Walter's breath on her neck, the way he'd reached around her, fumbling for her breast.

She shuddered to think of him touching her. Telling Pearl wasn't an option; Pearl wouldn't believe that Walter could be anything but perfect and she'd be terribly unraveled. Uma couldn't bear to hurt Pearl, but the kick in Walter's privates had served him notice.

Mitchell quickly noted her shudder of revulsion. "Did I do that, make you feel badly about last night? Look, Uma," he began earnestly. "I was wrong about Tessa this morning—"

Uma bent to crumble a baked fruitcake onto a plate for Rosy. The sight of Mitchell, injured and lying on her front porch, flashed through her again. She'd wanted to hold him and soothe him and—of course he would have none of that, because he was a big, strong macho man who managed his life without her. *Get out.* "Of course you were. She came to help you, and—and what are you doing with Rosy? Is something wrong with Kitty and Bernard?"

"I'm babysitting. Look, Uma, there are just some things that—"

"I know. You're like your father, exactly like him, in dealing with relationships. You just slam doors shut on people who are trying to help. Do you think I try to meddle in everyone's lives, Mitchell? Do you think for one minute that if you didn't matter to me, I would ask Tessa to explain something that hurts her so deeply? Do you think I'd put you both through that if I didn't think it would help you?"

Uma bent to scratch Rosy's ears and adjust her big pink bow. The pig danced warily and Mitchell bent to place his big hand on her bristly back, murmuring to her. She quieted instantly.

Uma remembered the certainty, the safety in Mitchell's hands, the delight and the ecstasy of consuming and being consumed totally.

Get out.

She would be in control, even if her heart was breaking. *Get out.* "Nice, Rosy. Nice girl. Now, why did you say you were babysitting Rosy?"

"I didn't," he snapped.

Uma knew the moment was critical, and that Mitchell had to be handled delicately, firmly. She needed a moment to think, to remove herself from the situation in which she might pick up a gob of fruitcake batter and throw it at him. She pushed that notion away—Mitchell had made her lose control during lovemaking and today at the garage. She would regain her composure and revenge wasn't for her—or rather, it hadn't been, until Mitchell entered her life.

He did know how to push her over edges she didn't realize she had. "Let me just go turn on the cartoons for Rosy. Come along, Rosy."

Settling Rosy in front of the television gave Uma time to think. Clearly, Mitchell was brooding over how to approach her. It mattered to her that he gave grave thought to a foray into words and action with her. Mitchell wasn't the kind of man to spend much time negotiating verbal land mines, but apparently, he would try with her.

She gave him one redemption point.

When she returned to the kitchen, Uma decided to help him say what he must to feel better. "I know you've been single a long time, and independent. And I've always lived with someone. First my father, and then Everett, and after my father's heart attack, this living arrangement was convenient, while I sorted out my life. I've decided to get my own house and move out."

At that, Mitchell's expression hardened. "Oh, no, you're not."

Uma didn't like his tone. She crossed her arms and watched Mitchell come to his feet. "And why not, may I ask?"

Mitchell frowned at her and slammed the washcloth onto the table; ice cubes scattered and fell to the floor. "One of the things I came over here to tell you is that I should have handled you a little better, especially after last night."

Get out. The words speared her again. "When I am certain that Everett's punch did not hurt you too badly, I am going to ask you to leave . . . nicely, if possible."

Uma didn't like her emotional display this morning. She wanted more than anything to have Mitchell hold her in that safe way.

"Everett would tell me that everything is going to be just fine."

"I won't." Mitchell stood and looked around the clutter of recipe books torn from the shelf, the empty egg cartons, the cracked egg shells, a visible matrix of if she was right and Mitchell was wrong, or if Mitchell was wrong and she was right to be upset.

Mitchell was wrong—dead wrong. All she had to do was to understand this new volatile Uma.

He stood there, huge and powerful and smelling like a freshly shaved lime, one of her favorite citrus flavors. He'd obviously dressed with care, the summer shirt expensive and probably a holdover from his office days, when he was in charge. *She* was in charge in her own kitchen. His shoes, definitely not small town, were polished to a high gloss. Italian, probably. Which said he did not fit in her life zone.

He did not fit in her kitchen, or in her town, but he fit perfectly in her arms and very perfectly within her body.

But not in her life. She hadn't done anything wrong, and Mitchell had shut the emotional door on her.

He moved toward her and Uma trembled. She wanted to hold him, yet pride said she was right and he had to make the distance, accept that she'd invited Tessa because she cared for him, and couldn't bear him thinking that he was responsible for Fred's death.

In defense of Mitchell coming closer, she held up the dripping egg whip in front of her. A long, slimy ooze slid to his shoes and Mitchell didn't look down. Instead, that honey-brown gaze caressed her face. "What's this all about?"

"What? What?" she asked desperately, as she fought the need to move into his arms.

"This. Thinking of moving out, all the cakes, all the bowls out of the—" He scanned the cluttered kitchen. "It looks like you've used every spoon in the place."

"I didn't have time to wash them. I was busy baking. You have to move fast when making fruitcake." She leaned back as Mitchell placed his hands on the countertop beside her hips. "It takes time to chop nuts and put them exactly so on the cakes, and—"

He sniffed lightly. "Uma, dear heart. Have you been nipping at the rum?"

"Of course not. That's for the fruitcakes." But, furious with Mitchell, she had taken just a sip.

He leaned closer, staring at her lips. "You look all flushed and warm and cute. You used to pout like that when you were a child. Except now, it's very sexy."

She couldn't breathe, yet she had to defend herself; Mitchell could not be allowed to—"Tell me why you're here."

Mitchell seemed to go inside himself, searching for answers. She waited, and it only seemed natural to ease away the toilet paper scraps he'd used after shaving. She wasn't the only one upset, and that helped raise her spirits. "The bottom line, Mitchell. Tell me what matters to you and we'll go from there."

"I want you," he said slowly, his expression wary. "I make mistakes. I've been married, but I know that I never gave any part of myself to Serene. I read *The Smooth Moves List* this afternoon—that book you recommended to Lonny—and there is a chapter in there about Single City . . . about sharing parts of yourself in a relationship, or choosing to stay independent of the other person, despite being in a relationship. Pretty confusing, deep stuff, the kind a woman would understand and not a man. I don't know that I can do that, but I want you in my life more than I've ever wanted anything. The bottom-line question is, do you want the same thing—do you want me in your life? At least, for right now?"

She knew what this admission, this revealing of his private thoughts and needs, was costing Mitchell. His earnest expression warned her to be very careful of her words. She could only express her needs in familiar language: "A relationship, once crumbled, is like a cookie. It can never be put back together and a new cookie must be made."

She didn't understand Mitchell's indulgent smile. Then his expression changed to sincerity, his voice deep and quiet. "I can't hand you everything. I'm not made like that. I'm pretty much the way I am. But I didn't mean to hurt you. I'm sorry for that, Uma."

She couldn't resist framing his face with her hands. His skin was warm and rough and familiar, the bones strong beneath her hands, as blunt and stark as the man. The shadows he bore lay within the lines, that fierce frown shielding his wariness. Once, he hadn't liked her to touch him, and now she could feel his pain, the ache within him.

"You're special and thoughtful, Mitchell. You've done wonderful things in your life, taking care of Roman and building a life, and then having the courage to come back to so much pain and open it, trying to see inside yourself. Few people would do that, especially in an unfriendly town."

He turned slightly to kiss her hands and his lips came away with a dusting of flour. "Think so?"

Uma ran her finger over his lips and smiled at his uncertainty; Mitchell, when he wasn't locked inside his shield, was definitely appealing and sweet. "See? We're relating. That's not so hard, is it?"

"I want you," he repeated. There was no uncertainty in that vibrating, raw, honest statement, or in the hard length of his body pressing against hers. His thumbs lightly caressed her hips.

Uma closed her eyes and inhaled his scent, familiar and tender and safe. She gave herself to the light, warm searching of his lips across hers and pushed the ugliness that was Walter away. On the cusp of desire, held by hunger and pride, she returned the light nibbling kisses and allowed herself to float in the sweetness.

There were peaks and valleys in a relationship with a man like Mitchell, and an excitement she craved. Dealing with Mitchell wasn't peace and harmony, but worth the ride . . . he was a man of textures and depth and consideration. He'd come to her because she mattered enough for him to leave his shell. Sex was a part of what he needed, but the fierce tenderness in his expression said it was only a bit of something greater.

But then sex was the bond to their tenuous contract now, Uma needing that riveting fulfillment as much as he did.

She smoothed Mitchell's tense shoulders, nestled close to him, and knew that he wouldn't touch her until—

"I want you, too," she whispered against his throat.

Mitchell held very still, and then his arms were tight around her, his mouth hot and searching and giving everything.

"Uma, I—" he whispered roughly as his hand found her breasts, smoothed them, then slid down to come up inside her shirt. Framed by her hands, his face was suddenly warm, honed by desire, almost arrogantly male.

He needed her desperately, honestly, and she knew that he did not expose his needs easily—nor did she. Yet she needed this rawness, this honesty between them, clearing away damage that words could do. She needed him locked with her, deep within and pounding with her through the fiery path where nothing else mattered.

In a flurry of hands and kisses and caresses, Uma's shirt flew away with her bra, and Mitchell's shirt came free to her searching hands, her tongue tasting him, teeth nibbling.

She was strong and free and happy, Mitchell's volatile reaction to her every move an inducement for another. The deep, rich sounds of hunger drew her on, erotic and enticing as his face pressed against her breasts, the heat and roughness of his skin sensitizing hers.

The tug of his lips on her breast heated every cord in her body, straight downward until it gathered and smoldered and tightened. The connect was immediate, unexpected, and stunning, riveting her in waves of heat. She didn't have time to apply logic and consider that her body had been revved since last night, needing Mitchell's.

She didn't have time to consider feminine foreplay and reassuring him that he was more than a sexual need.

Uma simply dug in for the journey, trusting Mitchell as he eased into a kitchen chair, bringing her legs to straddle his lap. She fisted his hair, sucking in her breath as his fullness entered, stretching, warming, pulsing tight and deep within her. Mitchell's hands began a rhythm she caught and locked onto and hoarded, the fiery height of desire rising quickly as his mouth slanted against hers, his tongue repeating the rhythm of their bodies.

The pressure built, coming faster and hotter, and Mitchell's hand caught her hair, his face honed by passion as he watched her.

"Don't watch," she whispered desperately. Waves of pleasure flowed over her, heat pouring through her skin, or was it his?

With a harsh sound, Mitchell drew inside himself, his eyes slitted, his body giving to hers. "Uma . . ."

Pushed to the fiery peak, Uma took in the pleasure, absorbing, treasuring it and the caress of Mitchell's hands. She leaned heavily against him, her face resting near his throat as his hands moved over her, his face rubbing hers. "I didn't intend to have you like this—"

She smiled and nipped his ear lightly. "Liar."

"I was thinking of a bed and more time and—"

The telephone rang shrilly, and Uma couldn't move. Mitchell tensed and reached for the wall telephone while holding her tightly within one arm. "What?"

His body was already hungry again, and Uma sighed, rocking gently against him. Mitchell breathed harshly and closed his eyes as she experimented with an exercise that had tightened her lower belly. He groaned slightly and then frowned as the caller began to speak.

Mitchell glanced at Uma, who was just smoothing his shoulders and wondering where she could nibble. He was like an unexplored, exciting territory just waiting for her. She traced his nipple, watching it peak.

"Umm. I'm helping Uma with a household project, Mike. Can't you take care of him?"

Mike's voice rumbled urgently, and Uma studied Mitchell, whose expression said he was torn between hunger and frustration. She decided tempting Mitchell could wait until she had his full attention. She eased to her feet, took the telephone, and braced it in the crook of her neck while she crossed her arm in front of her breasts and held a kitchen towel in front of her.

"Yes?" she managed to say, and knew her husky tone probably reflected their lovemaking just heartbeats ago.

Mike's voice cruised across the lines. "I need you to come pick up Everett. He's mooning about losing you to Mitchell Warren. Uma, the guy waited twelve years for you—the least you can do is to come pick him up so he doesn't embarrass himself even more."

"Uh—" Uma couldn't think, blindsided by the nude, evidently aroused male sitting before her, his arms behind his head.

The heat inside her body seeped outward, wrapping her in a full-body blush. She turned away from that dark intensity to try to focus on what Mike was saying. "Umm . . . Mike, do you suppose—?"

Mitchell's arms slid around her, cupping her breasts, his face hot and rough against hers, his breath swirling in her ear. The hardened length pressing between her thighs said he was going to finish what she had started, experimenting with him.

"I'll be there in a few minutes," she said as Mitchell's hand slid lower, caressing her.

She managed to hang the telephone on the cradle just before Mitchell gently bent her toward the counter. Blunt and hard, he eased intimately into her femininity and instantly the dizzying pleasure jolted through her. "This isn't . . . ah . . . very conventional . . . ah—oh, my . . ."

Mitchell's ear nibbles were very effective, she thought distantly as she gripped the counter, and in the living room, cartoon banjo music played happily as Rosy grunted.

She had her own problems, Uma decided, trying to keep a grip on the fast-moving heat within her, and then Mitchell touched her just there—

THIRTEEN

It was true—men did have wolfish smiles. Mitchell was absolutely smirking as they sat at Everett's table in Clyde's Tavern.

She scowled at Mitchell, whose shirt buttons were torn from their mooring. The flour smudges on his face weren't too noticeable, but the gob of batter at his temple was. She reached to brush his cheek and to remove the evidence that she had actually, actually—right in her mother's kitchen . . .

The last session of lovemaking, the one where she had clawed at a stack of neatly folded dish towels and heard her long, riveting cry echoing in her own mother's kitchen— *her mother's kitchen*—Uma's legs wouldn't have supported her. While Mitchell held her from behind and caressed her and she gradually surfaced *one more time*, Uma had tried to remember what was important, what pressing issue—other than Mitchell—had to be handled.

She was certain that their last time together had something to do with male possession, a primitive sealing of ownership. Uma shivered as Mitchell reached to lightly stroke the back of her neck with one finger. His sultry look said that collecting Everett was only a detour on the lovemaking trail.

Vince Gill's love songs throbbed from the jukebox. In the

light of the neon advertisements over the bar, couples slyly looked at the threesome featured in Madrid's newest gossip. After all, Uma Thornton was known to be a logical, controlled woman and just today she'd shot down Main Street in her car, tires squealing. Her neighbors had verified that Mitchell had left her house early that morning carrying a tool box and wearing a heavy growth of beard. Men at the bar shot curious glances over their shoulders as she sat between Mitchell and an evidently, but pleasantly, drunk ex-husband.

She glared back at them. She'd known them all her life, and what's more, she knew the stories of their ancestors, the good and the bad. She'd been at their weddings and their children's baptisms and listened to their tales of divorce woes. In one case, she had even acted as matchmaker. She leveled a stern stare at them. If she had a day out of her normal calm, she should be allowed. So what if she was sitting between her ex-husband, who had waited twelve years for her, and a new lover—a new, still-simmering lover? Neither man was showing signs of leaving the field to the other. She chose to battle the crowd, turning to them. "What exactly are you looking at?"

Immediately their heads turned away.

Straightening her shoulders, determined to preserve some dignity, Uma poured coffee into Everett's cup from the carafe Mike had brought; she received a woozy, happy smile from him. "No, thanks. I'll have another of whatever Mike has been bringing me."

"You've had enough of those. Drink the coffee," she stated, heedless of her sharp tone. The last thing she needed everyone in town to see was her disheveled, still stunned by Mitchell's last little surprise.

In her own mother's kitchen! Uma smoothed her hair and tried to think of her best fortune cookie reassurance. It escaped her.

That last time, Mitchell had wanted to prove his point—

that she was his. It was almost a controlled lovemaking, as though he were determined to hold her on the point of pleasure, just to make another point. She wasn't certain she liked that—her knees were still wobbly, her body full and heavy and sated, her breasts aching slightly from the light nibbling of his teeth, the suction of his hot mouth—

Uma inhaled raggedly and her flush deepened as Mitchell smiled at her. It was a knowing, sensual smile of a male who knew that he had pleased a woman to the maximum. She mentally labeled him as "Maximum." Maximum everything—concentrated, heavy duty, powerful, big maximum.

At her side, Rosy sat sniffing at the table goodies. In the mélée to get her to leave the television—because Mitchell insisted on bringing her with them to the tavern—Rosy's bow had slipped slightly.

Uma adjusted it and frowned when she noted the deep puncture wounds in Rosy's bristly hide. A questioning look at Mitchell drew a warning "Tell you later" frown.

"I love you guys," Everett was crooning. "First time I ever saw Uma all wrinkled and her hair sticking all out. She's always so perfect and cool, and now—"

Everett tilted his head to study her. "Now, Uma looks hot and kinda simmering and on edge. She was never ever like that when we were married. In fact, now that I think back, she was kinda boring. Every day was the same old routine. Everything in its place. A woman like that can put real stress on a man. I think maybe she was like my mother."

He reached to carefully pick something from her hair. He studied it keenly. "Looks like fruitcake—candied pineapple, I think. Is it Christmas?"

"It's the first week of August, and I was never like your mother." Uma shoved his hand away and tried to smooth her hair.

"Well, you were comfortable, like an old shoe. Maybe that was why I loved you. Why I still do."

"I love you, too, Everett. It's because we're friends and we grew up together. Those kinds of friendships usually last."

Mitchell's smile was angelic, innocent, and she knew he wasn't. Oh, how well she knew he wasn't.

While Everett patted Rosy and was momentarily distracted crooning to the pig, Uma leaned to whisper to Mitchell, "Just where would you learn something like that?"

"Huh?" he asked too innocently.

"You know," she shot at him in a low voice.

Mitchell's smile widened, humor crinkling the lines at his eyes. "Not here."

Hurrying to get dressed and hustling a protesting Rosy into her small car hadn't given Uma time for control or composure. She needed caresses and afterplay and—

"You're looking all steamy and sweet, honey," Mitchell said in that deep, husky tone that said he also would have preferred a longer ending to their lovemaking. He poured Everett another cup of coffee and leaned back to place his lips against her ear. "I was just thinking that one of those candied cherries might look tempting in your navel."

An electric quiver shot through Uma and headed straight for her oh-my. There it lodged and hummed and heated. She crushed the napkin in her hand, her nails digging in deep to her palm.

She wanted to drag him home and have him.

Uma put her hands to her face and found it hot. She'd heard about the sexually addicted, but that couldn't be happening to her; she'd always been so controlled.

In an effort to distract herself, she launched another topic. "What happened to Rosy? You never did explain why you have her."

Mitchell's expression changed, that closed, dangerous look he'd had when discovering the bullethole in her window and telling her about the danger to Shelly. As Everett's head nodded to his chest, Mitchell put a hand out to brace him upright and spoke quietly. "Kitty and Bernard brought her over. Someone knows their early nightly schedule to let her wallow in their backyard mud hole before cleaning her for the night. Whoever is causing trouble dropped a barbed wire noose around her neck and tied it to a post. The Ferrises had taken out their hearing aids, and they didn't hear her squealing until the neighbors complained. Fighting the wire, Rosy ran around the little slide they'd made for her and almost strangled herself."

"And they called you?"

"I'm Rosy's babysitter until this thing is over. I happened to tell them one time that I had worked as a security guard . . . so naturally, I'm qualified to keep their pig. They're more afraid for her than they are for themselves. Try giving a pig a bath when she's scared. I had to get in the shower with her. The wounds aren't deep enough to do damage. I'll put more antiseptic on them later."

Mitchell nudged the cup of coffee toward Everett. Clearly, Mitchell didn't want to continue the discussion now. "Drink that, will you, chum?"

"I love you guys," Everett crooned drowsily as he placed an arm around her and Mitchell. "I thought I just loved Uma. But I think I love you, too, Mitchell."

Mitchell looked up at the balloons fluttering in the breeze of the ceiling fan. "Sure. Can we go now?"

Lonny's patrol car followed Uma's compact red one—stuffed with tall, broad-shouldered men—to her house. She supposed she looked conspicuous with Mitchell filling the passenger side, and Rosy and Everett, equally big, pressed together in the back seat, Everett's arm around Rosy.

While Mitchell and Uma were helping Rosy and Everett out, Lonny stood on the sidewalk. "Hey, Uma. Did you know that you've got stuff in your hair?" he asked, picking out a bit of dough. He sniffed at it. "Fruitcake. Heard you were baking that after getting all worked up at the garage earlier."

She didn't want to discuss fruitcake or her "ungrip" on her emotions just then. Uma eyed him and smiled tightly. "Shouldn't you be getting home to Irma? Say, just how is that sexual potency formula working? Okay?"

Lonny zoomed out of her danger zone.

"Kitchen is a mess. Uma usually has everything in tip-top shape," Everett slurred as Mitchell urged him up the stairs to the Lawrence guest room. The two big men bumped against alternate sides of the stairway as they ascended to the bedrooms.

Rosy plopped to a rug as Uma set to furiously cleaning up the evidence of lovemaking in her mother's kitchen. Yes, she was thirty-six, but echoes of good-girls-don't haunted her.

Uma watched Rosy laboriously work her way upstairs as the Ferrises had taught her to do. Apparently, the pig wanted to get out of firing range.

The rapid clump-clump of a big man descending the stairs preceded the view of Mitchell's arms reaching down around the pig and hefting her upward. His return up the stairs was louder, due to carrying Rosy's weight.

It had been a very long day, from Tessa's upset to Mitchell this morning through the garage scene that Uma wanted to forget, right through the two very unconventional lovemaking sessions with Mitchell, to collecting an ex-husband from Clyde's Tavern.

Coming from upstairs, Rosy's squeals sounded more angry than frightened, but Uma hurried to her bedroom, where she found Mitchell kneeling on the floor, one arm wrapped around the pig and the other hand managing a tube of antiseptic. "You could help me."

"Or not," she stated, but for Rosy's sake, she knelt to help him.

Mitchell dosed Rosy liberally and then wrapped gauze around her chunky neck. "We're taking a stroll outside and then we'll be back. We need to talk."

Everett snored loudly in the guestroom and Mitchell

sighed deeply as he replaced Rosy's leash and led her down-stairs.

Who would want to hurt Rosy? Uma hurried to shower pieces of fruitcake batter out of her hair. As she collected the bits of candied fruit and nuts from the drain catcher, she was horrified at the amount of evidence Mike and Lonny must have seen.

Then, after a long day, she gave herself to the luxury of her shower, the warm spray, the scents—

And Mitchell stepped into the shower, his size crowding her against the wall. Through the steam, she recognized that sensual look. "Not one more time today. I need to get back into one piece, and my ex-husband is sleeping in the other room. I am starting to doubt who I really am. I knew, and now I don't—because of you. Peaks and valleys, all in one day, aren't me, and everyone knows it. It will take me forever to live down today. I was totally out of control—and it's *your* fault."

"I have no idea what you're talking about," he said, as he calmly began soaping himself. She was still crowded against the side as he stepped under the shower and shampooed in less time than she could turn around.

The shower curtain opened and closed, and the water and steam enclosed her in privacy.

So he was done? Not desiring her after making love that morning and twice that evening? Just like that?

It was silly to feel disappointed that Mitchell had had his fill of her, of the pleasure between them—*wasn't it?*

Uma dried furiously, wrapping a towel around her head and another around her body. She braced herself, turned the doorknob, and stepped into her bedroom.

Mitchell lay on her sheets, a towel resting over his hips, his arms behind his head. Rosy was already snoring gently on the braided rug beside the bed. In the guest room, Everett's snores sounded like a chain saw.

Unused to this intense intimacy, Uma hurried to her bedroom's dresser, extracted a prim set of cotton pajamas, and returned to the bathroom. After dressing and brushing her hair, she braced herself once more to see Mitchell.

This time, he was wearing his slacks and sitting up, scratching Rosy's ears. He patted the bed beside him and Uma sat down. "Who would want to hurt Rosy?"

"That's the question—who? Are you up to talking? I think you may know something that can add all this up. Lauren's killer, the dead shooter, Rosy, the accidents around town. Some small thing might turn into a lead."

"Yes, of course. What do you mean, 'accidents around town'?"

Mitchell hesitated, then said quietly, "Rosalie could have been murdered. Her daughter said that she never went upstairs. She always waited to have her family retrieve whatever she needed. She'd promised not to endanger herself by going up those stairs, and she'd kept that promise for years. Her sewing room downstairs was usually neat, orderly. But that day, she'd left her measuring tape on the floor and her sewing basket had tumbled onto the floor. The ironing board was upright, but the cord was unplugged and neatly wrapped around the iron—Rosalie used to leave it plugged in and just turned it off. She used it too much. And her appointment book was missing. She took very good care of that."

"Mitchell, if you're thinking that one of her customers pushed her down those stairs—she's altered clothing for almost everyone in Madrid for years."

He playfully waggled Rosy's ear the way her owners would. "There are a whole string of accidents that are starting to make sense. Whoever's out there is getting worked up to kill again. It's someone who knows the habits of the people here, their weaknesses and their life stories."

"Oh, Mitchell, I don't want to believe that—"

"Believe it," he stated grimly. "What do you know about Gerald Van Dyke?"

"His tractor ran over him. He was elderly; it was a farm accident."

"Try again. Lonny checked with his son, who said his father always was very careful not only to turn off the tractor and brake it, but to place blocks in front of all four tires. Van Dyke was meticulous about those blocks, and when he was found, they were a foot out from each. My guess is that someone moving fast pulled them out. The question is why they would want to hurt Gerald."

"Everyone loved Gerald . . . he'd been courting Rosalie for years, but she thought they were too old to get married."

"Maybe he saw something he shouldn't have. Maybe our guy didn't want witnesses."

She gripped his arm, feeling safe just by touching him, just as Kitty and Bernard trusted him with their beloved Rosy. "What can we do?"

"Talk . . . try to fit the pieces together. You know this town and the secrets in it better than anyone. And you could live with me." At his last words, Mitchell took her hand and brought it to his lips, watching her intently.

"You want to protect me."

He nodded and studied her hand in his. "I do. I think Shelly is the primary target, just by the evidence so far—she's had more accidents and that spray of bullets says she's made someone real angry."

"Shelly has never done anything wrong in her life."

"A lot of people think she has. This town holds a grudge. She was an unwed mother. She didn't give away her baby, like her mother wanted. It could be some friend of her mother's. We need to look at Mrs. Craig's friends, who she might have told about Shelly. Roman is staying with Shelly. He's put his plans on hold to open the garage for full business. Until this is over, he's sticking close to her and helping her with her cleaning business."

"She won't like that. Shelly is very independent."

"He's explaining the facts of life to her now. She'll want to protect Dani, if nothing else. She'll buy it until this is over."

Rosy's hooves began moving as if she were dream-running and Mitchell reached down to place a big, wide hand on her. "Night-night, Rosy."

Uma stared at Mitchell, trying to put the fiery lover of the kitchen into the man who had undressed and helped Everett into bed, into the man who was guarding a pig.

He shrugged at her questioning look. "Kitty told me what to say when Rosy is uneasy. The 'I love you, sugar-pie' part doesn't feel right somehow."

Those gold eyes darkened, narrowing on her. "So are you going to live with me or not?"

"Everything is happening so fast. Madrid has never been in the speed lane. I'd like to—I would prefer to adjust to these new events—I need to know who I am . . . I've changed . . ." she began properly, as she tried for logic when everyone in Madrid could be in danger and she had collected an ex-husband from Clyde's Tavern, and then there were the kitchen incidents, and of course, the way she had zoomed down Main Street.

Mitchell lifted an eyebrow. "No time. We need to bring this guy out in the open, to rattle him, to stir him up enough to make a move. He's caused Lauren to be killed. Shelly's wearing a scar that says he's serious about killing her, and he's only just warned you with that shot in the window. The BBs were warnings, too, after you'd been to my house. The shot was while I was here with you all night. He probably isn't out to kill you, or you would have been a clear shot at your desk almost any night of the week. Instead, he chose a night that we were together."

Uma tried to follow his logic. "You think that he doesn't like me seeing you?"

"I know he doesn't. And he doesn't like Roman or me coming back to disturb his plans. He's getting really good with a bow and arrow, and those other marks on the wind-mill paddles were from arrows glancing off—probably target arrows, like those used on the cows. It's likely that Shelly's car fire some time ago, and her accidents, were all planned."

"Could it be Walter?"

Mitchell frowned and asked, "Why?"

She shook her head, unwilling to tell Mitchell that Walter had been rejected by Shelly and her—Shelly's laughter when he exposed himself had made him furious, and Uma's knee in his privates had deepened that anger. Uma decided to have a very intimate chat with Pearl, not enough to upset her, but she would ask her just the right questions to get a sense if her friend's husband could be behind all this.

"He's a candidate. So is Mike. So are Lyle and the others."

"Mike?"

"Whoever it is likes Clyde Barrow–type guns, and Mike is a collector, though Lonny has already checked Mike's guns and they haven't been fired. And there's Everett, for starters. He had plans for you."

"I know. I'm sorry about that, but I tried to get him to move on. Everett isn't a possible. I know him too well."

"But I'm a complication. There's gossip. Those weren't ex-actly friendly nails in my truck tires," Mitchell pushed.

"Everett is good and kind and he likes everything in order, all shipshape. He could never hurt Rosy. He appreciates fine machinery and good appearances. He's not destructive at all."

"Sure. He's a saint," Mitchell said. "But someone did those things . . . they happened. You can't ignore them, Uma. Who-ever it is is starting to enjoy the game. That means he's done practicing and is ready for the real thing."

Mitchell took her hand and pressed it between his. "You're cold, honey. I know this is hard, but try to think—any little detail might help. Okay, we've been all through Lauren's pos-sible enemies. Now, tell me about Rosalie. Who were her friends, her customers?"

"So many people—she's been a seamstress for years. Everyone loved her."

"Someone didn't. I want you to live with me and help draw this psycho out so that he can't hurt any more people. The way I see it is that if we're real friendly, obviously living together, he won't like it. He'll come after me, not you, and I'll be ready."

Mitchell inhaled deeply, as if bracing himself to serve her a suggestion that might make her angry. "I thought we'd keep up the pressure on him, keep him so annoyed and busy that he'd be distracted from Shelly and Dani."

"I'll have to think about this, Mitchell."

"I want you more than I've wanted anything in my life," he stated rawly, unevenly. "I'll try. I'll really try to make you happy. But the decisions are yours as to the living arrangements—your call. For tonight, I'm sleeping right here, on the floor, next to my girlfriend Rosy. Everett is down for the count. We'll talk about this in the morning."

"That can't be true," Shelly said, when Roman had finished telling her of the danger in Madrid.

"Believe it." Roman's face was set in lines, as he watched her place aside her mending basket. He stood at the window, the drapes closed, the soft lamp light near her chair the only light in the room. In his usual jeans, shirt, and evening stubble, he looked tough and predatory, a contrast to the feminine room. He raked a hand through his shaggy hair and pinned her with those dark eyes. "Nothing is going to happen to either one of you."

"Dani? You think someone would hurt Dani?" Terror locked her fingertips to her armchair.

"She's a part of you—and of me. Though Mitchell and I agree that you are really the focus, and they've branded you with that scar."

Shelly's trembling fingers traced the scar at her temple. "Do you think that Uma will let Mitchell live with her?"

"He's going to protect her, one way or the other. And I'm going to protect you and Dani. That's how it's going to work. And Dani knows the situation. She's agreed to stay close— we're going to work on her bike and on her school work. She wants to test for her high school diploma, using a home study course."

The wry grin said he approved. "The kid is sharp, just like you. You did a good job."

"She's wonderful. But I'd rather send her away until this is over."

"I already suggested that to her, but she won't go. She wants to see you safe, and so do I, but she's not leaving."

Shelly still couldn't imagine anyone so dangerous prowling Madrid. "I'll be fine. There's Lonny and—"

"Dammit, Shell. This is serious. Where you go, I go."

She couldn't see him dusting furniture or lining kitchen shelves with paper. "I clean houses, Roman. Maids and cleaning women don't need bodyguards."

"I'll help. They'll get two for the price of one." His eyes were soft upon her. "You've turned white, Shell. We'll get through this."

"Lauren . . . whoever it was arranged to kill Lauren."

Roman took her hand, studying the capable rough palm. He folded it within both of his. "Those shots at the house and at Uma's said you're both on the list, too. Pearl's dog was poisoned, and she's almost had wrecks. But if Mitchell's plan works out, our boy will be so busy trying to get at Mitchell that he won't have time for anyone else. Whoever this is doesn't like him around Uma."

"Just don't alarm Pearl. She comes apart. Where's Dani? I haven't seen her for hours. If she's out there, we have to find her."

She was on her feet, tugging aside the draperies to look at the street, and Roman tugged her back. "Stay away from the window. That's a perfect shot. Dani is in her bedroom, studying. She's letting me break this to you. I don't think she had the heart to see you take this punch. But it's a reality—believe it. Someone in this good town is just getting warmed up to do some real damage, and it isn't going to be you or Dani . . . you can come out now, Dani."

Dani opened her door, a pair of headphones dangling from her neck. At Roman's warning look, she said, "So I took a break from the books. Music soothes the kid, and all that. How did she take it? Did you get the part where she's your Vargas girl and your Lamborghini all rolled into one?"

Roman eyed his daughter and his look said he hadn't. "Get a Coke or something, will you? And make sure those curtains are pulled in the kitchen, okay?"

Dani grinned. "Sure, Pops. It's so much fun to see you squirm."

"Smart mouth," Roman murmured with a grin as Dani left the room. "Well, you are," he said to Shelly. "My Vargas girl and my Lamborghini. Maybe you always have been. Since you've been through too much, I just thought I'd warn you, so you could see me coming—in a serious way, I mean."

Shelly placed her hand over her heart as Roman smoothed her hair, studying the lights in it. Her life had been harsh, but she knew what would happen each day. With Roman, anything was possible. To think that he would compare her to a calendar girl or to a finely tuned, sleek, expensive car stunned her. "Don't say things like that."

"You've got hair like silky fire. It catches the light . . . can you trust me on this, Shell? That I've never felt like this with anyone?"

He was too close, his hand caressing her nape, his thumb stroking her chin. Then, gently, he raised her face to his. "Shell?"

The storm of emotions swirled around her as she looked into those dark gold eyes, shadowed by the fringe of his lashes. He could make any woman swoon and he was focusing on her. The currents between them ran strong and vibrated within her until she looked away. "You're so unpredictable, Roman."

A corner of his mouth tugged up at that and he leaned closer, his lips just fractions from hers, his breath mingling with hers, his body warming hers. "So they tell me."

She couldn't move as his lips warmly caressed hers, slanted and teased and beckoned. She had to touch him and reached to place her hands on his shoulders. Roman inhaled sharply and opened his lips, nudging hers, his tongue tempting as his hand slowly moved downward to smooth her hip, then back up to rest on her side, just under her breast. She picked through the scents, the soap of his shower, to find that of his skin—dark and brooding and exciting—

Roman took her hands and placed her arms around his neck, tugging her full length against him, his body taut against hers. "It's like this with me," he whispered roughly. "But there's more. I just don't know how to give it to you. The right things to say to make it easier for you. You're so innocent that I—"

He closed his eyes and eased away from her. "I've been around a lot of women. But you're the one I want—if you'll have me. I'm trying to take this slow for your sake, but it isn't easy," he stated shakily.

She wanted to help him, to say something that would ease him, yet she feared herself and him.

And Dani was right, there was just something about nudging Roman that was exciting. "Tell me about the Vargas girl and the Lamborghini."

"Are you kidding? The two best things in any man's life. I've loved those calendar girls since I was—well, old enough to get steamed up in the back room with the door locked. Long legs, good hair, and pure woman in between. Just like you."

When he saw her blush, Roman spoke huskily. "Nice lines, purring like a Lamborghini motor, sleek and sweet and when touched just right, handling like a dream. I've got a whole bunch of mistakes behind me and a dream in front of me, Shell—you."

Dani chose that moment to come into the living room and sprawl full length on the couch, watching them. "So, Pops. Did you tell her that you and I are going to see good old Gram in the nursing home?"

Shelly thought of her mother's searing dismissal of her granddaughter. She couldn't let Dani be exposed to that. "Oh, no, he's not."

"She ought to realize she's got a granddaughter, and a good one. She ought to be grateful for all you've done for her. She certainly didn't do anything for you. Neither did I. That's why tomorrow morning you're going to Mitchell's—"

Shelly was furious now, her life being torn into shreds without her control. "I will not have you hurt my mother. Don't you dare!"

"Mom, give the guy a break. He's set to win her over. He's got charm, you have to give him that. She's a woman, after all."

Shelly knew that her mother would definitely say something to hurt Dani. Shelly also knew her daughter—she wasn't backing down from this meeting, not with Mr. Charm backing her up. "You two are just pure trouble. I'm coming, too."

"Not a chance," Dani and Roman said together.

"I'd rather you didn't see me in action, sweet cakes," Roman said after a pause in which Shelly wondered what happened to the pattern of her life, the safety of it. She felt as if she were on a swirling river, clinging to a mossy branch with her fingertips and the branch was creaking, giving way—

"Uma probably needs you. Mitchell is having this same

discussion with her, about keeping safe. We thought we'd drop you off and ride over to the rest home. Dani said she's going to look like Miss Sweet Innocent American Girl, didn't you, kid?" Roman was saying.

"Sure. I'm going to be a real sweetie," Dani said with a grin that mirrored Roman's.

Shelly threw up her hands. "I give up. You're not going to win my mother over with charm or anything else, so you might as well learn that right away. I've disappointed her terribly."

"Yeah, well. She's the disappointment. So am I," Roman said.

Dani rose and yawned. "I've got to get some sleep if I'm going to be sweet tomorrow. That's going to take some effort."

When her bedroom door closed, Roman said softly, "Shell, it's really important that you and Uma put your heads together and try to think of anything that might help uncover who is doing this. Any small thing."

Shelly eased onto the couch and Roman sat beside her. He eased a tendril behind her ear. "You look cute like that, all stunned and revved at the same time."

"I can't think of anyone—"

His arm reached to tug her closer. One look at his face and she knew he wanted her. "Roman, I know that you think you're doing the right thing, trying to protect us, but—"

"I am. Maybe I don't come from the best of folks, my mother running off and my father a drunk, but I want to do my best for you and Dani. I'm not going to treat her like my old man did me. She's never going to be worked until she drops. She's been hurt by your mother and it's eating at her. I've had enough things eat at me, and I don't want that for her. I'm going to give her what I can, and your mother is part of that enchilada."

"What things bother you, Roman? Your mother—"

A slash of his hand closed that thought.

"Your father, then," Shelly said softly and knew by the way Roman's head went back, that her guess was right.

"Neither one of them was a winner. That proof is in Mitchell and me."

"You should talk with Mitchell about what bothers you."

Roman shook his head. "I'm going outside and check the yard. Our guy likes to do his business at night."

He bent to his tool box sitting against the wall and took out a small, deadly looking automatic. He checked the clip and stuck it into his belt. "Don't think that I taught Dani how to shoot. She already knows how from that gang she runs with. If you've got time, we could use some food down at the garage tomorrow while we're working on the bikes. Her friends are coming in for some tips. I thought we might get some information from them . . . and I'm due for some family time and learning more about her. I figure her friends are maybe the best source. She's quite the girl, Shell. Just like her mom."

He reached into the tool box and lifted out a small wrapped box with a pink ribbon. "For you. Catch."

Roman watched as Shelly studied the pink roses on the paper. "You're my rose, Shell. You should have had something like that a long time ago. You can wear it or not."

He nodded and left the room while Shelly held the small, light box, fearing to open it.

Outside, Roman leaned back into the shadows, scanning Shelly's back yard. The old rose garden was overgrown and rambling, the arched trellis fallen. She didn't have time for herself, for what she enjoyed. She was sweet and innocent, and he'd taken too much already. But he wanted her in all the right ways, even if it was too late. The arguments of his father and mother echoed in the night. He didn't want his past to hurt Shelly, his bitterness about his father, the harshness that ruled their lives.

For Shelly, he needed either to forget his father's death, the guilt that he didn't help Mitchell, or to deal with it.

And the small diamond ring should have been bigger, coupled with a wedding ring. She deserved more.

Roman saw the racing wall in front of him again, felt the impact and the pain. But that terror was nothing like the fear of Shelly turning him away. Oh, he'd live all right, but a part of him would be missing . . .

In the morning, at Uma's breakfast table, Everett was embarrassed. "I know I've made a fool out of myself."

A very delicate situation, Mitchell decided. He'd let Uma and Everett settle the past and the present. He could only hope that Uma would let him be part of the future. This morning, she looked wary and a bit frightened, as though her world had just been torn apart.

Mitchell frowned as he finished the breakfast they had cooked silently together. He probably hadn't served the dangerous facts to Uma in the best way. But time and trouble didn't wait. Nor could he.

He wasn't exactly certain of what was happening between them, other than that he needed Uma, wanted her, and feared he might hurt her as he had the previous morning.

Shocking her in the kitchen—his need to show his possession of her before they collected Everett—probably wasn't something he'd find in her book. Okay, he was basically a primitive kind of guy, especially when it came to Uma. He'd have to watch that.

He knew why she and Everett had once fit so perfectly together. They hadn't walked on the darker side of life; they saw people as good and kind, and Mitchell knew they weren't—not always.

Everett looked at the eggs, bacon, and hash brown potatoes Uma placed in front of him. He turned pale, and

Mitchell pushed the plate away and replaced it with toast, juice, and coffee. Everett smiled weakly. "Thanks."

Mitchell dug into the plate he'd taken from Everett, and Uma blinked at him as though shocked that he could have another helping. He sensed her working up to a private discussion, the tension in the room was almost tangible.

Their eyes locked and held, and desire slammed into Mitchell. In his mind, he saw Uma's ecstasy, the way she took pleasure into herself, giving everything. From Uma's rosy, flustered look, she was also remembering the heated storm between them. Mitchell noted her nipples pushing against her dress before her blush deepened and she gripped a dish towel in front of her. From a few feet away, he could feel her pulse kick up, feel the softening of her body, recall the scent of it—if he didn't leave now, he'd be embarrassed to stand. "I just dropped in for breakfast and to see if you were okay," Mitchell said huskily as he rose. "I've got lawns to mow. See you."

Everett stood slowly, unsteadily, and extended his hand for a handshake. "I get the picture. You and Uma. Sorry I made such a fool of myself. But she's a rare woman, and a good friend."

Mitchell nodded and wondered whether, if the situation were reversed, he could have released Uma without a fight—but then, Everett was classy and Mitchell wasn't, not when it came to her.

He wondered if she would come to him that night. Or ever again. That she might not was terrifying.

Clyde polished his shoes, admiring the two-tone classic saddle oxfords. Mitchell Warren was just like his father, stepping in where he wasn't wanted—like the time Fred had stopped Clyde's father from whipping a horse that deserved it. Now Mitchell had Rosy in tow, but he couldn't always protect the pig. Or himself. He was far too visible, trimming hedges and mowing yards and cutting trees.

Mitchell was a top executive with a top paycheck. Why had he come back to Madrid?

It didn't make any difference. He'd be gone soon, one way or the other.

Clyde liked to move in the night, and eventually, Mitchell would step out into the night and find a bullet waiting for him. Dapper and well dressed, Clyde straightened in the mirror, smoothing his jacket and vest. Too bad he had to kill Rosalie; he really could have used her for more alterations. Fear wouldn't have worked on the old woman—threatening her children and grandchilden. Eventually, Rosalie would have made a mistake and exposed Clyde. He adjusted his hat at a cocky angle and checked the shoulder holster.

He had to carry on the outlaw's work. While Clyde Barrow had robbed banks and given away money to some of the poor people back then, his namesake could only try to right the wrongs in Madrid today.

Mitchell was big and tough, but not as smart as Clyde. When Mitchell was dead, Uma would settle for Everett, just as she should have long ago.

The gossips had broadcast Uma's sexual relationship with Mitchell, and that just could not be tolerated.

FOURTEEN

At ten o'clock the next morning, Uma hurried down the stairs from her office and out into the brilliant sunshine on her way to Mitchell's house next door. "Shelly is here. She needs you," he had said briskly, impatiently, on the phone.

Pearl's taut, frosty call earlier had asked Uma not to reveal anything she knew, Pearl would do her own research. "You *know* that Everett has left town. He's talking about moving to Denver," Pearl had said in an accusing tone.

"That will be good for his business. I'm sorry if you're hurting, Pearl. Truly sorry," Uma had said, meaning it. "Please call—or better yet, drop by for tea whenever you can. You had asked me to help sort your household things for that bazaar at the thrift shop. I know it's really important to you, something your mother started. I'll be glad to help you."

Uma ached for her; Pearl needed time to adjust to the lowered status of her ancestry, and she would.

On the sidewalk in front of Mitchell's house, Shelly stood watching Mitchell and Roman and Dani muscle Rosy into the motorcycle's sidecar. Shelly didn't look terrified, which was what Uma had expected; rather, she looked like she was trying to smother laughter. She turned to Uma and whispered, "I've seen a lot of rodeos, but nothing like this."

"Come on, you big slab of bacon," Mitchell was muttering as Rosy tried to jump out of the box prepared for her. "If we're going to be stuck with you, you're going to make it easier on us. We're not walking you everywhere."

"Sing lullabies to her, Mitchell. She likes that," Uma offered as Dani started to giggle.

Mitchell shot her a look, and Roman glared at his daughter. "Get on the bike, and no comments from the peanut gallery."

The scene was too comical, and Uma couldn't help laughing. She realized that it wasn't just the humorous situation; it was a release of the fear that had swallowed her, that a murderer prowled Madrid. Mitchell scowled at her. "She's got to go with Roman. He's pigsitting down at the garage today. He's cut one side of a bathtub down so she can hop inside."

When he placed his hand on Rosy, she instantly quieted. Uma shivered because she knew the strength of that touch, the emotions it could arouse or settle. The pig sat in the box prepared for her, and Mitchell clumsily adjusted the bow around her neck. A few Band-Aids were plastered at angles around Rosy's neck. Mitchell solemnly handed the tube of antiseptic to Roman.

"Oh, Rosy . . ." Dani crooned and held her earphones to Rosy's ear. The pig held very still as Rolling Stones music throbbed into the morning. She seemed to enjoy it.

Roman looked at Dani on the bike, Rosy in the sidecar, and Shelly, standing on the sidewalk. He walked to her with a meaningful look and she took a step backward, her eyes widening. Roman's arms looped around her and he dragged her close for a long kiss that left Shelly staring blankly at him. He added another little kiss on her nose. "Well, I'm off to school with the kids, honey. Kitty and Bernard are coming in this afternoon for a visit, and so are Dani's friends. Dani is going to walk Rosy with Kitty and Bernard. They feel safer, just in case Rosy gets away from them. Mitchell will bring you by later, and then we'll go clean those houses."

Shelly blinked and her lips moved, before she replied unevenly, "But I have houses to clean. I canceled this morning, but I have afternoon—"

"I just said that—I know we do. But you girls need some private talking time. Put your heads together and see if you come up with any candidates for Mr. Unfriendly," Roman said, swinging onto his bike. He revved it, and watching Rosy, carefully eased off into the street.

Shelly looked just as stunned as Uma felt. "You know, then," Uma said and Shelly nodded.

"It's awful. To think that someone killed Rosalie."

"Maybe others," Uma said gently, as they entered the door Mitchell had opened.

"Lauren," Shelly whispered inside the house as she held Uma's hand. "I feel her here still. So much is happening, Uma . . . all at once. Last night Roman gave me a ring—an engagement ring. He thinks I'm his Vargas calendar girl and his Lamborghini all in one. Imagine him saying something like that! Or that I'm his Rose. *Me.* Just plain Shelly Craig, cleaning woman. And now all *this*. He and Dani are going to see my mother. I know it's going to be a disaster and Dani will be hurt again. He just doesn't see—"

Uma understood Shelly's panic. "You know what I think would be a good idea? Cutting roses from Lauren's garden for her room. Let's go do that, and then we can talk. Mitchell says it's important that we put things together, try to remember anything that might help find this person. I think that should be our priority, don't you? To find this guy and stop him before he can hurt anyone else?"

Later, in Lauren's room, a full, lush bouquet of roses filled the room with perfume. "I don't like digging up dirty laundry—gossip and all the ugly things that happened in our town," Shelly said.

"Neither do I." Uma looked at Mitchell, who was leaning against the doorframe. "I think we should ask Grace to come back and help. She knows—"

"No." Mitchell pivoted and left the room. Sounds in the kitchen said he was making lunch and was none too happy, by the crash of pans and dishes.

"They do that. Just close off when something comes too near their hearts," Shelly said quietly. "I ached for them then and now. They had a horrible childhood, and Fred's death left another scar. Roman sinks inside himself at times, and it has something to do with his father's death."

Uma remembered Mitchell's reaction to Tessa's arrival. "They are difficult men."

"More than difficult—stubborn to the bone. Dani wants to meet her grandmother. I don't blame her. I would have told her sooner, but then, she didn't know her father's identity until now. And I couldn't risk—"

"I'll take care of it. Dani is right." Uma knew the brothers wouldn't be happy, but the risk was worth it—and Grace had a right to know her granddaughter.

Shelly hugged a pillow splashed with Lauren's needle-point roses. "Roman wants me to make a list of every accident I've had in the last year. He wants all the details surrounding them. He doesn't think they were accidents. I . . . I've been thinking I was losing my mind, worrying about Dani, distracted—I don't know. I can't bear to think that anyone in Madrid is so awful."

In the upstairs garage apartment that afternoon, Roman's gaze strolled down Shelly's body. She was clad in a T-shirt, jeans and tennis shoes, her regular working clothes. With the Vargas calendars behind her, she looked like one of the models, and was obviously nervous to be alone with him.

"Well? How did it go?" she asked too briskly, studying Dani's homework on his desk.

Roman couldn't resist teasing her. "How well did what go?"

"Oh, you know. The visit at the rest home? My mother? Dani said you both went."

"Super. Are we ready to start cleaning?"

"Not you. You're not going with me. But I've canceled my regular this afternoon, too, for the first time. Mitchell doesn't think there's any danger during the day, and that's when I clean. I can't have you underfoot every day and night. And you're not messing with my schedule after today. So just tell me what happened with my mother."

He could always count on Shelly, he thought, as those green eyes lasered through the shadows to him and the sunlight from the window caught the reddish tint of her hair. It was long and straight and silky. He wanted to wrap his fist in it and take that sweet mouth, but he wouldn't. She hadn't been treated like a woman, or a sweetheart, and he intended to give her that much.

"Tell me what happened," Shelly ordered fiercely again. "Did my mother say anything to hurt Dani?"

Roman thought of how the old woman had looked, bitter lines on her face, refusing to look at Dani—or at him. Her voice creaked with age and anger. "You think you two can just waltz in here and tell me that he's your father—a Warren, Fred Warren's boy, that no-good."

Her narrowed eyes had been green as Shelly's. "Look at you both. Now, who would want to claim you?"

"Your daughter did," Roman had said quietly. "She's like you, with a lot of heart—a fighter."

"Like me?" The old woman's head had snapped back as if taking a slap. "She shamed me, shamed our family. Look what we did for her. She was all set to go to college, and then you—a Warren—came along and ruined our lives. That is, if you're telling the truth now."

She'd glanced at Rosy sitting on the lawn, studying the newly watered gardens of the rest home. "What's that pig doing here, wearing that fancy ribbon?"

Roman had ignored her question and hadn't wanted Dani to hear his next words; he'd leaned close to Mrs. Craig's wicker armchair. He had adjusted her laprobe and whispered, "Listen to me, you old witch. Shelly loves you. She's working herself to death keeping you here. She's gone around you, trying not to upset you, but *I* won't. Dani is *her* daughter and *mine*. I thought we could all be a family, and maybe, just maybe, you'd like to take a spin with us someday in my motorcycle sidecar . . . or come to Shelly's for dinner. And if you really behave, you can probably stay overnight. It's your choice. Now, you can sit over here and chew on that bitterness until it eats you, or you can show Shelly the respect she deserves. She's raised a fine daughter, and Dani is going to college. You can be proud of her."

Mrs. Craig's stony face said she wasn't talking or listening to more, and tears shimmered in Dani's eyes. She'd been silent as they drove back to the garage, silent as she studied in his room. In the garage below, Roman had worked with Jace and his friends. The tough-looking girls who had gone up to chat with Dani had come down pouting. Sensing a gray mood in the garage, Rosy had stayed inside her bathtub.

Now, in the room above, Roman turned to Shelly, studying her as she stood in the August sunlight slanting into the room. Would she accept his engagement ring? He wouldn't blame her if she didn't. Pride—or was it fear?—stopped him from asking her about the ring, about marriage to him. He didn't know how to handle these gentler emotions. "Your mother is coming along. It's going to work out."

"I don't believe you."

Reacting instantly, he snagged her wrist and drew her into his arms, whispering fiercely against her cheek. He rocked her against him, just as someone should have been doing for years. "You've got to trust someone now, Shelly—I'm hoping it's going to be me."

Her body was stiff against his and Roman knew how difficult it was for her to accept another's help, especially his. She was trembling, fighting herself now, fearing to trust too much, fearing for Dani, an independent woman who needed support.

"I'm so sorry, Shell. I'm sorry I wasn't here for you. But I won't say that I'm sorry you gave me Dani. I feel . . . I can't tell you how I feel about her, just that she's a part of me already," he whispered against her cheek, smoothing her tears with his lips. He caressed her neck with his fingers, trying to draw out the tension, wanting to take it into him and protect her.

"You don't think he'd hurt Dani, do you? I just can't believe anyone could be so cruel as to cause Rosalie's and Gerald's deaths. None of this makes sense. Pearl's girls have spent the summer away and they'll be going to boarding school—they won't be in danger. Maybe I should send Dani somewhere, too, just until this awful person is caught . . . oh, I do hope he's caught before—it's just awful, Roman. Madrid has always been so safe, and then Lauren was killed."

"Did you and Uma come up with any ideas?"

Shelly couldn't yet admit that evil lurked in Madrid. "I know," he soothed grimly, when she shook her head. "But the pieces will come together."

He also knew that Dani wasn't going anywhere. She was just as stubborn as he, and she wanted to stay with her mother. Roman closed his eyes as Shelly relaxed slightly against him, his own doubt that she would trust him easing. "We'll get through this, Shell. I promise. Everything is going to work out."

And he prayed it would as Shelly turned slightly to him and their lips brushed. The taste caught and held and Roman took the sweetness into him, savoring Shelly in his arms. He saw himself in those green eyes before they closed, and with a quiet sigh, she opened her lips slightly against his and whispered, "You're afraid of me, aren't you?"

"Really afraid," he admitted unevenly, rawly. Her body was all soft beneath his easy caress, beneath her breast, her waist, and the gentle curve of her hips. "I want to do everything right with you this time, and I haven't ever been down this road before. I've lived with women, but when things got tough, I rolled on. I wasn't ready to make any commitment because there was always you."

"You're not so tough." She smoothed his hair, studying him with those meadow-green eyes.

"Just keep looking at me like that, and you'll find yourself beneath me on that bed." Roman wasn't too certain that he could leash his need for her; he'd never tried with another woman, but Shelly deserved every bit of patience he could manage.

"Maybe that wouldn't be so bad." Her lips were brushing his, lightly and with enough impact to send heat throbbing through his body.

He wanted her desperately, wanted to wrap himself in her, taking everything, making her a part of him, to hold her, to keep her safe and close and sweet. The ache was more than sexual, filling a need—it came from within his heart and both terrified and consumed him. What if he hurt her?

His body told him to dive greedily into lovemaking with her, to fill himself with her, to forget everything but Shelly.

His mind cautioned and wondered and feared and he eased away, holding her upper arms as she leaned toward him. Her soft, sensual expression sent him a jolt of sheer longing. "I don't know how to do this, Shell . . ."

Her eyes were soft, filled with him, and with something more than desire. He had enough experience with women to know the hot grab of desire, empty of everything but the satisfying of basic urges. Whatever was in Shelly's eyes now terrified him—it said she respected him, a tender worship.

Roman had had women racing fans adore him, but Shelly's expression seemed good and still and solid, as if it would never change.

He kissed her hard twice, slanting one way and then the other, then stepped back, more afraid of what tangled between them than he'd ever been of smashing into a racing wall.

"What was that?" Shelly asked quietly, her green eyes seeing too much.

Roman went to stand at the window, looking down at Maloney Street baking in the sunlight. "I don't know. You get me mixed up."

Shelly came to stand behind him. "You don't want to admit how good you are. You're afraid to believe in yourself. Believe in yourself, Roman. You're wonderful and kind . . . with the stuff heroes are made of," she added softly.

"Some hero," he muttered, more afraid of Shelly and his feelings.

She leaned against his back, her hands stroking his arms. "Jace came to see me today and apologized for acting smart. He said you'd made a difference in his life, because you'd managed to pull yourself out of nowhere and touch people's lives, like his. You've influenced him and his gang and they're assessing the rest of their lives. He said you're his hero, someone with enough—ah, male organs—to drop the macho act and tell it how it is, the problems in your life that you had to stand up to—like not taking drugs any longer than you had to for your knee. Dani and Jace are through, but he told me that he hopes he can find a girl to cherish, the way you said men should think of women—not to use them."

"They're good kids, just a little mixed up." Roman liked working with the young crowd, listening to their problems and trying to help. He'd held more than one boy as he cried.

"Not everyone thinks so. You saw something in them that

no one else could. You gave them something, someone to believe in them. That's important. You're afraid to admit how
wonderful you are, but I'm not. You're upstanding and brave
and true and unselfish, and you have a good heart. You're a
hero, Roman, like it or not."

That evening Mitchell stood beneath Uma's office window. In
stained work clothes, he looked big and tough and unmov-
able. She sensed that he'd stand there, watching her house
until—

She glanced at the woman in the shadows of the room, a
woman familiar with her mother.

A friend in Oklahoma City had collected Grace Warren
from the airport and delivered her to Uma's house. With
good bones beneath good skin, Grace was still a slender, stylish woman with streaks of gray sweeping back from her tem-
ples to blend into her raven chignon. The circles beneath her
brown eyes said she probably hadn't slept, but her sky blue
traveling suit was immaculate and stylish, reflecting her interest in clothing. Now retired, Grace had sold her small dress
shop, the finances invested, providing her with a good in-
come.

In Madrid on Uma's invitation, Grace feared her sons' reactions to her. Very much a lady, Grace sipped her tea as Uma
spoke to her father on the telephone.

When the call ended, her father's concern echoed harshly
in the soft room. His voice had been raised and quivered with
outrage. "You what? You think you love that Warren thug?
He's probably tied up with a crime syndicate. He's no good,
and neither is his brother. I'm coming home to settle this—"

"This isn't between you and me. This is between me and
Mitchell."

It had taken her a good half hour to calm Clarence while
Grace waited quietly. Uma chose to omit telling her father

about the dangerous situation in Madrid. He would only complicate matters by coming home now.

"I'll be fine, Dad," she'd said finally, and hoped it was true.

She glanced at the duct tape covering the bullethole in her window and shivered. Mitchell would stand there, in open sight of a murderer, until he got what he wanted—or until he died. If his suspicions were right—that the murderer did his dirty work at night—then . . .

If Mitchell just stood there and let himself be killed out of stubbornness, she'd kill him herself. Her fingers clenched into fists and she studied them. Until he'd come to town, she'd managed to survive without a storm of unsettling emotions—except for that infamous incident with Billy at the yard sale.

Mitchell touched her at a primitive, simmering, boiling, snapping point that no other person had drawn from her. She mentally ran through Charis's recommended slow count for controlling her emotions and pushed open the window.

Mitchell, in a stormy snit, was not exactly perfect to present to his mother.

"Mitchell, I'm just fine," she called down, and watched his expression harden.

"Get the hell away from that window," he returned fiercely. "You make a perfect target."

The order snapped her head back and strained her already ragged nerves. She preferred logical discussions, and this man was serving her curt one-way arguments. Her only option was to reply tit-for-tat. "Well, so do you."

His head tilted arrogantly and he served her another volley. "Then whatever happens to me will be your fault, won't it?"

Uma decided if he was already in a bad mood, she might as well give him one more problem. She held out her hand to Grace, who shook her head. "He sounds just like Fred. Demanding when he could be asking."

"Your son isn't perfect," Uma said. "But he has his good moments. This isn't one of them. Come stand by me; I'm not backing down from this. Mitchell and Roman should know the whole story of what happened to your marriage. They need to understand you and Fred."

"I don't know that I understand."

"You loved him, didn't you?"

Grace's expression was fierce, tears shimmering in her light brown eyes. "I adored Fred from the moment I saw him breaking those horses almost forty years ago. I've never loved anyone else."

I've never loved anyone else, Fred had said, when he'd talked to Uma's mother all those years ago. Uma glanced down at Mitchell, just as stubborn as his father, and prayed that she was making the right choice in trying to bridge the years of bitterness. It was in her nature to heal and help, and if he couldn't accept that, they were apt to find the same end as Grace and Fred.

Uma ached for all the lives that had been torn apart. "Then it's time all this was straightened out. And we all need to work together to help stop whoever caused Lauren to be killed. What you might know could be helpful in finding him. Grace, I'm not backing down because Mitchell is down there yelling loud enough to wake the dead. Dani deserves to know you. Come stand by me."

Grace moved slowly, gracefully, and Uma took her hand, framing them both in the window for Mitchell's view. His expression changed from stunned to bitterness, and whatever he was saying, low and fierce, wasn't sweet.

"Let me speak to him privately, please, Grace. One who cannot be changed must be moved," she muttered. She hurried downstairs and out onto the sidewalk to face Mitchell. His expression wasn't happy.

"What the hell have you done now?" he demanded instantly, his face hard in the dappled evening shadows. His eyes slashed at her, and the vein in his throat throbbed beneath tanned skin.

So much for intelligent conversation, Uma thought. "I've invited your mother back to Madrid. What she knows about old Madrid might be a help, and she has a perfect right to get to know her granddaughter."

"Of all the harebrained—" His expression was taut, those golden eyes pinning her, his body taut as he held Rosy's leash. His gaze ripped down Uma's loose cotton dress and back up to the twin braids running over her shoulders and breasts. Uma felt as if he'd reached inside and tugged her toward him; she felt the earth shake beneath her feet, and braced herself against that sensual tug. Yet he hadn't moved.

Instead, he issued a no-quarters-asked statement. "It's getting dark. Are you staying at my house tonight?"

She wasn't letting him push her now. "I have a guest. I can't very well leave your mother."

"You think that you can make everything just peachy, don't you? How do you justify her running out on us?"

"Grace did not run out on you, or Roman, or Fred. His pride forced her out. But you don't want to know the real truth, do you? You'd prefer to cling to your bitterness, digging in so deeply that you won't listen to the possibility that as a boy, you got the wrong impression and as a man, held it tight inside you, feeding on it."

"Why are you mixing in this? Don't you have enough to do running everyone else's lives?" Mitchell glared at Grace who had come to take Uma's hand. Then he turned and stiffly walked away, leaving the two women on the sidewalk.

"He looks so much like Fred," Grace said unevenly, her hand trembling in Uma's. The older woman laughed unevenly. "Acts like him, too. You love him, don't you?"

"I think I do. But at times like this, I could just—"

"I know. I'll be fine here, dear, if you want to go to him. I don't want to cause problems between you. . . . He's so much like Fred," Grace repeated, as tears came into her eyes.

Uma knew that Grace was close to breaking down. Uma placed her arm around the older woman. "Let's go inside. Mitchell will listen to reason. He's a good man. He just needs time to think."

Later, the sharp rap on the door and the broad-shouldered silhouette blocking the door window said that Mitchell had already done his thinking. Uma braced herself and smoothed her hair before opening the door.

"Oh, hello, Mitchell." She tried to sound casual, but her senses were taut and fearing that she had ruined their tenuous relationship.

"I'll be outside tonight, watching the house." He glared at her and handed her Rosy's leash. The pig trotted into the house, her snout sniffing for the remembered scents of fruitcake.

Shelly's pickup soared down the street and Dani burst from it the moment it stopped in front of Uma's house. "Hi, Unc," she said, shouldering past him as he held the door.

"Come in, Dani," Uma said. "Your grandmother has been waiting to meet you."

Shelly glanced up at Mitchell as she passed into the house. "Your brother isn't happy about this. But Dani has a right to meet her grandmother."

Roman's motorcycle purred to a stop behind Shelly's pickup. "Shelly, you come out here, right now," he yelled.

"Just a peaceful little family get-together. You couldn't wait to call Dani, could you, Uma?" Mitchell muttered, before closing the door between the women and the brothers.

Their deep voices sounded on the porch; Uma answered the sharp rap on the door to find Roman glaring down at her, Mitchell just behind him. "Yes? May I help you?"

May I knock your heads together to get you to see past your noses?

"I'd like to talk with Shelly, please," Roman said stiffly.

Inside the house, Shelly shook her head no, and Uma said, "I believe she's busy at the moment. She and Dani, myself, and *your* mother are going into the kitchen now to fix dinner. You're invited—if you behave yourself."

"Mitchell, she's your woman. She's meddling in things that don't concern her. Do something," Roman ordered as Shelly came to stand beside Uma.

Dani stood on her other side. "I am going to talk with my grandmother," she said with a fierceness matching Roman's.

"Everyone just wait a minute. Before this goes any further, I want to make one thing clear—" Uma held her breath and stepped out onto the porch. Mitchell's arrogant stance, his head tilted slightly, his arms crossed and his legs braced apart said he wasn't budging. "I know that the situation is dangerous—"

"Damned dangerous and you have to bring *her* here."

"Are you going to kiss me goodnight? Or are you coming in?"

"I'm not coming in."

"Then take this with you, hard head." Uma stood on tiptoe and reached her arms around his shoulders, kissing those firm lips.

Mitchell reacted instantly, letting go of the breath he'd been holding, and wrapping his arms around her tightly. His kiss tasted of hunger and frustration, diving deeply, sensuously, melding her to him until she could feel the rapid beat of his heart. Uma smoothed his hair and held him fiercely. Just as she sensed he was going to move off the porch with her, she eased away and Mitchell's expression closed. "War, is it?"

"Your father's pride tore them apart, Mitchell. Don't let that happen to us," she cautioned softly.

"You weren't there."

"My mother was."

"She heard Grace's side, not his."

Uma reached to caress Mitchell's cheek and despite his anger, he brushed a rough kiss into her palm. "Fred told my mother, too. I was there and too young to understand, but I saw him cry. He was heartbroken. It's time you told Roman what he said as he died. Grace has a right to hear it, too. I know what it was, because you were on painkillers and still delirious that night the house burned. You told me he said he loved her and that it was his fault."

Mitchell inhaled sharply and his eyes glittered down at her. Then he turned stiffly and walked off the porch, Roman staring after him. "My father said that?" he asked brusquely, raggedly.

"Yes. Give her a chance, Roman. For Dani's sake, and for your own." But Roman was already moving after Mitchell.

Clyde eased into position, drawing back the string of the powerful compound bow. He wasn't using practice arrows this time, rather the hunting arrowheads, meant to kill. In the trees bordering Uma's backyard, he was well hidden, yet he could see Mitchell Warren outlined in the streetlight sliding between the houses.

A cold trickle rose up Clyde's nape and he pivoted toward Lauren's old house. The house gave him the willies and he didn't know why. Lauren was dead, but some part of her was still lurking there, mocking him. *He could even smell her lemon cookies . . . as if she had just baked them.* He wasn't going in the house again—ever.

Clearly Mitchell and Roman were guarding the Lawrence house and the women in it. Dressed in black, the men weren't easy to see in the shadows. When the back door creaked and Uma stepped out into the night, dressed in a large white T-shirt that came to her mid-thighs, Clyde hissed and eased the bowstring. Instantly, both men crouched and moved to trap her between them, then Roman nodded, moved away.

Mitchell picked up Uma in his arms and hurried into his house.

Clyde considered burning Shelly's house, but then he didn't want all the players in one place as they were tonight. It was easier to pick them off when they were separated; all he had to do was to wait. He'd waited for years to make them all pay . . .

He breathed deeply, inhaling the scents of the summer roses on the trellis near his head, and silently mouthed his promise, his litany: "Before the last rose petal falls this year, those women will be dead."

He ripped a fragrant blossom from its thorny mooring and let the blood-red petals drift slowly to the earth. He ground the fragrant petals into the grass with his well-polished shoes; he'd always hated roses. The women chatted endlessly about tea, damask and old European roses, and whatever other boring nonsense interested them.

Uma had interfered in his life too many times. When she was dead, everything would fall into place . . . first, Shelly, and then dim-witted Pearl . . .

Clyde sucked in the night air as it chilled suddenly, bringing the scent of—of Lauren? The dead woman?

He shook his head, clearing it. The fragrances on a hot August night weren't that of a woman. *The air smelled like Lauren's lemon cookies.* He eyed Lauren's house and fought the fear that she might be in the night, waiting for him.

Then from the shadows he saw the cat's eyes, and moonlight caught the glow of white fangs as it hissed at him, its back arched. He thought he heard his real name whispered, the rose leaves brushing against each other as he moved, the thorns dragging at his jacket and slacks, threatening to dislodge his hat, trying to reveal who he really was . . .

He gave way to the prowling fear that Lauren wanted revenge. The sense that she waited for him pounded through him, his heart racing.

With a soft cry, Clyde hurried into the safety of the night and his secret place.

FIFTEEN

After his rousing argument with Roman, battles with Uma, and the discovery that she had brought his mother to Madrid, Mitchell wanted some very private time with the woman in his life.

She stood in the center of his kitchen, her hands on her hips her shirt stretched over those perfect breasts, her nipples etching dark peaks in the material. Her eyes narrowed up at him. "Just what do you think you're doing?"

"Let's get this straight. Parts of my life are out of bounds. You stepped over the line. I'm expecting you to correct your mistake."

"You're talking in memos again. You're not running a business empire here, Mitchell. I'm not an employee or an underling to be dictated to."

"I thought we had an agreement, a good one. An arrangement that suited us both." *She was his, and she knew it; that was a fact. She'd given him everything in lovemaking, with nothing held back, and they were one. Why did women have to complicate life? Dealing with them certainly wasn't easy, but then, he'd never wanted to, had he?*

"It may have suited *you*."

"Let's hear it. Whatever she's told you, I want to hear." Mitchell smiled tightly. He admired Uma; how she wouldn't back down. He breathed uneasily. A standoff with his mother was not what he wanted.

"She loved your father. He loved her, but he couldn't stop working that land, and it ruined their lives. They could have made it—just living there, and her working. But he felt he had to do as his father had done and his father before him—raise and break horses, selling them. He couldn't afford to do that, not with the expenses of food and grain and feed."

Uma shook her head. "She thought he'd come after her when he'd had time to think about what turned out to be their final argument, when he saw the ledgers and realized the truth, the folly of trying to do as his family had done before him. But he couldn't bend enough. Instead, he held his bitterness and frustration inside, and it devoured him. I don't want that to happen to you or to Roman. You're more like your father than you know. He got entrenched in that bitterness, and it took him to drink and trouble. And she wrote you, trying to explain. You look stunned. You didn't know that, did you? That she sent money for you and Roman? That she wrote and tried to call?"

Mitchell tried to rally his argument against his mother. "Dad promised his father the land would always be in the family. She knew that when she married him."

"They loved each other, Mitchell, and sometimes life just isn't sweet. He didn't want her working, and she wanted to help. They had a growing family, a piece of land that was a luxury to farm, her husband was killing himself trying to work it, and work at the garage, and she loved him."

"I don't want to talk with her. I'm not rehashing this." He felt backed into a corner.

"You're going to have a hard time ignoring her. The attachment with Dani is already strong. Dani needs her, and Everett has agreed to rent Grace his house. He's staying in

Denver for a time. He didn't give a woman there a chance, and he's trying to work through that. Grace is staying because of Dani and Shelly and me. Roman and you will just have to adjust."

"Not likely. You're saying that all you women are united on this. You've unionized and you're the spokesperson."

"I'm saying that you wanted to unravel what is inside you, and until you understand the past, you won't have the total package. I want that total package very much, not just pieces of you."

Uma forged on, her low voice slamming into him. "Children make a difference. You know how the baby you delivered touched you, reached inside you, and made you want to understand yourself? You've closed off the past and it's coming after you. Pride kept them apart, pure and simple. And children did make a difference in their marriage. She wanted more for you and Roman—"

"And herself. She left us, Uma. She left a husband and two sons for a better life. You like to fix things. Try justifying that."

He was feeling ugly and bitter and wounded. When he'd come into the house, carrying Uma, the gray cat had hurried in front of him. Now it leaped to the counter behind him, nudging and purring softly against his back.

Mitchell elbowed the cat away, and it gave way to sitting on the counter, watching him solemnly.

He thought he felt a gentle warning, but the storm between Uma and himself brewed hot and tight. "You started this."

He opened a drawer and took out a file folder of Charis Lopez clippings. "I've been doing some reading. *The Smooth Moves List*, too. You've got a real talent for ideal situations and how to fix them—in fairyland, where everything is perfect, but not in reality. Try dealing with reality sometime, Uma, and staying out of other people's business. I enjoyed the column 'Why Men Bristle.' It reminded me of a certain dinner at your house . . . the one with your ex-husband. You must just travel through life, viewing it from a distance, and coming up with these goodies. Like in the 'Single City' chapter, where like people will gravitate to each other—or opposites, and then the individual has to choose if they want to give up something to share with that person, or if they want to remain single."

When she turned pale, he regretted striking out at her. That was what he knew how to do best, wasn't it? Protect himself?

The cat leaped to the floor and wound around her legs, then the animal sat beside her, staring at him with yellow eyes. Mitchell had the feeling the cat had found him guilty of total insensitivity. Great. Now he understood cats and dead women.

"How long have you known?"

He disgusted himself, attacking her, like a wounded bear trying to take down everything in its path. "From the first. Your penchant for fortune cookies . . . Charis's neat little one-liners. Don't worry. I haven't told anyone."

"I wrote that when I was trying to sort out why it wasn't working with Everett. I had to have something to do in those hours at the hospital, after Dad's heart attack. So I outlined a book from some articles I'd stored away."

"Your relationship with Everett wasn't working, because of chemistry. He's perfect and so are you. You need flaws to fix. You need me—raw material to mold. I'm attractive to you. You can't help yourself. You're a do-gooder. You want life to be nice and sweet. And you need me to fix. Well, honey, what happened to my family can't be fixed."

"Of all the arrogance—"

She looked so defenseless, and instead of holding her as he wanted to, Mitchell jerked open the refrigerator and uncapped a bottle of water. "Here. Drink this."

"It's a natural consequence to relive or dissect mistakes when a marriage fails, I suppose," she said dully. "I wrote what I thought might happen."

"You did a good job of projecting," he murmured, remembering how after they had argued, they had made love—feverishly, hungrily.

Uma slowly sipped the water. "You think I'm trying to fix you, do you?"

"We're not going to be one big happy family. I came here to find what was missing, why I'm so different. I needed to prove that I was as good as anyone else. That I could earn a good paycheck and respect myself. My father didn't in the end, and I had to have that respect. But I'm not management and I don't like being cooped up in a city office. I like outside work, simple work with my hands—and not ranching on a two-bit place, either. You're complicating a basic man-woman relationship."

He didn't trust her narrowed look and that assessing "mmm."

Then Uma spoke slowly. "So you're afraid to talk with her. You're afraid you'll learn the truth and that frightens you. You've built a lifetime hating a mother who didn't deserve it. Gee whiz, what would you do without that bitterness to cling to?"

"Let's cut to the basics, shall we? The bottom line?"

"Mmm. Without the foreplay, the afterplay?" she taunted.

"You can sure hand it out, lady." Unable to resist, appreciating her determination and frustrated, Mitchell reacted. He reached to cup her chin and lift her face to his. Those smoke-gray eyes said she wasn't afraid, she wasn't backing down, and he admired her all the more.

Uma pushed his hand away and brushed away the tendril dancing along her warm cheek. "Now *you're* confusing the issue."

He noted that fascinating telltale little quiver that rippled through her. The air sizzled between them. He reached to smooth her cheek, to feel the passion in her. It licked at the ends of her hair, twining around them as her lids lowered, the light shimmering on her lashes as she met his stare. His body was already full and hard, needing her. Their physical bond was the truth that talking couldn't provide; he trusted that bond and what went with it, that river of deeper emotion.

"I don't feel like talking any more," she whispered unevenly as she flattened against the wall, watching him.

"Neither do I," he returned rawly as he braced his hand near her head and let the other hand slide downward, over the warm curves he needed against him. The hem of her T-shirt lifted to her briefs, and he smoothed his finger beneath the elastic, finding her warmth, stroking her gently, intimately.

Her body heated and melted beneath his touch, her hips moving against him, her lips ripe and hot against his. Her hands flattened to him, smoothed his shoulders, his throat, his chest. Her fingers rummaged through the hair on his chest and her mouth was on him, burning . . . she was his, a part of him, his hunger to complete them growing. *Oneness* . . . the word twined around him, the woman who was the other part of himself, completing him.

There was the passion they created, hot and feverish. She made him come alive, all his feelings storming, circling him—tenderness, need, desire, the completion he'd never known possible. Erotic and scented and soft, she was his other part, not gentle now, but hurrying to lift her T-shirt away, to find him with her hands—

Primeval? Basic? Truth in motion? Fire burning away all else, each touch raising the burn, the hunger?

Only for her, only for this one woman, Mitchell thought, as their hunger enveloped him, and he tore away his jeans.

Only for her . . . Uma . . . the only woman he had ever wanted . . . a special woman . . . Oneness . . .

On the edge of her passion, Uma's eyes were slitted, watching him, waiting as their bodies burned for each other, skin against skin.

Precious . . . gentle . . . valiant . . . truthful . . . feminine . . .

Oneness . . . Inside him, the words turned and gleamed and warmed. Passion and hunger rode them now, but Mitchell wanted more, wanted to give more—

Just there, before entering her, he saw everything—her quickening pulse, the hunger, the anticipation, the truth, the bonding. Uma could only give herself to a man she trusted and wanted as a part of her life. Her nails dug lightly into his shoulders and she closed her eyes as he moved his chest against her breasts, slowly, erotically, smoothing her body with his open hands.

He enjoyed the flavor of her, the nip of hunger, heat beating from her, the scent of her skin, the contours and softness, the way her breast fit into his hand, the peak rising at the brush of his thumb.

"What are you doing?" she whispered as he slowly moved around her, fitting himself to her, letting the curve of her bottom nestle against him, his face brushing against her shoulder, his tongue tasting her, both hands cupping her breasts, smoothing and caressing downward.

"I don't know, but it feels right."

He eased aside her hair to find her ear, sucking it gently, stroking, making her a part of him without the completion. There was more to their relationship than sex, more . . .

She turned slightly and he took her kiss, moving around to lift her in his arms. "I don't know what this is, but I like it," she whispered as he simply stood and held her against his chest.

"I think you may have a plan, Mitchell," she teased, nipping at his shoulder as he carried her into the bedroom.

"It's a new strategy," he answered as he eased her onto his bed and came down beside her.

"A very erotic strategy," Uma whispered as Mitchell's

hands and mouth and body claimed every inch of her without completion. He took her higher, only to ease the driving hunger, then slowly higher again. Intent on her pleasure, Uma sensed that he was taking her into him, into his pores, his senses, his rushing bloodstream, the heavy beat of his heart. In return, he was giving her everything he had protected from all others.

She couldn't breathe, holding the pleasure inside her, waiting for him to make them one. Then, as his face nuzzled and lips heated and suckled and tongue tasted, Uma held herself in check, wanting to give him as much, the slow, thorough erotic journey.

His breath stopped and held as she began to move slowly, brushing her body against his, moving her thighs, her hands open on him, feeling the strength he restrained when holding her, that burning rough skin, the friction rising between them.

Each touch lifted and seduced and burned, until Mitchell groaned deeply, rawly, and turned her beneath him, entering her fully.

Poised above her, Mitchell stared down at her, his hands taking her hair, holding her, though there was no need. A part of him now, lock and key, Uma moved boldly against him, watched his struggle to slow their journey, and cherished the pounding of his heart. Instinctively she knew that Mitchell had never given another woman this slow, erotic pleasure that she knew was meant only for her. Every touch was truth from his heart, opening for her, giving . . .

She'd waited a lifetime for him, she thought hazily, as her body began toppling over the edge . . .

Oneness . . . the word was her last clear thought.

Pearl glided the tiny black Miata that Pete had stolen for her into its garage, the space between the old motel's units. In a fury, she hurried outside to close the wooden doors and lock them. Always cautious, she glanced at the silhouettes of the small oil drills pecking at the earth, outlined by the moon, and then punched the hidden digital locking system's buttons.

Pete Jones wasn't much of a shooter, but he was handy enough to remodel this room with a battery-powered lock and several hidden panels in the walls and floors while he waited for Pearl. When the lock released, Pearl tore inside the motel unit and slammed the door behind her.

She jerked open a hidden cabinet and replaced the deadly bow in its holding place. She added a hunting arrow to the two already labeled "Uma and Shelly," and resting on prongs. Beneath the new arrow Pearl scribbled on the wall, "Mitchell."

This was where she could be free. This was where Clyde could come to her, no restrictions, no confining family, no endless daily routines—no Walter. No fat, disgusting, drunk-after-eight o'clock, rutting Walter.

How dared he father Shelly's baby? How dared he taunt her with Dani?

How dared Lauren grab the scarf intended to mark Shelly for Pete's bullet?

How dared Uma take up with a Warren?

Pearl ripped off her man's hat and rummaged her fingers through her hair, loosening it. She glanced around the masculine room—a plain cot, a table, and a lantern with matches. She sailed the hat to the cot and struck a match, lighting the kerosene lantern carefully and adjusting the wick.

Her daughters would be coming home next week from Walter's sister in Connecticut. She would take them to New York for school clothes shopping, and Pearl's roaming at night would have to stop—until school started.

Pearl kicked off her shoes, loosened her wide, masculine tie, and lit one of Walter's best black-market Havana cigars. She straddled a chair and placed her arms across the back as she smoked the cigar Walter thought was designated only for him.

Walter responded well to drugs at night, just a drop or two added to his usual whiskey sour to make him sleep heavily as Pearl moved around as she wished.

She blew a perfect circle of smoke in the air, then smaller ones. "No more perfect Pearl. Pearl is going to be strong now. Old pitiful, weak Pearl has to go, and new Pearl will handle her life as she wishes. First Uma—an accident, somehow—then grief will make Shelly's distraction fatal, and then Pearl. It's perfectly logical, and all before the last petal falls on the last rose . . . I see no problem at all, Clyde."

Uma's fingers prowled up Mitchell's chest and he lazily captured them, and brought them to him. "I think we should go hunting—"

"I agree—"

"Not there!" she exclaimed laughingly as he tossed the sheet over their heads and foraged downward. He nuzzled and made growling noises as Uma pulled his head upward.

She sat up, pressing the sheet against her as Mitchell lay back on the pillow, his arms behind his head, the picture of a very satisfied male. He traced a finger over her bare shoulder and Uma recognized that sultry, hungry look. "I was going with Shelly, but you'll do."

"Great. I'm second choice." He eased upright slightly to nuzzle at her breasts, suckling through the material.

Uma closed her eyes and let the warm, moist tugging zip through her body, lodging low in her. "Don't distract me."

"You *are* the distraction." Mitchell drew a line over her breasts and eased the material away.

"I can't think when you look at me like that."

"That's the general idea, hot stuff." There was that devastating, pure male grin flashing at her.

She caught his hair and bent to give him a raw, open kiss. "I need your complete attention."

Mitchell sat up and looped his arms around her, laughing

as he dragged her back on top of him. "What's up?"

She could *feel* what was up and quite ready. "Not that. We need to talk."

He withdrew just that wary bit, and she sensed his shields shimmering, warding off any talk of his mother.

"Roman knows that I'm with you, and he's watching my house, right?"

"Uh-huh." Mitchell's tone was flat and cautious.

"Mitchell, listen. It's just an idea, but we have to do something about whoever caused Lauren to be killed, and Rosalie, and the rest. I know this town better than anyone. You lived in the country and couldn't know the hidden places in Madrid, but as girls, we loved them—they were our secrets. The old root cellars, used to keep jars and potatoes, and our protection against tornados. There is an old root cellar behind our house. There are doors on the outside of old houses that no one in Madrid ever locks. They lead to basements. And anyone can hide in the root cellars, the basements, and hide deep in the overgrown bushes. Shelly and I put together a map of Madrid, and it is literally possible to cross from rooftop to rooftop through town. You can see everything that happens from on top of Mike's bar. If someone knew this town well enough, they could come and go as they pleased."

Mitchell was on his feet, striding out of the bedroom. Wrapping the sheet around herself, Uma hurried after him. "What are you doing?"

Nude, striding through the house in a gleaming flow of powerful muscles, Mitchell jerked open the back door and gave a low whistle. Several neighborhood dogs started barking, and Roman suddenly appeared from the shadows. "What's up?"

Mitchell turned to Uma. "Where is that root cellar?"

He was standing there, absolutely naked and as casual as if he were dressed, plunging through a business meeting in which he intended to win. Uma struggled to answer his question. "In the backyard, out in the brush between the field and the old rose trellis."

"Get on it, Roman. There's a passage that leads into the house."

"Holy—" Roman nodded curtly and slid into the darkness.

Mitchell waited a moment, and then closed and locked the back door. He paced the length of the kitchen, his big body tense and coiled. Uma stood back, stunned at the picture of Mitchell, nude and scowling, haunches hollowed with muscles, broad shoulders narrowing down to his waist, his masculinity shadowed as he stalked back again, looming over her. "Whoever it is could have come into your house and killed you in your sleep. You should have told me."

"Are you with me, or not?"

"As a backup to Shelly? Sure. Love to. Thanks for the invitation."

"Then get dressed and I'll get some clothes from Lauren's room. We were the same size. I don't want to alarm the neighbors, but if the house has been watched, maybe whoever it is doing this has left something on the rose bushes that are everywhere. I thought we could check the neighborhood without upsetting anyone, then work our way to Rosalie's house. I'd prefer that no one knew we were snooping through her house for clues."

Mitchell uttered a low curse, and Uma said, "No, it isn't a dingbat idea. If you're not up for it, Shelly will help me. Pearl is pretty shattered at the moment. I had to defend you against her."

His eyebrows lifted. "Defend me? How so?"

"You needed my protection, and that's all I'm going to say about it. Oh, I wish I had my sports bra—"

Moments later, Mitchell let Uma out of the house. "You look cute," he drawled, patting her bottom.

"I don't have any briefs on and I've never, ever gone out of the house without a bra since I was a little girl."

His "mmm" sounded as if he were anticipating a delicious event.

"You're full of surprises, honey," Mitchell admitted slowly as her small flashlight caught a thread on the rose bushes between his house and hers.

Roman appeared out of the night. Then, seeing Mitchell and Uma, he nodded. "What's up?"

Mitchell held up the single thread. "Our boy lost something. We're going on a little sightseeing tour. Take care."

"Take care," Roman answered, and slipped back into the night again.

They moved silently across the street to where the BBs had to have been fired. Another thread, a different color, clung to an opulent rambling scarlet rose bush. Uma held his hand as they moved between several other houses, pointing out the old cellars, the outside basement doors, until they were on Main Street, moving down an alley.

"I'm starting to enjoy this," Mitchell whispered as his hands eased her bottom higher and she climbed up onto the paint store's roof.

"If you do put in that big super center building and supply store that everyone wants, you're going to run a lot of little people out of business."

Mitchell stepped on a trash bin, grabbed a television antenna and hefted himself upward. "If you fall—"

"We did this all the time—Lauren, Shelly, Pearl, and me. I miss Lauren so," she finished fiercely. "Come on."

She made her way to the top of the roof and lay down. When Mitchell didn't lie down beside her to scan the street below, she looked upward to see him considering her backside. "No briefs, huh? Just you under those pants?"

"Not now. Mitchell, we're on duty."

"Uh-huh." He lay down beside her, but one big hand

found her bottom, caressing it. He bent to kiss her, and she tasted the passion lingering between them. "I just love it when you're so Double-O-Seven."

"You're enjoying this, and if you don't stop making fun of me, you can just go home."

He tugged her braid. "Whoops. Sorry."

Mitchell's expression said he wasn't; he was like a child enjoying a game, a playful little boy inside the man who held his emotions so tightly in check. "You're irritating me. Shelly would have been a better partner than you."

"Roman is set to marry her, you know. That might cut down this midnight roaming. You might be forced to ask me again. Now, why are we here?"

"Mrs. Dougan wouldn't give Elinor Stills a cutting from her rose bush, so Elinor decided to steal a start. She really needs to place better in competition, so she got up at two o'clock one morning and bicycled to Mrs. Dougan's, where she got her clipping. On her way, she noticed a sleek little back Miata cruising through town—no lights."

"Uh, makes sense. Pete Jones was the suspect in a Miata theft. They never found the car." Mitchell's hand prowled down to her bottom, then back up to her pants' elastic waistband. He lifted it slightly and turned to peer down at her briefless bottom. "Mmm. Interesting."

He bent to lightly bite her there and Uma stiffened, shocked at his play. He lifted his head to grin at her. "I love getting to you—seeing your face go absolutely blank before the blush sets in. You really don't know how to play, do you, honey?"

"Sure I do. I've played games all my life."

"Chess . . . Parcheesi . . . bridge . . . croquet?" he mocked. "All very ladylike."

"Any game you want to play, I can play."

"We'll see."

Uma put her hand over his face and pushed gently; she

wasn't certain how to handle Mitchell in a playful mood. "Jones has been dead for a year. Mrs. Dougan saw the Miata in May. I just found out today, when she called to gossip— and to tell me that Pearl is hunting things for her bazaar. I feel badly about having to put Pearl in her place. She's had such a hard life."

"I think you are the sexiest woman I have ever known," Mitchell whispered rawly as he drew her over him.

"Here?" she asked after an earthshaking kiss. Mitchell's hands were easing open their clothing. "We'll roll off the roof, and how would we explain that? Oh, Mitchell—"

Clinging to the rooftop by her fingertips, Uma held her breath as he slid into her, full and heavy and hot.

Fifteen minutes later, Mitchell helped a very shaky Uma down from the rooftop, catching her as she leaped into his arms. After gently placing her on the ground, he kissed her softly, and smoothed her disheveled braids.

"I certainly didn't see that coming," she managed, still stunned by the passion she hadn't expected to flame so quickly between them.

He tugged one braid, and there was that lazy pleased smile, so delicious she could almost devour him again. "You did okay."

Uma couldn't help but throw her arms around his shoulders and open her already sensitive lips to his. "What am I going to do with you?"

His smile said he already had a suggestion. "You'll think of something. Right now, take me to Rosalie's."

Minutes later, Rosalie's house was dark—except for the small flashlight Uma used to show Mitchell the receipts for cloth that Rosalie had special ordered for her customers. "See? This one isn't for cloth, but references her letter questioning what thread they recommended for a special 1930s fabric. Her appointment book was missing, but I started going through her tax receipts for the last year."

"Good girl."

"I think there's a connection to the bullets that shot up the old windmill—and Pete—but I can't make it. It might be something."

Mitchell jotted down the name of the manufacturer on a scrap of a paper and tucked it into his jeans. "Could be. Let's go home."

But Uma's flashlight had caught the small trash basket, overflowing with scraps. She bent to collect the one that wasn't summer flowers and cotton, but a heavier weave. "Do you think these scraps might match that thread?"

"Maybe. Keep it." He glanced outside the lace-covered window to where Lonny's police car was gliding beneath a streetlight. "Let's go."

In Mitchell's shower later, Uma gave herself to his gentle hands, to the sensation that she was finally home. Mitchell eased her out of the shower and began drying her. He traced the tiny stretch marks on her belly. "Tell me about Christina."

"She was my world—from the moment she was conceived."

He nodded slowly. "You're a woman who deserves a family. You never wanted to try again?"

"I think," she whispered honestly, "that she was so perfect that I feared nothing could compare, that I couldn't love another child as I did her."

The bathroom light caught the water droplets in Mitchell's hair, face, and shoulders as Uma studied him. She traced her fingertip across his brows, wiping the water there. He'd gone to another place suddenly, drawing away from her. "Mitchell?"

"I—" he began slowly, unevenly. The steamy mirror behind him revealed a powerful male back and a woman's soft, almost ethereal face looking up at him, her hands smoothing his hair.

Gentleness ran between them, and playfulness and passion so deep it tore at her control. With Mitchell she was free and alive—

He placed her fingertips on his lips. "When I held that baby, I wondered if Dad had felt that with us, a life so new and fragile. I felt as if I were cracking open, peering into an unknown storm of life that I'd never experienced. I just knew that there was a truth I didn't know—or that I was ignoring. And I had nowhere to go, not really, except back here."

"Your instincts were right. One's heart always knows where home is. All one has to do is listen to the call. For you, it was that baby delivered in the back of the taxi. It signaled to you that you had to work through your life and make sense of it. One—"

"Shut up, you," Mitchell whispered gently. "And come here . . ."

SIXTEEN

The morning sun was blinding as Roman climbed the old windmill, fighting the pain in his knee. He'd dozed on the front porch and had refused Shelly's invitation to come into the house for breakfast. Behind her stood the woman he'd detested for years, the woman who'd run out on the tough times, her husband, and her sons.

Morning was still cool, the trees slanting fingers of shade over the windmill as he sat and scanned the land he'd hated.

Shelly's small pickup pulled next to his motorcycle, and she spotted him immediately. In that long-legged stride, she moved toward the windmill and started upward on the boards serving as a ladder, and Roman's skin went cold. "Don't come up here."

She climbed steadily, the sunlight catching the burnished sheen of her hair, her body agile in its ascent. She stood on the platform and scanned the land. "Nice view."

"Sit down." Roman held her hands as she sat by him, legs dangling side by side.

"Nice view. What are you doing up here?"

"Trying to figure it out." Mitchell had told him of the unread letters Grace had written, and of Fred's dying words. *You're all I've got left of her, you and Roman. I loved that woman with all my heart . . . tell Grace I've always loved her*, his father had whispered amid his pain. *Everything was my fault. Take Roman and go to her—*

Shelly scanned the burned, overgrown house place and barn, the old garage where Pete Jones had been found. The sun caught the fluttering tendrils beside her cheeks, fiery silk that had escaped her ponytail. She pushed them back with her hand. "I don't want you cleaning houses with me. It's therapy of a sort, and I like it. It's my special time when I do my thinking."

Images swam by Roman—Shelly managing hard physical work and then caring for his baby—and he hadn't been there to help. "It's hard work. You deserve better."

"I worked out a lot of frustration cleaning those houses. They're mine—sort of . . . I want to thank you for what you've done with Dani. That hard makeup is gone. She looks—"

"Sweet, like you. Fresh and sweet and new."

Shelly swung her jeaned legs and a blush rose up her cheeks as she followed a bird's cutting flight across the sky.

"Hawk," Roman noted. "Looking for chickens, or mice."

Shelly took his hand and brought it to her lap, stroking it. "Tell me about that night, when the house burned. Tell me why you tighten up and close off when that's mentioned. The other day, Dani said something and you got that look, and your forehead beaded with sweat, though we were inside, in air conditioning."

The sun blinded him now, searing through the years to that night. On the ground below, he saw the flames devouring the barn, the house . . .

Yet in the distance, Lonny's buffalo were slowly moving toward the house. The past and the present, caught in time as the old windmill's blades began moving slowly.

"Mitchell has the scars. I've got the guilt."

"Tell me."

He heard Fred's screams again, horrible sounds of a man who had always been so strong, so—so hard, impenetrable, unmoving, stubborn . . . "Children are supposed to love their parents, right? I didn't love either one. Grace deserted us and nothing was ever good enough for Fred. He rode Mitchell one way and me another. Mitchell took the brunt. I've been sitting up here thinking how hard Dad struggled to hold this—this place. I wouldn't have. I'd have taken the easy road and just managed the garage—he could have done that, but not both things."

Yet Fred's dying words were for his love and for Roman's safety. "Why didn't you tell me?" he'd demanded rawly of Mitchell, who just shook his head.

"He loved her," Roman said slowly. "His dying words were his love of Grace. He wanted Mitchell to take me to her. My brother didn't want to. Maybe I resent that, or maybe I don't. But he should have told me."

"Talking is difficult for both of you. It hurt him and he didn't want you to hurt. Go on . . ."

Roman closed his eyes, fighting off the sounds of Fred's cries. "Dad was a drunk, and he kept this godforsaken piece of earth's crust out of spite. He could have made a go of the garage, but not both. We were ragtag kids, working too hard, without the right food or clothes—or a mother, or pictures of one. He destroyed everything of Grace. I remember his digging out her rose bushes, ones she loved and babied in drought."

He eased his hand away from Shelly's; he didn't want her to be touched by the darkness in him. "I didn't help Mitchell pull Dad from the fire. All I could think of was the hard work, the yelling, the shame of having a drunk for a father. I didn't do what I could have . . . instead, I watched Mitchell trying to save him."

"You've been carrying this all these years. You were only a boy, Roman. Grace loved him, too. Talk with her—"

"No, I won't."

Shelly eased to her feet and stood looking down at him, her hands on her hips. Then the flat of her hand swept against the back of his head, knocking him gently. "She's Dani's grandmother, and they are already attached to each other. Fred loved her, and she loved him. Maybe you'd better unlock your mind, mister."

She began down the wooden ladder. On the ground, she looked up at him. "I always thought this was a beautiful place. If Mitchell isn't going to do anything with it, maybe you might think about giving Dani something special, all her own, a family heritage. But you can't do that with bitterness wrapped around you, can you?"

"Lay off," he yelled at her.

"When I'm ready." Shelly turned and marched toward her pickup. Then she looked up at him and called, "It's never too late to change."

Moments later, Roman was still stunned. Instead of her pickup, Shelly had chosen to drive his bike back to town.

Grace smiled when Shelly passed her on the road, riding Roman's Harley. Shelly waved, but she was scowling and Grace knew that look—she'd worn it enough with Fred.

"Mom is in a snit," Dani noted as she drove expertly toward the old ranch. "He's done it again. She's hard to rile, but he sure knows how to push her buttons."

"Dani, pull over to this old motel."

"It's deserted. Dates back to Bonnie-and-Clyde days. Walter bought it, and people thought he was going to make a museum out of it, but there's not enough traffic on this road now since a main road has gone through."

"We spent our wedding night there," Grace whispered softly, and remembered how carefully Fred had touched her.

The European roses were still there, lush and pink, heavy blooms draping over the unpruned bush. She'd taken clippings for their home, loving them into life. "That's enough, Dani. When my things arrive, I'll show you how it was, the old place and your grandfather—my sons look so much like Fred, and just as stubborn, too. Let's go to the ranch."

"Just a minute. You deserve a bouquet, Grandma." Dani leaped out of the car and hurried to cut the roses with her small pocketknife. Holding the roses in front of her, she looked down and scraped the dirt with her biker boot, frowning. Then she grinned when she entered the car with the fragrance of roses, the lush pink blooms still touched by dew.

Grandma. Grace wallowed in the title, loving it, as Dani beamed at her. "I wish I could have held you as a baby and helped your mother."

"Well, we're here now, and together, Grams. All we have to do is to get Pops and Unc to see the light."

"They're like their father. That might not be easy."

"You came back, didn't you?" Dani asked, shifting expertly.

"Yes. They refused to see me and Fred—" Grace brushed away her tears, fighting the past.

The morning sunlight shone through the windshield as Grace thought of Uma and her softness, and how Mitchell had carried her so protectively into his home last night. She prayed that Mitchell could learn to bend, to give that wounded part of him into Uma's care.

Pain shot through Grace once more as she saw the old home place, the rubble that had once been her dream house.

"That's Pops, brooding up on the windmill," Dani said as they stepped from the car.

Fred, I loved you so. How could all of this have happened? For a moment she was frozen, the happy and the horrible memories swirling around her. Then pain bore Grace down to the ground, her hands covering her face.

Dani didn't waste time. She hurried to the boards leading

up to the windmill, and swiftly climbed up to stand over Roman. "Do something. She's hurting."

"Let her hurt."

Dani nudged his bottom with her boot. "Listen, Pops. It's a package deal. Little sweet me, my mom, and Grams."

"Lay off, kid."

"Boy, no wonder I'm stubborn, coming down through you. I've decided I'm going to buy this place when I can. I haven't had a heritage, and now that I do, I want what's mine. All of it, Grams and the land my grandfather tried to save for me."

Roman looked up at her. "You're hard, kid. But not tough enough to pull that one off."

"I've always wanted a horse. I like bikes, sure. But they're hard to hug. I'm going to work really hard, and get some money, and buy this place and live on it and hug my horse. My land, Pops, part of my heritage."

"Kid, you probably can't even ride a horse."

"Well, you'll just have to teach me, won't you, Pops?" The flat of her hand buffed the back of his head, just as Shelly had.

Roman watched his daughter briskly, agilely descend the ladder. "Women. Both up here on the same day, telling me what to do, whopping me on the head as if I were a wet-behind-the-ears kid stealing candy."

He saw Grace crouched on the ground and a part of his heart softened and turned. Then he looked out at the clear blue Oklahoma sky and shut his mother away.

There was no ignoring the rev of his bike as Shelly pulled to a stop. She swung off his bike and came to stand beside Dani, hands on hips, glaring up at him.

Roman scowled down at her. Those green eyes cut through the distance up to him, burning furiously, her mouth tightly pressed with anger. Her condemning stare never left him as she and Dani helped Grace to her feet.

The engagement sweetheart plan was not going well at all.

* * *

Mitchell slapped the unopened letters from his mother onto the kitchen counter. He was sweaty from an early morning job and the need to see Uma curled around him, memories of last night haunting him. He tipped up the fruit jar of iced tea and drank deeply.

The second week of August heat would be intolerable in the afternoon, and then he would come to Uma—if she wasn't with Grace.

The cat nudged his leg and Mitchell swiped a hand across his bare chest, dusting away the fine cuttings caught in the hair. He glanced at the scratches on his hands and ran water, soaping them, and wishing he could deal with the problem of his mother—and Uma's attachment to her—as easily.

The cat hopped onto the counter and settled next to the letters, and Mitchell had that odd sense of a woman's softness curling around him. He could sense Lauren's presence in the home she loved so much. Maybe she was a part of Uma, and by way of his love for Uma, Lauren was a part of him, too.

He instinctively knew her pain when she was shot, that last fleeting thought before the world went black—"I love you all so much. I'll always be with you."

He wiped his hands and face roughly with the towel. He wanted to hold Uma and know she was safe. He'd already called her twice, missing her as if she were a part of himself.

The cat's unblinking yellow eyes locked on him and inside him a chilling voice quietly said, "But she isn't safe."

Mitchell frowned and pushed away that sense that Uma was in danger—in the daylight hours, when the prowler never struck.

She was in her house, working desperately to meet a client's ad layout for a magazine.

Then later, she was showing Everett's house to Grace. *She was safe.*

If the threads and scraps he'd given Lonny for examination held any leads at all, maybe there would be an end to Madrid's danger.

Mitchell breathed deeply and hurled the towel away. His mother was another problem.

The women were united—Uma, Shelly, and Dani—all determined that he and Roman talk to Grace.

The cat leaped down and trotted into the room with Lauren's things, and as if drawn by the animal, Mitchell followed, the unopened letters in his hand. Whatever Grace had written, he was going to throw it back in his mother's face.

"Hello, Virginia," Grace said gently to the stone-faced woman staring out at the retirement home's garden.

Virginia Craig had always been a raw-boned, healthy woman, but now she sat slumped in a chair, a lap quilt over her legs. Her hair had once been auburn and sleek and neatly pinned, and she had moved with an elegance that Shelly now bore. She'd given birth to Shelly at midlife, and she and her husband had doted on their only child.

Dani's rundown on the situation was heartbreaking, and Grace felt she had to try to help. She took Mrs. Craig's thin, cold hand. "Virginia, I'm Grace Warren. Do you remember me?"

Virginia's head turned slowly on her thin neck, her green eyes shadowed at first; then they brightened and warmed. "Gracie? Gracie Warren?"

"I brought you a present, Virginia," Grace said, placing a ribboned box on the other woman's lap. She ached for the years of heartache between mother and child, daughter and granddaughter. "Would you like me to open it for you?"

Virginia's blue-veined fragile hands trembled over the box. "Yes, please."

Grace opened the box slowly. "You know we're two old ladies now, Virginia, and we have to do our best."

Those bright eyes stared at her. "Is this about my Shelly?"

"It's about our granddaughter." Grace took out the sweater she had carefully chosen for Virginia. It was green as Oklahoma's rolling spring hills. "Let me help you put it on. It's fairly cool in here. You like the gardens outside, don't you? I remember the lovely garden you grew, how big those tomatoes were, and how many quarts you canned. Goodness. What you know and can teach a young person."

"Dani . . . Danielle," Virginia whispered as she smoothed the soft knit of the sweater over her chest. "Your boy came to see me with Dani. He's got a sharp mouth, telling me off about how I treated Shelly and Dani."

Grace knew exactly how stubborn her sons could be, how abrupt, just like Fred. "I made a mistake with my husband. We had too much pride between the two of us, Virginia. Pride can be an awful, hurtful thing. It's like a river that starts to flow and can't stop or back up."

"Your boy was right." Virginia breathed slowly, watching the garden. Then her eyes began to shimmer with tears that overflowed onto the soft green knit. "I liked your boy, Gracie. Someone should have told me off years ago. There was only Shelly, and then—then suddenly she was a woman carrying a child, and not more than a child herself. Once I started on her, I couldn't stop. I loved her, but I couldn't stop. It was wrong and prideful."

Grace took Virginia's hands. "But we're going to change that, Virginia. We're going to be grandmothers. A little late for the both of us, but it's time we acted like it, don't you think? Dani may be leaving for college—"

"Leaving?" The fear in Virginia's voice trembled in the room. "I don't want her to leave!"

"I'm staying here in Madrid, Virginia, and you're welcome to stay at my house, if you want. We'll be grandmothers to Dani together. If you can put up with my sons' arrogance—

we still have trouble there—but for Dani's sake, I think we should be good friends, like we once were. You taught me so much. Will you think about it?"

"Your boy said he'd take me for a motorcycle ride. I'd like to show off to my friends here at the home that I'm still alive and kicking. About Dani . . . it's hard to give over once you've set your path, you know."

"I know. Oh, how well I know. Dani wants to buy that Warren place when she can. She's set on raising roses and horses and gardening. You could teach her so much about everything."

"It's a hard land, Gracie. It can tear the heart out of a person. You know that better than anyone."

"Shoot, Virginia. A hard land can't stand against you and me. We've been through the worst of times and the best, and we're not done yet."

Mrs. Craig looked out into the lush, manicured gardens of the retirement home, the white-smocked attendants pushing the wheelchairs. "You bring Dani to me. I'll try. She's right pretty, by the way."

"She looks like your Shelly."

Mrs. Craig beamed and nodded. "That she does."

Shelly eased into the closed, shadowy garage, to find Roman crouched, a big man grimly working on the motorcycle he wanted to give Dani.

"You're here to give back that ring, right? I don't blame you. I'm not a bargain," he said quietly, without looking at Shelly. He dropped a wrench into his toolbox and the metallic sound echoed coldly, hollowly in her heart. "I should have put her crib together, oiled her tricycle, carried her on my shoulders. Instead, I was riding high on myself—the big race-car driver. Look at me now—a has-been."

The light cruised over his shaggy hair, gleaming on his hard features as he turned to her. "Dani wants a horse. She wants to buy that old place. She wants her heritage. Some heritage. She's a rock-solid mechanic, an instinctive one for the sound of a motor. She won't need a computer to tune her bike, she'll feel it—and she wants a horse."

Shelly ached for Roman, for what he was going through, the years of pain to the present. "You can teach her about that, can't you? You broke and trained horses with Fred."

"Those nags just about killed us. My backside was so sore most of the time that I couldn't sit down to eat. Not that there was any decent food."

"She has a dream. She wants to own something that came down to her. That's not so bad, is it?"

Roman rose painfully to his feet, his hands on his hips, legs braced hip-shot, favoring his injured knee. In black jeans and a black T-shirt and biker's boots, he looked as if he'd seen the world and it had wearied him. "Dreams die," he said, his body all angles and taut with frustration.

"If you let them. If they aren't worth fighting for. What are you going to do? Let Dani struggle to buy that place, work herself to death, and not help her? Not teach her what you know?"

Roman's hand slashed at the air, signaling the end of the conversation.

She had to fight for him, the man she loved. "You're using Fred as an excuse, Roman. You act like him to back off from having to deal with logic that isn't your own. Don't you dare seal me off, not after all that hogwash about me being your Vargas and your Lamborghini girl. I didn't believe you anyway."

Silence swirled around the shadows and a muscle in Roman's cheek contracted as he scowled at her. "I may have said some things that weren't true to women who *knew* they weren't true, who knew how to play games. But not with you."

"All that bristling doesn't scare me, Roman. Don't try to intimidate me. It won't work."

"Are you going to give the damn ring back to me or not?" he demanded.

"You'll have to ask for it back. You gave it to me, and it's mine. I'm expecting everything that goes with it—but not some feeling-sorry-for-himself man who won't face how really wonderful he is."

"I'm not asking for it back."

"I'm not giving it back." Shelly pulled away the band that held her ponytail. She moved her head and the long burnished strands swirled and settled on her shoulders. The past still ate at Roman and she had to make him see that they had a future. Okay, maybe the woman that she was with him— alive and feeling her senses pound, thrilled by that dark, sultry look—loved testing him, pushing him, to find the man beneath. Maybe her time had come to play and laugh and rejoice in being a woman; she couldn't let that slip away without a fight. "Just try and get it."

"Feeling saucy, are you? I suppose you've got backup coming—Dani and Grace and Uma, just in case you can't handle me."

"Oh, I can handle you by myself . . . when you give me the truth about how you feel without words, and when I know in my heart that you will try to do your best by Dani—and me. That's all I want."

She backed up a step as he moved closer, eyes narrowed, studying her. "I know how this goes. The soft sell, getting me to talk with Grace, and everything is going to be peachy keen, right?"

"Wrong. I think it's time you put up or shut up. Or at least, stop looking at me like you do."

He took a step toward her. "How so?"

She moved backward again, lifting her foot to the first step of the stairs and standing up on it. "Like I'm special and you can't wait to have me."

She took another step higher and following her, Roman

eased onto the first step. "I guess that's how I feel. I was trying to watch that. To try to give you more, but all this night prowler business has cramped my style."

He reached in his shirt pocket and removed a small box. "Here."

Lying in a cotton bed was a feminine gold locket, etched with flowers and vines and engraved with her name and his. The heavier weight chain wasn't a match, looking as if nothing could break it. Inside the locket was a picture of Dani, clean and fresh and sweet looking as any teenager untouched by dirty rumors. Shelly braced herself against the heart-tugging gift. There was more that Roman had to give, and to take. If she stopped pushing him now, she'd just have to start all over, because she wasn't giving up—"What's this? A buy-off so you can ride on down the road?"

She took another step higher as that scowl jerked between his brows. "You think I'd give any woman something like that?"

"I don't know *what* to think. You sat up on that windmill today and looked like some old lonely wolf aching for his cave—or his floozies."

She took another step as Roman moved up one more. " 'Floozies'? I didn't know people still used that word. But sure, I've known some women."

"I don't want to be 'some women.' How do I know exactly how you feel about me?" Shelly clutched the necklace tightly in her fist and tossed away the box. "I bet you have a drawer-ful of these—"

His face hardened and he smiled coldly as he advanced another step higher. "Just two. I gave Dani one that matches it. I cut pictures out of Lauren's high school yearbook, one of you and one of me."

Shelly backed up three more steps, digging in to make her point with Roman, who didn't really believe in himself. She intended to push him to the edge, so that he couldn't doubt how he felt about her, or about himself. "So you really don't see yourself as a father, a married man, do you?"

"I said I'd try, and I wouldn't hurt you."

She backed up the steps until she stood at the top, looking down at him. "You're going to have to show me just how you feel." Shaking with her boldness, she moved back into his apartment. By the time Roman entered the spartan furnished room, she was wearing only her bra and briefs, and posed in front of his Vargas calendars.

"You're going to have to show me," she repeated unevenly, as she leaned back and licked her lips, in what she hoped was a seductive pose. "I want to know how you feel about me before the wedding night—if there's going to be one."

Caught in the shadowy light slicing through the miniblinds on the windows, Roman's hands gripped the hand railing on either side of him, his knuckles white. The bones of his face seemed to push against his dark skin, and his breathing seemed erratic, slow, dragging in and out, his nostrils flaring. The vein in his throat pounded slowly, the muscles of his broad shoulders bunched and hard, cords standing out in relief in his arms.

He stepped into the apartment fully, slowly closing the old door, and the hum of the air conditioner ate at the silence.

He stared so hard that she faltered, and wondered if she'd gone too far—sweet, shy Shelly, smalltown cleaning woman, trying to vamp a man who knew more about life than she even suspected. She had to know how fiercely he felt, and Roman's protective shield was keeping her from the truth—

She had to be bold now, her flesh shivering with Roman's burning slow look, taking her in from head to toe. Hands shaking, but trying to move slowly, artfully, seductively, she placed the necklace around her throat.

When she removed her bra, his indrawn breath hissed across the air conditioner's hum, and the pounding of her heart. Taking her time, she shimmied out of her briefs and with her foot, tossed them aside.

Roman still hadn't moved, and Shelly feared she'd gone too far. Or far enough?

She turned, and with her hands braced on her hips, her legs apart, she tilted her head. Her hair swayed to cover one shoulder as she looked at his beloved calendar girls on the wall. She'd had a baby, but she was lean and strong enough to fight for what she wanted—and she wanted all of Roman, to burn away the shadows hovering around him.

Behind her, the silence was terrifying. Then Roman's weight on the flooring creaked slightly, his footsteps nearing until the heat of his body burned her back, his lips warm against her ear. "What do you want?"

"Proof."

His finger slowly prowled down her bare back and up to her shoulder, where he drew the letter "R." His whisper was deep and raw, erotically warm as it swirled around her ear. "I wanted the sweetheart route this time, honey . . . taking it slow, giving you what you deserve . . . dinner, presents, that sort of thing. You're pushing."

"That's a sweet idea. Maybe later."

His teeth caught her lobe and he whispered, "You could be asking for more than you can handle. I'll understand if you want to back off."

She sucked in her breath as his open hand skimmed her side, curving to her hip and then rising to gently cup her breast, toying with her nipple until it peaked. Her voice came out low and husky. "Does a warning usually come with—?"

Roman turned her quickly and his mouth came down on hers—hard, demanding, open and hot, fusing with hers. His open hands stroked the length of her back, finding her bottom, cupping it briefly and pressing her to his arousal before moving to her sides.

She wasn't letting him intimidate her. Shelly arched into the kiss, opened for it, burned with it, locking him in her arms. She was a strong woman, and stronger, now that she had Roman, the friction between them bringing life and joy. His breath was hers, mingling as they locked, battling, pushing each other higher.

He pushed her away, quickly stripping his clothes away while he stared at her, eyes glittering, and Shelly couldn't resist running a fingernail slowly down his chest, an instinctive provocative feminine reaction to the raw sensuality pulsing between them. She eased back against the wall, the calendars framing her, and lifting her foot, slowly placed it on Roman's stomach. His hand wrapped around her ankle and held her there. "If you think you can use that bad knee as an excuse, think again," Shelly whispered.

Whoever she was now—not sweet Shelly, friend and daughter and mother—she reveled in her femininity, in the stark hunger in Roman's expression. She tossed away a lifetime of good-girls-don't and you'll-be-sorry, and threats of gossip. She tore away fears of Dani and sorrow for Lauren, and settled into one goal—Roman, all of him.

A downward look assured her there was plenty of him. She breathed heavily, feeling herself warm and soften as his hand slid from her ankle upward, caressing her inner thigh. She settled back against the wall, watching him, waiting, her body tensed for his next move.

Testing them both, she pushed her foot gently against his stomach, and Roman reacted instantly, not allowing her the distance. He eased her foot aside and stood watching her, a hunter locked onto what he sought.

She'd come after him. Maybe she was a hunter, too. That thrilling thought launched her out of the plain Shelly and into Shelly-the-desirable-woman.

A wonderful game, she thought, advance, retreat, entice, feel . . . oh, she wanted to feel him so badly—

Then Roman's mouth was on hers again as he lifted her and carried her to his bed, following her down upon it, holding her tight against him. Shelly dug her nails into his shoulders as Roman's hands skimmed her body, finding her warmth, tormenting her, and then he was a part of her, slowly easing to lock them together.

And then the storm began—

He'd hated this land, and now it called to him. He wanted to refuse the beckoning, yet it wouldn't let him go. Mitchell kicked the old stove pipe, rusted and overgrown with weeds and lying in the rubble of the burned house. The trees beside the rubble had once shielded the house from the heat and the fierce wind. The treetrunks were blackened, some of the trees dead, limbs broken, others alive with foliage and birds. The surviving trees had made the choice to grow and live, despite their scars.

He circled one tree and found the telling branch where a child's swing had hung. There was the old garden place, the fence to keep livestock out, looking like jagged, worn teeth. His mother had whitewashed that fence-

Mitchell pivoted toward the old barn, mounds of rusted metal roofing and burned wood, and in the silence of the morning heard the echoes of the horses screaming in fear.

He turned again and found the garage where Pete Jones had been found. The doors yawned open, the shadows inside echoing with Fred's curses as he tried to woo a tractor past its time into life.

Without hesitating, Mitchell took the gas he used for his lawn mowers from the back of his truck and poured it around the building. A lit match took the fire snaking around the weathered wood; rats and mice fled into the brush.

Mitchell watched the flames shoot up into the sky, gray smoke churning against the white clouds. In the distance, the oil rigs pecked slowly at the ground, while others remained still. Lonny's buffalo were grazing on the horizon, huge brown mountains of animals past their time.

Mitchell turned to the old house, seeing it through the years to when it looked like any average country home, a woman's touch in the roses and the gardens, the washed clothes flapping white in the hot sun, his mother hurrying to bring them in when the much-needed rain began.

A woman's touch. Uma's touch had curled inside him, easing the darkness. He'd come through time, back to where he started, because Uma made him *feel*. He could feel the other woman, Lauren, when he was in the house, the softness in her and the aching for a child, for a man to love only her. He could feel her sadness and her quiet joy.

He could hear a whisper even now, when he thought of how he felt about Uma. *Oneness* ... the women were wrapped together, through lifetime friendship and that moment of death, and Lauren wanted Uma to be happy.

"I'll do my best, Lauren," Mitchell whispered unevenly.

The wind stirred around him, heat from the flames burning as Fred's words whispered through the sunlight. *I loved that woman with all my heart . . . tell Gracie that I've always loved her . . .*

Mitchell took off his western hat and tried to understand why he would want anything to do with this land.

He tried to understand how Grace and Fred could love each other so much, then let themselves be torn apart.

But Mitchell knew . . . he knew he had a choice to move on as the old trees had done, or he could lose . . . lose Uma. Behind him, the burning garage collapsed. Taking his time, Mitchell hefted his water jug high in the air and let the icy water trickle over him. He poured water into a jar and sat on the back tailgate of his pickup, watching the flames devour themselves just as bitterness could devour any heart.

Uma. Oneness. Together. Man and woman . . .

He wanted to keep the best of the past, this small piece of

worthless land, because it was a part of him, in his blood, given to him by his homesteading ancestors, kept by his father against all odds.

Fred was right to keep the land, but he wasn't right to put it above letting Grace work, or spending time with his family. He could have made a good enough living through the garage, focusing on that, and just living on the land, instead of trying to bring it to life . . .

Mitchell kicked the hard-packed dirt. Well, then, but Fred wasn't a manager, was he? His father had felt deeply about keeping a deathbed promise to his father, and about his marriage vows. He didn't see the land in a bookkeeper's figures, black and white, or debtor's red. He was just a man trying to do his best and losing at life, pushing away those who loved him, too proud to tell them what was in his heart. And then life got too twisted and too much, and everyone lost. In his shame, Fred refused help from his wife, striking out at her . . .

Tell Gracie that I've always loved her . . .

When the flames died into coals, Mitchell began shoveling dirt onto the rubble, killing any chance of the fire spreading.

He'd fought his way off this land into offices and good paychecks and respect. Now here he was, a yard man, and a happy one when at his craft. He found peace in working with his hands and growing thorny old roses that scratched him when they could. He wanted a garden, and tomatoes to challenge Orley Long Trees' blue ribbons. A champion backyard gardener at ninety, Orley needed a little competition. Mitchell wanted a woman more than money, more than his pride . . . Uma . . .

He was soaked with sweat and feeling as if he'd been kicked by a mule, not the fear that if he didn't change, he'd hurt Uma, just as Fred had hurt Grace.

Then, out on the crest of a rolling hill, a stray horse raised his head, and gleaming like the devil, pawed the dirt, and Mitchell knew him for a wild one, escaped from some pasture, feeling his pride and freedom and full of himself.

Mitchell took a rope from the back of his truck, expertly fashioned a noose, and began walking toward the horse. There were some things he didn't want Uma to see, and one was him working off the past.

"Come here, you knothead," he murmured softly as the horse stomped and whinnied, and wide-eyed, rolled an ear toward him. The quarter horse was black and sleek and powerful and mean as hades and just what Mitchell wanted ... he thought of cool, sleek boardrooms and masked discussions, threats and compromises. But he'd rather do his fighting on the back of a horse, the honesty and truth beating into his bones. "Come here, you black son of a buck, let's have this out, you and me."

SEVENTEEN

Pearl crushed the delicate petals of a rose in her fist. *If Uma had her way, she would turn the Warrens into one big happy family. She'd brought Grace back to Madrid, a woman of such style and class that Pearl wouldn't be recognized for everything she had done. Still beautiful, soon Grace would be the leader of style and the center of the women's circles, replacing Pearl. The ladies would want Grace to head their thrift shop drives and power charities—*

Uma wouldn't be forgiven for tampering with Pearl's social standing—Uma and her mother must have falsified records, because Pearl knew her bloodline was spotless. Uma had to die for interfering, for making Grace comfortable in Everett's home, and for taking a low-class Warren to her bed.

Pearl swept up the stairs of her home, furious with the roses she hated. While Walter slept, snoring heavily in his early morning "siesta," a drug and alcohol haze, she'd worked to tear at the roses, digging them, cutting them, destroying the blooms beneath her shoes.

She paused at the bedroom, watching him drool as he slept. Her hand tightened around the garden snippers and she thought how badly she wanted to drive it into his throat.

He told her he'd spawned a child with Shelly, taunting Pearl about how good Shelly was in bed.

It wasn't just time yet for Walter to be even more addicted. If he couldn't function as she needed, she had to plan his removal to make Madrid feel sorry for her. The way he was taking to the drug she routinely placed in his afternoon drink, he could be managed easily when she wanted. Pearl pushed at her hair, controlling the anger within her as she had since childhood.

Until she'd become Clyde, she'd been powerless, but now she knew how to make them all pay.

She entered the room and crouched by Walter, disdaining the heavy alcoholic smell. "You will buy that Warren property, Walter. You *have* to have it. Mitchell Warren is no good. He's got Uma in his bed, and they are doing it all night. You have to buy that old land, force him to show how unfit he is for Madrid. They are doing it all night, Walter, rubbing all over each other, Uma hot for him. Get him out before he starts a business here and people look up to him, not you. He's not your equal, Walter, and he's doing it to Uma every day and night."

Satisfied as Walter stirred restlessly, taking her subliminal coaching, Pearl stood and smiled coldly. She swept from the room and into the small feminine room that was all her own, her retreat within the house where no one, not even her daughters, dared enter.

Her daughters, pale, lifeless girls. She felt no maternal instincts for them, and they would do as they were told.

Her hands were bloody, her designer silk blouse and slacks torn. She tore off her clothing, kicking it aside as she went to scrub her hands. In the ornate bathroom mirror, leaves stuck in her hair.

She had to move quickly, to confine and disarm Uma before she could do more damage to the release of Pearl into the powerful woman handling her own destiny. Clyde was merely an end to changing herself and handling the problems of a lifetime.

Pearl plucked the leaves from her hair and talked softly, outlining her plans as she changed into the hidden softer, flowing 1930s style clothing of Bonnie Parker. She studied herself clinically in the full-length mirror. After her obvious grief over Uma's and Shelly's death eased, she might adopt the style; it suited her.

Lonny's Oklahoma drawl traveled lazily over the telephone lines to Uma. "Looks like someone is handling a big problem. Mitchell just asked LeRoy Stein if he could help him break horses. LeRoy does that in the early morning, and it's hot as hades now. Mitchell didn't care. He's out there now, busting broncs just like his old man did when he was fighting losing everything . . . and I'm stuck with pigsitting the Ferris's Rosy. I'll be glad when this is all over and they aren't scared for her. A pig really shouldn't be riding in the back seat of a patrol car."

Uma's hand went to her throat. With Grace's arrival came a fresh blast of old memories, and Mitchell was dealing with a gut-wrenching reaction. She pressed the save button on her computer, praying that her fussy client would like her new design. She'd promised herself she'd return Pearl's call in a few minutes, but for now, Uma had to get to Mitchell.

She called Dani. "Your uncle. That man. He's breaking horses and I've got to stop him from breaking his neck. Could you please take Grace to Everett's and help her with what she needs? She wants to spend the night and should have everything she needs—just change the sheets in the guestroom—"

"Grace says she could use a nap. I want to come. I want to see how to handle a horse, because someday I'm going to have one. Can I?"

At LeRoy's ranch, a big hound dog chasing a yellow cat ran in front of Uma's car. She braked, the car skidded, turned sideways, slowly slid, and then bumped into Mitchell's big Dodge pickup. The bump wasn't enough to jar her anger at Mitchell. The screech of metal against metal sounded as she put her car in reverse just enough to be able to open the door.

Dani leaped out of the passenger side and hurried at Uma. "Wow, Uma. You just don't get all lit up like this."

"Call me 'fireball,'" Uma gritted through her teeth and smoothed her sleeveless loose dress, trying to grip whatever calm Mitchell was intent upon destroying. "Your uncle needs some sense knocked into him. If the horse doesn't do it, I may."

"You love him, don't you? He's the only one who's ever gotten you so riled and on edge. You never used to talk like that. Such violence. Not your usual 'let's talk about it reasonably' mode," Dani teased.

"Mitchell understands action, not logical conversation, give and take. If that's how I have to reach him, I will."

Mitchell was in the corral, easing down onto a gleaming red horse called "Devil." The scrawny little ancient cowboy holding Devil's reins wasn't winning the battle. Devil had broken more bones in the local rodeo than any other horse. With a long–sleeved shirt rolled back at the cuffs, leather gloves, jeans, and workman's boots, Mitchell looked as if he'd been jerked out of drover times. The expression on his face said he was in a fighting mood and the bad-tempered horse was his choice for a battle.

Images of Fred doing the same thing slid across Uma's mind as she hitched up her skirt and kicked off her sandals. She hefted herself up on the corral boards and over the fence, marching toward Mitchell.

LeRoy started a jagged-toothed smile that died at her cold stare. "Don't you dare let him do this, LeRoy."

From the dust on Mitchell's face and clothes, he'd already been in the horse's saddle several times—and had been tossed. The horse skittered and sidewalked as LeRoy held him, and Mitchell's hard voice cut across the early afternoon air. "Get out of the corral, Uma."

He was beautiful, macho, sweaty, stubborn, and outlined in the hot, burning sun as the only man she both loved and wanted to kill. "What's this going to prove?"

LeRoy's panicked expression didn't matter to her. "Ms. Uma, you can get hurt. Old Devil here isn't high on manners. I can't hold him much longer. Once I let go, he's a sidewinder."

She pointed to another docile horse tied to the side of the corral. "What about him?"

"Old Sweetheart? You know that most of my stock are for the rodeos. He's fine until you put some weight on him—"

Uma looked up at Mitchell. "If you do not get down off that horse this minute, I am going to ride *that* one."

He swung down, almost vaulting off the horse. "When are you going to learn to stop messing in my business?"

Mitchell glanced at Dani who was now in the corral. "Get out of here."

"I want to pet the horses. You're probably just mean to them. You should try some animal psychology. That's what I'm going to do," Dani said.

Mitchell jerked back to Uma, glaring down at her as he ripped off his gloves. "I've had a bellyful of everything this morning. Don't you start on me. And by the way, you're a bad example to Dani. Dani, take Uma's car back to town. We'll be back later."

He had that stiff-backed, male-ordering command sound to his voice that raised Uma's temper a notch higher. "Gee, Mr. Man. You're so . . . so—bull-headed, thoughtless, ignorant, lowdown—"

The disbelieving sound coming from LeRoy said he was shocked. "Ms. Uma!"

"Oh, LeRoy. We just haven't figured out this relationship business yet. *He's* the problem."

"Let's not share *our* problems, dear," Mitchell said in a warning tone. When she opened her mouth again, ready to tell him exactly how much he had terrified her, Mitchell scooped her up on his shoulder. He walked through the gate LeRoy had just opened, carrying her to his pickup.

Mitchell stopped near at the new dent and scrapes on his pickup, then rounded it with her in his arms. He dumped her into the passenger side and closed the door. "Well, at least you put the dent on the same side."

Uma settled into the seat and crossed her arms over her chest. No one had ever handled her so—so improperly. She must have looked like a sack of grain, slung over his shoulder. It just wasn't seemly. "One who is strong does not have to demonstrate that strength for it to be known. That . . . was . . . not . . . very . . . nice."

He drove down the dusty road toward the cottonwood creek, stopping abruptly in a shady spot. Leaving Uma in the pickup, he strode down to the water, tore off his clothes, and hurled himself into the water.

In Uma's entire life, she'd never gone skinny dipping. As a child, she and her friends used the city pool, then later, occasionally swimming at Pearl's luxurious one.

She picked her way over the path in her bare feet, lifting her skirt away from the bushes. In the water, Mitchell was diving and coming up, throwing back his hair in a spray of water. The water wasn't deep in August, but shaded by tall cottonwood trees.

"Are we over our snit now, dear?" she asked as the golden leaves caught the hot sun searing through the trees. She wondered what had set Mitchell off, to pit himself against a beast who had already broken more men's bones than she wanted to count. "You know, Tommy Eagle is still nursing his ribs from the last time that animal was in the rodeo. George and Lyle and all the rest have tried to break him."

Mitchell turned over on his back and floated, ignoring her.

Last night and this morning, he'd—

If he could swim buck-naked in the middle of the day, so could she. Uma wondered what Uma the controlled, sensible woman must think of her as she removed her loose dress and bra and briefs. Mitchell's eyes didn't leave her as she eased into the water quickly, shy of the bold daylight, and quickly lowered until only her head was exposed. "If this is the only way to talk with you, Mitchell Warren, then I suppose the end justifies the means. What happened to upset you?"

"I'm not upset."

"Ohhh! Of course you are. No one in his right mind would try horse breaking in one hundred-degree heat—"

"I thought I stood a better chance of wearing him down," Mitchell said logically.

"You're a skilled businessman. You hated ranch work. You said you never intended to do anything with that land. Why in heavens name would you just up and decide to break horses again?"

"Because I can."

His tone said he wasn't giving information freely. Uma closed her lips and decided to play his game her way. Conscious of her nude body, and bracing herself against a lifetime of modesty, Uma eased into a floating position, her hair spreading out around her. She gave herself to the sensual movement of the water, gently ebbing against her breasts.

"I've never seen a woman blush all over before."

"It's a new experience, shedding my clothes in broad daylight, but a rather delightful one." She waited and hoped he would share his darkness with her, that whatever taunted him would ease. She gave herself to the quiet day, the flow of the water over her body, to being with the man she loved.

His body shaded hers as he stood beside her. "Who would know that sweet, very proper Uma would enjoy skinny dipping?"

"Mmm. I've changed since you came into town. I don't know that it's for the best. I'm edgy and I think about you all the time, and a good percentage of that time, I'm pretty darned frustrated with you. I'm used to harmony and peace and safety, and you're none of those. With you, every day is a land mine of the unexpected. I've never, ever liked surprises, and you're a walking, talking one. And then there's the sleep that I'm missing, though last night was an experience not to be missed."

Mitchell bent to take her breast in his mouth sucking gently—just for a brief moment. "There you were—Ninja woman, slinking around buildings and rooftops. Tell me, would you really have ridden that horse? *Can* you ride a horse?"

"I would have made do. I find that when you're involved and acting macho . . . macho Mr. Man, I can do anything. The people that I know usually listen and use logic and we chat and resolve. You're just too . . . too . . ." She wouldn't let him derail her. Something horrible had upset him. It still hovered around Mitchell with the sunlight and the shadows. "You know what I mean."

"I'm like Dad," he said bluntly. "I cut you off the same way he treated her. From the sound of her letters, they loved each other and she really tried to make their marriage work."

Clearly, Mitchell had been wrestling with open doors to the past and finding what was behind them painful, which explained his need to face the physical reality of a horse, rather than tearing himself apart emotionally. "That's true. He came to the house one day, a man unable to hold more, and asked if he could talk to my mother, Grace's friend. Mother knew both sides . . . Grace had confided in her, and in the end, Fred did, too. He just couldn't take that simple first step after denying her for all those years."

"His pride kept them apart. He didn't give her letters to us. He didn't want to lose the only part of her that he had left— his sons. She would have come back at any time, and he was ashamed."

She reached to take his hand. "That was all in the letters?"

"No, I read between the lines. I remembered the things that he had said, and fitted them together with her letters, and I knew how I would feel—down on my luck, knowing that I hadn't treated a good woman right, ignoring her when she wanted to work, to make things better . . . and not understanding how to deal with myself, how to apologize and beg her to come back to me."

That was what had set Mitchell off, realizing that his father's bitterness had ruined lives . . . realizing that he'd spent precious years ignoring a woman who desperately loved her sons, wanting only the best for them and ready to fight for them against the man she loved . . . and Mitchell had shared his anguish with Uma. "That's pretty insightful."

"Too bad your *Smooth Moves List* wasn't around then. He made all the mistakes with a woman he loved, and eventually she had to do something to try to help him and us. He returned the money she'd sent. And you knew all that, didn't you?"

"It was for you to work through and to understand. I felt as if Lauren's house was the right place to soothe you, to give you a softness to open yourself to the truth. When you said you felt Lauren move in the house—"

"Hopefully, when those results on those threads and scraps come back, we're going to get that—" Mitchell promised roughly. "Her life shouldn't have ended that way."

"Any candidates?"

"Mike knows more than he's saying. I don't think he's the

one, but he knows something, and he's afraid. There's some connection between his addiction to the 1930s outlaw guns and the slugs at Shelly's house, on the windmill and used on Pete."

Mitchell eased her to her feet. The water swirled around them, his arousal brushing her lower stomach, his hands beneath her arms. His palms massaged the outer curve of her breasts and he studied the softness flowing within his hands. "Walter Whiteford."

"Walter? Why?" she asked automatically because her body's awakening was pushing away clear thought. Only Mitchell had the ability to make her feel so sensual, the sunlight warming her upper body and the water caressing her lower limbs. His sleepy expression belied his tense body, the way he looked lower, past her belly to the hidden nest that waited and warmed for him. His hands opened on her hips, gripping her, his fingers splayed.

There was enough pressure to hold or release her as she wished. Uma held his upper arms, feeling the power in them, the security, preparing to hold her anchor in the coming passion.

"He's been wanting to buy the ranch. When I turned him down this last time, he was furious, and I didn't like what he had to say. I think Mike can use some pushing, and Lyle, too. You're the most exciting, feminine woman I've ever known. I don't want to talk any more now." His expression tightened as he looked downward, watching his body slowly enter hers.

"I love you, Mitchell." She couldn't stop the words from flowing into the sunlight and shadows, around the water that rippled gently against their bodies, over the treetops and down to the willows swaying into the water.

He paused, his eyes closed as he completed the lock of their bodies, lifting her to wrap her legs around him, taking her weight.

"Uma," he whispered unevenly, and the deep sound of his voice tore at her senses, enveloping her.

She knew instinctively that Mitchell had never given himself to another woman like this, with such aching hunger, both tender and earthshaking . . .

Dani: proof that Walter had been unfaithful; he'd bragged about his relationship with Shelly to Pearl. Living proof of his infidelity could not be tolerated.

Pearl had to move quickly. Her daughters were coming home from Walter's sister for just a few days before that New York shopping spree she'd promised them. Then she'd herd them off to boarding school. Then the election for mayor—Walter was already on the town's council; it was a logical next step.

She'd burned with excitement all day, working herself up to fever pitch, making herself strong.

She had to clean up Madrid to her satisfaction, remove the woman who had borne Walter's child, and the woman who had slurred Pearl's ancestry. Uma was also the Keeper in Madrid, and she'd known Pearl when she was a sniveling child, protected her. But Pearl didn't want people to remember her that way. She'd removed evidence before, and in her own mind, she thought of herself as a methodical cleaning woman.

Clyde, her coming-out personality, had served his purpose, an insulating buffer from which she would emerge as powerful and in charge of her life. She'd needed to step into Clyde to shed her burdensome, lifetime inhibitions.

While Walter snored in his room, his nightly drinks laced with drugs, she paced her small feminine retreat, her anger brewing.

The fool. The Toad, as she thought of Walter, now that she was stronger, didn't see what was happening. He didn't recognize Mitchell Warren as a political threat. Madrid wanted

Mitchell's influence on big business. He had been a top executive, and as such he could manage a town—or as Farley
Parks, an old-timer, was spouting at the coffee shop, "A man
doesn't get that high up without something in his noggin."

If the Toad could not pull votes as Madrid's mayor after all
she had done for him, he was disposable. She couldn't carry
him forever. If he was showing poorly just before the election,
she would simply do away with him and step into that office
herself. Sympathy went a long way in Madrid, and she knew
how to use that.

She knew also how to use Uma, one of the most important
people in the fabric of Madrid.

Pearl shrugged as she rocked her back against the wall, fueling her hatred of Uma. "How dare she malign my bloodline! How *dare* she!"

She studied her manicured nails, admiring the glossy finish. Uma had a weakness—her softness, her need to nurture
and help, her selflessness. Pearl smiled tightly, then began
priming herself as poor, helpless, defeated Pearl, battered by
life and needing her close friend. She wiped the tears from
her eyes, sniffed, and called Uma.

Uma's voice sounded distracted, as though she was working on her computer.

"I'm so sorry, Uma," Pearl burst out, throwing herself into
the role. "I shouldn't have spoken about the Warrens that
way. I miss you so. Please, please, forgive me."

Her sob was perfect, caught right in her throat, her voice
bordering on the hysterical edge that Uma had never ignored. She smiled coldly as Uma said, "Pearl, what's wrong?"

"I just can't manage without my friend. I'm horribly sorry.
I was just so upset by all this work, and the charity bazaar is
coming up. Please, please forgive me."

She studied her nails while Uma's familiar soothing voice
cruised over the telephone. "Oh, good. You'll come, then?

First thing in the morning? Oh, how can I ever thank you?"

Pearl replaced the telephone and began to dance around the room, clapping her hands. "Uma and Shelly and Mitchell . . . Uma and Shelly and Mitchell . . ."

EIGHTEEN

At eight o'clock the next morning, Uma swung into the work she had promised to do with Pearl, helping clean her overstuffed closet. While Uma wondered how any woman could manage to buy so many clothes, Pearl rummaged the garage for more packing boxes.

The small room that Pearl labeled her "retreat" was softly lit from the sunlight passing through the window's ruffled sheers. A delicate table stood next to a cream-colored velvet chaise longue laden with mounds of the clothing and shoes that Pearl had decided to donate to charity. The lid to a small secretary stood closed, and across its top were stacks of decorating and fashion magazines.

In contrast to her cozy "retreat," Pearl's walk-in closet was massive, and mirrors lined her huge private bathroom.

Uma glanced at the deadbolt on the door and decided that if Walter was in the vicinity, locks might not be a bad idea, even for his wife. She remembered how shattered Pearl had been when she'd returned from her honeymoon. She'd been terrified, but she'd stayed with Walter against Uma's advice. Until Pearl had had enough, no one could help her.

Uma yawned, feeling sated after a night spent with

Mitchell. The walkie-talkies that Roman and Mitchell had insisted that Dani use in case of trouble had remained quiet throughout the night.

She smiled softly as she folded a summer lawn dress and placed it into a cardboard box marked "Dressy." Shelly had that simmering, bubbling, blooming look of a woman well loved and wanting more. Roman had that quiet, tense expression of a man just waiting to get her alone.

The night had been quiet and that odd, cool stillness had come to Uma in the early morning, just as it had when Christina had died and when Lauren had been killed . . . as if all the world had stopped, waiting.

She hugged a raw silk jacket close to her. Whoever stalked Madrid knew the lives there; Uma prayed for just one clue, that if Mike knew anything—Walter . . . Mike . . . Walter . . . Uma breathed quietly as she remembered how excited Pearl had been when Walter had personally loaned a financially strapped Mike money in return for the mortgage of his house and Clyde's Tavern.

Uma held the jacket close to her and looked out at the bright sunlight and listened to the slow dragging beat of her heart. A crow landed heavily on the branch outside the window; the branch bobbed with the weight, sunlit leaves shimmering as the bird seemed to peer at Uma through the glass.

Her hand passed over the jacket, smoothing it, and paper crackled within one pocket.

Uma reached into the pocket and pulled out a crumpled snapshot. She opened it carefully to find Walter standing by Shelly. It was one of Lauren's first photographs with her new camera, and Uma remembered it had been in Lauren's things, in her albums. Excited, she'd taken pictures at one of Pearl's parties, capturing Walter and Shelly as they had talked. Walter's head was inclined toward Shelly, his body position intimately close. Uma remembered the picture because Shelly's expression had shown subtle distaste.

The picture had been crushed; Shelly's face and body had been punched with holes.

Pearl entered the room, a glass of sweet tea topped with a wedge of lemon in each hand. "Mine is the one with the peppermint sprig. My great-great-great-grandmother Matilda used to serve—"

When she saw Uma's expression and the picture in her hand, Pearl walked to the small secretary and placed the tea on top. She calmly reached to an ornate picture frame and removed a key, unlocking the closed front door of the secretary.

"I see you've found the proof," she said quietly.

"Proof of what?" Uma asked as she found herself facing the large automatic in Pearl's hand.

Above it, her friend's face was a cold mask. Her careful makeup seemed etched on her face, almost cartoonish in contrast to her pale skin, her eyes glittering. The usual soft, vulnerable shape of her mouth had tightened as she spoke with command. "Let's take a drive. We can talk later. Just remember, dear, that if anyone stops us, you could cause them to die just by betraying me. And yourself, of course. I'm a very good shot."

She lifted the glass of tea with the lemon wedge. "But first, you must drink this. I couldn't be so rude as to ignore my duty as a proper hostess."

Uma took the glass and slowly ran her thumb down the outer beads of perspiration. An icy drop formed and plopped to the lush silver carpeting as suddenly she heard Lauren whisper again, "I'll always be with you."

When Uma hesitated, Pearl lifted the deadly muzzle of the gun. "Drink it. It's got just a little of my special ingredient that Walter is getting to love so much . . . just a little something to relax you."

I'll always be with you . . .

"Why?" *Was it possible that Pearl had something to do with Lauren's death?*

"Oh, not here, darling. I can't explain here. You must know that there is a proper time and place for everything. If you want to know all the details of my little plan, you must be a good little girl and drink what Mommy has prepared for you. Surprises must be planned, you know, so drink and relax, and yours will come, all in due time. Oh, don't worry, I'm not going to kill you now."

"You're not going to stop here, are you? With me?" Uma asked.

Pearl smiled tightly. "It depends how good you are. If you're a bad girl, Mommy will punish your friends. I suggest you drink that . . . you don't think I'll shoot, do you? Think about the bullets in Shelly's house, that scar I put on her head . . . think about Rosy and the barbed-wire necktie I gave her . . . think about your computer crash and all those little distracting accidents that Shelly has had this year. A magnet in my purse was all it took to ruin your computer files, dear. The perfect hostess as always, you were getting tea for me, leaving me alone in your office."

"Shelly? You did all those things to Shelly?"

"I managed them. And then they just happened. I just turned on the stove when she wasn't looking, cut her gas line—you remember her car fire? But she really did them to herself, like by turning that key."

Because Uma feared that Pearl as she was now could actually carry out her threats, Uma drank slowly. She waited for just the right distraction, but Pearl leaned against the secretary, focused on her. "It's just a little something to take the edge off, dear, don't worry. I need you. But then, I've always needed you—and that's your weakness, the eternal need to nurture and help. I've never had to worry about maternal urges. They must be a bother. You're absolutely stuffed with maternal urges."

The drink was taking effect; Uma's body began to feel heavy. "Pearl, you have daughters. Don't do this."

Pearl shrugged and thoughtfully stroked the nuzzle against her cheek. She took the glass from Uma and placed it carefully on a coaster. "They'll do as they're told. I did."

Uma tried to ask, "Proof of what?" but the words weren't clear, only a sheer fuzziness that deepened as Pearl wrapped her arm around Uma's waist and managed her out of the room and down the hallway. "That's right, dear, lean on me. Everything is going to be fine. Just be a good little girl."

Uma gripped the curved walnut banister as they slowly made their way downstairs. She wanted to fight, but her body was too heavy, her mind suddenly unclear—

Then Pearl was easing her into a car seat, strapping her in. "Safety first," Pearl said cheerfully. "Buckle up."

Cold metal circled Uma's wrist, clicking shut and imprisoning her, and then the other locking her hands together. A heavy cloth dropped over her. Uma felt the seat recline beneath her, until she was almost lying down, and she could feel the car easing out of the garage. Beneath the heavy cloth, she could barely breathe, the heat suffocating. "I want to go home. I want Mitchell."

"Well, of course you do." As she drove, Pearl patted Uma's knee. "We'll be there in just a minute. I want to show you something very special. Comfy?"

Uma felt herself helped out of the car and into a building, and then she was on a small creaking cot. "There, there, dear. Take a nice nap," she heard Pearl say in the distance. "I'll be back soon with Shelly. Won't that be nice? All of us together? With no interruptions? And then we'll have that little chat I've been promising you."

Sunlight slanted across Shelly's face, nudging her slowly awake. She opened her eyes to see that shaft of sunlight gleaming on Roman's shoulder—

Shelly flattened to Roman's bed, the wall on one side. Roman, his head propped on one hand was on the other side, studying her. In the shadows, his hair was rumpled, a dark stubble covering his jaw. He toyed with a strand of her hair, bringing it to his lips. " 'Morning, sleepyhead."

Shelly's blush began at her toes and began a warming path upward. "Um. I don't suppose you would know what time it is?"

He chuckled and the deep, rich, intimate sound curled around her. "Not exactly the first words I was hoping for from you this morning, but they'll do."

She couldn't breathe, lying naked beneath the sheet that she tugged up to her chin.

"People do it in the daylight, too, you know, honey," Roman said, and his finger tugged at the sheet. "I want to know that I wasn't dreaming."

"Um. I'd rather not."

She held firm to the sheet and Roman's hand cruised over the gold chain at her throat and lower, smoothing her breasts. "Is this the same woman who pushed me last night?"

She'd met him in fire, taking her share, giving, pitting herself against Roman without shame. Without shame . . . the words prodded her. She closed her eyes, unwilling to meet his searching gaze. "I have work to do."

"Are you sorry?" he asked abruptly, cupping her cheek and turning her to him.

"No. But this is a new experience for me."

"I've been in a few women's beds. Maybe more than my share. That isn't going to happen again. Not after you," Roman said slowly as his thumb stroked her cheek. "You're all wide eyed and sweet, Shell. So sweet . . ."

He bent to brush his lips across hers. "I've never wanted to linger and talk with any woman. This is new for me, too."

She tried to breathe and pushed away the brief, nagging workday that waited for her; she knew that if Dani needed her, she would call . . . Shelly sensed that this moment with Roman might not come again, and she loved him so. He seemed poised on a discovery that he wanted to unravel with her.

"I love you, Shell. I never thought I'd say those words, but that's how it is. I'll try real hard, Shell."

He looked away, his lashes catching the light, his mouth tight as if he wasn't certain of her response. She stroked his cheek and turned him back to her. "I've always loved you, Roman Warren. Always, and I always will. I've known that since I was just a child, watching you play 'Eagle' and swaggering around, trying to impress the girls . . . which you did very well, by the way."

He swallowed roughly and those light brown eyes shimmered with tears. "It's been a long, hard road, Shell. I thought I had everything once, and I had nothing. When that was ripped away, I thought about ending it."

Intimacy, she thought, loving him more. There would be quiet talk in the mornings and at night, sharing the years between and the ones together. She smoothed his hair, enjoying the texture, watching his changing expressions, the uncertainty hovering around him.

"How you look at me," he whispered unevenly. "As if I'm someone special."

"You are. Very special and sweet."

He snorted at that. " 'Sweet.' That's the first time anyone has called me that."

"Well, I just know certain parts of you that no one else does."

When his lips smiled lazily, smugly, she traced them. "Those parts, too, but I mean what's inside, where you're good and kind and loving."

If she told him he was blushing, he'd deny it. She decided to hoard that secret for herself. Because Roman was uncomfortable with his good qualities, he moved toward a safer reaction—easing down the sheet from her body.

His gaze took in all of her, slowly, warmly. And then his hands began their magic—

A flash of time and heat and storms later, Roman's breathing slowed, and he relaxed slowly into Shelly's arms. He'd just told her he loved her again, by the cherishing touch of his hands, by the slow, drugging kisses. Still luxuriating in their lovemaking, Shelly stroked his back, enjoying the floating after-pleasure as his face nuzzled her throat.

"You'll wear a white dress, Shell . . . at the wedding . . ."

"Hmm?" She smiled lazily, drifting exquisitely, as he nibbled at her ear.

"Our wedding. You'll wear a bridal gown. Something long and sweet and virginal, and at the church . . . what's wrong? You just went stiff as a board."

Shelly held her breath; if there was one thing she didn't want it was to be the focus of attention at a church wedding. She'd lived with gossip for years, and a wedding like that would only create more. "I'm a private person, Roman . . . I don't think so."

Roman eased away, watching her. "Why not?"

She sensed his brewing frustration, that agile mind leaping through all sorts of conclusions, including the one that said she was ashamed of him. "I'm not ashamed. I'm just a private person."

"Dani wants my name. It would look a whole lot better if you and I got married first."

She placed her open hand on his chest. "Roman, you're moving too fast. I—"

"You like to be independent and call the shots." There it was, right on the edge, Roman's frustration that he hadn't been a part of her life and now she wasn't letting him into it.

"Let's not argue. I have to get to work."

"You're staying right here until this is settled. I want to wake up to you every morning and hold you all night long. I want to know that you're safe and so is Dani. I don't want another night where you're in the house with someone else, and I'm on the outside. I want—"

"Is everything about what you want? What about what I want?"

"What you want to do is to run everything your way. Maybe I'm saying it wrong, but you're my woman now, and that's that . . . 'My woman,' funny, I remember Dad saying that in just about the same tone, fierce-like, as if he'd fight the world for Mother. That's what I'd do for you, Shell, but you've got to let me in."

Now he was on the side of the wall and she was on the outer side of the bed. Shelly sat up and started to leave the bed and Roman's arm looped around her waist, dragging her back into bed with him. He pinned her beneath him, holding her wrists in his hands.

"Let me go." She tried to buck his weight from her and Roman's expression darkened.

"If you want me again, you've got just the right moves, honey."

She flattened to the bed, lying still. She wasn't afraid; he wouldn't hurt her. "Let me go, Roman."

"What's wrong with us getting married in a church and you wearing what a bride should wear, and doing the whole thing up right?" he demanded.

"You don't understand—"

"No, I don't. But this is going to have to come from you. I thought you'd want what most women want, what I hope Dani will have—all her family and friends there, wishing her well. That's what I want for you."

Roman released her hands and eased to the side. He lay staring at the ceiling, his hands behind his head. "I don't want to sneak around, Shell. I want the woman I love to have everyone know that I love her. Is that so wrong?"

He frowned at her as she rose, clenching his discarded shirt to her body for protection. "Go ahead. Go to work."

"I'm sorry—" She hadn't meant to hurt him, to toss away the lovely offer he'd served her, and now he'd stepped back into his shield, closing her off.

"Sure. Dani will probably stay with Grace again tonight. I'll cook supper."

She'd just ruined one moment and wondered if she should push now. "Roman, I really am sorry. I've just never—"

"You're scared, Shell. So am I. We're going to make mistakes," he said curtly. "Especially me . . . is there something else you wanted to talk about before you run out of here?"

"I'm not running. I have a job; it's my day to do the Morrisons. What are you going to do?"

Silence.

Shelly took a deep breath and plunged right into what she hoped would happen in Roman's day. "It's important to me that you talk with Grace."

Now the silence was throbbing, almost tangible, as Roman stared at her coldly. "Have a nice day."

Shelly's knees shook as she descended the stairs and walked out into the hot August day. From the looks of him, Roman wouldn't be dropping the subject of their wedding, and he could be very, very persuasive.

And tonight, they would be alone in the house.

Uma pushed herself through the layers of fog and found herself in a small barren room, lying on a metal cot. One tug of her hand proved she had been handcuffed to it. At the sound of a motor, she sat upright and held her breath as a rock-hard headache stunned her.

The door unlocked electronically and Pearl pushed Shelly into the room at the point of a revolver.

"Shelly!"

Pearl tossed another pair of handcuffs on the bed and pointed the automatic at Uma. "Put them on, Shelly, dear. And please use the other end of the bed. Just put one on the metal bedframe. You wouldn't want Uma to be punished because you didn't obey me, would you?"

Shelly's green eyes were wide in her pale face. "Uma, she said that Mitchell had beaten you and you didn't want anyone to know, that you wanted me to come to you. That isn't true, is it?"

"Mitchell would never hurt me."

"I didn't think so."

Pearl eased luxuriously into the wood chair and looked at her manicured nails, admiring them. "Well, dear old chums, here we are. For your information, Mitchell is going to murder both of you, and then, horrified at what he has done, he's going to kill himself. There are one or two little problems to tidy up after that, but I'm really good at this. Little Pearl. Huh. Who would have thought it?"

"Where are we?" Uma asked, stunned that Pearl could be dangerous.

"At the old motel," Shelly answered quietly as she shook her head. "I can't believe this is happening."

"Believe it." Pearl rose and stretched and pushed the flat of her hand against the board wall and a door swung open to reveal a closet.

Pearl removed a man's suit and held it high, admiring it. She stroked a torn section on the sleeve. "I had these made. Exact copies of Clyde Barrow's wardrobe. I admire him so. Inside, that's who I really am, someone like him—edgy, dangerous, taking what I want, and yet maintaining style. Rosalie fitted the last to me, and then she had to die, of course. That old cat tore this one and the rose bushes another. I guess I'll just have to find another seamstress."

"You killed Rosalie?" Uma tried to stand and the handcuff on her wrist clicked firm and taut on the bedframe. From the distance of a few feet, she knew that it was true; the scrap of material in Rosalie's trash matched the suit's color exactly. The threads Mitchell and she had found were of the same shade. She didn't want to believe that Pearl could be stalking and killing—

"Just a little push down the stairs. Rosalie was old and disposable, and eventually she'd have told. Then Gerald Van Dyke happened to see me there, dressed as Clyde Barrow. I just couldn't let him live. He'd have wanted to be with her, anyway. I did them a favor, killing them both. *Now* they're together."

She glanced at both women, who were tugging desperately at their handcuffed wrists. "Sit down, dears. The bed is bolted to the floor. Pete was a wonderful fix-it man. I hated to lose him, too, but then there was that awful more-money thing when he killed Lauren—he wanted more for a second pass to get Shelly. You two are both so easy. Uma can't resist a chance to get into someone else's life and comfort the abused, can you, dear? And Shelly would do anything for Uma. This may be easier than I had planned. You're both so gullible."

Uma couldn't move, frozen as she sat on the cot with Shelly, their hands gripping tightly together. She couldn't believe Pearl's admissions. If she'd killed Pete, then—her body chilled despite the heat in the room. "Tell me that you didn't cause Lauren to be killed."

"She was a mistake. Shelly should have died that night. That scarf I wanted Shelly to try on? That was the mark Pete needed. Only Lauren grabbed it and he shot the wrong . . . friend." Pearl replaced the suit and took the gun, tapping it on the table as she frowned at Shelly. "Walter has had indiscretions before, but they have never produced a child. Dani is the evidence of Walter's indiscretion with Shelly and she'll have to be removed. I can't have her—"

"Pearl, Walter is *not* Dani's father, Roman is," Shelly cried out. "You can't hurt her."

"But I must, and I know you're lying. She's evidence . . . proof. Walter told me so himself just a month or so before I knew I had to act last year. I couldn't seem to do anything as Pearl Whiteford, so I had to invent another person, one with strength and cunning, and that was when I created Clyde—my Clyde, fashioned after Clyde Barrow. I found I could do amazing things when I thought and acted like him. I made contact with Pete. Walter repeatedly told me how good you were in bed—"

"He lied to you, Pearl. I wouldn't let Walter touch me . . . ever. He's not Dani's father."

"Walter never lies to me. I would know. He said you enticed him, flirted with him and it wasn't his fault—that a man is a man and can only resist so much. It was then that I knew you had to die—and Uma just knows too much. She's even tried to sully the name of my esteemed ancestor Matilda Radford. I can't have that."

Pearl shook her head and tsk-tsked. "I really have to clean all this up. I'm on a schedule, you know. When the last petal falls on the last rose in Madrid, I'm going to have everything neat and nice in my life. Oh, I may have to weep and mourn and wail a bit, but that's just acting, and I've managed that for years—haven't I, Uma? Well, I have work to do. There's bottled water in the ice chest on the table and an old covered pot beneath the bed, if you need the bathroom. You've each got a free hand and you'll manage. You always do. You're both so capable, and now, so am I. Ta."

After the door locked behind Pearl, Uma closed her eyes, and in her mind, that night over a year ago came swirling back, the stillness she felt, the way that Pearl preened with her new scarf, offering it to Shelly—the way Lauren took it playfully . . . *I'll always be with you* . . .

Shelly's face was pale, her eyes enormous and haunted. "Every accident I had . . . Pearl had been nearby or had just left. The skillet fires . . . the misplaced knives, a broken glass in the dishwater . . . *how could she?*"

I'll always be with you.

"We've got to get out of here. She intends to kill— Shelly, she killed Rosalie and Gerald. And she thinks of Dani as proof . . ."

"Dani . . ." Shelly struggled futilely with her wrist, the abrasions from the cuff starting to bleed.

Uma took Shelly's free hand. She couldn't bear to see her friend struggle, hurting herself. And she couldn't bear to think that Pearl could be so evil, so demented. Pearl had caused Lauren to be killed—sweet, innocent Lauren, who'd only wanted to tease Pearl with the scarf that night.

Again, the image that wouldn't go away slid in front of her—Lauren's summer dress, stained with blood that was warm and sticky on Uma's hands. "Don't . . . don't, Shelly. We'll think of something. We've got to be calm. Didn't you tell me that you had to sometimes unlock Dani's bedroom door with a hairpin?"

"Uh-huh. So?" Shelly followed Uma's look at her hair and then hurriedly removed the bobby pin there. "It's worth a try."

Mitchell looked up at the old windmill, the blades still at ten o'clock in the morning. He was hot and sweaty and tense and ripping into the old house's burned rubble; pitting himself against it gave him something to do. He hefted an old board, tugged it from the overgrowth, and tossed it into a pile he intended to burn. Glass and other debris would go into a rusted barrel.

He circled an old wringer washer with a rope, then walked back to the tractor and slowly pulled the rusted washer away, disturbing the field mice that scampered back into the rubble.

If Rosalie had been killed, the murderer was also a serial killer.

With Lonny's help, Mitchell had made calls to the manufacturer of the thread and the unique matching fabric. Four different seamstresses had ordered the fabric, a unique blend of material used in the 1930s. Lonny's calls to the local law said that all four seamstresses had died by accidents and their appointment books were missing.

Mitchell swung down from the tractor and hefted a grappling hook into the pile of shingles that had once been a roof. It caught and held as he tugged on it. With snakes and rats in residence, he moved carefully, beginning to methodically pull the old rubble apart, sorting his thoughts as he worked.

Mike knew something, his eyes darting to the side when Mitchell questioned him about the Colt Model 1911 .45-caliber automatic slugs that had been dug out of Uma's office wall and from the windmill and from Shelly's house. The big man's fear was hard to miss, and Mike had stiffened at questions concerning the Browning automatic rifle that had probably peppered the windmill.

While Mitchell was waiting for slow-thinking Mike to understand how serious it was to aid a murderer, and that other people might be killed, he decided to clear Warren land and his thoughts. Taking the old house apart was only physical and easier than sifting through layers of bad times and new emotions.

Uma had changed him; he wanted a life with her. He wanted peace, as much as he could wallow in with a woman that fascinated, frustrated, and loved him.

"I love you," she had whispered, and the words that he wanted to serve her wouldn't come to his lips, locked inside him.

She deserved a man who said he loved her, and acted like it.

Mitchell couldn't give her what she needed, if he acted like his father, closing doors, letting pride make him unreasonable.

That new life he'd delivered in a taxicab had started his voyage toward unraveling the darkness within him, that dark closet that held so much that he was afraid to open it.

Just as Uma needed to be cherished, Grace deserved to know that Fred's dying words were for her. "Now *that* one is going to be hard," Mitchell noted to the crows perched on top of the windmill, watching him.

The incredible softness within his house had influenced him. Lauren seemed to touch him somehow; he was sensitive to her life, her joys—the roses and her kitchen and the need to have children. "We'll get him, Lauren. And Uma won't have your blood on her hands anymore. I promise you."

At five-thirty, the rubble had been pulled apart, growing piles of pipe and metal beside those of wood to be burned. He was sweaty and dirty and fiercely afraid that he couldn't give Uma what she deserved. *I love you.*

Why wouldn't those words come easily to him?

Instead the word "oneness" curled around him, the sense that Uma was forever a part of him. Mitchell watched a rabbit hop away from the disturbed rubble and into the brush, then glanced at the approaching Lincoln town car. Walter burst from it, stalking toward Mitchell. "Hey, you. Warren. I'm on to you now."

Taking his time, Mitchell stripped his leather gloves and stuck them in his back pocket. He removed the red bandana serving as a sweatband and wiped his face and bare chest with it. Clearly Walter was in a snit, not just his natural offensive self. "How so?"

Walter paced back and forth and then delivered a rapid-fire attack. "You may be a big hotshot from a major corporation, but you're not buying your way into the position of

Madrid's mayor. There are people who want you to get Rogers to build here, to stimulate the town's economy."

"I've been asked to think about contacting Rogers. But I'm not working for them anymore."

"People think you're so high and mighty, that you have important business contacts. I say you're lowdown, Warren, you're just here to make trouble . . . to pay Madrid back for treating your dad as he deserved. You'll be gone soon enough."

"And if I'm not?"

Walter had never been so bold, but agitated now, he puffed up in his three-piece suit and glared at Mitchell. "Not one person in this town will vote for a man who beats Uma Thornton."

Mitchell threw down the bandana. He wanted to hit Walter, but the man wasn't strong enough to face him without some backing, some proof. "Where did you get that?"

Walter's hand slashed through the summer evening. "Everyone is talking about it this morning down at the coffee shop. It's common knowledge that she's changed. She ran you down at the garage that day and lit into you. She's sharp with Pearl, and she's never been that. She's always been kind to my wife, poor little delicate thing. You had even messed up Uma that day you and she went after Everett who was drinking at Mike's. I heard you beat her so bad that she's hiding out today, ashamed to show herself, poor thing."

"Where is she?" Fear snaked over Mitchell, freezing him inside, despite the hot August sun.

"No one knows. She's probably just waiting for the bruises to fade. I tell you, Warren, you'd better get out of town fast. Uma is respected here, or was until you came back, ready to wreck our lives, our town. I'm the best thing for Madrid, and I'm not letting you get the mayor's office. I'll run you right out—"

Mitchell reached out to catch Walter's tie, wrapped it around his fist, and lifted to stretch it tight. "I said, 'where is

Uma'? If you have any idea, now would be a good time to say so."

Walter struggled for breath, his hands trying to grip the taut Italian tie as his eyes bulged with fear. "I don't know . . . I don't know. I just know that I went to comfort her—"

" 'Comfort'?" Mitchell lifted his fist just an inch.

"She isn't in her house," Walter said quickly, his expression that of stark fear. "She isn't anywhere, and Roman is looking for Shelly. Shelly is probably with Uma, trying to help her—"

He breathed deeply when Mitchell released his tie and hurried toward his pickup. Walter rubbed his throat and huffily straightened his clothing. He decided he would wait until another time to chat with Mitchell—a time when other people were there to help him.

Fearing for Uma, Mitchell raced toward town. He couldn't breathe, his heart racing as his truck skidded to a stop by the Lawrence house. He shoved open the door, calling, "Uma?"

Deadly silence answered him, and Mitchell pushed up the stairs, two at a time, his body cold. Uma's office was neat . . . and empty.

The bullethole in the window reminded him that she could be—

He swallowed, hurrying down the stairs and through the kitchen and out the back door to the garden. The roses she loved were beautiful, glossy and rich, and perfumed, and too still, the air seeming thick and layered and cool on his naked chest . . . too still, as if they were waiting . . .

Tail twitching, the gray cat watched him from his back steps. The cat leaped aside as Mitchell hurried inside to call, "Uma!"

The word echoed hollowly back to him, and the house was still and cool and trembling, as if—he could feel the stillness inside him, the prickling of the hair at his nape and on his body, and he knew that Uma was in danger—that the stalker had chosen his time.

Mitchell had made a mistake . . . he'd been certain that the danger walked in the night, but now it was only evening and still light, the sun barely fingering through the growing shadows on Lawrence Street. "Lauren, take care of her . . . Please . . ."

NINETEEN

"**M**ike, whoever you're protecting has got Uma and Shelly. We'd appreciate any help you can give us." Mitchell knew better than to push the big bartender too far; he got confused easily. Beside Mitchell, Roman stood in Mike's small, cluttered hobby gun shop, located in his garage. Children's excited yells sounded in the other part of Mike's house, his wife calling to quiet them, the television was too loud.

Outlaw guns lined the rough walls of Mike's shop, a model 1887 ten-gauge "riot gun" gleaming on the rack with a Remington "Whipit" gun, and a Remington Model 11 "sawed-off."

Mike, seated at his workbench, held his head in his hands, sobbing quietly. "I had to fix the guns, repair them, show her how to use them, or she'd take everything—the bar, the house—and she threatened to—"

Wrapped in anguish, he reached out an arm and swept his gun repair tools from the workbench; they clattered to the floor. The surprised poodle sitting at his feet yelped, and he picked her up to press his face against her coat. "She said no one would believe me. She said she'd . . . she'd hurt my kids, and my little Lily . . . and she'd see that I lost everything, the house and the bar. I inherited the bar from Dad. I had to do as she said. I knew that when she just said, 'Whoops. Spot could be a dot on the road.' This is my Spot, my dog. My poor cute little puppy, and I knew she'd hurt my dog."

"Who, Mike? Who?"

Mike shook his head and tears covered his ravaged face. "I knew I should have told Lonny. Now, he'll be mad. It was Pearl Whiteford. She found some guns that she thinks Bonnie and Clyde must have stashed in that old motel her husband bought for storage. Who knows if they were really Clyde Barrow's, but she thought they were and they needed repair. She came to me. At first, I thought it was just a rich woman's fancy, something she'd give her husband for a present . . . and then, after the body—that Pete Jones—was found and Lonny came to me for information on the guns, I had some idea, but I didn't want to think about it—that I might have been responsible for that Colt .45."

He reached behind gun repair manuals and brought out a whiskey bottle, tipping it high. "I don't drink, can't afford to when you run a bar, but I need this."

While Mitchell and Roman waited, their nerves taut, Mike wiped the back of his hand across his mouth. A slow-thinking man, he had to be allowed time to tell his story. "She went nuts. Came in here one night through a window while I was working, dressed like Clyde Barrow. Had the hat, the tie, the suit, everything. That's when I knew—and that's when she told me that I was going to prison and nothing could protect my family . . . all because I repaired those guns for her. I knew it was wrong, but I—"

"The old motel . . ." Mitchell said quietly, meeting Roman's eyes.

"What do I do? Can I help?" Mike asked urgently. "I don't want anything to happen to Uma and Shelly. Uma tutored me to get through high school and she helped me on setting up the bar."

"You stay here and take care of your family," Mitchell said quietly, as he and Roman moved toward the outside door. "Don't say anything to anyone. We don't know who else is in this."

"Pearl is real smart, crazy-like," Mike muttered as his five-year-old boy burst into the room, holding a truck that needed repair. The big man's eyes pleaded with Mitchell and Roman. "I'll stay put and take what I deserve," he promised unevenly.

A half hour later, Roman rode beside Mitchell, the horses borrowed fromw LeRoy moving quietly over a back trail to the old motel. Expert horsemen, they kept to the shadows of the trees. No words were necessary; both men feared for the women, terrified that they might already be killed.

I'll always be with you . . . Mitchell remembered how Uma rubbed her hands, still seeing Lauren's blood. With a good heart, Uma had been blind to the madwoman, and now she was in danger—*Uma* . . .

It had taken forty-five minutes to convince Mike that he had to tell everything, and now, at almost eight o'clock, rain-clouds darkened the summer night, layering close to the earth, the air damp on Mitchell's face. Roman grimaced occasionally as he had to put weight on the stirrup, his knee paining him, but he never slowed or complained.

The old motel lay in shadows, the windows boarded, the garages locked. Mitchell eased around the back and Roman waited at the front corner. When they met, Roman said, "Small car marks going into the garage. No sounds inside. Dani had said there was someone using this place, but I didn't think about it because the Whitefords use it for storage."

Mitchell slipped a small tool kit from his pocket and tried the massive lock. It came free, but an alarm sounded inside. The brothers looked at each other, and together, pushed their shoulders against the old wooden doors. It wouldn't give, and Mitchell and Roman backed the horses up to the doors; Mitchell flapped his western hat in front of their heads. On cue from their rodeo experiences, the horses back hooves lifted and kicked and the doors flew open, torn from their hinges. Inside the garage, Roman turned off a digital alarm.

Mitchell moved the horses to one of the motel doors, and they kicked the doors open, alarms ringing. Inside, the sweep of Mitchell's flashlight proved the small room was filled with storage boxes. Another room, more boxes, and then the third unit, which was empty and neat. A mussed cot was bolted to the floor, a table with an ice chest near it.

The flashlight's beam pinpointed a hairpin on the floor, which Roman scooped up and gripped in his fist. An elastic band with Uma's long mink-brown hair was on the bed with a note in her handwriting that said, "Tell anyone and we die."

Mitchell wrapped his hand around the opened bottle of water. "Still cold. They haven't been gone very long."

"New wood," Roman noted, as he moved his hands over the walls. At one point he pressed harder, and with a click, a secret closet opened to reveal clothing. Holding a small men's suit high, Roman shook his head.

Replacing it, he noted another inset of new wood and pressed it. Another small, high closet opened to reveal a lethal compound bow and accessories. The arrow quiver held steel-tipped practice arrows, but there were three hunting arrows carefully hung in line. Below them were marked the names Shelly, Uma, and Mitchell.

"Lauren wasn't in the plan," Mitchell noted softly.

"That must have really gotten Pearl—to know that Pete had killed the wrong woman. Just an innocent bystander. That was probably why Shelly got that scar and her house peppered with slugs . . . Pearl was really mad and lost it."

Mitchell lifted the compound bow out of the closet and tested the pull. "She's stronger than she looks. The old windmill was a moving target—she practiced on that."

"And from what she did to Rosy, she likes to see pain, enjoys watching it."

Mitchell pushed away the image of Uma, bleeding as Lauren had done. *He had to find Uma.* "Let's go."

The brothers grimly mounted their horses. "Which way?" Roman asked, his grim features etched in the dim light.

Mitchell tried not to let his terror ride over logic. "Any root cellar, any old shack, any house."

"Not the Whitefords. That's too obvious."

"Pearl doesn't like messes. She's meticulous about that. She'll pick somewhere else."

"That old garage where they found the body?"

Mitchell shook his head. "I burned it to the ground."

"Does Pearl know?"

With a look at each other, the brothers nudged the horses into a run toward the old Warren ranch. They took the back trails, rounding over the hills and down into the valleys. Then, in the low-lying clouds of the brewing storm, Lonny's buffalo churned; beyond them was the old windmill, paddles circling quickly in the rising wind.

The wind pushed against the two women tethered to the windmill, while another stalked back and forth, waving the glint of a gun. Roman cursed silently, and Mitchell's body ran cold as they dismounted and tied the horses to a stand of brush.

"I hated tending those roses," Pearl was yelling fiercely in the wind. "My mother actually threw me into the bushes when I didn't get good grades, when my dress was wrinkled, when I cried. I hated her. She loved them more than me."

"Pearl . . ." Uma was trying to talk softly to the raging woman, dressed in a man's suit. "Pearl, you don't want to hurt your friends."

Pearl pointed the gun at Shelly. "She had Walter's child, shaming me. He told me so."

She pointed the gun at Uma, and Mitchell went cold as the men moved, crouching, easing closer in the cloud shadows that hurled across the rolling hills. "You had the audacity, Uma, to tell me that my esteemed great-great-great-grandmother ran a bordello. You can't malign my family that way. I'm going to shoot both of you, and then I'm going to kill him, my yard man. I can't have him winning an election for mayor. I really can't have that, not a Warren. You chose a Warren over me. *Over me.* I tried to warn you off, but you just weren't paying attention, Uma," Pearl crooned.

"But she did," Mitchell said slowly, rising to stand just yards away from Pearl. He hoped he could hold Pearl's attention, long enough for Roman to come up behind her. Mitchell started walking toward the woman with the gun. It was the Colt .45, and Pearl was good with it, good enough to kill Pete.

Her eyes were wild, her face white, her smile a grimace. "You," she whispered. "Now I've got all of you in one place."

"They love you, Pearl. Don't do this," Mitchell said quietly, slowly walking toward Pearl.

"Stay back. I'll shoot them."

Mitchell shot the flashlight's powerful beam at Pearl, and blinded, she held up one hand covering her eyes, and fire leaped from her other hand, the .45's slugs hissing by him. "Turn it off, or I'll shoot them right now."

The searing burn on his arm said the .45 had skimmed his flesh, blood dripping down his hand. Roman hadn't had time to get around the back of the windmill and they needed more time. Mitchell killed the flashlight beam and started walking toward Pearl again.

"Lauren is here, you know. She's always near Uma. That's what she said when she died that night, 'I'll always be with you.' Lauren is waiting for you, Pearl. Remember how my house feels, how you felt that Lauren was still there? She's with Uma and Shelly now, waiting for you."

"Lauren is dead," Pearl cried wildly, glancing into the night shadows. "I was there. She didn't say anything."

"She told me. She's here. In the wind. In the trees. Listen to her. *Feel* her."

"She's dead . . . she's dead . . . I saw Lauren die."

"She's stayed to protect Uma and Shelly. She's their friend, and your friend, too. You don't want to hurt your friends. Uma understands how badly you've been treated. You're her friend. You don't want to hurt her. Who will you talk to? Who will you tell about your new clothes and your elegant parties? Who will help you send out invitations and help with your charities? And Shelly—she's really an excellent housekeeper, Pearl. They're hard to replace."

Pearl looked confused, as if torn between two worlds, and she wavered, looking fearfully into the night, turning one way, then another. The sounds of the buffalo moving through the night seemed to terrify her. "Lauren? Are you there? I didn't mean it to be you. It was Shelly. Shelly had Walter's child. He told me so . . . Lauren?"

Just then Roman stood, and startled Pearl misfired into the ground. The shot shook the damp air, and the weapon sprang from her hand. In the distance, the already nervous buffalo began to stampede toward the windmill, the sound of their hooves like thunder. Wild with fear of the huge approaching beasts, and seeing the two big men closing in on her, Pearl began to climb the wooden bars of the windmill.

"Mitchell, help me," Uma cried out, and he hurried to her. His hands shook as he used the small tool on her handcuff and it came free. Uma hurled herself into his arms and Mitchell buried his face against her throat, his body shaking, gathering her close and safe against him. He realized then that in the aftermath of fear, his heart pounded louder than the buffalo hooves.

The ground shook, and both men flattened themselves protectively against their loves, holding firmly to the old windmill as the buffalo swept past, thundering into the dim light, flowing like one beast over the hill.

Then Roman quickly freed Shelly, who was crying in his arms, and then Uma was pushing Mitchell away. "I've got to help her."

Fearing for her, his grip on her wrist tethered her. Uma's eyes begged him. "She's sick, Mitchell. I've got to help her."

"No." He looked up to where Pearl stood, on the platform in front of the whirling paddles, looking terrified. If one of the paddles caught her, she could lose her balance and fall. "Let her go. For what's she's done, maybe it's better. Maybe it's justice."

"I have to, Mitchell," Uma whispered desperately, and hurled herself into his arms, holding him tightly. "I love you, Mitchell. But I love Pearl in a different way. She's been tormented all her life, a victim. Walter lied and drove her to this. I can't have her death on my conscience."

Mitchell framed her face with his hands. "I love you, Uma. Don't do this."

She smiled sadly, the wind licking her hair around them in a storm of silk. "Will you love me any less if I do?"

When he couldn't speak, torn by fear for her and what she intended, Uma stroked his cheek. "You've told me in so many ways that you love me, you know. You've shown me in every action, in how you've tried to move from the past, because you cared. I won't start life with you like this, when I could have helped Pearl. I should have tried to help her sooner . . . I knew she was deeply troubled and at a breaking point. I was so tied up in my own life, in my grief for my baby and in trying to keep safe, that I didn't act. I won't have her death on my conscience. Try to understand."

"Uma has to go, to help Pearl, Mitchell," Shelly said quietly as she came to take Uma's hand. "That's who she is. Don't ask less of her."

Taking a deep, searing breath and fighting his terror, Mitchell stepped back. "I won't be happy if you let anything happen to you. And Lauren won't be happy, either."

"I know. Could you just save the lectures until we're home together?"

"Uma! I need you," Pearl cried wildly. *"I'm afraid. Help me! Lauren is here. Don't you feel her? She's here! She's come for me. I've been a bad girl. She's going to punish me!"*

She sounded like a frightened child rather than a murderer, small against the blades whirring behind her, the wind whipping at her hair and clothing.

Uma cupped her hands together and called, "Lauren is not going to punish you, Pearl. She wants you to be safe. She wants you to come down."

"I'll go," Mitchell said darkly, resenting his own softness for the woman who had caused so much pain.

Uma stayed him with a hand on his arm. She looked down at the blood staining her fingers. "You're hurt."

"It grazed the skin. I'm fine." In the present nightmare, he saw Uma skip mentally back to when Lauren was killed, the woman's blood on her hands. "Lauren, Uma. Think of how Pearl had Lauren killed, of how she tried to kill Shelly. She knows how to use you, how to reach inside and—and it's a long way down, if she takes you with her."

Uma shook her head slowly, sadly. She tore her skirt once, then again to fashion the scrap into a length which she tied around Mitchell's arm. "She wants me. She's not in control now. She's just poor Pearl, and I've got to help her. You've got to trust me in this, Mitchell."

"No. You're not going up there. It's not a matter of trust. It's a matter of reality. She could take you down with her."

Mitchell fought the terror inside him as Uma smiled softly. "Lauren wouldn't want Pearl to die like this, Mitchell. Neither do I. I'm the only one she'll listen to. And who would take you to the doctor and listen to you cry about the stitches this wound will need? I couldn't put anyone else through your grumbling and ranting and bullying, could I?"

She smoothed his face, her expression tender. "Mitchell, I am who I am, and I need to help Pearl. I couldn't live with myself if I let this happen to her. You see, my mother only found out about how badly Pearl was treated much later. My mother felt that she should have done something, that she should have recognized the signs of abuse. To the day she died, Mother felt badly about Pearl. Those are old ties and debts that others might not honor, but in our family it's left to me. So I understand why it was so important for your father to try to work this land—because he'd promised someone he loved deeply. In a way, I inherited Pearl, good or bad. I can't just write her off. I *have* to do this, Mitchell."

Faced with that logic, Mitchell shook his head. "You promise me that you'll come down safe."

She stood on tiptoe to kiss him. "When one begins a journey, one must finish it. You're not getting rid of me that easily. Not when you've just told me that you love me. Not when we have the rest of our lives to go skinny dipping."

Uma gripped the wooden bars leading up to the windmill and stepped up to the first one. Mitchell's hands on her waist tightened, as if he wouldn't let her go. "I'll be fine, Mitchell, but not if I don't get her down safely."

"Just a minute. Your hair could get caught." He deftly wove her hair into a long braid and secured the tip with the elastic band Roman handed him.

He bent to her long dress and tore it at her thighs. "You're not getting tangled up in this thing, either."

There was just that brief squeeze of his hands as if he would lift her away from the windmill, and then she was moving upward.

Uma focused on Pearl, high above her, the windmill's blades catching the wind. "I'm coming, Pearl," Uma called, just as Pearl seemed to waver on the edge of the platform. "Why don't you sit down and we'll have a nice chat? I've been wanting to know how you manage those beautiful parties . . . how you get your ideas for folding those napkins, and where did you find the napkin rings this last time? Then there are the caterers—"

Uma pushed herself up the wooden bars, fear licking at her stomach, tightening it. She moved onto the old wooden platform and took Pearl's outstretched hand.

"I've been bad," Pearl whined.

She had killed and caused to be killed, and yet Uma saw the child within her that needed love. "I love you, Pearl," she said above the wind and the whirring of the blades behind them. "Lauren loves you, too. She wants you to come with me, so we can be together, like we've always been. Lauren, Shelly, you and I . . ."

I'll always be with you . . .

"Mitchell—ah, you're holding me too tight. I can't breathe," Uma said in the doorway of Mitchell's house, where he stood holding her close against his chest, as if fearing to let her go. "Put me down."

"Uh. Sorry." His voice was uneven, his body tense with the lingering fear that held them both. He eased her to her feet, but gathered her tenderly back against him, tucking her head beneath his chin. He rocked her against him, taking the shaking of her body, her reaction after the nightmare, into his own body. "I keep seeing you crawling up that shaky old windmill, the wind tearing at your clothes. You could have fallen at any minute. I told Lauren to keep you safe. I felt she was with you up there."

"She was. I felt her around me. She made me feel safe." Uma held Mitchell tighter, his body anchoring her from the past hours of nightmare; she took comfort in the gentle soothing of his hands on her hair.

Uma saw him again, on the ground, looking up at her. Every ridge and plane on his face was edged by fear, catching the dim light, the wind tearing at his clothes.

She heard again the eerie sound of the windmill blades, churning in the wind, and Pearl's childish cries.

"Well, you weren't safe. You were clinging to the windmill with one hand and holding her hand with the other."

"I can't stop shaking. She was so terrified, and I was, too. She's so sick, Mitchell. Even sedated, when Lonny took her away, she was raving about her mother, and how she hated roses. She wanted Walter, and I doubt he'll even visit her in the institution, if that's where she's placed." Uma decided to have a little chat with the man who had pushed Pearl over the brink. Each summer the Whiteford girls came back from their aunt's like any other vibrant teenagers, then within a week, they were quiet shadows.

"Walter will manage," Mitchell said grimly as he kissed her temple. "And she'll have you."

"Yes. She'll have me." She wouldn't desert Pearl, though she had done horrible things. "And nothing is going to happen to Mike. He's paid enough already. I'll see to that. Lonny will help."

"You're going after Walter, aren't you?"

"Yes, I am. I'm going to research his sister very well, and if she wants those girls, Walter is going to sign off as the father he'd never been."

"Walter and I need to have a little chat—"

Uma stood on tiptoe and pressed her lips to his. "Stop. I can handle Walter. He can't very well play the poor, innocent duped husband, if I tell all I know, and I will if he—"

Mitchell lifted an eyebrow. "That's called blackmail."

She shrugged and smiled softly. "One must use the elements at hand to complete a necessary task. Walter is that. There are a few outlaws in his ancestry that he doesn't know about. He wouldn't want them to come out. I imagine he'll be relocating. You might not be a yard man there, anymore."

The midnight storm crashed and battered the house that had been Lauren's; rain hurled against it in gray sheets. Then suddenly, it stopped, and a quiet, cleansing rain pattered at the windows. "Lauren is leaving," Uma whispered quietly. "Do you feel her leaving?"

Mitchell listened to the stillness of the house, the quiet shadows at peace. "Yes, I do. Her work is done. She's protected you."

I'll always be with you . . .

Mitchell and Uma stood in the quiet barren house, and only the scents of lemon cookies, fresh lumber and paint remained. "Mitchell? Do you smell lemon cookies?"

He lifted her in his arms, holding her tight against his chest. "I found Lauren's recipe book, and thought I'd try baking the cookies. They were good."

"Mmm. I'm so tired," she murmured, and then yawned and placed her head on his shoulder. Mitchell would take care of her, his arms strong around her, and she'd come such a long way. She'd come from the shadows where she'd lost a baby and fought living as a woman. She'd come to Mitchell, the man she loved, and who loved her in every touch, every look. Uma had traveled from a lonely, safe life to bond with Mitchell, a man she adored.

She sighed and cuddled close to him. Everything else could wait until morning.

"Mom!" Dani and Grace stood on Everett's front porch as Shelly hurried through the quiet rain to them.

Roman stood with his hands in his pockets, hunched against the rain and loneliness. Shelly stopped on the sidewalk, poised between her daughter and her lover.

She hurried back to Roman. "You're not getting away from

me tonight. Come in. Dani needs to know that we're both safe—her father *and* her mother."

"Grace," he said flatly, the one word holding the reason he wasn't coming into the house. "Go on, if that's what you want to do. I'll be at the garage. Call me if you need me."

"Hardhead."

"Hey, Pops, where are you going?" Dani called, and ran through the rain to him, his beautiful, wonderful daughter, a part of him and a part of Shelly.

And a part of Grace. The thought stunned him as Dani hugged his arm and Shelly pressed against his other side.

"Coming in, Pops?" Dani asked anxiously, and he knew she needed to know that he was safe, that all of them were safe—her family, the family she'd wanted for so long, the father she'd missed.

Dressed in a long robe, Grace stood on the porch, her face pale in the layers of mist and gentle rain between them.

"You two are getting all wet," he said, delaying leaving . . . and choosing to go inside. "You'll catch cold."

"Mommm . . . Grams and I made cookies—gingersnaps with molasses, the old-fashioned kind," Dani pleaded, inviting Shelly to push him. "Oh, please, please, please, Pops . . . uh . . . I mean, Daddy."

"You're giving me a headache, kid," Roman grumbled, but couldn't wipe the grin off his face. It was clear that neither female was leaving him alone, one on each side of him, their arms wrapped around his. It was a good feeling, his love and his daughter wanting him. He felt warm inside, wallowing in the tingle of love.

Then he looked at the woman on the porch and knew the time had come to know his mother. Her expression said she feared his rejection; but that wasn't coming. He looked down at Shelly, her hair flattened to her head as her eyes pleaded with him. He bent to take a brief kiss and watch her eyes darken, because they both knew what would happen later between them—the fierce welcoming of life and their future together. And Dani was right, it was a package deal; he wanted Shelly to be happy. "Man, you're stubborn."

"You're worth it."

"Lonny called and told us everything. Pop is a hero, isn't he, Mom? Risking his life for you, and that time for me?"

"We'll get you a hero medal, if you come in," Shelly offered, with a smile that said she wasn't certain of his reaction to the situation.

Grace helped an elderly woman ease out the screen door. In a warm long robe, Mrs. Craig was smiling. "What's this?" Roman asked, amused at the four women watching him, waiting to see what he would do. If Shelly married him, he'd have to learn to juggle all of them—including Grace—and that might not be so bad. "A pajama party?"

Dani grinned in delight, her eyes sparkling. "The rest home heard about tonight and Grandma called Grams. She's staying just the night. She thought you might need her help. If you come in, I'll have almost my whole family together."

Mrs. Craig waved her thin hand. "Hey! You! Boy! I want my motorcycle ride when you youngsters rest up!"

If that old woman was game enough to make peace after a hard bitter road, so could he. "Sure. I could do with a few cookies after tonight," he said. "Take me to them."

Later, alone with Shelly in her house, Roman kneeled to unwrap carefully the gauze circling her scraped and bruised wrist. "You fought hard."

"There was a lot at stake." Sitting on the bed, she watched his big hand delicately lather antiseptic cream on her skin before he rewrapped the gauze.

"What do you need? A shower? Something to drink? An aspirin? Tell me," he whispered urgently, smoothing her hair with his hands. They flowed over her once again since that awful scene, checking her body, smoothing her arms and her legs. Then he eased his arms around her gently and drew her to him, resting his head on her breast. He spoke humbling, heartbreakingly, a side that no one had seen but her, the tender man. "I thought I'd lost you, Shell. I couldn't handle that. Everything else, all the old problems between Grace and Dad, fade by comparison. Tell me what you need."

She smiled at this loving man, so anxious about her, and trying his best to move into the first stages of a relationship with his mother. Only a hero could bridge the gap from a bitter past into a loving one, and Roman was that hero, her love. "I have everything I need right here, with you. Just hold me tonight—and forever."

Uma awoke to the man sleeping beside her, his arm wrapped around her. In the predawn hours, the lines on Mitchell's face had eased, his eyelashes sweeping shadows across the jut of his cheekbone, a wave of his hair crossing his forehead. He was a part of her, in her heart, a kind, good man, an enduring one, if not exactly sweet at times.

His eyes opened slowly to meet hers. "Hi," he whispered, as his hand slowly began to caress her.

"Hi," she returned, loving him.

Mitchell's kiss lingered and held and brushed gently. "I didn't think this feeling would ever come to me—peace, feeling like I've found what I need, what my life has been about. You've given me that."

"And you made me see that I need life, to be in it, to be a woman."

His hand caressed her breast. "Oh, you're a woman, all right."

She eased against his body, sliding her bare thigh against his. "Show me."

Mitchell showed her so well and long and good, that she

slept heavily against him, feeling safe and warm and cherished. Mitchell knew how to cherish, to hold her tenderly, and yet to draw everything from her until she bloomed, and climbed and took and gave.

In the morning, she smiled drowsily, snuggling beneath the sheet in his bed. The scent of brewed coffee enticed, blended with the low, indistinct murmur of a man's voice and a woman's. A glance at the bedroom clock told Uma that it was eight o'clock and the sunshine coming softly through the window told her that another clean, bright day had begun.

Pearl . . . Uma held Mitchell's pillow and ached for Pearl, and Lauren. Their lives had been so twined together that she would always think of them. Today, there would be police reports and details to wind through, but a new beginning needed that cleaning so life could grow sweeter and better.

She nuzzled Mitchell's scent, keeping him and the night and their love close to her, wrapping herself in it—and the scent of the roses that were freshly clipped and near their bed. Uma dreamily reached out a hand to smooth them, perfect satiny blooms, a mixture of the old pioneer roses that were a part of her life.

With a sigh, Uma sat up and stretched and luxuriated in Mitchell's lovemaking. He'd been tender but possessive, tempering his strength to her . . . she smiled softly, feeling the heaviness of her breasts, the delicate aching of her muscles, because she'd pushed to the limit, hoarding every sensation that made them one, burning away everything else.

After a quick shower, she wore Mitchell's loose cotton shirt and undershorts into the kitchen. Her torn clothing of last night had been thoughtfully removed by Mitchell.

Seated on bar stools near the counter, Mitchell and Grace were having coffee and sweet rolls, talking quietly, earnestly. They turned to her, and Mitchell quickly rose to come to Uma, kissing her. "Good morning, sleepyhead."

"What's this?" she asked, snuggling against him.

"I invited Grace over this morning . . . I wanted to talk with her. The past is over, and last night—"

Mitchell inhaled sharply, his body tense as once more he fought the terror of losing Uma. "Last night put everything into perspective. Enough years have been wasted . . . I'll try to work through my feelings for Grace, because as a man, I see things differently—as a man who loves a woman deeply and wants the best for her. It isn't going to be easy. But I've told her what Dad said. She should have that, and it was important to me not to wait. I want our life—yours and mine—to start fresh, as it should be, with family. I couldn't go there, because after a night of talking, Mrs. Craig and Dani are still sleeping. And I wanted to be here, with you."

Uma's throat tightened with joy, and she held him tighter, this man she loved and who loved her enough to work through a bitter past. "This is a wonderful surprise, Grace. I'm so glad."

Grace's vulnerable expression said she was struggling against tears. "It is wonderful, so wonderful."

"It's a beginning," Mitchell murmured softly against Uma's hair.

"Yes, a beginning," she returned, her heart filling with love as she smiled up at him.

EPILOGUE

In the first week of September, Mitchell turned the handle of the old-fashioned wooden ice cream churn in his backyard. He decided he'd stay on the sidelines of his family's ongoing evening mélée. With the old gray cat to keep him company, it was Mitchell's first attempt at the pineapple ice cream recipe that Everett had sent—after Uma had called him with the news of Madrid, the danger, and the joy of her upcoming marriage to Mitchell.

Everett and Uma would always be tied together, as friends, and Mitchell understood her need to tell him, to invite him to their home.

Mitchell frowned slightly; Clarence had returned, stiffly rejecting any approach from Mitchell and reprimanding Uma. He was entrenched in the Lawrence house, refusing to visit their home. Uma stayed firmly with Mitchell while wooing her father gently. Mitchell knew how persuasive she could be.

Inside the house, negotiations weren't going well on any front: Dani had no immediate plans for college after completing her high school equivalency course; she wanted to revel in her family. Shelly balked at the church wedding that was important for Roman to give her, and Grace and Mrs. Craig thought it important that Dani have a coming-out party, to announce her new last name when the legalities were completed.

Amid the feminine skirmishes, Roman was losing, struggling for calm and reasoning.

Finally, the lone warrior slammed out of the house and plopped down on the bench beside Mitchell. "Let me churn that thing. It's a madhouse in there. Dresses and parties and petit fours and Shelly—well, Shelly is going to have to be tied and shoved into a church, and soon. She's the only woman I've ever had to push into marriage, the first one. It's not doing much for my ego. This is going to be our only wedding, and we need to do it up right, with all the trimmings."

Despite the thickening ice cream, Roman worked furiously at turning the handle. "According to Everett, that ice cream should ripen. You can stop turning it now," Mitchell advised.

Roman's groan was long and weary, reflecting his frustration. "I don't know if I'm doing the right thing by her, or by Dani. Maybe I should get work somewhere and save up to buy a house—"

"Dani won't go for you leaving and neither would Shelly."

"I don't know if I can make the garage pay off, not here. If we were in Daytona or Indianapolis or any big city, I could go for a custom racing car business, or bikes. But not in Madrid. I could end up fighting a losing battle, and that would be just like Dad. I can't do that to Shelly, not what he did to Grace."

"I don't know why you can't have that business here, build specialty cars or bikes. It's all in advertising, and you've got contacts, don't you?"

"Sure, contacts . . ." Roman turned to Mitchell, his eyes lighting. "You're saying have them come here. Or ship to them."

"Right."

Roman nodded, examining the new idea. "I'm a really good mechanic. I could do that."

He listened to the raging feminine debate about churches and coming-out parties, the whens and wheres and hows not agreeing, then sighed slowly. "It's nice out here. No wonder you took up this ice cream making, using the old-fashioned hand churn, instead of the electric one. You're hiding out."

"*Now* you've got it. I think we should split the land half and half, twenty and twenty acres. Uma should have a new house, one we've built together—that's important to her and to me. She'll need a proper office, not a converted bedroom. I want to garden and raise big, fat tomatoes. Basically, I like being a yard man. I'll keep my jobs in town, too. My first project is the city park. I can't wait to get started on that—a next spring job, if I can get the city council to agree."

Roman stared blankly at him. "There's no way I can buy half from you. I'm broke."

Mitchell served Roman the plan he'd been considering for a month. "You won't be. I was a top sales executive. You build 'em, I'll market 'em. And Dani can have that little spread she wants so badly. Warren and Warren. Think about it."

Mitchell nudged his brother as the women's voices rose. "I'm needed inside."

He stood and stretched and inhaled the roses that would soon be gone. Clarence was in the next yard, trying to appear busy while he was obviously interested in the houseful of women. "Hey, Clarence. Would you mind coming over and checking on this ice cream, seeing how long it needs to ripen? I've got to go inside," Mitchell said casually, but hoped that the older man would take the invitation.

"I'll think about it," Roman said quietly.

"You're good at what you do, and I'm really good at what I do, which is negotiation business—and right now, I'm needed inside."

Mitchell stepped into his kitchen to find Shelly with her

arms crossed. Dani was glaring at her. "I'm not leaving my family to go to any college. I'm staying right here."

"You need a coming-out party," Mrs. Craig said. "I want people to know my granddaughter."

Grace looked as if she thought every inch of reconciliation and family togetherness could be shredded, and Uma was frantically jotting down notes. "Let me have that, dearest," Mitchell said lightly.

He ran down the list of notations she had made. "Okay, let's cut to the bottom line. Everyone wants something different, but this is how it will work—first of all, everyone back off Shelly. She has to *want* a wedding like that herself, and you're all pressuring her too much."

"Oh, I want a wedding. I just don't want all the *fuss*."

"Check. I'll handle the wedding."

Uma stared blankly at him. "But Mitchell—"

He leaned down to kiss her parted lips. "It's just a wedding. How much more difficult can it be than managing a national sales meeting? And Dani, you're right about staying with family, because that's important to you now. Meanwhile—Uma, research what college classes she can take through the computer or mail or television. Shell, see that she gets tested for abilities. The high school counselor will help. We'll put together a package she can work on right here. It's called teamwork, and we're all players. I'll plan her coming-out party."

He smiled at the women. "See? Now you can all focus on me, and not each other. I'm a manager, and a very good one. This is all going to run smoothly, with your cooperation. Once this initial rough patch is over, you can return to your designated duties, but for right now, I'm assigning them."

He placed his hand on *The Smooth Moves List* and left it there just long enough to watch Uma's anxious expression, wondering if he would expose her secrets. Of course not; he wanted Uma's secrets all for himself.

"First of all, this is a really good book about relationships. I want each of you to use it as a study guide on give and take. This whole operation depends on cooperation of involved departments. I want a list from Shelly of what she would like in her wedding. We'll work from there. Get on it, Shell. And while you're at it, confer with Uma. You might want to make it a double wedding. Uma, I'll need a list from you as to what you want in a wedding. We might get all the plans to dovetail nicely . . . if all parties agree. I remain neutral and flexible. My only definite, unchangeable goal is to marry Uma—and soon."

In the gaping silence, with the women staring blankly at him, Mitchell nodded and left the house. Roman and Clarence were talking quietly, a towel draped over the wooden ice cream churn. "Let's get out of here," Mitchell said as the silence grew inside the house. He picked up the tomcat, and when it purred, he tucked it under his arm, petting it.

"Let's go down to the ice cream shop and hide out. I've got a feeling it won't be safe here much longer."

"You're taking that tomcat?" Clarence asked, obviously wanting to make friends with the animal as it watched him warily.

"Sure. You can feed him your ice cream. He'll like that."

A month and a half later, Uma lifted her face to the October chill and noted the last of the roses in Lauren's garden caught by the early frost. She wrapped her shawl around her, nestling inside the soft familiar wool. Next summer they would bud and bloom in rich, vibrant colors, just like the love between Mitchell and her.

But then Lauren's house would be another woman's; Grace had come through a terrible journey to be reunited with her sons. Their relationship needed more mending, because the road to family had been deep and wounding. But the Warrens, all of them, were working on peace and "give and take."

Uma slowly swept her hand over a frost-nipped bud. "Don't worry, little rose. Next year, you'll bloom on Warren land. You came from the past and endured and brought me the pleasure of other lives, the settlers, and the families here in Madrid. I'm the Keeper, they say, and I'm keeping you."

I'll always be with you . . . "Yes, you will, Lauren. We'll always remember you, keeping you with us."

Warren and Warren's first project had been to build two matching chests in the garage, beautiful, big walnut chests to hold portions of Lauren's life, a friend Shelly and Uma had loved dearly. The brothers worked and talked together now, and often a rich, unexpected chuckle escaped Mitchell. Uma hoarded the sound with pleasure as she listened.

She was in life's swift-moving lane now, hers and Mitchell's, not an outsider, hiding away from a life of richness and depth.

Uma looked at her hands and instead of Lauren's blood, she found the gold and promise and love of Mitchell's wedding band.

At a sound, she turned to see the man she loved watching her, his expression shielded as it was when he thought of the baby she'd lost—and the lingering doubt that he could make her happy.

Uma walked slowly toward him. "When one loves with an open heart, anything is possible."

"When an exciting woman snuggles close to a hungry man, she can expect—" Mitchell gathered her close against him and nuzzled her hair. His lips nibbled at her earlobe and he blew softly into her ear. The familiar erotic technique brought the sensual quiver she couldn't hide and would get him everything they both wanted.

Uma laughed outright at the unexpected flirtation, the joyous sound curling into the fragrant garden, to be carried on the timeless Oklahoma wind . . .

Fall in love . . .
With Avon's most dashing heroes!

The irresistible Earl of Huntingdon is looking for a marriage of convenience only in *To Marry an Heiress*, Lorraine Heath's Avon Romantic Treasure. Yet from the moment he waltzed with Georgina Pierce, he imagines spending many passionate nights with the American heiress. Then he discovers that Georgina's fortune has been squandered, and there's nothing left for him to do . . . except fall in love.

Richard Wesley III is the handsome attorney in Sue Civil-Brown's Avon Contemporary romance *Breaking All the Rules*. Richard just lost a case, and Erin Kelly is determined to put things back on track for him. If only Erin's outlandish plots to help didn't cause more trouble than they solve . . . and if only her sparkling green eyes and fiery spirit didn't make his head spin.

Gunnar Olafson appears like a warrior in a dream in *The Rose and the Shield* by Sara Bennett, an Avon Romance. This Viking mercenary was hired to defend young widow Lady Rose's lands, but she doesn't know he is sworn to betray her. Gunnar never expected to be bewitched by the exquisite beauty, and now must choose between her love . . . and his honor.

Jake Reed didn't think he's the marrying kind in *A Chance at Love*, Beverly Jenkins' newest historical romance. But when Loreli Winters shows up on his doorstep with his two adorable orphaned nieces, he knows he's going to need a wife to help him raise the girls. Now all he has to do is convince this enchantress to abandon her plans to be a mail order bride—and marry him instead!

Avon Romantic Treasures

Unforgettable, enthralling love stories,
sparkling with passion and adventure
from Romance's bestselling authors